A KISS OF PROMISE

Will's eyes, smoky with passion, revealed all his thoughts—and the intensity of them scared Marta Carolina. His countenance was too awesome for her to stand, his resolve and determination too strong. Unintentionally, innocently, she had pushed him beyond his threshold of endurance. But she wasn't prepared to pay the consequences. She couldn't remember a time when she had been more frightened . . . of him . . . of herself.

He whispered in her ear, "Open your mouth."

With no mind to resist, Marta Carolina followed his injunction. She opened her mouth, and she also opened her eyes. The beauty of her desire-darkened irises stayed his movement. She heard his quick intake of breath. She was as enraptured by Will's face as he was with hers. Gone was the anger and the flinty resolve. Now he was warm and soft. She lifted a hand and touched his face. She drew her fingers over his cheeks, loving the feel of the stubble. She outlined the thick eyebrows and the nose. She felt ▓▓▓▓▓▓▓▓▓▓▓▓▓▓▓▓▓▓ hrough her insides, but sh▓▓▓▓▓▓▓▓▓▓▓▓▓▓▓▓▓▓ a crisp for one kiss . . .

SATIN SECRET

EMMA MERRITT

ZEBRA BOOKS
KENSINGTON PUBLISHING CORP.

ZEBRA BOOKS

are published by

Kensington Publishing Corp.
475 Park Avenue South
New York, NY 10016

First printing: July 1987

Printed in the United States of America

I dedicate this book

to the Lady of Cofitachequi,

to the Chicorans,

to the Timucuans.

Native Americans, Great Americans!

Prologue

On the coast of England
December 1586

Under cover of night and heavy fog, steps echoed through the sleeping village as a cloaked man walked toward the Boar's Head Inn. When he reached his destination, his hand curled around the iron handle, but he didn't immediately open the huge door. He paused and looked about, his eyes straining through the thick milky veil as if he were looking for someone . . . or something. His quest stopped when he focused on a point across the road where oblique forms merged with the mist to become eerie, shadowy figures. When he heard the soft wheeze of the horse and saw the hazy diffusion of light appear, disappear, only to reappear three times, he exhaled in relief.

Then, supposing the door to be locked at such a late hour, he tried the latch. He was surprised—but then again he wasn't—when it quietly swished open. After all, the landlord was expecting a visitor, was he not? The man moved into the dimly lit entry. Happy to have a respite from the harsh weather, he smiled to himself and lifted a gloved hand to draw back his hood and reveal a head of jet black hair, brushed in deep waves from his forehead and temples.

Again he paused—a deliberate cessation of movement that seemed to be casual, yet none of his actions were casual. All were planned and calculated to the most minute degree. He pulled the exquisite gauntlet gloves from his hands and, heedless to its cost, crushed the expensive leather in one fist. Unconsciously, he ran a finger over the small mustache that topped a sensuous lip and gently trailed his hand over the short, immaculately trimmed beard. Although his eyes, the same color as his hair, as vibrant and alive, flicked around the shadowed room, his gaze was thorough. Not one item missed his accounting: the wall hangings; the floor coverings; the statues at each end of the mantel—a bust of Queen Elizabeth I on the left side, a black marble statue of St. Peter on the right; and the lone occupant, a portly man in his early sixties. When the guest's gaze finally fell on the small table near the fireplace, his smile widened and his eyes glistened with the sheen of victory.

He tucked his gloves into his doublet, and his boots rapped a measured cadence on the wooden floor as he stepped out of the hall, down the two steps into the recessed dining room. When he neared the landlord, hovering in the corner, he courteously dipped his head and said in a low, resonant voice, "Good evening to you, Master Smyth."

The innkeeper looked at the stranger quizzically for a moment.

"The name is Smyth, is it not? Henry Smyth?"

"Aye, my lord," the host returned amiably, nervously drying dishes with the bottom of his apron. "Henry Smyth it is." He set the pewter tankard on the counter and moved to the fireplace. Bending, his back to the stranger, he picked up a log from the wood box. He, too, strove for casualness, but he was not as accomplished an actor as his guest. "And who might you be, my lord?"

The man, tall and slender, his whipcord body solid muscle, laughed, the mellow sound filling the room. "Some call me Will'am Dare, good host. Others call me El Desafiador." His hands capped his hips. "Perhaps you've heard of me. The One who Dares."

A grin softened the haggard features of the old man's face, and he threw the log on the blaze and straightened. "Most of us folks hereabouts have heard of you, sir—" he dusted his hands down the sides of his apron "—and we're mighty proud of what you're doing. We be wishing to see the Spaniards drove out of the Netherlands. Now what can I do for you on this chilly night, sir?"

The man who called himself Will Dare unfastened his cloak and tossed it over the back of a chair, the firelight-reflecting off the golden threads woven through the honey and green damask. He sat down, leaned back in the high-backed chair, and stretched his legs toward the fire. "If it's not too much to ask, I would have some food and a cup of ale. I have traveled many miles, Master Smyth, and I have many more to go before I can call my task finished." With that same deliberation with which he had executed all his movements, his words, his thoughts, he lifted his hands, twined his fingers together, and cradled the back of his head.

"Nay, my lord, food and drink 'tis not too much to ask," Smyth replied, his eyes appreciatively running the

9

length of the guest's body from the doublet, enriched with magnificent lace and drawn thread work, to the expensive leather riding boots. "I will have my daughter prepare you supper, and I shall get you a cup of the finest ale in all England." The host took a few steps before he asked, "And shall I be preparing you a room for the evening, sir?"

"No, good man," the guest replied. "No room for the night. I must leave for Hampton Court as soon as I've eaten and rested a bit." He pointed to the nearby table. "I see you play chess."

"Indeed I do, sir," Henry Smyth replied, his faded blue eyes suddenly sparking to light. Proudly he said, "And right well if I might say so myself."

"I, too, play." With the sleek smoothness of a cat, El Desafiador lifted his hand and stroked his beard. "Perhaps after I've supped, Mister Smyth, you would care to indulge me in a game."

As Henry moved toward the kitchen, he flashed his guest another toothy grin. "To be sure, my lord, I would."

When the door closed behind him, Henry fairly beamed. To his daughter and only child, the sixteen-year-old girl across the room, he whispered. "'Tis someone who called himself El Desafiador, Betsy love."

Betsy dropped the wooden bowl into the dish water and spun about, her skirt swirling around dainty ankles. She wiped her hands on her apron. "Is he the one, Papa? Shall I go tell the bishop?"

"No," Henry returned, "'tis not time to tell the bishop. I don't know if he's the one. He's asked for food and drink but no bed. Said he must be getting on to the queen's palace as soon as possible." He walked to the

10

cupboard and opened the door, taking out a loaf of freshly baked bread. "As soon as he's supped, he wants to play a game of chess."

Betsy clapped her hands together and danced around the room. "Perhaps he is the one we've been waiting for, Father."

"Could be, lass," Henry agreed, "but 'tis too early to tell. Hurry and get him some victuals, gal. We'll know soon enough if this feller is the one or not."

After the guest had dined, he beckoned the host. "Come, good landlord, you promised to indulge me in a game of chess."

Henry dragged a second bench near the reading table. "A good game of chess I always enjoy, my lord." He moved the candle holder closer to the checkerboard. "But I must confess one of my chess pieces is missing."

"Ah, yes," El Desafiador said, "I had noticed. You are missing the queen piece." He reached into his doublet and withdrew a tiny figurine which he held out. Then with that predator ease—with those subtle movements that were such an integral part of him, he rose and approached the table at which Henry Smyth sat. "God save the queen, Henry Smyth."

"Aye, sir, God save the queen." Henry took the queen piece and brought it close to the candle, the tiny flame flickering over the exquisite miniature sculptured in ivory and gold. "'Tis a fine queen piece, sir. Which of us shall use it?" With no more ado he proceeded to set the pieces on the board. He knew this man was not Will Dare; he was an impostor.

The man's eyes narrowed as he watched Smyth. "I would like for you to add it to your set, Master Host."

"Well, now," Henry replied, his fingers deftly setting

the pieces to order on the checkerboard, "I rightly appreciate that, sir. Other guests will be happy to play with a complete set."

Betsy cracked the kitchen door. "Papa, I'm through for the night. Do you have any other errands for me to run?"

"Aye, lass," Henry said, wanting to get his daughter out of the house. Using a previously arranged and coded message, he said, "Mistress Ford has been ailing. I would like for you to carry her a crock of your soup, and hurry, lass. I don't like you to be about by yerself at night."

"Aye, Papa," Betsy replied, pulling back and shutting the door. She scampered to the clothes peg, unhooked her cloak, and swirled it about her shoulders. Something was wrong, and she had to get help. Her eyes darting around the kitchen at each unfamiliar sound, she ran to the back door, opened it, and was soon lost in the dense fog.

The guest sat at the table and peered into the shadowed visage of the old man. Then he dropped his gaze to the checkerboard. He reached out, his long, slender fingers closing over the head of the queen piece he had previously handed the innkeeper. He pretended great interest in the small figurine.

"I think perhaps you have some important papers for me—papers that Santica gave to you which must be delivered to the queen immediately."

"I don't be knowing what you're talking about, my lord," Smyth said. "I don't know anyone named Santica, nor do I know anything about the papers."

As quick as a flash of lightning across the sky and as lethal, all pretense of friendliness was wiped from the impostor's countenance. He bounded to his feet and rounded the table. "I know you're lying," he gritted between clenched teeth, his hand balling into a fist as he grabbed the front of Smyth's shirt and jerked the old man to his feet. "Now give me those papers and give them to me this moment."

"I don't know what you're talking about, my lord."

"We shall soon find out," the traitor said.

He shoved Smyth into the seat; then he picked up the candle and moved across the room. Three times he waved it in front of the window—a signal to his accomplices who waited outside. Soon the front door of the inn flew open and two men rushed into the room, dragging Betsy with them.

"And look who we found leaving through the back door." One of the men—a fat, unkempt man with greasy hair and beard who wore sweat-stained clothing—laughed as he tossed her down the steps and she fell into the main room.

"A good night's work, Mason Small," the man who called himself El Desafiador declared. "We'll get the truth out of this man one way or the other. And she—" he walked to Betsy, knelt down, and threw the hood off her head "—may be the way." He trailed his fingers over the creamy smoothness of her face. "Such a winsome lass!"

"No," Henry cried, divining the traitor's intentions, "don't harm her. She's done nothing to deserve this. She's innocent."

"In this war, old man," the man barked, "no one is innocent." He returned his attention to Betsy. "And where is your crock of soup for the ailing mistress, lass?"

"Don't tell them anything, lass!" Henry ordered.

"We have ways to loosen the tongue," the impostor said with a wave of his hand to the tall, thin man who still hovered near the entryway. "Come, Alfred. Let's show them."

Mason Small held Betsy while Alfred struck Henry Smyth across the face again and again until the landlord's head slumped against his chest, blood dribbling from his mouth to stain the front of his cambric shirt. Still the old man would not confess.

The impostor pushed Alfred out of the way so he could peer into the landlord's face. "Tell me!" he demanded. "Tell me where the papers are hidden."

Tears streaming down her face, Betsy cried, "Tell them, Papa. Tell them where you've hidden the papers." Anxiously she waited; her father was such a stubborn man, so loyal and true to Her Majesty.

"The queen," Smyth muttered, the words nothing but garbled sounds coming through bruised and swollen lips.

"I'm tired of games, old man," the man snarled, his fist jabbing Smyth in the face the last time. The innkeeper crumpled to the floor.

The girl broke away from the man who held her, ran across the room, and knelt beside her unconscious father. "'Tis no game he's playing," she screamed. "He's telling you where the papers are. In the queen's bust. Do something to it and the panel opens."

"What?" Alfred growled, his head bobbing about as if it were an apple dangling on a string. Then he saw the sculpture on the left side of the mantelpiece. "What must we do?"

Betsy tenderly cradled her father's battered face in her hands. "I don't know."

The impostor walked across the room and carefully ran his fingers over the bust of Queen Elizabeth I of England, pressing his thumbs in several places as he

14

searched for the lever to open the panel. Time hung suspended. The only sounds in the room were the crackle of the fire and the heavy breathing of the three men. Then came a gasp of pleasure that immediately preceded the groan of hinges and swish of wood as the secret door smoothly glided open.

"Have you found the papers?" one of the men asked, unable to bear the suspense any longer.

"Aye, I've found the papers." A large smile graced the impostor's handsome face. "We must hasten, lads, and get them translated. They are written in Dutch."

"What about the girl and the old man?"

The man who imposed himself as Will Dare didn't answer immediately. He picked up his cloak and hooked it about his neck; then with meticulous care he pulled his gloves on. "Kill both of them," he finally drawled. "Make sure it looks as if Will Dare perpetrated the murder. I want the English to think he is a Spanish spy, a traitor to England, and a murderer."

The impersonator, feeling a heated gaze on his back, turned and looked around the room until his gaze collided with the sightless eyes of the black marble statue of St. Peter, and a shiver ran his spine. Those eyes peered into the inner recesses of his soul and laid open his sins for the world to see.

The village was quiet, all lights doused as the young sailor rode through the evening fog toward Henry Smyth's tavern. Sweet memories of his lady-love brought a smile that softened the angular lines of his face. Timothy Turner reached into his doublet to touch the ring that he had so recently bought his betrothed—a ring to solemnize their engagement.

He dismounted, tethered his mount, and raced to the door of the tavern, which stood slightly ajar. His hand, palm flat, pressed against the wood, worn smooth by years of use, and he shoved, the hinges creaking ominously in the silence that was as heavy as the fog.

"Mister Smyth!" Timothy called not one but several times, his voice echoing through the empty, blackened house. He cautiously made his way down the steps across the main hall to the fireplace where one or two coals still glowed with life. Hurriedly but carefully—all his movements were careful—he rebuilt the fire; then, still squatting, he turned around.

He leapt to his feet. "My God!" His cry was an unrecognizable croak. In disbelief he shook his shoulder-length blond hair and his gray eyes grew bleak with despair when he saw Betsy Smyth lying on the floor, her arms and legs twisted unnaturally.

"No," he murmured, running to the inert form and falling to his knees, "it can't be true." He took her cold body into his arms and cradled her. He willed the strength of his love and the warmth of his body to give her new life. But he could not impart life to her. He was too late. "No, Betsy, my love," he cried, tears streaking his face to drip onto the bruised and swollen face, "you can't be dead. You can't be dead."

In a daze Timothy finally laid Betsy's body on the floor and straightened her dress as best he could. Then he followed a trail of blood to the table on the far side of the room where he found Henry Smyth's body. Close by was a quill and a toppled inkwell, the trail of black writing fluid mixing with Smyth's life blood. In an outstretched hand, cold and fisted in death, the old man clutched a

16

piece of paper. Timothy twisted and pried and finally tore the paper loose. When at last he opened it, he read the message—one word that ended in a glob of ink: "El Desafiador . . ."

Timothy placed the paper in a leather pouch which he tucked into his doublet for safekeeping and strode the width of the room, something slithering across the floor as the toe of his boot hit it. Bending his head, he gazed at the strewn chess pieces. A sad smile hovered on his lips. Henry Smyth had indeed enjoyed playing a good game of chess. For a moment Timothy could hear Henry's gusty laughter filling the room, the jovial sound blending with the crackling of the blaze in the fireplace, adding to the warmth and welcome of the tavern. Timothy could see the old man's eyes sparkling with victory. But all too soon death chilled the sounds and sights to bring the young sailor back to the present, back to reality. He looked around until he found the destroyed checker-board, splinters of wood and marble squares of alternating color scattered across the floor.

"Nothing," he murmured. "I have nothing left of Betsy." He fell into the nearby chair and dropped his face into his hands.

Only when Timothy ceased his crying and carried his grief safely hidden inside, did he move through the hamlet to wake the villagers and alert them to the fate of Henry and Betsy Smyth.

Timothy had no recollection of the passage of time. In a daze he saw to the burying of the Smyths, but he was a different person from the happy, carefree sailor who had ridden into town only a sennight ago. A moment of time reeked eternal change in young Timothy Turner. Plans for a future with Betsy as his wife were dashed in one

17

cruel blow. The young dreamer was forever gone to be replaced by the cynic—a man set on revenge—a man who lived only for that one moment of revenge.

After the funeral, the kindly priest asked, "Are you home for good, Timothy?"

"No," the young sailor replied, "I promised Sir Anthony Chadwick that I would sail with him one more time. After that—" his voice hardened like iron and was as sharp as a two-edged sword "—I shall find this man called El Desafiador and I will kill him!"

Chapter I

Semiconscious, Marta Carolina Lucas de Santiago lay on the beach, her sodden nun's wimple entangled with long black hair and twisted about her face and shoulders. The tattered remains of a somber-colored habit clung to her body, revealing more than covering her youthful curves. When she drew in deep gulps of air, pain shot through her body. Thought and sensation slowly and agonizingly returned, but she remained perfectly still with her eyes closed as she tried to get her bearings. Her face was burned from exposure; her lips were cracked and dry.

Spain. She remembered Spain. The ship. Her leaving for her land grant in Mexico. St. Augustine was to have been their first port. Her companions from the convent, Sisters Angelica and Maria Theresa. The ship . . .

Marta Carolina's thoughts were too hazy, concentration too painful. She tried to sit up, but her limbs felt as if they were glued to the earth. Finally she lifted her arm

19

and wiped the caked sand from her lids; then she opened her blue eyes, blinking rapidly against the brightness of the overhead sun. Slowly she moved her head to one side, looking about. She saw the beach merge into a dense forest. When she heard the lapping of the waves against the shore, she turned her head in the other direction. She gasped and, despite the roaring in her ears and the spinning in her head, bolted up. The last of her precious belongings were strewn along the beach; her chest, the lid open, was bobbing with the surge of the tide.

The surge of the tide brought with it memory!

The ship boarded by pirates; everyone around her dead . . . Out of the haze of unbidden thoughts returning, Marta Carolina suddenly remembered Sister Maria Theresa! Where was she? No sooner had the question formed than Marta Carolina saw the lifeless body, the brown church robe a banner of her faith in life, a shroud in death.

In that instant Marta Carolina Lucas de Santiago remembered everything! After a dreadful sea battle, pirates had boarded the ship on which she and her two companions were traveling to her inheritance in Mexico. Only Sister Angelica's ingenuity had kept Marta Carolina and the other nun alive. Taking the two women below deck, Sister Angelica had ordered her young charge, Marta Carolina, to don a nun's gown.

"I don't know if anything will save us, child," Sister Angelica had said when they were in the small cabin the three of them shared. "But a disguise and prayer are the only protection which I can offer you."

Then the three had slipped into the hold and had hidden. An involuntary shudder racked Marta Carolina's slender frame when she remembered the horrible men who ultimately found them and dragged them from behind the food casks. Before they discovered the women were nuns, the pirates killed Sister Angelica.

As if they were smitten with conscience, Marta Carolina recalled, the pirates hesitated to kill her and Sister Maria Theresa outright. Depriving the two women of everything except a trunk of their personal belongings, the pirates set them adrift in a small rowboat. Now Sister Maria Theresa was dead, and the small rowboat nowhere to be seen. Marta Carolina was alone.

The tranquility of the autumn afternoon was suddenly shattered. A group of Indians, their faces ferocious with paint, suddenly tore out of the forest and circled her. Their heads were shaved on either side, and their cockscombs were painted vermilion red. She had no time to shrink in fear, and before a scream could leave her lips, she was roughly yanked to her feet.

Her head was spinning, and her eyes were dark with fright. She teetered on unsteady feet as she turned her gaze from one scowling visage to the next. Now Marta Carolina was alone against a band of Indians! Then her eyes moved beyond her captors, to the beach. Sister Maria Theresa! Her baggage!

Marta Carolina broke the hypnotic, fear-binding moment. Disregarding her own plight, she lunged through the human prison in the direction of the nun. At the same moment one of the braves grabbed a handful of wimple and sea-matted hair to yank Marta's head back so hard she buckled to her knees. Since this one had demonstrated his ownership of the prisoner, the other braves broke the circle and trotted along the beach. Several retrieved her trunk and clothes; others knelt beside the dead nun.

When they touched Sister Maria Theresa's body, Marta Carolina screamed, "No!" Before she could move toward the woman, however, the Indian turned and walked toward the forest, dragging Marta Carolina with him. Dizzy with renewed pain, she cast one last, tearful look at her friend as she stumbled behind the Indian.

When they reached the camp, the Indian shoved her to the ground, but Marta Carolina was not so easily subdued. As he knelt over her to tie her hands, she lifted her leg and bent her knee, striking at his groin. The Indian easily deflected the blow, muttering imprecations under his breath as he threw his weight over her legs, and using the same thong, tied her feet together. Still mumbling in his own language, he yanked on the leather to make sure it was secure, then leaped to his feet and dashed to join the rest of his party.

Marta could hear them shouting in the distance, but none of the band ventured near her. Eventually she heard nothing except the soft afternoon sounds of the forest. She twisted and squirmed, trying to unfasten the cords that bound her, but the more she worked with the thin leather thongs, the more they cut into her wrists.

Finally, exhausted, her strength spent, she gave up and dropped into a fevered and fitful sleep, golden dreams tainted by ghoulish nightmares. Her family alive and well one minute—dead the next. First her mother and baby brother—both dead in childbirth; then her father—a man broken by grief rather than age. Aunt Karolina and Uncle Juan Martin Lucas de Santiago! They were dead. The one because she chose to aid Elizabeth, queen of England, in her scheme to return a Dutch ruler to the throne in Holland; the other because a political marriage of convenience turned into one of love and Juan Martin couldn't betray his wife. The two were branded traitors! Now Sisters Angelica and Maria Theresa, Marta Carolina's closest friends and her traveling companions, were dead; both had died protecting their ward.

At last, dreams abandoned Marta Carolina, leaving her to a restless sleep. When she awoke, it was dawn. Her dress, now dried of the ocean water but still filled with salt, was dampened by her own perspiration and plastered to her slender body. Attuned to her surroundings, she heard the sudden quietness that settled around her. She rolled on her side, scooted close to a large tree, and using it as a support, pushed herself into a sitting position. Exhausted from the effort of moving, she rested her throbbing head against the tree and slowly looked around the clearing. In the still, oppressive heat of early autumn, her heart turned cold when she saw single file, their arms laden with their salvaging, the returning Indians.

Marta Carolina watched them drop first her chest, then her belongings on the ground, and all but one of the braves squatted around them. The one who remained standing, her captor, the one who had dragged her from the shore, was staring at her; then he was moving toward her. Again Marta Carolina was hypnotized by fear. With smooth movements he discarded his knife and his tomahawk, tossing them aside. As he walked, he untied the thong that held his breechclout in place, and the leather apron slithered down his legs to the ground.

A scream—a loud, forceful scream—formed inside Marta Carolina, reverberating through her body, echoing through her head, and deafening her, but she couldn't give it voice no matter how hard she tried. Knotting in her throat, it cut her breath off. Her heart hurt so badly she could hardly stand the pain; she swam in and out of blackness. She heard the crude knife as it sawed through the leather thongs that bound her; she felt more than saw the naked Indian when he lay beside her, his strong, lean hands grappling for her body through the thick layers of dark material.

Then she heard her dress rip and felt the warm autumn heat touch her breast through the thinness of her chemise. The savage was tearing more than her clothing. He was shredding her integrity; he was violating her body. With an inner strength she didn't know she possessed, she twisted into a sitting position and balled her hands into fists that pounded on his smooth, rock-hard chest. This pounding was the immediate prelude to her loosening the scream that fear had bottled in her body.

The Indian, undaunted by her flailing, easily flipped her on her back, the jar vibrating her into insensibility. He pulled one hand back and slapped her across the face, a slender line of blood trickling from the corner of her mouth. With the other hand the Indian fought the binding garments. When the material wouldn't give, he gave an angry snarl. Shifting position, he pushed her skirts up and tore through the softer undergarments. Disregarding her cries of protest and her resistance, he moved between her legs. However, before he could penetrate her innocent flesh with his engorged muscle, he heard the fierce war whoops that seemed to fill the air around him.

In an instant the woman was forgotten. The Indian's weight fell on Marta Carolina, knocking the breath out of her, as he lunged for his knife that lay nearby because he didn't have time to locate his tomahawk. Another Indian flew out of the forest and landed on him. For only a second she bore the weight of both of them before they tumbled off. Relief swept over Marta Carolina. She had been saved! She gasped but nothing filled her lungs. She couldn't breath! Fear replaced relief. As she struggled for air, her chest heaved, and tears burned her eyes. Finally she sat up and leaned weakly against the tree trunk and took in long, deep breaths. Oxygen painfully refilled her lungs. The tightness in her chest slowly eased, and with it the pain.

She sighed in relief, and suddenly became aware of the battle going on around her. Her captor fought, but the enemy, in growing numbers, converged on the group who sat around the campfire and admired Marta Carolina's possessions.

She rolled her bruised body over and braced her weight on both hands. When her head stopped spinning, she reached up and straightened her wimple; she pulled the torn pieces of her bodice together. Slowly, using the trunk of a tree for support, her back against it, she pushed to her feet. Her head as well as her vision was clearing. Her eyes darted over the frenzied fracas. Now was the time to run for her life, she decided. Anything was better than the fate which awaited her here. She took several tentative steps, stopped, and looked over her shoulder. She spared her belongings one last glance. Everything she held dear in the world was scattered on the ground around the small campfire. Her herbs, her medicines! The recipes which the good nuns had given her. The apothecary in her wanted to take the time to salvage them.

But life was more precious. She spun around and raced away. Although she used her arms to clear the path before her, the undergrowth was thick and bushes

25

slapped her face, stinging and cutting the tender flesh. She was too conscious of impending danger, however, to think about her pain. She unwittingly blinked back the tears. She ran and she ran, her feet taking wings.

When her feet were too heavy for her to pick up again, when her muscles revolted against the mere thought of movement, when breath came in deep guttural gasps, she collapsed on the floor of the forest. Her fingers gripped into the cushion of pine needles; her face nestled into the cool comfort. Into her aching chest she gulped the sweet scent of rosin. If only she could rest awhile. But she couldn't. She had to keep going. The Indians would be after her. She had to get away.

Fighting the weight of her dress, she struggled to her feet. She looked around in fright, not knowing where to go. She couldn't remember from which direction she'd come. She heard the unfamiliar noises of the forest, and they frightened her. She imagined the Indians upon her, and she suddenly bolted. Again she ran, looking first over one shoulder, then over the other, until all she could hear was her labored breathing and the pounding of her heart, until she stumbled to her knees. She pushed herself up and ran again. Eventually she crumpled to the ground. She drew deep, ragged breaths into her chest.

She knew she could not stop; she must go on! Using her hands, she pushed up and rocked back and forth on her knees. She heaved the much needed air into her lungs and reached up to wipe hair and shredded material from her face; gingerly she touched the abrasions and welts on her cheeks. Finally she stared at the gnarled roots of the huge tree that splayed around her. Then she closed her eyes and summoned the last reserve of her energy. She drew in that last deep breath and opened her eyes.

Planted directly in front of her were two moccasined feet!

Slowly her eyes climbed one of the long, straddled legs, encased in tight leather breeches that were stuffed into black knee-high boots. Her gaze moved upward over the chest, also covered in the soft fawn-colored leather clothing, over the folded arms, to the glaring face, devoid of paint. Cut short, curly hair was brushed away from the finely chiseled face, and eyes, raven-black—the same color as his hair—never moved from Marta Carolina's countenance. If her eyes had been the window of her soul, the savage would have known her deepest and most intimate secrets, so piercing was his gaze.

But Marta Carolina Lucas de Santiago had never been a maiden to quail before anyone, and she wasn't about to start now. She'd heard tales of these natives, and the thought of her squirming at the feet of an American savage revolted her; it gave her spirit. Defying the brave who loomed like a giant above her, she tossed her head, straightened her wimple, and stood—although a wee bit unsteadily. But even when she pulled to her full height, she found him a good head and shoulders taller than she.

"I see you have found the paleface, my brother." Another brave moved out of the cover of forest and spoke in Scupperongac, breaking the silence that seemed to bind Marta Carolina to the man who stood in front of her. "Have they hurt her?"

"I think not." The Englishman's onyx eyes then moved from the startling blue eyes—that turned to indigo with fear—down the tiny body, covered with so many layers of coarse, dark material. "All I can see are small cuts on her face and hands."

The Scupperongac brave spoke again. "Is she one of

your people, Will Dare?"

Will shook his head, his thick hair softly brushing against the neckline of his leather jacket. He addressed Kee-lee, one of the village chieftains of the Scupperongacs, a powerful tribe of the Great Forest Confederation who lived close to the English settlement in Roanoak. "She comes from the land over the sea, Kee-lee, *Werowance* of the Scupperongacs, but she is not from my country."

Vision was one of the most valuable weapons an Indian possessed; therefore, he was highly skilled in its use. No one knew when, what, or how much he was seeing. Kee-lee's obsidian eyes seemed to be centered on her countenance. Yet he caught the lift of her chin, the straightening of her back, and the squaring of her shoulders. Although his features remained immobile, the Scupperongac smiled at the woman. He admired her spirit.

Will reached out and touched Marta Carolina's garment. When he did, she jumped away from him and her eyes narrowed angrily. "Keep your hands off me, you savage."

Understanding Spanish, Will started to reply, but quick thinking stopped the verbal retort. He closed his mouth, but he didn't drop his hand. Rather he closed his hand around the material and jerked Marta Carolina to him. However, even the roughness of his action was tempered with a gentleness that Marta Carolina sensed more than felt.

"Do you understand her language?" Kee-lee asked the Englishman, his eyes quickly assessing the forest about them.

"Aye." Will's free hand closed around one of Marta

Carolina's. Holding it in his, he brought it up and studied each of her fingers. Unconsciously he brushed the sand from the palm and tenderly touched the skin around the abrasions. "She's speaking Spanish."

"Spanish," Kee-lee repeated more to himself than to the other man as he thought of Will Dare's mission. The Indian's gaze shifted to his friend. "Is she one of your enemies to the south?"

"One of them." Will quietly answered the question, but his attention was on his captive.

In the outer periphery of her consciousness, Marta Carolina heard the men talking, but she wasn't even curious about their conversation. She was caught up in the demeanor of these new captors which immediately alleviated her fears and was so at odds with the behavior of the first group of Indians.

She was caught up in the virility of this man who stood so near. He was protective and kind, she thought. He wouldn't be brutal to her. Her extended hand lay on his, and she was unable to pull away. Fascinated, she watched as he ran the ball of his index finger over the top of her hand. No touch had rendered her this helpless before, nor had any man's touch caused shivers of delight to race through her body. Slowly as if Will Dare had given the order, Marta Carolina lifted her head and gazed fully at him. At the same time that she was attracted to him, she was horrified. How could she be drawn to a savage?

His hair, brushed into deep waves, framed the classical lines of his face. His eyes were large and blacker than polished ebony, Marta Carolina thought; they sparkled with life. At her scrutiny, curly lashes deliberately drooped over them, but she still saw in their depths traces of warmth and laughter. Her gaze shifted to the sensuous mouth—the finely shaped upper lip, the full lower one. Fleetingly she wondered what he would look like with the mustache and short clipped beard that was so in style on the Continent.

With interest Kee-lee watched Will Dare and the captive. His mouth curved into a smile, and gentle laughter warmed the forest. "The wise men say the best way to forget a woman who has broken your heart, Will Dare, is to put another on your platform."

At the brave's words, Will's eyes again swept over the tattered remains of Marta Carolina's religious habit. He dropped her hand as if it were a piece of red-hot metal which he feared would brand him and stepped back.

"'Twill be a long time before I can replace Ellen Graystone, my friend, and certainly not with such a one as this."

Kee-lee shrugged as he observed Marta Carolina's disheveled appearance. "From what I can see and tell she is a tiny thing, but how can you make such a reply, Will Dare? You haven't seen the woman yet. She's so covered in all those clothes."

Will could pull his hands away from Marta Carolina; he could even back up a step or two, but he couldn't take his eyes off her. Something about her compelled his complete attention. "Even if I were to strip the clothing away and see her, brave *Werowance* of the Scupperongacs, I could not take her to my platform. She is a woman dedicated to God."

Kee-lee's eyes narrowed, and he again surveyed Marta Carolina—from the top of her wimpled head to the frayed shoes that barely peeked from beneath her skirt. "A shaman?" His question was full of doubt. When Will nodded, Kee-lee asked, "How do you know this?"

Will chuckled. "Her clothing, my friend. Only God is allowed to see this body which she has dedicated to him."

At the same time both men heard the soft cooing sound of a dove. Their heads lifted, and they looked around.

"We must be leaving," Kee-lee informed him. "We saw signs of the main hunting party. They will soon rejoin this one." He motioned with his head toward Marta Carolina. "What are you going to do with her?"

Although Marta couldn't understand Scupperongac, she knew the Indian was asking about her, and she knew the decision rested with the one who had found her. Her gaze shifted from one man to the other as she, too, apprehensively awaited Will's answer.

His face furrowed. "I don't need the added burden of a woman on this trip." And certainly not a nun! His eyes troubled, he turned toward his head toward Kee-lee. "But in all good conscience I can't leave her behind."

"Are we to take her with us then, my brother?"

The peacefulness that had settled over Marta Carolina was dispelled. The indecision of the Indians, the questions they threw back and forth at one another, the shrugs, the frowns, all shattered her feeling of well-being. Again she was filled with fright. She had to get away; she had to escape. Frantically she looked around.

"We have no choice," Will replied, resignation dulling his voice. "We can't take her back, and we certainly can't leave her here."

As the two men turned, Will reached out, his hand going toward Marta Carolina's shoulder, but she dodged his grip and jumped away. "No!" she cried, once more seeking refuge in flight.

Will, however, moved quicker than she and blocked

31

her escape. "Yes!" he exclaimed authoritatively in Spanish, his hands clamping down on both shoulders. Unceremoniously he hauled her back. "I'm not chasing all over this forest for you the second time. You've already caused me to lose enough valuable time."

Startled, Marta Carolina stopped fighting. She gasped, "You speak fluent Spanish."

"I do." Will ingloriously propelled her through the forest.

"I mean," she said, "you have no accent."

"I don't."

Irritated, she again jerked away from Will. Turning, she dug her feet in the sandy loom and planted both hands on her hips. She threw her head back and glared up at him. "Don't treat me so condescendingly!"

Seeing one of his braves approaching, Kee-lee walked in the opposite direction to greet him, but Will planted himself firmly in front of Marta Carolina. "If you stand here any longer, Sister, you won't be acting like a compromised maiden, you will be one. In case you're not quite clear about what happened earlier, let me tell you. You were about to be raped. I happened to rescue you in time."

"Come, Will Dare," Kee-lee called softly. "We must be on our way. The main party is coming back."

Will nodded his acknowledgment. Unconsciously he caught Marta Carolina's arm, but not understanding Scupperongac, she didn't budge. She jerked from his clasp. "Who are you?"

"We don't have time to exchange social amenities," Will growled. "We must get back before—"

"And I, señor, am not budging from this spot until you tell me who you are and how you come to be speaking

32

perfect Spanish."

"If you wish to stay here and take your chances with the other Indians, Sister, you may. As for me, I'm leaving." Without another word, Will Dare turned and walked into the forest, joining Kee-lee and the other brave.

Her chin jutting out defiantly, Marta Carolina resolutely stood her ground. She watched the three until they were lost in the cover of trees. Then she was alone again, the forest closing in on her. As she stood there by herself, the unfamiliar sounds grew louder and more pronounced; they sounded more ominous. Picking up her skirt so she wouldn't stumble on it, she ran after the Indians. But she couldn't find them. They were gone.

"Wait," she screamed. "Wait for me!"

No matter how fast she ran, she couldn't catch them. They had abandoned her. Gasping for breath, she wrapped an arm around the tree and rested her cheek against the trunk. Why had she acted so abominably? She didn't know anything about survival in this new land. What was she going to do? Where was she going? As suddenly as the sounds of the forest creatures had begun, they stopped. Nothing stirred. The air was so quiet, the beating of Marta Carolina's heart was like a drum.

"Señor," she called. "Señor, is that you?"

Silence replied.

Having no intention of abandoning Marta Carolina, Will had sent the two Scupperongac braves to the canoes. Now he stood behind the tree and watched the nun. He wondered what she was doing stranded between the two Indian kingdoms of Scupperong and Chicora, and although he didn't like the idea at all, he fleetingly wondered why such a young and beautiful woman had entered a convent.

"Please, señor," Marta Carolina cried, "I know you're around here. Please help me."

Will moved from the covey of trees and slipped up behind Marta Carolina. Before she knew what had happened, he grabbed a handful of wimple and hair and pulled her back. His other hand held a knife at her throat.

"This, Sister," he quietly told her, his voice menacing, "is what happens to Europeans who don't understand the ways of the forest and its people. If you're to survive, you must listen to me and obey me. Do you understand?" Marta Carolina slowly nodded. "Good," Will replied, his tone ending the conversation. He sheathed his knife, and this time when his hand clasped her elbow, Marta Carolina submissively followed his guidance.

After they had traveled a bit, Will moving steadily through the forest with, Marta Carolina stumbling behind, she spoke. "Not once in my life, señor, have I been hauled across the countryside like a bag of manure. If I'm not defying your authority, señor—" her voice was heavy with sarcasm "—may I ask your name?"

Will's chest lifted in the lightest of chuckles, and he glanced over his shoulder. "Ahh, Sister, I must confess if you were a bag of manure I would have fewer problems at the moment. I would easily toss you aside and be about my business.

"What is your business?" Marta Carolina asked.

Will smiled and shook his head. "Certainly none of yours, Sister."

"How did you come to learn Spanish?" Marta asked. When Will didn't answer, she said, her voice slightly tinged with desperation, "I must know. I must find my people and get to them." Again she was answered by silence, but she was persistent. "From whom did you learn Spanish?"

Understanding her fright and her loneliness, Will relented. Careful to rely on the truth, he said, "My mother was Spanish."

"How wonderful!" Marta Carolina exclaimed. "And your father—" she thought of the Scupperongacs who had been with Will "—your father was Indian." When Will said nothing to correct her erroneous surmise, Marta Carolina beamed. "I am so glad that I met you, señor. Now I have hope."

"Yes," Will replied, her words heavy on his shoulders. They placed on him a responsibility he could ill afford. "I am your only hope." He stopped walking and turned around. "It is I who must protect you."

The suddenness of his movement caused Marta Carolina to bump into him. Reflexively he caught her in his arms to keep her from falling. But once she had regained her balance he didn't turn her loose. She fit perfectly against his body. She was soft and easy to hold. So he kept her in his arms and gazed into her beautiful eyes—eyes the color of the overhead sky—eyes that changed to indigo when she was frightened—eyes that darkened to midnight when she was obstinate.

Eventually she murmured, "From . . . from predators."

"From predators," he murmured. Eyes the color of the ocean.

Softly she said, "Two-footed as well as four-footed."

Will didn't pretend to misunderstand her. "Perhaps, Sister," he as softly returned, "two-footed more than the four-footed."

"What is your name?" Marta Carolina's voice was

hardly above a whisper. With intuitive knowledge she knew Will would answer her this time. "I cannot go around calling you señor."

"Guillermo in my mother's language," he said, "and Ca-leb-a-dam-a in Scupperongac." He didn't add, Will'am Dare in English.

"Ca-leb-a-dam-a," she repeated, tasting the beauty of his name. She smiled. "Does it mean Guillermo?"

"Nay. It means Man-who-is-bold. Ca-leb is the word for bold and a-dam-a is the word for man."

"Are you a man who is bold, señor?" Marta Carolina was so innocent and naive, she wasn't aware that she was flirting with the man and for the moment totally forgot that she was disguised as a nun. Now that she knew he was half-Spanish she wasn't horrified about her attraction to him, and she reveled in her emotional awakening and delighted in the new and joyous sensations that raced through her body. At the same time they were frightening in their quest for sensuality, but they were warm in their promise of passion fulfilled.

Will pensively nodded his head. "Aye, I am bold. I dare do anything."

His hands tightened on her arms, and he pulled her closer to him. Mesmerized by his touch, Marta Carolina was following his bidding. Her sweet virginal mouth was pouting for the taste of his. But then the abrasive material of her habit stung Will's hands, and he looked down. He remembered: This woman was a nun! Breathing deeply, he dropped his hands and stepped back. He cleared his throat. Not even he dared to touch a woman dedicated to God.

To cover his embarrassment, he said gruffly, "Come on, we need to hurry."

36

Disappointed that he hadn't kissed her, Marta Carolina ran behind him. "Don't you want to know my name?"

"Nay," Will replied. "I think we'll both be better off if I only think of you as 'Sister'."

Damn, he felt like a fool for having momentarily lost control, a double fool for having lost his control with a nun. He had been too long without a woman, he thought, absolutely too long.

"But I don't want to leave it at 'Sister'," Marta Carolina called breathlessly. "I'm Marta. Marta Carolina."

"Do you ever heed advice or follow orders, Sister Marta Carolina?" Will was exasperated, and his steps lengthened.

"Only if I have absolutely no alternative," Marta Carolina returned on soft laughter, the caressive sound winding a web of desire around Will. Young and romantic, this tall, handsome man fit all her fanciful, girlhood dreams.

For the second time he spun around, Marta Carolina colliding into his chest. His hand closed over her upper arms. "Then, by God, Sister Marta Carolina, you have absolutely no alternative."

He hauled her to his chest and stared into her face, looking into those eyes that were rounded in surprise and fear. But as she pondered the raven-black irises of Will Dare, her fear subsided. She saw no anger to correlate with his harsh words; rather she saw something more wondrous, something infinitely more alluring that stirred in the very depths of his eyes.

Frustration gave Will's voice a husky seductiveness. "I am a man, Sister, a man who has wants and desires. Unlike you I'm not married to the Church nor do I wish to be. And shortly you are going to find yourself divorced from everything you count holy if you don't remember that you're in the wilds of the New World. We're a primitive people in a primitive world with no Church to protect the innocent. The Indians won't respect your habit or your vows, and unless one of them has pity on you, you'll become the village whore."

Marta Carolina's temporary well-being was destroyed, her dreams shattered, but she no longer feared the man—she feared the emotions which this man of the wild could stir up in her. Although he spoke Spanish fluently, although he spoke with cultured sophistication, Marta Carolina knew he was a primitive; he was a rugged man. His every move reflected prowess, alertness, and the necessity to survive. This animalism was covered only by a thin veneer of civilization.

If she were to save herself, she had to get away from Will. She tried to twist out of his grip, but he held her tight. Her hands balled into fists and she pounded on his chest, but Will didn't turn her loose.

"From now on, Sister Marta Carolina, you are a shaman, a woman of God to be respected, and I'm the only one who can protect you from these Indians." He released her and shoved her away. "Never forget that!"

Marta Carolina stumbled backward and rubbed her arms where he had held her so tightly. She didn't understand how this man could have changed so quickly. "But—but you—you were the one who wanted to—to kiss me," she stammered.

"Yes." He was so irritated with his own weakness his answer sounded like a sudden clap of thunder. "I wanted to kiss you. In fact, dear Sister, I wanted more than just a kiss. I want to make love to you. Now do you understand why I don't want your friendship. I could so easily forget that you're a nun, and it wouldn't be because I love you. I would take you because I want a woman—any woman. I could so easily build the fire of desire in you that you would willingly desecrate your vows to God. Afterward both of us would hate ourselves and each other.''

For the first time in her seventeen years, Marta Carolina didn't know what to say or do. She wanted to confess to this primitive man, this half-Spaniard half-Indian, that she wasn't a nun. She wanted to tell him the reason why she was dressed like a nun. She opened her mouth, but the words wouldn't come. As she looked at the undisguised lust that swirled in Will's eyes, as her eyes lowered, and she saw the evidence of his arousal, she was rendered speechless . . . frightened . . . also breathlessly wondering. Her cheeks flamed red, and she lifted her head to stare into Will's face. Her silence—her secret—would be her protection.

Swallowing, Marta Carolina said, ''I'm sorry, I didn't mean to behave so unbecomingly. I have never—'' involuntarily her eyes strayed lower to the bulge in his breeches ''—I didn't know.''

''How could you have known?'' Will murmured, moving so that his back was to her. When he spoke his voice was oddly gentle, at variance with his gruff tones only moments ago. ''You're so young and trusting, Sister, you couldn't have known what you were doing? Sixteen, perhaps, or seventeen?''

A smile trembled on Marta Carolina's lips. ''Seventeen.''

He nodded. ''I thought so.''

''I've lived at the convent since my mother died ten years ago,'' Marta Carolina rushed on to explain. ''The good sisters raised me. Sister Angelica looked after me as if I were her own child. After my—my family died, she was the only one whom I had. She was traveling with me—she was the—"

His desires under control, Will faced Marta Carolina. Even if they hadn't been, he would have turned to her; her confession was a tender cord that wrapped around his heart and drew him to her. "She was the other woman whom we found on the beach."

Marta Carolina shook her head. "No, she was the one who died protecting me when—" Marta Carolina could say no more; tears rushed down her cheeks.

Will spiritually reached for Marta Carolina, but by sheer will power he kept himself from touching her. "Don't cry, little one," he soothed. "I'll take care of you. I'll see that you get to your people in St. Augustine."

"Thank you, Señor Ca-leb-a-dam-a."

Instinctively Will's desire to protect her welled up inside him; he moved closer and his sensuous mouth curled into a warm smile. He cursed his earlier weakness and determined to be strong. Holding out his hand, he said, "Come, little Sister, let's be on our way."

Chapter II

The canoe, a long hollowed log, smoothly sliced the water as Kee-lee paddled toward the riverbank. "We'll stop here for the night," he announced, looking over his shoulder at Marta Carolina who knelt immediately behind him, stuffed between burden baskets laden high with goods for bartering. Her head was bowed, her shoulders slumped. "We can fish and hunt for the evening meal. The shaman needs to eat and to rest."

"Are we there?" At the rear of the canoe Will rested his paddle in front of himself, leaned his elbows on it and surveyed the unfamiliar countryside.

Kee-lee smiled at the impatience of his friend. "Not yet, Ca-leb. You must give us time. The kingdom of Chicora lies another night's sleep to the south of Scupperong. The forts of the Spaniards are even farther south."

Something in the tone of their voices alerted Marta Carolina to a change in their usual travel pattern. She lifted her head and also looked about. Because the Indians were speaking in Scupperongac, she didn't know

41

what they were discussing, but at the moment she was too weary to care. Her clothes were gritty from the dried ocean water; her hair matted to her head; she itched all over, and although cushioned mats covered the bottom of the canoe, her legs were numbed from her long journey on bent knees. Lifting a hand, she pushed her fingers beneath the wimple to wipe the perspiration from her brow. From the way the Indians were pointing, she knew they were going to land. For whatever reason, Marta Carolina was thankful for a brief respite from water travel.

Conversation stopped as the three canoes made for shore, and the lead paddler agilely leaped aside to wade through shallow water and beach the vessel. Because the current was so swift, one brave held the canoe while the others began to unload. They left Marta Carolina and her belongings for Will.

Will hoisted her trunk on one shoulder and waded out of the water, yelling, "Jump out; then hold the canoe, Sister, so the braves can get the camp set up!" He pointed to the Scupperongac who held the bow of the vessel. "I'll come back and help you as soon as I get this ashore."

Following instructions, Marta Carolina stiffly waded through knee-deep water onto the muddy edge of the bank and grabbed the bow of the canoe, but the sleek lines of the vessel deceived her. She was unprepared for the weight of the bark, which was built sturdily enough to carry a cargo of several tons. Also she was unfamiliar with the swift current of the deep, wide river. Added to her ignorance was her physical disability. Her muscles recoiled from having been cramped in such narrow confines all day, and the primitive vessel slipped down the muddy incline into the water. Marta Carolina made a desperate lunge for it, her fingers barely hooking over one side. But her slight weight and strength, hampered by her long, wet dress, weren't enough to stop its descent. The bark continued to slide into the water, dragging Marta Carolina with it.

Will heard the splash of water first, then her screech. Dropping the trunk with a thud, he turned and yelled, "Don't turn that canoe loose!"

Marta Carolina was in the river now, being dragged by the current. *Damn you!* She opened her mouth to voice her protest, but the words turned into a gasp, a sputter, then a cough when the cold water sloshed into her mouth. *I'm more important than this damn canoe!*

Deeper into the swift water she went, her feet barely touching bottom. Still she struggled to hang onto the canoe, moving farther and farther from the safety of the riverbank. Then she stepped into a hole and sank beneath the surface of the river. For a moment Marta Carolina was too stunned to do anything. Like a windmill gone out of control, she lost her grip and began thrashing wildly in the water. When she broke surface again, she sputtered at the top of her lungs.

"Grab that canoe!" Will exclaimed, long strides carrying him toward Marta Carolina.

Grab that canoe! Is that all you can think about? That damned canoe! What about me? Who's going to grab me? The fears whirled in her brain as she flailed her arms and bobbed up and down. *Can't you see that I'm drowning?*

Then Will realized that Marta Carolina could not swim. He yelled to no one in particular, "She's drowning!"

His words galvanized the braves into action. They leaped to their feet, and immediately behind Will they

43

raced to the river. Will splashed toward her, shouting. "Everything will be all right." The braves swam after the canoe.

All right! Marta Carolina thought. All right for you. I'm the one who's drowning! Her head emerged, the sodden wimple clinging to her face, water running in little streams down her face.

"Here," Will said, compassion softening his voice as he reached for her, "catch my hand."

Marta Carolina was so frightened that Will's hand didn't offer her the safety she desired. She lunged for his shoulders, the force of her movement and the weight of her wet garment sending both of them spiraling to the bottom of the river. Her legs wound around his thighs, and her arms manacled his shoulders, cinching his hands to his sides. In the death hold she kept him under water. Finally Will managed to get his head above the surface and freed himself from her viselike grip.

"Don't fight me," he gasped.

Marta Carolina, however, was too frightened to listen or to reason. One hand clamped around Will's throat, the other over his eyes and head. Exerting all the strength he possessed, he swam to the shallows and crawled ashore, dragging the struggling woman with him. Wet and bedraggled, the two of them gulped air into their lungs.

"Much more of that, Sister," he finally gasped, sitting up, "and you would have drowned both of us."

"I'm sorry," Marta Carolina apologized in a small voice. She lifted the hem of her dress and twisted it to wring water out.

"Why didn't you tell me you couldn't swim?"

"Why didn't you ask?" she retorted. Then: "I didn't think I would have occasion to swim. I had no idea the damn canoe would have a mind of its own."

Will's lips twitched into a grin. The good sister was indeed rankled by her experience.

"Or that it was that heavy."

Will lifted his hands and raked his fingers through his hair, by now a riotous mass of curls. Then he stood, lifted her trunk, and set it on his shoulder. "Come on," he said, a tender note of amusement in his voice. "Let's find somewhere for you to dry off and bed down for the night before you do any more damage."

Without a word Marta Carolina trudged behind him, not stopping until he set her trunk on the ground. When he turned to look at her, he could hardly suppress the smile that tugged his lips. The wimple was plastered to her head and neck, and strands of black hair, escaping the confines of the veil, were pasted to her cheeks. Rivulets of water clung to her lashes and trickled down her cheeks, off the tip of her nose and the point of her chin.

Feeling his eyes on her, Marta Carolina lifted her head, and their gaze locked. They seemed to create their own time and place. Too innocent to understand the sensations that were coursing through her body, Marta Carolina stared at Will in perplexity, silently begging him to explain what was happening. She opened her mouth to speak, but as her eyes lowered to Will's lips, the words died because coherent thought was forgotten.

She saw the dark shadow of beard above the fine curve of his upper lip, the sheen of water on the full lower one. Though his lips never quivered, she saw the beautiful touch of humor in his eyes—warm and glowing, all encompassing—and now that the danger was over, she knew he wanted to laugh . . . but he didn't—not aloud anyway.

45

As Marta Carolina stared at Will she wondered what it would be like to be kissed. No new thought! She had often fantasized what it would be like to kiss a man, but never before had she imagined a particular man by whom she would like to be kissed. Now she knew. Her mouth opened, and her lips naturally rounded. Unconsciously they begged for Will's touch.

Will, watching and reading all the expressions that flitted across Marta Carolina's countenance, felt his heart hammer erratically beneath the buckskin garment; he felt perspiration bead over his upper lip. Desire burned through his body, leaving him hot and turgid. Unable to control the physical evidence of his excitement, he finally dropped his eyes; he broke the mesmeric bonding . . . but as if she were a magnet and he the metal, his gaze slowly returned lower this time to the swell of her breasts, their fullness emphasized by the wet garments that clung to her small, voluptuous frame. A rip in the material exposed skin that was creamy and soft in comparison to the coarse brown material of the habit. Spellbound, Will once again felt desire as it raged through his bloodstream, stretching his veins until he thought they would burst. As he felt his arousal straining against his breeches, he abruptly spun around

"You need to bathe. You're covered with mud." He cloaked his feelings with gruffness. "Let's find a place where you can clean up."

Disappointed because she thought he was angry with her, Marta Carolina innocently reached out, her fingers splaying on his lower arm. "I'm sorry," she whispered. "I didn't mean to lose the canoe. I was so frightened of the water that I didn't think. Please forgive me, Guillermo."

Will started. The musical softness of Marta Carolina's voice reminded him of his mother. She had called him Guillermo, but no one had called him by that name in a long time. Again he heard Marta Carolina softly say his name, the sound so caressive he wanted to take her into his arms and to love her hurts and disappointments away . . . or maybe to let her love his hurts and disappointments away. But he stifled the urge. He drew a deep, tremulous breath and looked at the small dainty fingers that rested on the deerskin sleeve.

Still he didn't move; still he didn't look at Marta Carolina. He couldn't, not without losing control altogether. And although Will Dare acknowledged that he was a rake, that he had tumbled many a maiden without another thought after the deed had been done, he had principles. He had never taken an unwilling lover or an innocent, nor would he take a woman of the cloth . . . even if she pronounced his name so that it sounded like a caress.

My God! What had he been thinking!

He gently removed his arm from her clasp, but even when she no longer touched him, he could feel her warmth. "I know you didn't do it on purpose, Sister, and I'm sorry for my outburst. I don't care more for the canoe than I do you," he apologized. "I—I just have many concerns on my mind."

"And I'm just one more worry," Marta Carolina softly said.

Now Will moved slightly so he could look at her. He smiled, fine lines splintering from the corners of his eyes. "Yes, Sister Marta Carolina—" his deep voice was full of the gentle friendliness that Marta Carolina wanted to hear "—you are a worry, and if you don't get those dirty,

47

wet clothes off, you're going to be an even bigger worry because you're going to be ill." He took several steps. "Now while I hunt you a secluded spot so you can bathe, you sort through your trunk for dry clothes."

A smile on her face, Marta Carolina watched Will until the forest closed around him. Eventually she knelt and opened her chest to look at what remained of her possessions. Not much, she decided with a heavy heart. The corsairs had taken her most prized possessions: the Lucas de Santiago jewels and the beautiful chess set with the ivory and gold chessmen which her aunt Karolina had given to her.

Marta Carolina rummaged through the trunk until she found the small leather satchel. She opened it and extracted her herbs and medicines. She touched the diary in which she had recorded the recipes she had gathered while living at the convent. She opened the book and breathed her relief when she saw the pages intact, the ink not even smeared. She returned it to the satchel.

Then she lovingly touched the packet of letters which her tía Karolina had written her through the years; she opened the parchment that legally transferred the land grant in Mexico from her uncle Juan Martin Lucas de Santiago to her. This *repartimiento* was all she had left. Because her aunt and uncle had been executed as traitors, all the Lucas de Santiago property and possessions had been confiscated by the Crown.

No, Marta Carolina thought with a smile as her fingers brushed the bottom of the satchel and she chased the lone chessman, *I have one small memento!* Finally she clasped the exquisite ivory and gold figurine in her hand and held it up. The symbol of her word: the queen piece. Marta Carolina was still puzzled about the promise that her aunt had extracted.

She rememberd the last time she had seen Doña Karolina Lucas de Santiago—a house prisoner of the Duke of Parma, the governor of the Spanish Netherlands. Already condemned a traitor and sentenced to die, Doña Karolina had asked permission to see her niece before she was executed. The duke had agreed to the visit because he wished to find a particular letter that had found its way into Doña Karolina's hand. It outlined in detail an assassination plot on Queen Elizabeth's life in case the coming armada failed. By all costs he had to get the document. Several of his most important spies who were key figures in Elizabeth's court were named as conspirators in the plot. The Duke hoped Doña Karolina might confess the letter's whereabouts to the niece; therefore, he sent to the convent and brought the young girl to Holland.

Marta Carolina remembered how frightened she was when she and her chaperon, Sister Angelica, arrived in the Spanish Netherlands where they had been ushered immediately to the house where Doña Karolina Lucas de Santiago was being incarcerated. Because they arrived before dawn, the house was dark. The maid, a candelabrum in hand, led them through the chambers and halls to the large reception room upstairs where Sister Angelica waited while a soldier led Marta Carolina to her aunt's room. When the jailer unlocked the door and threw it open, a tall woman turned from the opened window.

"Tía?" Marta Carolina had cried, her eyes adjusting to the shadowed room. "Tía Karolina, is that you?"

"Sí," the soft, husky voice replied, "it is I." She lifted her hand and beckoned her niece to the window. "Come and look! Stand here with me but a moment and look at the beauty of God's handiwork." She laughed softly as she laid an arm on Marta Carolina's shoulder and pointed to the sky. "Do you remember the game we used to play when you were a child?"

Marta Carolina nodded her head, her eyes sweeping the star-studded heavens. "Tía—" she began urgently.

"Can you find it?" Doña Karolina asked as if she and Marta Carolina had all the time in the world.

Again Marta Carolina nodded, but she felt no enthusiasm for the childhood game.

"Show me the queen of stars," her aunt insisted, her attention never leaving the heaven's above. "Show me the morning star."

Slowly Marta Carolina lifted her hand and pointed. "There," she said. "That's the star of destiny, Tía."

"Sí," Doña Karolina replied, her voice reflective, "that's the star of destiny." She hugged Marta Carolina tightly. "And with the morning star you'll find your destiny, my little niece."

The tall woman, so regal in prison, so stately in death, led Marta Carolina to the narrow cot that sat in the corner of the room. Aware that she was being spied upon—her every word listened to, her every action watched—Doña Karolina said, "I wanted to visit with you one last time. I hope you didn't mind my asking to see you."

"No," Marta Carolina replied quietly, "I'm honored that you asked for me."

"I don't want you to judge me too harshly," Doña Karolina said. "I'm condemned a traitor and sentenced to die." She lapsed into a contemplative silence which Marta Carolina didn't interrupt. "But I don't feel as if

50

I'm a traitor." She laughed softly. "Really, the word is relative. To the people of the Netherlands I'm a heroine; to the English I'm a business associate; to the Spanish a traitor. So different to so many, yet neither I nor my beliefs change from one country to the next."

"The duke claims you have papers which implicate certain Spanish officials in an assassination plot against the queen of England."

Doña Karolina had been prepared for the duke's devious machinations. She had known he would use Marta Carolina as a means of getting his hands on the letter. If only he had known his opponent better, Doña Karolina thought. He would have known that she loved her niece too much to embroil her in political intrigue. "That's what he claims, *querida*."

"If you turn these papers over to him, Tía," Marta Carolina continued, "he said he may be able to grant you mercy."

"No, my darling," Doña Karolina replied, "I will ask mercy of no man; therefore, I shall not be disappointed when I receive none." When she saw the tears almost spill out of Marta Carolina's eyes, she added, "Don't grieve, *querida*. Had I to do it over again, I would make the same choice. I have no regrets except one."

"What is that, Tía?"

"That I will not live to see you mistress of your own house with children of your own."

"Ahh, Tía." Marta Carolina smiled. She knew her aunt was saying things to cover up her sadness. Though her heart was breaking, Marta Carolina would play her aunt's game. "I have yet to meet the man who has made me wish to give up my work at the hospital."

"But a woman's place is in the home," Doña Karolina

said, voicing the same argument Marta Carolina heard no less than once a week from Sister Angelica, "not nursing the sick and impoverished in a convent hospital. That is for the good sisters who devote their life to God and the Church. God's will is for you to marry, to have a family, and to rear children."

"I'm perfectly happy working as an apothecary, Tía," Marta Carolina patiently reminded her aunt, "and I do believe I'm in his will."

"Do you never plan to wed?" Doña Karolina asked.

"I wouldn't say never, Tía," Marta Carolina replied, "but I must find a man who loves me as much as Tío Juan loves you; I must be as much in love with him as you are with Tío. Until then I shall work with my medicines." Marta Carolina chuckled. "I can understand Sister Angelica chastising me, but not you, Tía. You have always been so unorthodox. Quite rebellious at times." Her voice saddened. "Otherwise you would not have had the strength to stand with your conviction. You wouldn't have chosen to aid Queen Elizabeth, a declared political enemy of Spain."

Doña Karolina nodded and quietly conceded, "You are so right, Marta Carolina. I am unorthodox, and you are so much like me."

"After all, Tía," Marta Carolina softly reminded her, "I am your namesake."

"At times," Doña Karolina said, "I think you are my niece rather than Juan's." She reached up to touch the hair that was burnished a blue-black in the dawning light that had begun to pour in through the open window. "So much a part of my soul you are; so much like me." A catch in her voice, she said, "Since your parents are dead and your uncle and I have no children of our own, you

52

are our direct heir. You will inherit everything we possess."

Doña Karolina paused as she thought of her husband. She had not seen her beloved since the day they were arrested. The Duke of Parma had, however, allowed them to correspond. Doña Karolina had begged the governor to release Juan Martin; she would confess to any crime as long as they would release Juan; she had begged and pleaded for her innocent husband. He was not a traitor to the Spanish cause. His only sin had been his love for her.

But no one had listened. The price of Juan Martin's life was the original letter which implicated a group of spies whom the Duke had personally hand-picked and placed in Elizabeth's court, a letter which Doña Karolina no longer had in her possession, a letter she could not recall; therefore, her beloved must die with her. The price of glory had come too high. It had cost her her beloved's life.

Doña Karolina straightened her back and pushed her grief aside. She had one last duty to perform before she died. "Your uncle has a *repartimiento* in Mexico, Marta Carolina, an extremely large one." As if her niece did not understand what she was saying, Doña Karolina explained, "Thousands and thousands of acres of rich property, *querida,* and you own everything that is on or under them. The savages, the crops, and the underground minerals after you pay the King's tribute. Do you understand me?" She caught the young girl's shoulders in both her hands and looked directly into her face.

"Sí, Tía."

"At the moment your distant cousin, Don Rafael is managing it. I have spoken to Sister Angelica, and she agrees with me that you must go there and start your life

53

anew with Don Rafael and his family. As long as you stay here, you will be reminded of your sadness. You may even be persecuted for my crimes. No one will believe that you are innocent and that I did not leave important papers and documents with you." When Marta Carolina made no immediate reply, Doña Karolina persisted, "Promise me that you'll go to the New World, Marta Carolina."

"I promise, Tía," Marta Carolina compromised, "that I shall go to Mexico and see the *repartimiento*. If I'm happy I shall stay and make my life with Rafael and his family. If not, I shall deed the *repartimiento* to him and carve my own destiny."

Satisfied that this was as much of a promise as she would receive from her niece, Doña Karolina had stood and crossed the room to stand in front of the small table by the window. "I taught you how to play chess, Marta Carolina. Do you still play?"

Marta Carolina nodded.

"I would like for you to have this set," Doña Karolina said. "It's my most prized possession, and the only set I have left." She smiled sadly as she gently touched all the delicate figurines. "I've lost several of the pieces . . . the moving about I suppose. Both the bishops, the black king, and the white queen are gone. I miss her the most. After all she's the principal mover." Pounding on the door interrupted Doña Karolina. Before she could grant entry, the door opened, and the jailer barged into the room. He turned to Marta Carolina.

"Your time is up, señorita. Sister Angelica is waiting for you in the reception room."

Marta Carolina looked from the man to her aunt. She knew this would be the last time she would see Doña

Karolina alive. She felt as if a weight had been laid upon her heart and was pressing the very life out of her body.

Doña Karolina forced herself to smile though her eyes were shadowed with sadness. "Our roles are reversed this time, are they not?" she said. "'Tis you leaving me rather than my leaving you. But—" she looked around the sparsely furnished room "—I shall find you a gift."

Marta Carolina's eyes misted, but to give in to grief now would only hurt her aunt. She fought the tears, raising her head proudly, knowing Tía Karolina would expect this of her. "You—you don't have to give me a gift this time, Tía. I promise that I won't cry." So you can see me, she silently added.

"Of course I do." Doña Karolina's voice was crisp. "Every time I've been separated from you since you were a tiny child, I've given you a gift." She smiled through the tears. "Whether I see you or not, I don't want you crying when you leave. I want you to remember me with a smile." Doña Karolina pointed to the chess set. "Here, child. Take this and remember me."

Suddenly the older woman's face lit up. She retrieved the solitary queen piece and tucked it into Marta Carolina's hand. "This is a symbol of your promise, my little namesake." As she kissed her niece on the cheek for the last time, Doña Karolina whispered into her ear, "Good-bye, my darling. God bless." Valiantly keeping the tears at bay, Marta Carolina picked up the chess set and walked to the door where she stopped and turned her head to look over her shoulder. Doña Karolina whispered, "Every time you see the morning star, *querida,* remember me. Remember me with a smile."

"Sister!"

Will's voice cracked through the dusk-laden night.

Marta Carolina jerked out of her reverie and looked up, her large eyes shadowed with memories and sadness. Will squatted down beside her. As if he knew she were lost in the past, he smiled.

"Count your blessings, little Sister. At least you're alive."

Marta Carolina swallowed the lump in her throat and a sad smile quivered on her lips. "Sí, señor, I am alive." She then closed the trunk lid and stood. Speaking briskly to cover her grief, she said, "Come. Show me where to bathe."

Will understood Marta Carolina's grief and took no exception to her brusqueness. He stood and quietly moved ahead of her to stop only when he reached a secluded cove on the river.

"Are you afraid to bathe here?" he asked as he recalled her earlier fear of the river.

Marta Carolina's cheeks reddened. "No, I'll be fine. I won't stray too far from shore." She waited a moment before she said, "Señor, I know you think my fear of water is foolish—"

"No," Will softly negated, "I don't think it's foolish, but I do think it might be the death of you—" his lips quirked into a partial smile. "—or maybe the death of me."

Marta Carolina laughed with him. "As a small child, my older cousin Rafael and I often rode on horseback near the river that ran by our house. One day my horse stepped into a hole and broke her leg. She stumbled and fell, causing me to hit my head on a boulder and to lose consciousness. I fell into the water and was carried away by the current. Had it not been for the quick thinking of my cousin I would have drowned." Tears sparked in her eyes. "I have had a fear of water since then, señor. I have a recurring nightmare in which I am drowning."

Will caught both her hands in his and held them tightly for a moment. I understand, his touch seemed to say.

"Call me if you need me," Will replied, his softness the understanding which she needed.

"I shall."

As soon as he disappeared, Marta Carolina stripped out of her clothing and stepped into the icy water. Shivering, she dipped below the surface and cleansed both her body and her hair. Then she hurriedly washed her soiled garments. Clutching them in her arms and wading out of the water, she hung her habit and wimple across the low branches of a nearby tree to dry. She was drying off when she heard the noise in the bushes.

Although she was cold, her movements stopped, and she looked around. She heard the crackle of leaves. Someone was coming toward her. She dropped the towel and grabbed for the clean habit, holding it in front of her naked body.

"Who's there?" she called. No one answered. She heard steps approaching; twigs and leaves were cracking. "Who's there?" she called the second time, her voice rising.

Her words caught in her throat when out of the autumn foliage came a bear, dark and hideous. He reared up, his paws swinging through the air. Frightened of the creature, other animals raced out of the forest straight toward Marta Carolina, past her. Screaming at the top of her voice, she ran toward the camp, her habit catching on a low-hanging branch. Rather than stop to untangle it, she dropped the gown, clutching her wimple in her fisted hand, and continued to run.

Will heard the scream of terror. "Marta Carolina!" The cry tore from Will's throat as he and the Scupperongac braves rushed to the river.

"It's after me," she yelled, throwing herself into Will's arms. "It's after me."

"What's after you?" Will asked. Unconsciously his arms circled the small, trembling body as he visually scaled the woods, looking for her attacker.

The Indians, silent-footed, ran beyond him.

"It chased me," she cried, pointing in the opposite direction from which she had just come and burrowing her face into Will's soft leather shirt. "It came out of the woods and chased me."

"Shhhh." Will lowered his cheek until it rested on the crown of her head, until it rested against her soft, silky hair. He tightened his arms about her and snuggled her against his massive strength. Of their own volition his hands moved over the creamy smoothness of her back.

"It was—it was horrid," she mumbled, inhaling Will's scent, a masculine odor that blended an herbal fragrance with the sweet must of the buckskins which he wore. She brushed her cheek up and down, loving the friction of the soft leather against her face. She listened to the rapid drumbeat of his heart, her breathing heightening with his.

"What did it look like?" Will asked, his raspy voice making the mundane question sensuous.

"Large," Marta Carolina replied, the tiny fist creeping up Will's torso to lay on his chest. "Large and furry." She shuddered as she remembered the animal. "It was coming for me, Guillermo."

"Ca-leb!" Kee-lee's voice rang out, growing louder the

closer he came. "Your shaman has brought us great magic. Without too much effort we have found something to go with our fish for the evening meal."

Will looked up to see Kee-lee and the other braves move into the clearing, their faces wreathed with smiles. From Kee-lee's hand a dead rabbit hung. Having discovered the critter scampering in the direction toward which Marta Carolina had pointed, Kee-lee and the Scupperongacs never thought to search farther.

Will stared at the small animal for a minute before he, too, smiled. The more he thought about Marta Carolina's scream and her fearful exaggeration, the funnier he thought it was. His chest rumbled with suppressed laughter, but he wouldn't give voice to it. Even now he felt the erratic thumping of Marta Carolina's heart against his, the tremors that still shook her slight body.

Pulling away, Marta Carolina turned her head and looked at the rabbit that dangled from the Indian's outstretched hand. When she saw the grins on their faces, she was indignant. Did they think she was such a simpleton that a small creature like that would frighten her!

"I did see a bear!" she exclaimed when she looked up and saw the same laughter in Will's eyes. She pulled out of his arms.

The sudden movement caused his hand to graze her breast. Simultaneously Marta Carolina's eyes flew to Will's and she sucked in her breath. In the wake of passion, the argument was forgotten. Like Adam and Eve when they tasted the forbidden, Marta Carolina and Will were suddenly aware of her nakedness.

Will lifted his hand and reached out, his fingertips touching Marta Carolina's cheek. So young, he thought, and so beautiful. His hand, in whisper-soft movements, stroked the black eyebrows that arched above those Spanish-blue eyes, the smooth line of her nose. His hand cupped her chin, and he held her face immobile as he gazed into its beauty. Her eyes were so blue he thought he would drown in them. They were so trusting.

"Guillermo," she whispered, swaying toward him.

Will couldn't remember when he had ever wanted to kiss a woman as much as he wanted to kiss Marta Carolina. His body, of its own volition, refused to quell the desire that burned through him, the flame centering in his loins. He forgot that she was a nun, but he didn't forget that she was an innocent. Yet he lusted for her. He dropped his hand from her chin and caught her shoulders, his fingers like bands of white-hot metal against her flesh. He pulled her to him at the same time that he lowered his head.

Before his lips touched hers, he saw the crushed wimple in her hand, reminding him of her station. A flimsy piece of material it was; yet it was the strongest barrier Will had ever come up against. It kept him from making love to Marta Carolina. Exerting all his will-power, swallowing the bitter lump of disappointment, he slowly straightened and set her aside.

"Put your clothes on, Sister," he said, his voice a parody of its normal resonance. So Marta Carolina couldn't see his arousal—an occurrence that was happening entirely too frequently for comfort—he turned from her and ran his hand through his hair. "I'm sorry," he murmured. "I—I didn't mean to take advantage of—"

"I'm not sorry," Marta Carolina replied, "and you didn't take advantage of—"

"Then, by God, you ought to be!" Unable to restrain his emotions much longer, Will wheeled around. "Don't you understand anything, Sister!" He brushed past Marta Carolina and picked up the discarded habit. He yanked it off the branch and thrust it into her hands. "I've already explained to you what's happening between you and me. Lust! Lust and nothing more."

"Now I understand why Sister Angelica wanted me to leave the convent and come to the New World!" Marta Carolina's mouth curved into a winsome smile. She was on the verge of confessing to Will that she was not a nun. "She knew I would meet a man like you, Guillermo. She knew I would fall in love and would marry."

Before she could tell Will the truth, however, he exploded. "Love! Marriage!" He spat the words. "What I've been proposing, Sister Marta Carolina, is hardly love and marriage. I have been thinking of nothing more than a tumble in the —" he flung his hand around "—in the bushes. I'm offering you no incentive to leave the cloth of the Church."

Holding the habit in her arms, clutching it as if it were her only means of support, Marta Carolina stared incredulously at Will. "I—I don't understand."

"For God's sake," Will whispered, jerking the habit out of her arms. "Put your clothes on."

He held the gown up, twisting it around several times before he discovered the neckline. Grabbing Marta Carolina by the upper arm, he pulled her to him and dropped the dress unceremoniously over her head.

"And keep it on," he added as Marta Carolina pushed her arms through the sleeves. "I have enough problems without seeing you naked all the time."

"Guillermo—" Marta Carolina began.

If he heard her say his name one more time, his resolve would snap. "Don't call me Guillermo!" He reached for the wimple. "Call me Ca-leb."

"Ca-leb," she said, her voice making a caress of the Scupperongac word.

"Damn it!" he exclaimed, irritated because this snip of a girl was getting under his skin. "Don't call me anything, will you! Just be quiet. Behave in a manner befitting a nun. Grab your missal and your rosary and go somewhere and quietly pray for the sins of the world. If you will do that, Sister, I'll get you to your Spanish colony in St. Augustine in one piece, your virtue untarnished. And you might also pray for your own wayward ways," he muttered under his breath.

He flopped the wimple haphazardly on her head, but he couldn't fasten the neck band. The gentle evening breeze picked up tendrils of hair and wrapped them around his hand. Muttering imprecations under his breath, Will unwrapped the silken strand, but he held it across his palm and looked at it for a long time. Finally he dropped it.

His voice was slack. "I'm going back to camp, Sister. When you're dressed, fully dressed, please join us for supper."

Although she didn't know why, Marta Carolina had a lump in her throat, and her eyes stung. Ca-leb-a-dam-a, this man whom she had only met today, had the power to hurt her deeply. He exerted a power over her that no other man had ever had. She had been so sure the life of an apothecary, sheltered in the convent had been for her—so sure that she had argued first with her tía Karolina and later with Sister Angelica. Now she

62

respected the older women's judgment.

Remembering the desire that ravaged her body only moments ago when Will had held her, Marta Carolina knew beyond a doubt that a sequestered life—certainly not a nun's life—was for her. Yet now she must wear the nun's garb as protection from this man else she would succumb to the passion that his very look ignited in her body—a passion that promised nothing but a—a tumble in the grass.

She took the wimple off her head and quickly braided her hair, pinning it to the nape of her neck. As she replaced the veil, she fastened the band and walked to the river to lean over the water where she studied her reflection for a long time.

Ca-leb had told her to behave in the manner befitting a nun, and since she was impersonating a nun, from this moment on she would be a nun. Pray for the sins of the world, he had said! Pray she would. But her prayers would be for her own sin—for lusting after Ca-leb-a-dam-a.

Her virtue was at stake where this man was concerned; more, her integrity. She must maintain a distance between her and this primitive man of the wilds. Although she had been denied the sophistication of courtly manners and experience because she had been reared and schooled at the convent, Marta Carolina intuitively knew Ca-leb-a-dam-a was a worldly man, selfish in that he was accustomed to taking what he wanted without thought of the consequences.

He was truthful, she had to concede. He had told her that he only lusted after her body. He was also ruthless, she knew. Perhaps it was well that she wore the habit; it would be her armor against her own feelings. If she didn't keep a barrier between her and this half-savage, if she didn't pretend to be a nun, he would have no qualms in making love to her, no qualms in discarding her when the act was done.

But he would never give the one thing for which she was starved . . . love.

Chapter III

By the time Marta Carolina returned to camp, two of the Scupperongac braves were cooking the evening meal. Some were gathering pine needles and piling them for beds; others were securing the canoes. On the far side of the fire by himself, Will sprawled lazily, propped on one arm. He had promised himself that he would ignore her, but the moment she appeared, he became a man manipulated by forces stronger than his will and determination. He turned to gaze at her. Despite his resolve, he couldn't keep his eyes off her. He couldn't touch her physically, but he would look . . . by God he would look!

Marta Carolina deliberately sat away from him and kept her eyes averted, but she felt Will's intent gaze on her. For long grueling minutes, she stared at the spit on which the rabbit roasted. She counted the flames that leaped into the air only to disappear. Then she looked at the fish that cooked on large flat stones which circled the fire.

As she smelled the tantalizing aroma of the food, she

realized how hungry she was. With the exception of the cornmeal which the Indians had graciously shared with her when they rescued her, she hadn't eaten in two days—perhaps more. She was losing track of time.

Kee-lee pushed several more sticks of wood into the fire, and he covertly studied the paleface. Although he had been exposed to many palefaces since the English had settled on Roanoak Island during the past four or five winters, he had not seen one whose eyes were so filled with sadness. Marta Carolina smiled with her lips and occasionally with her eyes, but Kee-lee observed that she had no laughter in her soul. Happily married to a Lumbroan princess, Little Doe, Kee-lee was a man acquainted with joy and well-being; therefore, he regretted the absence of such laughter in the shaman. Truly it would make her magic stronger.

"Come. Eat," he said, using the few words he knew in English. He beckoned to Marta Carolina, a gentle smile warming his stern countenance. Friendliness shone in the depths of those obsidian eyes.

Reacting to the offer of food and companionship, Marta Carolina cast him a beautiful smile and moved closer to the fire. Following his example, she began to flake the tender fish from the bone with her fingers, and she hungrily stuffed it into her mouth. Both of them laughed when in her haste she missed her mouth and the succulent crumbs fell to her lap.

As the flames of the fire continued to dance through the darkened evening, shadows played on Will's immobile visage. He lay back, still propped on his elbow, and in morose silence watched Marta Carolina. Although she was modestly—in fact, she was totally—covered in the somber color of the nun's habit, he could still see her

66

beautiful body. He remembered the touch of her naked flesh against his; he remembered the feel of her small body in his arms. How wonderfully they had fit together!

He ached for her; his loins hurt with longing. Damn it! he silently exclaimed, pushing himself into an upright position. Why did she have to appear in his life at this time? Why did she have to come on the heels of Ellen's rejection and departure? That's why he was panting after her like she was a bitch in heat!

Never taking his eyes from his food, Kee-lee sensed Will's anxiety. The Scupperongac war chief was ever sensitive to his friend's changing moods. "What is wrong, Will Dare?" he asked. "You have been so quiet since you returned from the river."

Will shrugged his shoulders but said nothing.

Kee-lee faced the Englishman. "If you want the woman," he said, his approach simple and direct, "why do you not take her to your platform. She wants you."

"I cannot," Will muttered bitterly, "she's made a vow to God that she will give her body to no man."

Kee-lee's obsidian eyes swept over Marta Carolina. "I do not think she has made such a vow, Ca-leb, my friend. One who has made such a commitment as that to the Creator would have laughter in his soul. She has none." He continued to study Marta Carolina. Nodding his head, he said, "Yes, my friend, I think she waits for the warrior who can give it to her." Moving slightly, he picked up the forked stick and turned the spit so the rabbit could brown on the other side. "Perhaps you are that warrior."

"Nay," Will replied, "I'm not that warrior. Only love can bring laughter to the heart of the lover, and I have no love to give. I have given that to another, and she

67

destroyed it, my friend."

"You are thinking of the paleface woman, the one called Ellen Graystone?"

"Aye," Will murmured, visions of the fair-haired beauty swimming before his eyes.

"She was not the woman for you, and you know that, my friend."

Not wanting to discuss Ellen, Will jumped to his feet and strode away from the camp. At the edge of the forest, his back to Marta Carolina, he leaned against a tree and closed his eyes.

Such a short while ago since Ellen had gone . . . only two months . . . yet it seemed like an eternity. Will could remember her departure as if it were yesterday.

The Roanoak colonists had been elated with the arrival of the English ship. At first they thought it heralded the safe return of their Governor White with the promised provisions for the coming winter. Soon they learned it was Sir Roscoe Bennett, captain of the *Leviathan*. Initially the settlers were downcast, but on hearing Bennett's good news their disappointment was short-lived.

"My friends," Sir Roscoe had announced, legs astraddle, his hands on his ample waist—so ample, in fact, that his doublet paunch needed no extra padding. "I bring good news. England has defeated the Spanish Armada. Truly we are the mistress of the seas." Lifting his hands, he yelled, "God save the queen." Following his announcement, boisterous hurrahs were lifted and victory fists jabbed the air.

Ananias Dare, the interim governor of the small English colony during John White's absence and Will's older brother, had ordered fresh water to be loaded on the

68

ship; the captain in turn had provender unloaded for the colonists.

"Dine with me tonight," Sir Roscoe cordially invited, looking at the Dare brothers, a complete antithesis of each other. "I would learn much about your settlement so I might report to Sir Raleigh. Also I have much to tell you about the homeland." He looked at Will. "And I have a message for you, young Will Dare." The captain lowered his voice, and his grave eyes narrowed into a meaningful slit. "From Drake himself."

"Isn't it wonderful, Will," Ellen had gushed later when Will told her about the invitation. For the first time in ages, her eyes sparkled, her voice was animated. "England has defeated the Spanish, and our ship has come. We can go home." She clapped her hands together and repeated meaningfully, "We can go home to England, Will!"

Will nodded, but he was too preoccupied with his own thoughts to pay much attention to Ellen's gushing. Bennett had brought a message from Sir Frances, but what?

Ellen looped her hand through Will's arm. "What's wrong? You've been so quiet since the ship arrived. Aren't you glad about our victory over the Spaniards?"

Will sighed. "I'm afraid this battle is just one of many in a long war," he replied. "Sir Roscoe said the queen was already talking of a counterarmada. It won't be long before the war comes to the shores of the New World."

"Ah, Will," Ellen pooh-poohed his concerns aside, "you worry too much."

"Perhaps," he replied. "Perhaps not." He remembered the Spanish ship that had been cruising the coastline earlier.

Ellen concentrated on their supper invitation with the captain. "What shall I wear?" she asked, her brow furrowing in irritation as she thought of her skimpy wardrobe. "My brown gown," she decided. "It always shows my eyes to their best advantage."

On and on she chattered, and although Will nodded and murmured the appropriate answers at her pauses, he wasn't listening. Again he was lost in thought.

That night after a resplendent meal in the captain's cabin, Sir Roscoe toasted the victory of England over the Invincible Armada. His smile faltered when he saw Will's apparent disinterest, which he misinterpreted. "A toast to our victory at sea!" he thundered a second time, looking directly at the younger Dare.

Will spared him the courtesy of a nod and a partial curve of the lips. He lifted his tankard. "God save the queen."

Behind the facade of indifference was concern, however. Will was worried about the safety of the queen; he fervently prayed that God would save her. If Phillip of Spain had his way, Will thought, Elizabeth I of England didn't have many more days to live. Unless he found the man . . . the man who had deliberately and maliciously branded him a traitor, a spy, and a murderer!

After the happy gush of gossip in which Ananias participated as much as Eleanor and Ellen, Sir Roscoe eased his frame into his chair and sipped on his ale. "I have more news to give to you," he announced with a flourish. Again he visually singled out Will. "We English privateers now have a personal agent on pension in Havana who will be sending us sailing schedules for any of the wealth-laden fleets leaving the New World for Spain."

Will's eyes narrowed, but he made a pretense of studying his glass of wine. With a casual nonchalance, he asked, "Who is this agent, Sir Roscoe?"

"Rodrigo Fernandez," Bennett replied, slowly drawling out each syllable of the name. "He will also be assisting the queen in preparing her counterarmada by giving her information on the defensive strength of Spanish ports on the Continent and throughout the Spanish dominions prior to her attack."

"Rodrigo Fernandez," Will murmured in perfect Spanish, running his finger around the rim of the pewter goblet. "Isn't he the spy who worked with Sir James Palmer, the queen's ambassador in the Netherlands?"

"Aye," Bennett replied. "The same."

"After what happened to Palmer, is the queen sure she can trust Fernandez?" Will asked.

Bennett's lids dropped over his watery eyes, and he leaned back in his chair, crossing his hands over his stomach. For a long while he contemplated Will before he said, "Her Majesty doesn't blame Fernandez for Palmer's death; she blames the Duke of Parma. He's the one who apprehended and executed him."

"What does Drake think?" Will persisted.

Bennett threw back his head and guffawed. "Ah, yes, Drake," he muttered. "Drake had been acting quite like the queen's admiral. He has been in a huff since the queen made the proclamation. Says he won't use any information which a Spaniard sells to us. Hates 'em he does. Said to tell you not to trust 'em either. The devils won't rest, he declares, until they've killed the queen and taken over England. And he swears and declares upon his mother's grave that Rodrigo Fernandez is the leader of the scoundrels. Told me to tell you that, he did."

As quickly as he shifted his weight and pushed the chair back, Bennett changed the subject. "Well, good folk, I shall be lifting anchor on the morrow." He smiled at all of them. "Any of you who wishes to return to England may have passage aboard the *Leviathan*."

Later that night Will and Ellen stood in front of the governor's house, a large log building, which although a crude structure, was the grandest of which the small village boasted. Ever since Ellen's sister Catherine, had married Lone Wolf, War Chief of the Scupperongacs, and had gone to live in Scupperong, Ellen had been staying with Ananias and Eleanor Dare.

"I'm going home, Will. I'm going back to England." Ellen's voice was desperate as she continued the dead-locked argument. "This may be my last chance. I don't like it here."

"A little while, Ellen," Will begged. "Give me a little time. Then both of us will go home."

"Time for what?" Ellen asked.

"I must travel to Florida," he replied.

"Florida!" Ellen exclaimed incredulously. "Why must you go there?"

"I must find out the strength of the Spanish forts along the coast of the New World."

He wanted to tell Ellen of his search for the man who had framed him—the man who also was plotting to kill the queen—but he couldn't. Her Majesty's life depended on his silence. One small slip could prematurely set the assassination plot into motion. Besides, he had promised Sir Francis Drake that he would remain incognito and would await direct orders from him. Even now the orders from Drake were indirect, but Will knew time was running out. He had to find this Rodrigo Fernandez, his only link to freedom.

"But John Cartwright has already taken a group to spy on the Spaniards." Ellen's voice penetrated Will's consciousness. Suspicious now, she asked, "What's happened to you, Will? Since Sir Roscoe announced our victory over the Spanish, you have been acting strangely. Why are you so eager to travel to Florida?"

"I can't tell you now, sweet Ellen," Will whispered as he pulled her into his arms. "I will later. I promise. For the time being you must trust me."

Not to be persuaded with sweet words and kisses, Ellen pushed out of his arms. She wouldn't be bound with what she considered to be empty promises. She was beyond compromise, beyond reason. She was a woman with purpose, resolved to carry it out no matter what the cost.

"Return to England with me," she demanded.

"I told you I have a task I must perform before I return," Will told her. "After that I'll go with you."

"It's now or never, Will!"

Ellen announced the ultimatum firmly. Her coming to America had been a mistake. She had spent all the time here that she intended to spend. She wanted a life of grandeur and wealth; she wanted excitement and beauty—all of which could be found at the queen's court.

"If you love me, you'll go with me."

"I love you, but I can't return to England before I complete my task. Will you wait for me?"

"Perhaps," Ellen replied.

She knew at that moment she loved Will and had confidence that if he promised her he would follow her to England, he would keep that promise. She knew Will would never want the kind of life that she desired; she also knew herself well enough to know that she was not the woman

73

for Will. She was selfish and unable to risk danger to be by his side. More gently she added, "My destiny lies in England."

Thinking of Ellen resurrected older, more painful memories for Will—memories he couldn't forget or push aside as he did most of the time. He remembered that night two years ago, that night during the autumn of 1586, when he had been on a special mission for Sir Francis Drake. Disguised as El Desafiador, he had traveled to the Spanish Netherlands as an informer; however, his real task had been to get vitally important information from Sir James Palmer, the English ambassador to the Spanish Netherlands who had been arrested as a spy.

Palmer had discovered a large, concentrated spy ring, and the prime mover was in the queen's court. If the Armada which Phillip was amassing did not bring about Elizabeth's downfall, an alternate plan was to be executed, one that could not easily be foiled because all the perpetrators were trusted persons—key figures—in Elizabeth's court. Elizabeth Regina of England was to be assassinated. However, before Palmer could get the documents and information to his contact, he had been revealed as an English spy and subsequently arrested. Will visited Palmer one time in prison, but he hadn't seen the man face to face; they were forced to talk to each other through a confessional booth. Nor had Palmer been able to give Will any secret information—just the code name of Her Majesty's personal associate in the Netherlands—Santica. Palmer's untimely execution ruined Will's chances of learning more, and Will's only contact—Rodrigo Fernandez—told him he must find Santica.

The elusive Santica! Will hadn't known how to fi her. No one knew who the queen's personal associate the Netherlands was, not even Sir James Palmer. Th Will had received the mysterious message: *Meet me at th church. You will find me in the third row from the entrance. Wearing a white dress and veil of mourning, I shall be kneeling in prayer.* Immediately Will had contacted Fernandez and had shown him the message. Then Will had proceeded to the meeting place.

Will never saw Santica's face; he heard only the low feminine voice. "Henry Smyth has the documents which you are seeking. You will find him in Dover at the Boar's Head Inn. Give him this," she instructed, pressing a small object in Will's hand, "and say 'God save the queen.'" Will looked at the small black chess piece—a black queen—as Santica warned him, "This is part of a matched set which only he will recognize."

"What if Henry Smyth should not be there?" Will asked. "Is there another in Dover whom I may contact?"

"Yes," she whispered, her eyes fearfully bouncing back and forth as she saw the building fill with worshipers who seemed to be converging on them. "Search for the bishop."

Will left the church and returned to the prearranged meeting place—a tavern on the outskirts of Brussels— where he was to await Fernandez.

"All you must do is present yourself to this Henry Smyth at the Boar's Head Inn," Fernandez inquired, "and say 'God save the queen'?"

If Will had learned anything during his service with Sir Francis Drake, he had learned to distrust the Spaniards. That night he had been reticent to tell Fernandez all that had transpired between him and

Santica. For safe measure he said, "You must also present a queen's piece to the old man. That will identify El Desafiador."

"Of course," the Spaniard murmured, "Santica has always used chess pieces as her codes." Soft laughter filled the room as he reached up to stroke his finely shaped mustache. "You'll be happy to learn, señor, that at this very moment Santica has been arrested, and if you'll look about—" Fernandez waved around the room "—you will see that you are surrounded by Spanish soldiers, and you, too, are under arrest."

Will kept his hands on the table, never betraying by word or movement the queen's piece in his doublet. Already he was planning his escape, and how easy it had been! At the time he hadn't pondered the ease. He remembered the harrowing ride through the Spanish Netherlands and the hideous double murder at the Boar's Head Tavern that awaited him. He didn't have time to investigate before he heard a man call from the door. In his haste to blow out the candle so he could hide, Will knocked over the black marble sculpture that rested on the end of the mantel. Quickly he sat it upright and darted into the kitchen to peer through a crack in the door.

The blond-haired youth cautiously made his way across the room to stoke the fire into a full blaze. Then he had discovered the murder of Henry Smyth and the young girl. Will watched as the stranger wrested a sheet of paper from the dead man's cold, unyielding hand. He heard the man's exclamation.

"El Desafiador!"

Then Will understood. He knew why the escape had been so easy. Rodrigo Fernandez had planned it to be this way. He had set the scene so Will Dare would be blamed for the double murder and that he would arrive immediately after it had happened. Unawares, Will had slipped out of the house and headed for Plymouth where he awaited Sir Francis Drake—the only one who would believe his innocence.

Will would never forget Rodrigo Fernandez, and he had promised himself two years ago that he would not rest until he had found and punished him. And now this autumn, the autumn of 1588, he tasted the closeness of retribution for the first time.

Will didn't know how long he walked through the woods, thinking, but when he eventually returned to camp, the Indians were lying on pallets of pine needles, their blankets wrapped around them. Marta Carolina was sitting close to the fire, leaning against her trunk. The flicker of the flames hued her face in golden shadows.

"You should lie down, Sister," Will said softly as he moved nearer to her.

Startled, not having heard his approach, Marta Carolina jumped.

"We're going to rise early on the morrow, and we have a long journey ahead of us."

"You said you would take me to St. Augustine?" She spoke more than asked the question. When Will nodded, she stood and brushed her hands down her skirt. His acknowledgment seemed to reassure her. Without another word, she turned to walk to the pallet Kee-lee made for her. Lying down, she pulled the bearskin blanket over her body. She tensed when she heard Will move past her and lie down, but eventually she relaxed and dropped into a short fitful sleep.

She awakened, not quite sure what had roused her,

but she couldn't go back to sleep. Ghosts of the past troubled her too much. The shock was wearing off, and being in a strange place, her aloneness closed in on her more than it would have normally. She didn't want to cry, but the tears would not be stayed. They seeped from beneath the closed lids, soon to stream down her face.

Unable to sleep, Will heard Marta Carolina thrashing on the pallet next to him. His fingers gripped into the pine needles, and he breathed imprecations under his breath—not because he was callous but because he understood exactly how Marta Carolina must feel. He wanted to comfort her, but he also knew that his body responded to her as a man responds to a woman. He knew that it was not comfort his body wanted to give. Finally Will conceded victory to Marta Carolina. He rolled off the blanket and scooted close to her. His hand clasped her shoulder.

"What's wrong?" he demanded, his concern edged with roughness.

Ashamed that he had found her crying and stung over his gruffness, which she misunderstood, Marta Carolina snapped, "I'm doing exactly as you suggested, señor. I'm praying for the sins of the world. They are many and so burdensome, I find all my time filled with them. I find my heart heavy with grief."

Will groaned and pulled her into his arms. Lying beside her, he cradled her small body next to his larger one. "What are you doing over here in the wilds of this New World, little one?" he asked.

Shock forced Marta Carolina to talk. "If it were not for the English corsairs, Señor Ca-leb," she sniffed, "I would not be here. I would be in Mexico."

"The English pirates!"

"I think so," she said. "I—I heard one of them speak in English."

Will didn't think so. If English privateers had been in these waters, they would have harbored at Roanoak. But he didn't speak his doubts to Marta Carolina. Rather he listened quietly as she told her story.

"Sister Angelica, Sister Maria Theresa, and I hid below the deck, but the pirates found us. They dragged us from behind the food casks and before they saw our habits, they killed Sister Angelica." Marta Carolina shivered with renewed fear. "They were—they were going to-to—" she couldn't finish her sentence "but because they thought—because we were nuns, they were smitten with a conscience. Perhaps they feared God's retribution if they . . ."

She sniffed and paused for a moment then said, "Deprived of all our personal belongings but one trunk of clothes between us, Sister Maria Theresa and I were set adrift in a small rowboat." As she remembered the cruelty of the pirates, her voice hardened with a hatred that was foreign to the convent-reared woman. "They laughed and said our fate was in God's hand. He was the one who would determine whether we lived or died." Her voice became so low Will could hardly hear her. "We drifted for two days and nights before the storm came. I'm not sure what happened after that. When I regained consciousness, I was on the shore, and Sister Maria Theresa was—she was—"

"Don't think about it," Will ordered, contouring her head with his hand and pressing her face against his chest. "Let's talk about something else," he said, groping for happier memories. "Tell me about your parents."

"I—I don't have any parents," Marta Carolina replied,

gulping back her tears. "I was six when my mother died giving birth—both she and the baby boy. My father never recovered from their death. He carried me to the convent, and he entered a monastery himself, dedicating his life to God."

Will was stunned by her confession and hurt by all the grief she had borne in such a short period of time. More, he was surprised that she was such an innocent. How much her life paralleled his own.

"You've lived at the convent all your life?"

"Since I was seven," Marta Carolina replied.

"What did you do with your time?" Will asked, then added teasingly, "Stay on your knees and pray all day in one of those little cells."

"No," Marta Carolina drawled, her voice thick with amusement, "I didn't spend all my time closed up in prayer." She chuckled. "Nuns are people like everyone else. They laugh; they love; they hurt. I received a wonderful education at the school, and I worked beside the other sisters at the hospital. They generously shared their knowledge with me. They taught me to be an apothecary, and they gave me all their recipes for medicines."

Marta Carolina's words surprised Will. Any woman who wished to be mistress of her own home learned about herbs and medicines, but the studies of medicine were left to men. Why had Marta Carolina chosen to become an apothecary? Why had her father deserted her when she was yet a child? Will could not understand a man who turned his back on his responsibilities and family.

"Your father had no other family with whom he could leave you? Someone outside the convent?"

"He did leave me with family," Marta Carolina pointed

out. "His spiritual family. The only other family he had was his brother with whom he wouldn't allow me to live."

"Why?"

"They lived too far away from us, and my father wanted me near." She sighed. "I often wish, though, that Father had allowed me to live with my aunt."

"You sound as if you're quite fond of her."

"I was," Marta Carolina said, thinking of Doña Karolina. "I was named for her."

"Carolina," he murmured, giving it the Spanish pronunciation rather than the Dutch. "Such a beautiful name."

"My aunt was a beautiful woman," Marta Carolina confessed, her mind temporarily filled with lovely memories.

"Was?"

"Yes, she's dead." She paused shortly before she said, "After Father placed me in the convent, Tía would come see me once a month. We would spend the several days together, talking and playing games. Knowing I was close to tears when it came time for her to go, she would hand me a present which I couldn't open until after she had gone. 'Always remember me with a smile, little Marta Carolina,' she would say."

"And that is what you must do," Will softly admonished. "You must remember all of your family with a smile. But you must also thank God for his blessings. You're alive and well. You're young and you've a life ahead of you. You can't let the sorrows of the past burden down the happiness of your future." He felt Marta Carolina's head move against his chest as she acknowledged with a nod.

"That's what Sister Angelica once told me."

"What are you doing on your own so far from Spain?" Will asked.

The sensations Will evoked in Marta Carolina confused her. She wanted to tell him the truth; she wanted him to know that she was not a nun—not even a novitiate—in fact, had never considered becoming one, but she also feared the feelings that he stirred inside her. She felt as if the habit were her only shield against this man, and until she was sure what her feelings were she would wear the protective cloak of the Church.

"At the death of my aunt and uncle, I inherited a *repartimiento* in Mexico. I wanted to give it to the Church; however, the Holy Mother didn't think the idea prudent. She wanted me to travel to Mexico to see it first. A wise woman, she didn't want me to regret my decision when I was older." Marta Carolina laughed. "Little did the Holy Mother know that our ship would be attacked by corsairs." Again Marta Carolina felt the vulnerability that comes to one when all her possessions have been stripped from her. "Everything I own was stolen. Everything but my memories and a few odd belongings."

Marta Carolina curled against Will, seeking solace for her wounded soul and body; innocently her body touched him in all the most sensitive places, and he wished he were numb. He wished she did not evoke the passionate sensations that vibrated every inch of his powerful frame.

"Tell me something about yourself." Because she rested her face against his chest, her voice was muffled.

"My life is not one you would be interested in, little one. At best it is nondescript."

"Let me be the judge of that." Her eyes adjusted to the moonlight, Marta Carolina pushed up on one elbow and looked down at Will. "Already I know that your mother is Spanish and your father Indian."

Again Will did not correct her about his parentage—a perfect time to do so, but he didn't. At present, the less she knew about him the safer both of them would be.

"You speak Spanish fluently, and you converse quite readily with the Indians in their tongue. You even speak their hand language. Yet you don't look like them."

Will chuckled, and Marta Carolina watched the moonlight ease the chiseled sharpness from his face. "How am I different from the Indians, Sister Marta Carolina?" He rolled on his back and lifted his hands over his shoulders, twining his fingers together and pillowing them under his head.

"For one," she pointed out, "you don't wear your hair in long braids."

"Curly hair is difficult to braid," Will returned. "I find it much easier to care for when it's short."

"How dashing you would look, Señor Ca-leb, as a Spaniard. I can just see you at court. In your purple doublet slashed and paned, with great sleeves slit to show stitched linen beneath. A high collar to clip your throat about with a little starched ruff atop. And a rare stiletto beard, black as your closely cropped hair."

"Ah, mistress," Will clucked disapprovingly, enjoying the gentle bantering, "can you see me strutting around court like a peacock, setting the style for the dandies?"

Marta Carolina giggled. "No, Ca-leb of the Scupperongacs, I cannot imagine you in any European court. Somehow, you seem to be at home out here in this wild, primitive country." She sighed, then after a short while asked, "Do you live far from here?"

"A two-week journey," he replied.

"Do you have any family?"

"Only a brother is living," Will replied.

"Where does he live?" she asked, ferreting for information.

"The same village as I."

A disappointed "Oh," then: "How old are you, Ca-leb?" Marta Carolina pulled her legs up to her breasts, folded her arms around them, and rested her chin on her knees.

Will looked at the pull of the material across her shoulders, and he wondered what it would be like to span his hands around her small waist. He wondered what it would be like to taste her lips with his, to mold her naked body to his. His thoughts made him a caldron of emotion; his wishes were molten desire boiling through his blood to settle in his groin.

Marta Carolina turned her head, the moonlight gently touching her profile. "Did you hear me?"

"Sí," Will whispered, glad the cloak of night covered his aroused sexuality.

"How old are you?" she repeated.

Will sat up and peered into her face. "Marta Carolina," he murmured, dropping the respective title of Sister, "I have lived so many years that you cannot begin to count them. Compared to me you are a mere babe."

"I'm not a babe."

"How well I know that," Will returned dryly.

"When you're not comparing yourself to me, how old are you?"

Fearing the exchange of intimacy which Marta Carolina's question was innocently intimating, Will changed the subject. "Lie down and go to sleep, Sister. We're going to be getting up quite early in the morning, and you're going to need all the rest you can get."

Following his orders, Marta Carolina lay down and snuggled under the bearskin blanket. "What are you going to do when your mission is completed, Ca-leb?"

"Return to my village," he answered, then asked, "What are you going to do once you've seen your *repartimiento?*"

"I don't know," she replied. "At first, I thought I was coming over here in order to keep a promise to my aunt, but lately I've been wondering if that is the real reason." She turned her head to look up at him. "Since I've met you, I have begun to feel differently about life."

Will propped himself up on an elbow and leaned over Marta Carolina. His body told him to take the woman. She was ready for the plucking, but his conscience forbade him. And at the moment his conscience ruled supreme.

"Little Marta." His words were as sweet to Marta Carolina's ears as his breath was warm against her skin. "You are so young and sweet. So innocent."

"If I were not—if I told you that I was not a nun—" Marta Carolina said, but Will interrupted her.

"Marta Carolina, you don't need to get involved with a man like me," he softly said, "nor should you deal in lies. Your entire life has been devoted to giving and to serving others, to loving. Even if you told me this moment that you had not taken your final vows yet, it would make no difference in the way I feel."

"I don't understand," Marta Carolina whispered, a heaviness settling in her heart.

"I want to make love to you, little one. I would enjoy it, but I don't want to love you. I don't want you to love me. I want to teach you all the secrets and joys of making love to a man, but I'm rather like your father. I don't

85

want the responsibility that goes with loving. I have a task to perform and nothing—" he hesitated as a picture of Ellen flashed across his mind "—no one can deter me."

"After the task?" Marta Carolina asked.

"I can only think of one day at a time." His hand cupped her face. "Certainly not the future." In the moonlight he could see her face but not her eyes, yet he knew the beautiful blue orbs were swimming in tears. Because he had inflicted the hurt, he was sorry, but at the same time he had to be truthful with her. "I will tell you this: that aunt of yours was wise. You need to consider carefully your decision to remain in the convent, but don't base that decision on your feelings for me. I suspect your feeling toward me is one of gratitude." He leaned over and planted a gentle kiss on the tip of her nose. "Now go to sleep, little one. You have plenty of time to ponder your decision."

After Will moved back to his pallet, Marta Carolina lay quite still. Fear and loneliness gripped her as she listened to the nocturnal sounds about her. Unable to go back to sleep, she tossed and turned; she pondered Will's words.

All her life she had been taught the difference between lust and love. To lust was sin; to love was godly. But now that she bumped headlong into lust, she wasn't sure one could draw such a harsh line of demarcation.

Whether the feelings Will stirred up in her were sinful of not, she didn't know. She did know, however, that they were wrong . . . wrong for her. Despite what Ca-leb said, she felt more for him than mere gratitude. She might be innocent and naive, but she had womanly intuition which told her that she could not whore herself with Will . . . no matter how much she might love him, and love him she might. He had plainly stated he didn't love her. He couldn't. He wouldn't!

Will heard Marta Carolina as she tossed about, and he wanted to go to her. He guessed what she was feeling. He was feeling it himself. He wanted her so bad he could hardly stand it.

You ought to be proud of yourself, Will Dare, he thought. You've made the right decision. You've behaved like a gentleman. Quite chivalrous, in fact! You've retained your honor; you've protected hers.

Suddenly a scream pierced the night.

Marta Carolina leapt from her pallet and scrambled to Will's. "What was that?"

"An animal of some sort," Will sighed as he scooted over and let her slide under the cover with him. "Probably a panther." Evidently he was doing penance for all the sins he had ever committed—in this life and those before and the life to come. In spoon fashion he drew her trembling body close to his. "If you're going to sleep with me," he said, "lie down and get still."

"I feel so much better," Marta Carolina said as she snuggled her bottom against the curve of his thighs and hips. "Good night, Ca-leb."

Good night! Will inwardly groaned. How much worse can the night get? Aloud he only said, "Good night, Sister Marta Carolina."

A little later she asked, "How old did you say you were, Ca-leb?"

"Twenty-six," he breathed. "Now will you go to sleep?"

Entr'acte

Timothy Turner hunched over a secluded table in the corner of the tavern and stared blankly at the amber dregs of ale in his tankard. So much had happened since the death of his dear Betsy. His capture and imprisonment by the Spaniards, the defeat of the Invincible Armada. So much had happened and yet so little. And so much time had passed.

Where was the elusive El Desafiador? he wondered. His trail ended at the Boar's Head Inn. No one had heard a word of him since that fateful December two years ago. He was kindred spirit to an apparition. He appeared from and disappeared into nowhere.

Timothy cursed time—it had been his worst enemy. Hand in hand with fate, it conspired to keep him from finding El Desafiador. Captured and imprisoned for eighteen months by the Spaniards, he had been forced to abandon his pursuit. Timothy's gray eyes clouded in retrospect. Yet three months ago fate had proven fickle to time. The defeat of the armada had been his key to freedom; it had given him his ship. He slipped into the past, shedding three months as easily as if they were unnecessary garments he stripped from his body.

His faded cap sat at a rakish angle on his golden head, and an unkempt beard hid his face. Captured by the Spaniards and subsequently tried and condemned as an English pirate, Timothy Turner was sentenced to life imprisonment as an oarsman in the galley. More like an interment, Timothy thought as he listened to the battle sounds around him—Phillip's Armada had finally engaged in battle with the English. But was he above fighting the Spaniards? Nay, he was down here. Buried alive.

In the gun decks the noise was hellish; in naval gunnery battles it always was. An experienced sailor, one who relished the excitement of a good fight, Timothy closed his eyes and lowered his gaunt face to rest it on the handle of the oar as he imagined the battle on the upper decks.

There he could see flashes from the English gun ports; then he could see splashes far and wide of his random shots. Once in a while he could hear a thud when a ball hit the hull, or the twang of a cut stay, or a crash when a halyard was cut and a yardarm fell down—or, worse, when a shot came through the upper deck and sent splinters humming across the decks, splinters that wounded more men than the shots themselves; a cry of agony.

Turner could tell the battle was not going well for the Spaniards—how badly, though, he did not know, either. At the moment he wasn't sure which was greatest—his hatred for the Spaniards in general or his fermenting hatred for Will'am Dare, the Spanish spy in particular. He was lost in dark, bitter thoughts about both of them when he heard Don Pedro Avilar's desperate cry. He watched the commander of the vessel—a squat, Spanish aristocrat with no knowledge of the sea but one conscripted for service by the king—hurry through the door. A young subordinate officer dogged the commander's heels.

"Señor Turner, I need your help most desperately if any of us on this ship is to survive."

Although Don Pedro spoke Spanish, Timothy understood the man. An opportunist, the Englishman never dwelt on what could have been. He was a man who squared his shoulders and caught calamity by the head, turning it into an advantage every time. In the eighteen months since he had been a galley slave, he had learned Spanish, and he had questioned every Spaniard with whom he had come into contact concerning this man called El Desafiador. From Don Pedro, Timothy had learned that this renowned Spanish spy was also called Will'am Dare.

Timothy and Don Pedro shared a mutual respect for one another. One was a reputed soldier from one of the best families in Spain, one whom the king chose to command this particular vessel; the other, Timothy Turner, was reputed to be one of the most seasoned of English sailors, having sailed under Hawkins himself.

"I am a soldier," Don Pedro lamented, silently wondering about the wisdom of the king in sending him on this mission, "not a sailor. I know nothing about sailing a ship. Our pilot has been killed, and neither my men nor I know what to do to save the galley."

Timothy interpreted the words for the other oarsmen to hear. A gleam in their eyes, they looked from one to the other. How long they had waited for this opportunity! They waited for Turner's reply.

"You must set me and my sailors free, Don Pedro. Otherwise, we cannot help you."

"How do I know that I can trust you?" the Spaniard asked, deliberating his dilemma, his dark eyes bouncing frantically from one oarsman to the next.

"You don't," Turner replied, well in control of the situation.

"They have no weapons," the subordinate officer said to Don Pedro, "and we greatly outnumber them. They can do us no harm."

Don Pedro nodded his head. He motioned to the jailer and took the keys, unlocking the chains that bound Turner. He in turn freed his fellow shipmates.

"Now, Don Pedro," Turner called, moving up deck, "we must take in sail. Send your soldiers below decks out of the oarsmen's way, and we'll row for the coast of France."

"I shall send most of the soldiers below decks," Don Pedro agreed, "but not all of them."

Turner had expected this, so he was not perturbed. He nodded his head and barked orders in English to his crew members. They were prepared. From the very moment of their incarceration they had begun making toothpicks out of broken swords, which they sold. Secretly they had been making themselves stilettos. Now they awaited the agreed-upon signal.

They listened to and obeyed Turner's orders and soon the galley was in shipshape. The majority of the soldiers were below decks. At the right moment when they were out of danger of both English and Spanish ships, Turner threw his cap on the floor and stabbed Don Pedro to the heart. The signal. The slaves rose up in mutiny and killed every Spaniard on board.

As soon as all the Spanish banners were stripped from the ship and the English flag hoisted, Turner was proclaimed captain and the ship was renamed *Lady Fortune*.

"And now, lads," Timothy yelled above the huzzas, "what shall we do?"

"Take to the seas, Captain, and kill as many of the Spaniards as we can and take as much booty as we can."

"Aye," Timothy Turner replied, "we shall take to the seas." A smile touched his lips; purpose glistened in the steely gray eyes. "But first we must seek harbor in France. From there we will return to England."

And from there to the four corners of the world to find El Desafiador, he thought as he strode the deck.

He was now ready for revenge. He would hunt until he found Will Dare. He would slowly torture the traitor and murderer, enjoying each excruciating moment of his dying.

"How about another drink, wench!"

A boisterous voice called about the noise, and a tankard clanged against a table top, jostling Timothy back to the present. He looked around the raucous tavern. He was no nearer to finding Will Dare now than he had been two months ago when he captured his ship from the Spaniards. The man called El Desafiador seemed to have vanished into thin air.

"How about another drink yourself, Captain?"

From behind, Timothy heard the sultry voice. He turned to stare into the lovely face of the tavern wench who winked broadly at him. The gray eyes swept up the voluptuous figure in approval. "I would rather have something more than a drink of ale, wench." He caught her around the waist and pulled her into his lap. His lips touched the small indentation at the base of her neck. "The name's Timothy, love. What's yours?"

"Abby."

"What are you doing later tonight, Abby?" As he spoke, his breath warmed her skin.

She set her pewter tray on the table, locked her arms around his neck, and pressed her bosom against his chest. "It all depends on what you have to offer, sir, as to what I'll be doing." Her eyes were atwinkle. "My time is quite valuable, if you know what I mean."

Timothy reached into his doublet and extracted a beautiful gold chain that he'd stolen from Don Pedro when he took over the Spanish galleon. He dangled it in front of the woman. "There's plenty more where this came from, wench."

"I take it—" she reached for the jewelry "—you'll be a-wanting a room for the night."

Timothy nodded his head. "The best in the house, wench."

"I'll see that you get it," she promised. "And more. Now for a refill on that ale."

When she started to rise, Timothy's lips moved over the fullness of her breasts. His chin rested in the cleavage. "I would also be buying information, wench."

"That would be even harder to come by." Abby's voice lowered, and her eyes darted about the dingy room. "And much more expensive."

Timothy chuckled. "My purse as well as my codpiece is full, wench."

Abby dimpled alluringly. "Then perhaps I be a-knowing what you want to know."

"Do you know an Englishman by the name of Will Dare?"

Thought creased Abby's brow. Finally she shook her head. "Not a Will Dare, but I do be a-knowing a Dare, I think." Again she lapsed into silence. "Ananias Dare, it was. He and his wife stayed in this very same tavern when they was leaving for their venture in the New World."

For the first time since sweet Betsy's death, excitement sang through Timothy's body. So the man's name was Ananias; that concerned Timothy little. This could still be the same one. This could be the elusive El Desafiador.

"Did you hear him referred to as El Desafiador?" he asked eagerly. Abby shook her head. "I've been told that he's a handsome devil," Timothy said. "Close-cropped raven-black hair and eyes. A stiletto beard the same color. Quite a ladies' man."

"That ain't the man who stayed here," Abby said. "He was much older, white-headed. Certainly not a ladies' man." Abby chuckled. "I remember thinking, how could such a beautiful woman as his wife marry him." She snapped her fingers as a thought came to her. "But there was a handsome devil who came into the tavern with Drake hisself, governor. No beard and mustache, but he had the black hair and eyes."

Not interested in Drake or his acquaintances, only interested in the Dares, Timothy asked, "Did this Ananias mention anyone in his family by the name of Will?"

Again Abby was lost in thoughts. Finally she shook her head. "So many joined them, I can't remember, and not all of them stayed here. I don't even know where this Ananias came from." When she saw Timothy's downcast countenance, she promised, "I'll be sure to let you know if I can remember anything else."

Timothy reached into his doublet and extracted a ring which he dropped down her bosom. "Thanks, love, that's all I can ask of you."

After Abby left, Timothy slumped into morose thought again. Plymouth was his last lead. Where would he go from here? Begin all over again? He wasn't sure how much longer the crew would indulge him in his bid for revenge. What about sailing to the colony in the New World? He could question this Ananias Dare himself. Timothy's countenance lifted. He would tell the crew they were sailing for the Spanish Main and for treasure.

Chapter IV

Thinking she was back in her room at the convent, Marta Carolina smiled and stretched. She opened her eyes and gazed at the ribboned sky, gently colored by dawn. After awhile she turned her head and gazed about; then she blinked in surprise. With the exception of the pallet on which she lay, she saw no evidence of a camp. The bearskin blankets and mounds of pine-straw had disappeared; the fire-pit was nothing more than darkened ash. She threw her blanket aside and bolted up. The Indians were gone. Every one of them was gone. She was all alone. Frightened, she jumped to her feet and ran around, all the while searching for Ca-leb.

"Ca-leb," she called, wondering if he had abandoned her also.

With both hands she picked up her skirt so she wouldn't stumble over the hem, and she ran from one side of the clearing to the other; finally she headed toward the cove where she had bathed yesterday. When she rounded the bend in the river, she stopped short. Relief momentarily flooded through her; she saw Will standing waist-deep in the water. She lifted her hand to wave at him and opened her mouth to call, but she did neither. Unidentified emotions—hot and disturbing—surged through her. She was mesmerized by the man who bathed in the river. Spellbound, she stared at his naked chest. She was embarrassed; at the same time she was too attracted to him to look away.

Although she had labored at the hospital with the nuns, Marta Carolina had never seen a fully naked man before. Most of her work had been in the preparation of the medicines not in the administering of them. The good sisters, ever conscious of her innocence, had always protected her. She knew she should turn and quietly retreat before he sensed her presence, but she couldn't. She couldn't tear her eyes from him.

Will, aware that someone was watching him, turned around, his eyes colliding with Marta Carolina's. All his resolves, all his good intentions quickly dissipated in the wake of passion resurrected. He was a man, she a woman. No barrier could separate them. The washcloth dropped from his hand, but neither of them heard the gentle splash as it hit the water. Never taking his eyes from her face, he waded toward her, the water smoothly sluicing off his bronzed skin.

Marta Carolina's eyes, of their own volition, moved from Will's beard-stubbled face to his neck and shoulders. She drew in her breath sharply when she saw the thick black hair swirl across his pectoral muscles down his abdomen and stomach . . . lower . . .

Marta Carolina saw him as he moved closer to her, but she never moved; she was mesmerized by his masculinity. She couldn't tear her eyes away from his body. She couldn't control the quiver of desire that raced through her when she saw the soft groin muscle engorge with reciprocal emotion. Her stomach quivered convulsively, then seemed to tie into a knot. A hot, moist throbbing began in her most secret part, and for the first time in her life she knew want.

So weak she thought she would melt to the ground, Marta Carolina lifted her head to meet Will's face. Instead of the tenderness which she expected to find, however, his visage reflected his inner turmoil. His eyes were thunderous, dark with passion, smoldering with self-disgust; his mouth set in determination.

Marta Carolina had thought about this man's being ruthless and selfish, but as she encountered the suffering and anguish on his face, she realized that thought had no substance, no reality, compared to all the negative sides of his personality so blatantly revealed for her to see. Her desire quickly abated only to be replaced with fear. She threw her hand up to her mouth and backed away.

But Will was not to be deterred this time. His steps lengthened, and he moved directly toward her. Wimple and habit were forgotten. Will's sensibilities swam with visions of her loveliness. As though she were standing there naked, Will saw her hair hanging down her back, shimmering blue-black in the golden rays of morning sun.

In his mind's eye his hands spanned her tiny waist, and he lifted her up, her abdomen resting against his arched torso. In his fantasy he saw her breasts, rounded and firm, the aureoles pert and ready for a man's possession. He could feel them brushing against his chest, her hands splaying through his hair. He heard her tinkling laughter as it joined the happy sounds of the forest; he saw her smile. Altogether Will saw only a woman—a woman who was begging to be loved—a woman to whom he wanted to make love—a woman who had tormented him beyond endurance.

His eyes, smoky with passion, revealed all his thoughts, and the intensity of them scared Marta Carolina. She fled down the path into the forest. His countenance was too awesome for her to stand, his resolve and determination too strong. Unintentionally, innocently, she had pushed Ca-leb-a-dam-a beyond his threshold of endurance. But she wasn't prepared to pay the consequences. She couldn't remember a time when she had been more frightened . . . of him . . . of herself.

She looked over her shoulder. Will was directly behind her. She saw the big hand as it reached out and caught her, his fingers painfully digging into the soft flesh of her shoulders.

"Not this time," Will grated. "You've been throwing yourself at me ever since we rescued you, Sister Marta Carolina. Now I'm going to give you exactly what you're asking for." He yanked her around so that she was facing him. "You want to know what it's like for a man to make love to you. Well, you're going to learn this moment."

"No!" Marta Carolina's fists pummeled his chest. "Turn me loose."

Will's hand moved to her face to cup her chin. He lifted her head, and his lips moved unerringly toward hers. Although she was small, Marta Carolina was strong and she was afraid. She jerked from Will's grasp.

"I said turn me loose," she gasped as his hand slid across her cheeks. Opening her mouth wider, she sank her teeth into his hand.

Will grunted with pain, momentarily turning her loose. Before Marta Carolina could run to freedom, however, Will had caught her again.

"I'll teach you to tease me, wench." Tumbling her to the ground, he used his weight and superior strength to throw her on her back. He angled his leg over hers to still the thrashing, and his chest lay across her bosom. His hand moved to her face, his fingers biting into the tender skin of her chin.

"No," Marta Carolina muttered as his face came closer and closer to hers. She tried to twist away, but Will held her fast this time. When she could endure the hard, ebony eyes no longer, she closed hers and tensed for the brutality of his possession.

But when Will's lips touched her, they were so gentle Marta Carolina could hardly believe it. Her fighting ceased; her resistance fled. Her body trembled convulsively, but she didn't know how to reciprocate his demands.

Will truly forgot that Marta Carolina was a nun; he didn't see the wimple and the somber-colored gown. He saw only a desirable woman who wanted his touch, who enjoyed his touch. His lips slowly nipped around Marta Carolina's, and the heel of his hand tenderly brushed her breast until he felt the nipple harden.

He lifted himself slightly and whispered, "Open your mouth."

With no mind to resist, Marta Carolina followed his injunction. She opened her mouth, but she also opened her eyes. The beauty of her desire-darkened irises stayed his movement. She heard his quick intake of breath. She was as enraptured by Will's face as he was with hers. Gone was the anger and the flinty resolve. Now he was warm and soft. She lifted a hand and touched his face. She drew her fingers over his cheeks, loving the feel of the stubble. She outlined the thick eyebrows and the nose. She brushed in the fullness of his lips.

Will's head slowly lowered and slanted toward Marta Carolina's lips, his mouth opening. Remembering his words, she kept her mouth open, and she shivered anew when Will's lips touched hers—fully touched hers. Warm and moist, his tongue tentatively traced the sensitive inner lining. She felt as if flames of fire were leaping through her insides, burning her . . . incinerating her. But she would have gladly burned to a crisp so wonderful was Will's kiss.

In no hurry, he moved his lips over hers again and again in many delicious ways; his forays were gentle and tentative, each one claiming a little more territory than the one before. Finally his lips settled in a deep, demanding kiss. The demand frightened Marta Carolina, and she struggled beneath him, but Will was not to be put off. His hands joined the assault to move over her body as his lips sank deeper and deeper into hers. Will knew he was blazing a trail across virgin territory. With reverence he touched what no man had touched before.

Marta Carolina groaned as his tongue brushed against her lips. She reflexively twisted her body, thrusting her breast into his palm. Her hands slid around his neck, and her fingers twined through his hair. She kneaded his scalp at the same time that she pressured his head down against hers. Of its own volition her mouth opened wider to accept the fullness of his tongue, and she reveled in the wanton delight that possessed her soul and body.

When Will finally broke the kiss, Marta Carolina lay absolutely still, and he leaned over her, a hand planted on each side of her body. He labored to drag air into his lungs; his chest heaved with the effort. They stared at each other for a long minute. Then Marta Carolina raised her hand and ran her fingers through the crisp black hair.

"You're different from the other Indians," she whispered, her voice still husky with passion. "They have no hair on their bodies."

You are different! The words reverberated through Will's mind as he looked at the slight figure completely hidden in the voluminous folds of material, nothing exposed but tiny hands and a face. She was different, too! Filled with recrimination and self-disgust, he rolled away from Marta Carolina, and for the first time in his life he was ashamed of his nakedness. And he hated her for making him feel this way.

Marta Carolina was aware of his change of attitude by the expression on his countenance. When the warmth and softness was replaced by that chiseled hardness, she, too, felt the same recrimination, and she was ashamed.

"Guillermo—" she said.

"For God's sake," Will breathed deeply, unable to say at what point his desire had turned into disgust and hatred or hatred into desire, "don't say one word. Don't touch me again. Don't come near me again." He looked at her, his face drawn with suppressed anger. "I detest you for what you've done to me. Do you hear me? I detest you."

Without another word, he stood and walked away from her. Unable to help herself, Marta Carolina unashamedly looked at him: the broad back, the trim waist and buttocks, the long legs, all of them lean and muscle-corded.

After Will had disappeared, Marta Carolina stood. Too embarrassed and troubled to return to camp, she aimlessly wandered through the woods. How could her life have changed so drastically in such a short period of time? she wondered. How could she be so attracted to a man whom she periodically hated and feared?

Puzzled over these questions, she continued to walk, picking plants and digging for roots. Eventually she sat down on a large boulder. She heard a shuffling noise, but she didn't move. Her episode with the rabbits had cured her of impulsive screaming. By the time she looked up, the shuffling noise had turned into a huge brown creature with long shaggy hair, his teeth bared, his paws clawing the air. The bear she had seen yesterday! Her resolve forgotten, Marta Carolina leaped to her feet, her scream echoing through the forest.

Dressed in breeches and boots only, Will stood on the bank of the river. He heard Marta Carolina's scream. Dear God, he sighed. What had happened to the woman now? Another rabbit?

Will picked up his shirt and was about to drop it over his head when he heard Marta Carolina scream again. This time she was closer, and her call more frantic, more desperate, fraught with fear.

Will dropped the shirt and picked up his knife. Then he ran in the direction of Marta Carolina's scream. As he reached the clearing, he saw the bear swat Marta Carolina, its claws tearing through the thick material of her dress. The blow hurled Marta Carolina to her feet.

Heedless of the danger, Will ran to Marta Carolina. Waving his arms, jumping up and down and making noise, Will lured the bear away from her. "Run," he yelled. "I can't keep him occupied for long."

The bear growled and turned his attention to Will. He swiped through the air with his powerful paws, his long bladelike claws sinking into Will's chest, knocking him to

103

the ground. Marta Carolina gasped when she saw the deep, bloody slashes across Will's torso. Lying flat on her back, using her elbows to propel herself, she inched away from Will and the bear. Her arm hit something hard; she looked. A large tree branch.

As Will maneuvered away from the bear, he saw Marta Carolina. "Damn you! Get out of here!" he gritted.

The animal slapped at Will again, his claws slicing into his neck. Will groaned and stumbled backward. The bear lunged for him. Marta Carolina knew she had to do something to help Will. If she didn't, the bear would kill him. Picking up the nearby branch, she ran behind the bear and hit him over the back. Quick for an animal so large, he turned around and swiped at Marta Carolina. She managed to jump out of his way, but her feet caught in the hem of her gown, and she sprawled on the ground. As the huge grizzly lumbered closer, she rolled underneath a protruding boulder.

Taking advantage of the bear's distraction, Will leapt on his back and circled his thick, hairy neck with his arms. With the other hand, Will plunged the blade of his knife into the bear's chest. The beast reared up and bellowed, but he couldn't dislodge Will or the weapon. He spun around time and again, the circles making Will dizzy, but he held on, and he continued to plunge the knife through the thick skin. Finally, in one last effort the bear jostled Will loose. Will fell to the ground, the back of his head hitting the boulder on the other side of where Marta Carolina lay hidden. With a low groan he collapsed, and the bear fell on top of him.

Forgetting the danger, Marta Carolina came out of hiding and stopped only to pick up the branch as she ran toward the bear. "You killed him!" she shouted over and over again as she pummeled the animal.

Then she realized the bear wasn't fighting anymore. She held the branch suspended in the air, but the beast made no effort to move. Kneeling, she began to dig for Will beneath the heavy mass. When she couldn't budge the huge creature, she ran to her discarded branch. Using it as a lever, she pried him off Will. Blood matted the long, shaggy fur; the knife was sunk to the hilt in the side of the bear's neck. Slowly Marta Carolina dragged Will's body from beneath the dead beast.

"Guillermo," Marta Carolina whispered, wondering if he were alive. He didn't move, and he was covered with blood—his and the bear's. She lowered her head to his lips and listened for his breathing. Then she laid her hand over his heart to feel the faint beat of life. Lifting her gown, she tore off layers of her chemise and tenderly wiped the blood away. Exposed were deep slashes on his face, neck, and chest and bruise marks on his face, but her training at the convent came to her rescue. She was too intent on saving Will's life to be squeamish. She ran to the river and rinsed the rags. When she had wrung them out, she rushed back to Will and gently cleansed most of the dirt and blood from him.

Hurrying to her pallet, she picked up the blanket and returned to where Will lay. She worked until she had him lying on the bearskin. Then she slowly dragged him to the riverbank where she cleansed his cuts and placed a wet compress on his head. She willed him to regain consciousness. To make him more comfortable she pulled his boots off. Only then did she notice that his left ankle was horribly swollen and discolored.

She hastened to her trunk and dug through her clothes for her medicine and the swaddling which the nuns had taught her to use to bind wounds as well as babies. When she returned to Will, she knelt and unfastened the leather satchel. She uncorked one of the vials and rubbed the healing oil over his gashes. By the time she was finished, Will's chest was completely covered in a white bandage.

She scooted down the blanket to look at his foot, the ankle engorged and fevered. Capping the vial, she returned it to the satchel. She opened a wooden box and extracted some herbs which she crumbled into a mortar. She poured a yellowish mixture on top of the leaves and began to mix it with a pestle. The odor was so strong, her eyes were watering, but she didn't even take time to wipe the tears from her cheeks. Using her hands, she wiped the poultice around his ankle, which she also bound in swaddling.

After she washed the mortar and pestle, she returned them to her medicine box and filled a cup with water. Setting it aside she dug through the labyrinth of vials until she found the one she was looking for. She poured several drops into the cup of water.

Supporting Will's head up with one hand, she forced several swallows of the liquid down his throat. Having administered to his wounds and given him a sedative, Marta Carolina could do no more than wait. She wasn't sure where the Scupperongacs had gone, but she knew that she had to take care of both herself and Will until such time as they returned—if they returned.

For the first time since Will had rescued her, Marta Carolina wished she were the nun she pretended to be. Folding her hands, she raised her face to heaven and sent a prayer up for Ca-leb's life. It was her fault the bear had mauled him; it was because of her that he lay near death.

Moments later practicality took over. She knew they would need food, and by nightfall when the autumn chill came they would need a fire. First she gathered wood. Then she rummaged through her chest until she found a cord and a hooked needle which she could use to catch fish.

Using Will's knife, she dug under stones until she had her a nice supply of fishing bait. From here she went to the river where she sat on the bank beside the unconscious man and fished while she waited. Finally as the noon sun beat relentlessly down on them, Will groaned and stirred. Marta Carolina tied her cord to an exposed root and scampered to where he lay. On her all fours, she leaned over him.

Disoriented, he opened his eyes and looked around for a moment. His vision was so bleary he couldn't focus all that well. He saw the glow of Marta Carolina's face in the brilliant slashes of sunlight that filtered through the dense evergreen forest. The sun danced off the wimple, and for a moment he thought she was someone else.

"Ellen," he whispered in English, lifting his hand to beckon her. "You've come back."

Marta Carolina recognized that he spoke English, but she didn't understand the language. Following the injunction of his hand, she moved closer.

"Ellen," Will whispered. "My beautiful Ellen."

His hand touched her face, and he smiled—a beautiful loving smile that he had never bestowed on Marta Carolina. Her heart wrenched because she knew. He thought she was someone else. Someone called Ellen. She could tell by the caressing tone that the woman meant something special to him. But now was not the time to speculate on his rambling. She had to tend to

107

his needs.

His hand dropped, he closed his eyes, and his head rolled over. "Guillermo," Marta Carolina ordered, "you must fight if you wish to live. I can treat your wounds, but I cannot give you the incentive to live. That comes from within." But her words did not penetrate. Once again Will had sunk into unconsciousness.

After she had caught enough fish for the two of them, she cleaned and filleted them. Then she spent almost an hour building a fire. It had seemed so easy, she thought, looking at her blistered hands, when she watched Kee-lee doing it last night. Once it was going, she circled it with the stones and laid the fish out to cook.

Having dragged all their possessions to the river, Marta Carolina, leaning against a tree herself, sat close to Will. As an apothecary she was closely attuned to nature, and she had spent much of her life scouring the countryside for her plants and roots. Even now in this foreign land, she was growing accustomed to the individual sounds of the forest around her, so accustomed that she knew when she heard the unfamiliar bird call.

She tensed. She sensed the presence of other people. Without drawing attention to her actions, she eased to her feet and moved closer to the fire. Using the forked stick as Kee-lee had done, she turned the fish. All the while she was looking around. She reached for Will's knife and tomahawk. She had no training in the use of either, but she knew she would use them to the best of her ability.

When the Indians broke out of the forest, Marta Carolina was not surprised. She leaped to her feet and placed her small body between them and Will. She drew the tomahawk back in one hand, the knife in the other,

108

and stood facing the strange warriors.

She was frightened, but oddly wasn't shaking. She knew what she had to do, and she would do it. As the men cautiously moved toward her, their hideous weapons brandished, she stood her ground. Her fears she conquered with purpose. Her blue eyes moved from one to the other, but she never quailed. She promised herself that she would die fighting.

Before the Indians reached her, however, a piteous squall rent the air. The Indians stopped short; their heads never moved but their eyes darted in the direction from which the sound had come. Then they heard a shuffle and scrape as an animal moved through the forest. Quietly they spoke among themselves. Although Marta Carolina was as puzzled about the noise as the Indians were, she didn't take her eyes off them.

She wished something would happen—anything. Her palm was so damp with apprehension that the shank of the tomahawk was slipping through her fist. Her stiff arm, raised above her head, sent excruciating pain messages through her body. Perspiration beaded on her forehead to run down her temples and into her eyes. The salt burned and blinded her; she blinked rapidly.

She heard the animal's call again, closer this time; and something, a small ball of brown fur, bounded out of the woods. However, because her vision was blurred, she wasn't sure what. She batted her lids several times; then she recognized the fluff of fur at the same time as the Indians. They tensed and turned, ready for the enemy. Behind the bear cub would be the mother.

Thinking they were going to kill the baby, Marta Carolina galvanized into motion, running across the clearing to the small animal. "Don't kill it," she yelled, dropping the weapons as she fell to her knees and pulled the ball of fur into her arms. "It has no mother." Oddly, she felt an affinity with the orphaned cub.

Slowly, in synchronized movements, the Indians lowered their war clubs. Their fierce scowls were replaced by puzzled sternness. They watched Marta Carolina and the cub. Finally one of the braves took a step, the movement announcing his leadership of the group.

He was older, perhaps in his late thirties, but he was a virile man. He was lean and wiry, his gaunt features handsome. His hair was parted in the center and hung in two thick braids. Around his forehead was a headband of sheet gold. His cheekbones were high and prominent. His nose was clearly defined, and his eyes, a chocolate brown rather than black, glittered with admiration for the paleface woman. His mouth was finely shaped, beautiful in its firmness.

Unlike the Scupperongac braves, he wore leather breeches and a sleeveless vest that hung loose from his broad shoulders, fringe decorating the bottom. Around his neck hung many necklaces: some of them gold chains, the others strands of pearls. One was made of polished bear teeth. Around his forearms were fitted bracelets of gold, designs etched into the metal. He carried a bow in his left hand, a spear in the right, and over his shoulder hung an elaborate quiver filled with arrows.

In fluent Spanish the Indian asked, "What are you doing here, señorita, so far from the fort of your people?"

Marta Carolina gasped. Would she never cease to be amazed by these primitive forest people? How had they come to speak Spanish? As she gazed into the fiery eyes, she decided that the truth was her only salvation.

110

"I am not from the fort—" she started to explain.

"You speak their language!"

Marta Carolina dodged the swiping paw and the nudging mouth. "I am one of them," she admitted, "but I am from Spain. I was traveling to the fort when my ship was wrecked and I was cast ashore."

"Who is the man?" the chief looked at Will.

"He's—he's the one who rescued me," she replied. "He—he is Ca-leb-a-dam-a, and he belongs to the Scupperongac tribe."

"What are Scupperongac Indians doing this far south?" The Indian's tone was quiet, almost unassuming; the question was innocent enough, but the air was fraught with tension.

Swimming in and out of consciousness, Will heard the Indians as they interrogated Marta Carolina. He squirmed, his movements stiff, but he felt no pain. Surprised, he blinked, waited a moment, then lifted his head. His hand groped around as he searched for his weapons, but he found nothing.

"What are the Scupperongacs doing this far south?" The Indian repeated his question.

Will sat up and breathed deeply in an effort to clear his head. In as strong a voice as he could muster, he answered in Spanish, "I will speak for myself. The Scupperongacs are guiding me to the Spanish garrison beyond the land of the Chicora."

Marta Carolina's happy gasp of surprise was lost on the Indians. They now had their back to her and were looking at the man who spoke. The chief asked Will, "What are you called?"

"By the Scupperongacs I am called Ca-leb-a-dam-a. The Bold One," he translated into Spanish. "The one who dares." Keeping his face expressionless, Will asked, "What are you called?"

"I am called Strong Bear." He pointed to the long, sharp bear teeth that adorned his necklaces. "These are my totem."

"To what tribe do you belong?"

"We are the Chicorans."

"This is not Chicoran country, Strong Bear. What are you and your braves doing this far north?"

"We are hunting the Spaniards. On their horses and with their dogs they have marched through the Chicoran kingdom, killing our men and children and stealing our women. They burned two of our villages. We found a trail which indicated they had traveled to the Great Forest of the North." The Chicoran openly scrutinized Will. "Are the Spaniards your friends?"

Will shook his head.

"Then what are you doing with the woman black robe?"

Awaiting his answer, Marta Carolina pushed the cub aside.

"She was shipwrecked and captured by a hostile tribe," Will explained. "I rescued her." Will watched the way Strong Bear looked at Marta Carolina. He didn't like the desire he saw brewing in the depth of those dark brown eyes. The woman and I have killed a bear," he said, at the same time signing so the other braves could understand him. They nodded and emitted a murmur of appreciation.

"That is a good sign," Strong Bear replied absently, wondering what the paleface woman looked like beneath all those clothes.

"It is too big for her to butcher." Will laughed softly.

112

"Because she comes from the land over the sea, my brother, she does not know the ways of the Forest People. She does not know how to dress it. If your braves will help her butcher the bear and prepare a fire, we will cook food for your evening meal."

Again Strong Bear inclined his head in agreement. "That is kind of you to share your kill with us."

"It is kind of you to receive us as friends. To show our thanks we ask you to take all the bear meat which we do not eat to your village for your people," Will replied. To Marta Carolina he ordered, "Lead them to the bear."

Marta Carolina slowly stood, the bear running circles around the tail of her skirt. She glared at Will. Not a word of appreciation for her care and administration. Not one word of thanks. He sat up and immediately started barking orders. The two of them stared at each other for a full minute.

"Lead the braves to the bear." Will barked the order. He knew—Marta Carolina didn't—it was most important for their survival to have the respect of these braves. They must reckon him a warrior. He willed Marta Carolina to understand the precariousness of their position; he willed her to obey. Unmindful of the cub who scampered behind her, Marta Carolina finally turned and walked away.

After Strong Bear spoke to his braves in Chicoran, they followed her. Then he sat down on the blanket beside Will. For a long time they did not talk. Will deferred to Indian custom. He would let Strong Bear speak first and so guide the conversation.

With a bluntness which Will found characteristic of the woodland Indians, Strong Bear said, "Even though she is your enemy, you want the woman black robe."

Returning to camp to get Will's knife, Marta Carolina heard Strong Bear's assertion. She stopped before they could see her and waited for Will's reply.

"Yes, I want the woman. I killed for her." He looked at Strong Bear. "I would kill for her again." He left no doubt to his meaning.

Strong Bear stared at Will, then nodded. Raising his voice, he said, "Come, woman black robe. What do you want?"

Marta Carolina was not embarrassed that she had been caught eavesdropping. Rather she was angry, and she didn't mind their knowing. Moving from the cover of the forest, she walked to the spot where she had dropped Will's knife and tomahawk. "I returned to get the knife," she said, stooping and picking it up. When her eyes touched Will, he knew she had overheard his remark.

Marta Carolina had been irritated when Will had regained consciousness and had begun barking orders to her, but now she was angry. The audacity of him! Speaking about her as if she were his property, his possession. She belonged to no man and certainly not to him. He had made it clear that he did not want her. With a defiant tilt of her head, she walked away.

Strong Bear and Will watched Marta Carolina until she disappeared down the path. Then the Chicoran turned his head and scrutinized the bandages which swaddled Will's body and ankle. "The black robe tended to your wounds?"

"Yes," Will answered, gently probing the bandages, wondering why he was feeling no discomfort.

"Where are the braves who travel with you?"

"They have gone ahead to scout."

"What are they looking for?"

"Four men from my town traveled south to spy on the Spanish forts and to report back to us. Because we have seen no signs of their having passed through, we are worried."

"My braves and I did not encounter your men."

"Perhaps the trail you are following is the one left by my scouts. That would explain why it was coming from the North Land."

"That could be."

His leg cramping, Will moved and flexed his ankle. Although it was swollen, it didn't hurt, but it was tight and stiff. He knew walking on it would be a painful chore. He was frustrated. His mission had been delayed long enough, and now this would slow him down even longer.

Strong Bear's strong fingers probed the swollen area. "You need to rest several days and let this heal."

"I don't have several days."

"You must take the time."

Will heard the familiar bird coo. Angling his head and cupping his mouth, he made a similar sound, letting his companions know it was safe to come into the camp. Only then did Kee-lee and his braves move into the clearing. The Scupperongac's blanket was draped over one shoulder in bundle fashion. The four corners formed a handle which he gripped in one hand. As he set the bundle down, he looked from the Chicoran chief to Will who sat on the blanket. Before Will could speak, Kee-lee's hands began to move in fluid motion as he talked the silent language—the universal language of the forest people.

"I am Kee-lee of the Scupperongac. We come in peace. We wish to trade as we travel through your country to the forts of the Spaniards."

115

Strong Bear replied in the silent tongue. "I am Strong Bear of the Chicorans. We welcome you to our nation, and we wish to barter goods with you. We grant you peaceful passage through our kingdom." Speaking in Spanish as he signed, he said, "While you greet your friend, I will help my braves skin and dress the bear which Ca-leb and his woman have slain. We will exchange gifts and talk after we have eaten the evening meal."

After Strong Bear had walked away, Kee-lee knelt beside Will. "Your magic is strong today, my brother." He addressed Will with affection and admiration. "You have fought the great bear and have won."

"I have killed a great bear," Will admitted, "but I'm not so sure which one of us won, my friend." He pointed to his leg. "I shall be moving slowly for a few days." As he shifted and repositioned his leg, he grunted, "Now, tell me, what did you find?"

As always Kee-lee's answer was direct and to the point. "The bones of three people swinging from the trees at an old deserted paleface fort." He unfolded the blanket. "And this." He handed Will the tattered remains of a cambric shirt and leather jerkin, several metal buttons, and the stock of a matchlock musket.

Will reached for the stock and ran the tip of his fingers over the initials. "John Cartwright," he whispered.

"One of your braves?"

Will nodded. Clutching the piece of wood tightly in his hands, he said, "One of the four!"

Chapter V

Having watched the Scupperongac braves as they made the cooking frame the night before, Marta Carolina ably—however, more slowly—constructed another for the cooking of the bear, but when the Chicoran arrived with a large piece of meat and glanced dubiously at the spit, she realized it was too flimsy. He laid the roast on the cold rocks that circled the fire pit and returned to the forest. Marta Carolina lifted a hand and wiped the perspiration from her face. What was she to do?

Strong Bear, Kee-lee, and Will were sitting on the blanket, talking. The others were in the forest; some of them butchering the bear, others gathering plants. One of the Chicorans, his blanket cupped basket-fashion and filled with nuts, ran into the clearing. When he saw the cooking rod, he smiled.

"One moment, señorita. I will show you how to cook the meat," the Indian volunteered.

After several more trips into the forest, he knelt, and, using a piece of wood, scraped away the coals from last night's fire. Then he dug a pit which he lined with leaves and sheets of bark. This done, he filled the hole with the nuts and covered it with another piece of bark.

Patting a thin layer of dirt over it, he said, "We will have roasted nuts to eat with our meal." Quickly he stacked the wood over the oven and circled the stones around it. In those smooth movements that Marta Carolina was coming to associate with the Indians, the Chicoran leapt to his feet. "Now I will show you how to make a rack for cooking over the fire."

He trotted into the woods, returning shortly with an armload of reeds. He dropped them by the fire pit and knelt. Using his flint knife and sinew thongs, he whittled and cut until he had constructed an elevated grill which was supported and kept away from the flames by four large stakes driven into the ground. He looked at the diminutive woman and grinned.

"Now, señorita, you can strip the meat and lay it across the rack."

"Thank you—" A lovely smile lit Marta Carolina's face. "I'm sorry, but I don't know what you're called."

"Thunder Cloud," he replied. "And what are you called?"

"Marta Carolina," she answered as she knelt beside him, and the two of them sliced the bear meat into small strips, "How is it that you speak Spanish so fluently?" she asked. "Do you live at the Spanish fort?"

The Indian shook his head. "The people who follow the black robes," he said, "have been in our kingdom for more winters than I have seen. Even now I've heard that a black robe lives in one of our villages."

Because the Chicorans used the term inclusively for all Spaniards, Marta Carolina wasn't sure if he meant

118

a priest or not. His next words, however, answered her question.

"He is a shaman also. He wears a robe like yours."

Conversation was stopped. Another brave came running from the river, several large sturgeons impaled on his spear. Speaking in Chicoran, he addressed Thunder Cloud. From his gestures, Marta Carolina knew what he was saying. She didn't need any translation.

She took the fish, quickly scaling and filleting them, proud that she knew what to do. Then she spread them on the large stones that circled the fire pit. As the blaze crackled and sputtered to life, Marta Carolina turned her head and gazed at Will, in particular at the bandages that covered his upper body. He and the two Indians were in deep discussion. Their voices were low; their countenances serious.

Marta Carolina was quite proud of her nursing. The bandages looked as good as any the sisters had ever put on a patient, and the salves and drugs had numbed his pain. She was glad she had brought her apothecary cabinet with her. But even with the medicines, Will was not going to be able to set his full weight on his sprained ankle for several days. He would need a crutch.

As she rocked back, balancing her weight on her toes rather than on her knees, she remembered Will's delirious rambling. Why had he spoken in English? she wondered. And who was Ellen?

"I must go get more firewood," Thunder Cloud said, using the forked stick to turn several pieces of the meat that had browned on one side.

"I'll do it," Marta Carolina said and jumped to her feet before the Indian could protest.

119

Picking up Will's hatchet, she scurried into the forest and moved from tree to tree until she found the right one, a forked lower branch which she chopped off and stripped clean as she carried it back to camp. She laid the branch near the fire and returned to the forest to gather fuel for the fire.

When she had dumped her load of wood close to the cooking pit, she raced to her chest and searched until she found her oldest undergarment. Pulling the chemise out, she closed the lid, picked up the branch she had just cut, and sat down by the pit, so she could tend to the evening meal with Thunder Cloud. After she cut the chemise into strips, she wrapped them around the forked end of the branch to cushion the crutch for Will.

When the meal was ready, she picked up the crutch and walked to the blanket where Will, Kee-lee, and Strong Bear sat. "The food is ready. Shall I bring it over here, or do you wish to move closer to the fire?"

"We'll move closer to the fire," Will answered. The sun had lowered, and the autumn chill was settling around them.

Before he could push to his feet, Marta Carolina handed him the crutch. "Here. I made this for you."

Dumbfounded, Will looked at it; then he looked at her. Finally he murmured, "Thank you," and pushed to his good foot, tucking the forked limb under his arm and moving to the fire.

Marta Carolina naturally fell into slow step beside him. She heard his deep intake of breath and knew his ordeal was taking its toll on him. Before he went to sleep, she would give him another dose of medicine.

"You must lie down to rest as soon as you can, Ca-leb," she said.

Will nodded. "But that will not be too soon. We have yet to exchange gifts."

"Cannot that wait until morrow?"

"No, it's a custom which must be followed before we eat."

When they reached the campfire, they all sat on bearskin blankets in front of the blaze, Will and the Scupperongac braves in a line facing Strong Bear and the Chicorans, Marta Carolina next to Will. Kee-lee set a basket beside Will. Because Will was the one requesting aid and information from the Chicorans and was following Indian custom, he was the one to bestow gifts. First, he took out a beautiful pouch filled with tobacco and decorated with European beads; then he pulled out a string of white wampum.

"This—" Will said, speaking in Spanish, as he held the tobacco pouch out to Strong Bear "—is a gift of thanks for receiving us as friends."

Strong Bear grasped the pouch. "Thank you, my paleface brother." He turned the soft leather over and admired the embroidery and bead work; then he opened it to smell the tobacco. Although he appreciated the gift, the Chicoran Indians themselves did not smoke. Only the medicine men did. "I will take this pouch of religious herbs to our shaman. He will be most happy to receive a gift of such great value." He angled his head, directing his gaze at Will. "I have never seen such beautiful embroidery."

"Thank you, Strong Bear, Chief of the Chicorans." Will touched the brilliant thread that decorated the buckskin. "The peace woman of the Scupperongacs, Autumn Woman, embroidered this herself."

"I have never seen sinew or beads like these," Strong

Bear murmured appreciatively.

Marta Carolina craned her neck so that she could see more clearly. Her eyes opened wide. She had seen the like before! European thread and beads! As quickly, she lifted her head and turned an inquisitive face to Will.

"Autumn Woman, the peace woman of the Scupperongac, brought them from the land across the sea," Will explained, ignoring Marta Carolina's gaping. "She embroidered them as a symbol of our goodwill to your tribes."

"Is this Autumn Woman one of yours?" Strong Bear asked.

Marta Carolina was more eager for the answer than Strong Bear.

Will nodded. "She was known as Catherine Graystone before she married Lone Wolf, War Chief of the Scupperongac, and was adopted into her husband's tribe."

Catherine Graystone, an English woman! Marta Carolina thought. Who then was Ellen? What was Caleb's relationship with these English people?

"Tell this woman that I accept her gift of peace. I will speak to our great council all that you have said to me."

"I can ask for no more." Will held the wampum belt out. "This is a string of white wampum from the Lenapi of the Northland Forest, Strong Bear. This ensures you happiness and health. A string of white wampum for the continuation of peace between our tribes."

Strong Bear didn't immediately reach for the wampum. Although his tribe did not use them as did the tribes farther north, he understood their significance. "According to the belief of the Northland Indians, my paleface friend," he said, "wampum is like the heart of your people. Anything which you say with wampum will live forever and never be forgotten by your people. The Creator has declared that anyone who accepts a string of wampum must fulfill the promise made when the gift is accepted."

"That is true," Will replied, his hand still extended. He waited for Strong Bear's reaction.

The Chicoran chief reached for the wampum belt. "What would you have me do?"

"I would have you give us information about and safe passage to the Spanish garrison that lies on the other side of Chicora."

Strong Bear measured Will's request in silence. Thinking perhaps the paleface and his people would be a strong ally against the Spanish, he deemed it expedient to help them. Never taking his eyes from Will's, not once allowing his thoughts to be reflected in either his eyes or on his countenance, he nodded. "This I will do. We will begin our journey at the rising of the sun."

Marta Carolina smiled, pleased with Strong Bear's answer. She was about to move to the fire so she could serve supper when Will spoke again.

"I would like to leave tonight."

She spun around and stared incredulously at him.

"Why the haste, my brother?" Strong Bear asked.

"I fear for the safety of my people who scouted ahead of me." He turned to Kee-lee, signing as he spoke in Scupperongac. He translated all that had been spoken, then said, "Please tell Strong Bear what you saw."

Marta Carolina watched in amazement as Kee-lee's hands moved, and he spoke. She was puzzled now that they were no longer speaking Spanish and filled with questions. Who had scouted ahead of Ca-leb? What was

123

their purpose? What was Ca-leb's mission?

Kee-lee told Strong Bear about the three bodies he had found at the ruins of the old Spanish fort on the Waccamaw River.

Strong Bear nodded. His hands gestured in reply. "We know the place of which you speak, but we know nothing of the deaths of the three men. We thought we were following the trail of soldiers of the black robes. I will send five of my braves back to our village. They will send runners to find out what has happened at Waccamaw."

Will's expression didn't change, but his eyes were dulled with disappointment.

Strong Bear continued to sign, "I will stay behind and lead you to ruins of the Spanish fort tonight."

Turning to Marta Carolina, Will said in Spanish, "Now we will eat."

"When are we leaving?" Marta Carolina demanded. Then she saw the spark of excitement in the depths of Will's eyes. "Tonight!" Will nodded his head, and she exploded. "You're not strong enough to travel. You need to rest."

"Serve the evening meal," Will said softly, his eyes dangerously hard.

"I will not—"

His voice soft but as unyielding as his eyes, Will said, "Serve the food!"

They stared at each other for only a minute, but the gaze seemed to last forever. As always when they looked at each other, they transcended time—place—identity. This time Marta Carolina was in no doubt as to the victor. She sensed the importance of her obeying his words. Finally she moved to the fire. She would serve the food! She recognized the flinty gleam of resolve in the depth of those glittering black eyes, and she knew that nothing, that no one would keep him from his mission—whatever it was.

Marta Carolina could hardly wait for the meal to end, so she could question Will. But even then her curiosity had to be pushed aside. The camp was astir with activity. Strong Bear took his braves aside, spoke to them, and in a matter of minutes all of them, Strong Bear included, had disappeared into the forest. The Scupperongacs broke camp. By the time the canoes were loaded, Strong Bear returned, his arms full of branches needed to make torches for their night journey.

His body aching, his cuts throbbing, Will limped away from the group, leaning heavily on the crutch. He was standing by the river when Marta Carolina joined him. Taking the weight off his throbbing ankle, he rested against a tree, his arms folded over his chest, and he stared into the darkened heaven. "You're not really a Spaniard, are you, Ca-leb?"

"No." He knew what she meant, so he added, "But I didn't lie to you. My mother was Spanish."

"Where was the lie then?"

"I let you assume my father was Indian."

"He was English?" she asked flatly.

"Yes."

"Why did you not tell me the whole truth?"

"At the time I didn't think it mattered," he replied. "Who I am, what I am, that could matter little to you. Once I've delivered you to St. Augustine, our paths will never cross again. Each of us has his mission; each of us has his own life to live."

"Your name is Guillermo in Spanish," Marta Carolina said. "What are you called in English?"

125

"I am called Will'am or Will" came the succinct reply.

Marta Carolina put her arms behind her and twined her hands together. Using them as a cushion, she leaned her hips against the opposite tree. "Who is Ellen?"

Will started. A moment passed before he asked, "How did you know about Ellen?"

"You spoke her name when you were regaining consciousness."

"I'd rather not talk about her."

"You love her?" Marta Carolina persisted. She had to know.

"Look, Sister," Will barked, reminding her she had no business questioning him, reminding her of her robes and the dedication she was supposed to have made to God and Church. He jerked away from the tree and inadvertently put weight on his injured leg. Pain shot through his body. The effects of the medicine having worn off, his head was pounding. "I'm not ready to make my confessions yet." Unconsciously he reached up and rubbed his hand over the knot on the back of his head.

"You're hurting?" Without waiting for an answer, Marta Carolina rushed to her chest. Shortly she returned with a cup. Handing it to Will, she said, "Here. Drink this. It will numb the pain so you can travel. I wish you would remember that you've been badly mauled by the bear," she grumbled.

Balancing his weight on his good foot and the crutch, Will took the cup of smelly liquid and stared long and evenly at Marta Carolina. After he finally drank the bitter concoction, he said, "Thank you." He returned the cup to her and turned clumsily on the crutch to hobble away.

Marta Carolina did not tarry long after Will had moved back toward the shore. She rinsed the cup and replaced it in her chest. Then she, too, moved to the riverbank, staying her distance so the braves could load the canoes. When they were ready she followed Will's instructions and climbed into the canoe behind him.

The three canoes, torches glowing from their bow, the light flickering across the water, sailed quickly and smoothly downstream. Because Strong Bear had sent his warriors ahead, the villages along the way were apprised of the strangers' coming, so they attracted little attention. In the lead canoe Strong Bear knelt in the bow, paddling and guiding. Will, in the same canoe, was next, his sprained leg stretched out. Then came Marta Carolina. Behind her, in the stern, was Kee-lee. The only sounds that could be heard were the sounds of the forest and the gentle ripple of water as the paddles slid in and out.

"What will happen to the bear cub?" Marta Carolina finally asked.

"Strong Bear's warriors will take it back to a nearby village where the Indians will care for it until it's large enough to care for itself."

"Fatten it up for the kill," she murmured.

"Don't worry about it," Will softly advised. "The Indians live by the law of the forest, tenaciously guarding the rights of all creatures, man and beast. They kill nothing unnecessarily."

Marta Carolina shrugged and mumbled, "Perhaps you're right." Then they lapsed into a long period of silence that wasn't broken until she asked, "Where are we going."

"To St. Augustine," he replied evasively.

"Eventually," she replied on a deep sigh, "but where are we headed immediately?"

"To a deserted fort."

"One of ours?" Marta Carolina asked, excitement at the thought of its being a Spanish fort causing her to squirm.

"Sit still," Will ordered. "You'll turn the canoe over." Then he said, "yes, it's a Spanish fort, but it hasn't been occupied in many years."

"Why are we going there?"

Cramped, his leg throbbing incessantly, Will carefully readjusted his body and inadvertently scooted closer to Marta Carolina. "Kee-lee found three bodies. We think it may be part of our group who was scouting ahead."

"Englishmen," Marta Carolina said, remembering the stock of the matchlock gun Kee-lee had given to Will.

"Englishmen," Will confirmed.

"You are one of the English, not the Indians," Marta Carolina said, for the first time verbalizing her worst fears. When she had heard Will speak in English she had begun to have qualms concerning him, but she had pushed the doubts aside. Now they refused to be harnessed. Spain and England were enemies—old, declared enemies. Was this enmity between their nations strong enough to bind her and Will?

"I am English," Will returned truthfully.

"Why—why are you traveling to St. Augustine?"

Will hesitated only temporarily before he explained his mission to her. He concluded with, "And this is the only way we can learn the strength of the Spanish forts in Florida."

"Are you planning the Spaniards any harm?"

"No, and we hope they are planning us no harm."

Marta Carolina sat quietly for a little longer, watching the flicker of the torchlight on the water. The ordeal of the day taking its toll, Will's head lolled forward, and his shoulder slumped. Gingerly, slowly—having learned her lesson about sudden movement in canoes—Marta Carolina slid back. As gently, she touched his shoulders.

"Lie down," she ordered, pulling him back so that his head rested in her lap.

Although the movement hurt, he was so tired he welcomed the chance to rest. His head on her lap, lulled by the medicine, he murmured, "Ellen Graystone was the woman whom I wanted to wed."

Pain shot through Marta Carolina's heart; she felt as if someone had just stabbed her with a stiletto. Thinking about the smile he had given her when he whispered Ellen's name, she asked, "Why did you not marry her?"

"She preferred to return to England rather than stay here with me."

"So—do you still love her?"

"Yes."

He answered without thinking, but Marta Carolina's words kept reverberating through his mind. Do you still love her? Although his answer had come quickly, the more he thought about it, the less sure he was about his answer. Did he love Ellen? He had thought he loved her! Was sure that he had loved her. But could he have desired . . . lusted after Marta Carolina the way he did and still be in love with Ellen? Questions and answers merged, both eluding him. At the moment he was too tired to think about it, too weary to sort through his confused thoughts. One fact clearly registered: He knew for sure that he had not been thinking of Ellen when he had taken Marta Carolina in his arms. He turned, putting his weight on his uninjured shoulder, and dropped off into a fevered sleep.

Marta Carolina sat still so long, her limbs were stiff. Her body clamored for relief. Yet she would not move; she wouldn't disturb Will. She wondered if she would ever understand this man. He was such an enigma to her, and she was an enigma to herself. Why should her heart feel so heavy when he admitted his love for the Englishwoman, Ellen?

Now she had even greater reason for not telling him that she was not—had never been and had never entertained the thought of being—a nun. Before she hadn't told him because she needed to protect herself. Silence had been her only emotional safety. As long as she had hidden behind the sisterhood, she could play with the fire of desire without getting burned.

From this moment on she must continue her deceit because Will was English—an English soldier. Now that she thought about it, she could see the soldier in his carriage; she could hear it in his tones. Everything about him bespoke a knight. As such he was her sworn enemy. But his mother had been Spanish, and he felt a reverence and respect for the sisterhood. As long as he thought she was a nun, he wouldn't touch her. She would be safe.

Last, she wouldn't tell him because he was in love with another woman, with this Ellen Graystone. Marta Carolina wondered what Ellen was like. What kind of woman did Will love? These disturbing thoughts occupied her through the night. When she saw the first pearly gray sheen of dawn, Strong Bow lifted his paddle.

"Awake Will Dare and tell him that we have arrived," he said in Spanish.

Marta Carolina lowered her head and looked at the handsome profile, rendered so soft and vulnerable in sleep. Her lips almost touched his ears, and her warm breath splayed against the side of his head.

"Will, we are at the fort."

Will snuggled his face deeper into her lap, loath to have his sleep disturbed.

She touched his shoulder and shook him gently. "We are here, Will. Wake up."

He opened his eyes and blinked several times. Then he breathed deeply.

Marta Carolina smiled. "Strong Bear said we were at the fort."

Cautiously Will sat up, grimacing as he moved. His shoulders and chest ached; his leg throbbed. He pushed his hand through his thick black hair, now a mass of unruly curls.

After they disembarked the canoes, the Scupperongacs pushed them ashore and docked them. Strong Bear and Kee-lee moved to the remains of the old Spanish fort. Will walked more slowly behind them, Marta Carolina at his side.

Kee-lee pointed to a tree. "That is where I found them, Ca-leb. Because of your belief that your dead should be buried beneath the ground I did not leave them on the trees."

Will's eyes moved to three freshly dug graves. "Thank you, my friend."

He limped around the ruins, looking for any clue that would let him know what had happened to the colonists. Who had killed them and why?

"Chicora is not far from here," Strong Bear said. "Let us travel to it. Perhaps they will have news of your scouting party."

The canoes hoisted above their heads, the Scupperongac braves followed Strong Bear as he moved through the thick forest. Because of his leg, Will again followed behind, his progress slow. Marta walked with him. As morning turned into afternoon, they continued to travel. Although his leg pained him, Will never uttered one complaint. When they reached a small creek, Strong Bear stopped. He turned and spoke in Spanish, signing for the Scupperongacs at the same time.

"We will rest here."

The Scupperongacs set the canoes down and trotted to the creek for a drink of cool water as did Will and Marta Carolina. Then they sat down and ate their parched corn. As soon as Strong Bear had finished eating, he stood.

"While Will Dare rests, I am going to scout ahead. I will return for you shortly."

Glad for the rest, the Scupperongacs grunted their acknowledgment. While they conversed with one another, Will returned to the creek and motioned for Marta Carolina.

"Will you remove the moccasin and the bandage?" he asked. "I need to soak my foot to get the swelling down."

Marta Carolina quickly knelt, unlaced the moccasin which he wore because of the swelling, and pushed the leg of his breeches up to his knees. Sitting on the bank, Will dangled his leg in the cool water. He leaned his back against a tree trunk, closed his eyes, and sighed his relief. He didn't know Marta Carolina had mixed more medicine until she pressed the cup into his hands.

"Drink this," she said. "It will lessen the pain."

He smiled his gratitude and lifted the container to his lips, emptying it in one swallow. The medicine soon took effect. He relaxed and was almost asleep when he heard the subtle change in the forest. He tensed; the Scupperongacs leapt to their feet, but not soon enough.

By the time Will was on his feet, his crutch under his arm, he and his companions were surrounded by strange warriors. Then the circle of Indian braves was broken, and he saw a woman move through. She was young and slender, no older than Marta Carolina, he thought. Her black hair, parted in the center, hung straight and smooth down her back. A diadem of gold and pearls kept it out of her eyes.

Marta Carolina gasped in surprise. She had never seen anyone who could compare to this woman . . . to this warrior. She stared in rapt silence at the Indian who stood in front of her. An oval face, with high well-defined cheekbones, framed eyes that were like polished ebony. Marta Carolina's gaze descended her smooth, almond-colored skin to full, rounded breasts. Around them she wore a brassiere, hammered out of gold with a large opening in the center of each cup.

When Will heard Marta Carolina gasp, he returned his attention to her. As he watched her astonished eyes quickly skim over the exposed flesh and the dark aureoles, he grinned. When color brightened her cheeks, he softly chuckled. Too soon from Spain she had yet to learn that the Indians regarded nudity differently from the Europeans.

By now he, too, was interested in this strange woman/warrior, and he curiously stared at her. The straps of the halter were triple strands of pearls. Her short apron, exposing the entire length of her legs, was made of material, Will was sure. The colors were vivid, the designs artistic. On her back was an ornate quiver, filled with arrows. In her left hand she carried a bow; in her right a spear, the shaft of gold, decorated with pearls.

Marta Carolina observed the warrior's gaze as it

deliberately moved from the Scupperongacs to Will. She inwardly seethed as the Indian openly perused Will's body, her eyes moving down, then up. When the woman's face encountered his, she smiled boldly. Will returned the gesture. Marta Carolina clenched her fists to her side; she wanted to slap the returning smile off Will's face.

The woman turned her head and saw Marta Carolina. Her smile vanished; her gaze hardened. Hatred openly gleamed in the dark irises. She lowered the spear and moved toward the Spanish woman, hatred burning in her eyes. When she tapped Marta Carolina's breast with the point of the spear, Will dropped his crutch and lunged to Marta Carolina's rescue. The woman/warrior barked a command, and one of her braves, disregarding Will's wounds, caught him by the shoulders and dragged him back. Will twisted against the grip of his captor, but the brave's fingers dug into his cuts, sending excruciating pain through his body.

"You are my enemy, woman black robe. I am going to kill you," the warrior/woman said in fluent Spanish. "We do not want you in our kingdom. You and your people have brought nothing but grief to our people."

"You can't kill her," Will shouted, thrusting his shoulders forward, again straining against the iron-gripped fingers that held him.

The warrior/woman turned to Will. "Are you a follower of the black robe?"

"No," he replied, astounded by the woman's forceful-ness and intrigued by her commanding demeanor.

"Then why do you wish me to spare the woman's life?"

"She belongs to me," Will replied. "She is my woman."

The warrior/woman was interested. "Who are you?"

"I am Will Dare. My village is in the Northland close to the kingdom of Scupperong. I travel with Kee-lee, chief of the Scupperongacs, and his braves." He waved his hand toward Kee-lee who stepped forward.

"I am Kee-lee, *Werowance* of the Scupperongacs." His words flowed from his gesturing hands. "I am traveling with Will Dare. In my baskets—" his hand swung to the large baskets which his braves had strapped over their shoulders "—are the goods which we bring for barter."

"You are welcome, Kee-lee of the Scupperongacs," she said. "We also welcome the opportunity to trade with your people." With a visual brush at the baskets, the woman quickly dismissed the Scupperongac chief. She returned her attention to Will. "What are you doing in the kingdom of Chicora?"

"The Spaniards have been sailing up our coast in their ships. We fear they are preparing for an attack on our village. I and several more of my people began a journey to the Southland to learn how many Spanish garrisons there are, how large they are, and how many soldiers they have."

"That is good," the woman said. "Come. Now we go to our town."

Not knowing what her position was or her title, Will said, "Please, señorita, I must beg you to let us continue our journey to the Southland. As much as I desire to, I do not have time to travel to your town. We are waiting for the return of our friend. With your permission, as soon as he arrives we will depart."

135

Chapter VI

"Señor," the warrior/woman said, a strange smile on her face, "I do not grant permission for you to depart. You will travel to my town with me."

Her words demanded obedience, and Will could see that her warriors were prepared to enforce her command.

Strong Bear appeared in the clearing in time to hear the remark. His expression stern and fixed, he angrily pushed through the circle of braves, strode to her, and grasped the shank of her spear in his left hand to lower it. Speaking in Chicoran he asked, "Where have you been, White Blossom?"

The woman stared at the intruder for a long time before she answered, also speaking Chicoran. "I have been on the same mission as you, my father. I, too, have been trailing the soldiers of the black robes. The big chief of the Hisitos, *Cacique* Rippling Water, sent for help. The soldiers of the black robes and their dogs were moving directly toward his village. My braves and I answered his call."

Concern for his people's welfare momentarily replaced

Strong Bear's anger. "Were you in time?"

White Blossom nodded her head. "For some reason the Spaniards did not continue their journey into the heart of Chicora Land. They returned to their fort. In their haste they left one of their soldiers."

"I was told about him when I entered the city."

"I would have killed him," White Blossom said, "but the queen ordered us to bind him in a house away from the village because he is extremely ill. The evil spirits have entered his mind. His speech is strange, and he cries out and screams. We cannot question him." She looked beyond her father to Will. "And now we have more soldiers of the black robes." Hostile chocolate brown eyes riveted to Marta Carolina. "We also have a woman black robe."

Strong Bear followed the piercing gaze of his daughter. But his eyes, when they lighted on Marta Carolina, unlike his daughter's were filled with tenderness; his voice softened noticeably. "I have promised them safe passage through Chicora."

White Blossom turned to look at Strong Bear. Her face remained impassive, a reflection on her excellent discipline as a warrior, but her eyes swirled with contempt. "After all the people of the black robes have done to us, why would you grant them free passage through our lands?"

"You question your father?" Strong Bear's tone was gentle, but the impact was like a sudden clap of thunder; it was like the strike of the whip across tender flesh.

"No," White Blossom denied, "as your daughter I respect my father too much to question his judgment, but as White Blossom, War *Cacique* of the Edistos, question the wisdom of Strong Bear, *Cacique* of the Council of all

137

the Chicoras. I wonder if he so soon forgets the atrocities committed against our people by our enemy from over the water."

"No," Strong Bear replied, bowing to Chicoran custom by explaining his actions to a lesser chief, "I have not forgotten. Nor shall I ever forget." He swept his hand toward Will and Marta Carolina. "Although the brave comes from the land over the water, he belongs to another kingdom, my daughter. He is not a soldier of the black robes. The people of the black robes are his enemies as well as ours."

White Blossom's eyes swept over Marta Carolina's travel-worn habit. "She is a black robe."

"She is," Strong Bear agreed quietly, his words warm and tender as he looked at Marta Carolina, "but she is also a shaman with great magic, my daughter. She has medicines which equal if they do not excel those used by our shaman. Also, my daughter, she and the paleface brave, the two of them, with no more than a knife and the branch of a tree, killed a bear today. That is a good omen. The teeth they have given me because they are my totem; the bearskin shall become my blanket; the meat they have sent to our people." With great difficulty Strong Bear pulled his gaze from Marta Carolina and looked once again at his daughter.

White Blossom was angry. She could see the tenderness her father felt for the woman black robe, and she despised this weakness in him. "For a few gifts you will let them move freely through our lands?" she asked contemptuously.

Strong Bear shook his head. "Now you speak as a spoiled child rather than a war chief. You should know I would not allow the palefaces such liberties."

White Blossom's eyes narrowed. "What is your reason for bringing them to our town?"

"I told you, my daughter, but you were listening only with your ears, not with your heart and your mind." He smiled. "The black robe is a shaman. I bring her magic to Chicora and to our queen."

"Do you also bring her to your lodging and your platform, my father?"

"My plans for the woman black robe are not your concern," Strong Bear replied curtly, irritated because his daughter had seen the heart of the matter.

"Have you so soon forgotten what they did to us?" she cried vehemently. "Have you so soon forgotten what they did to your wife and to my mother?"

Strong Bear lifted his hand to silence her. "Enough," he said. "As a daughter you have no right to question my motives about another woman, and you have over-stepped your authority as a chief of the Chicoras."

White Blossom was instantly repentant. "I'm sorry, my father. I have much to learn before I shall be as tall in wisdom as Strong Bear, Chief of the Council of all Chicoras."

Strong Bear's eyes sparkled with pride. White Blossom deserved to be a warrior. "We can learn much from the paleface and the woman black robe."

Marta Carolina and Will apprehensively watched the two Chicorans as they talked; they listened to the inflections of their voices, and both wondered what they were saying. Finally Marta Carolina saw the woman nod. Only then did Strong Bear release his grip on her spear. He turned and walked to Will.

Speaking in Spanish, he said, "Will Dare of the Scupperongacs, I would introduce you to my daughter,

White Blossom, War Chief of the Edistos—a tribe of the Chicoras."

The woman was beautiful, even more so when she smiled. Will could see how men would be captivated by White Blossom's dark beauty. Respecting her position as chief, he gave her a friendly smile and bowed low. He reached for her hand and brushed a kiss. "It is a pleasure to meet you, Señorita White Blossom."

Blinded by jealousy, Marta Carolina exaggerated all Will's actions toward White Blossom. To her, friendliness became flirtation, and she was angry, angry enough to fight. She could never recall having felt this furious before. Always she had been taught to be gentle and soft-spoken. Her mother had been such a woman, one easily manipulated by those whom she loved and those who loved her. Marta Carolina could never recall one time when her mother's voice had been raised in protest much less anger. Then at her mother's death, Marta Carolina had been placed in the convent to be reared by Sister Angelica who was also a gentle woman.

All her life Marta Carolina had been reared to repress and suppress her anger. "'A gentle answer turneth away wrath,'" the Holy Mother had always quoted, and the scripture had stood Marta Carolina in good stead as long as she lived in the convent with similar souls and tended the sick who were at the mercy of the sisters.

Now for the first time in her life, Marta Carolina felt anger as she had never before felt it. As if she were a caldron sitting over a fire, emotions—emotions she couldn't identify much less name—boiled inside her, threatening to overflow the frail human vessel at any moment. Anger, jealousy, hatred, resentment! Her eyes disdainfully raked over the tall form of the

140

warrior/woman. Then she looked at Will Dare. She couldn't stand the way he was bowing over White Blossom—kissing her hand—as if she were royalty.

Marta Carolina wished she could rip the nun's habit from her body and let Will know that she wasn't a member of the sisterhood. That she, too, was endowed with such femininity. For the shortest of moments she wished she could don the apron and the gold brassiere to show him how beautiful and delectable her body was. But she was caught in a web of deception that was harder to wear than the clothes of the church. She loved . . . She stopped short, her own confession startling her. Yes, she loved a man who didn't love her. He said he wanted to make love to her, but he didn't love her. Now he had found another. Did he want the Chicoran woman also?

"Come," Strong Bear said in Spanish, signing as he spoke so the Scupperongacs could understand, "we will go to our town. They are expecting us."

He grasped Marta Carolina's arm and guided her to the front of the group, the two of them leading the way to Chicora. She glanced over her shoulder to see Kee-lee and his braves following behind. At the rear were White Blossom and Will, walking slowly because of Will's injured foot. Pain speared her heart so sharply and so deeply, she jerked her head forward and moved through the forest beside Strong Bear.

They walked for hours through the forest, and Marta Carolina could have sworn Strong Bear was leading them in circles so they would be disoriented. Frequently she looked over her shoulder to see White Blossom and Will talking so friendly and easily. Fleetingly she would wish she hadn't tended his wounds. She hoped they were hurting him! She wished . . .

141

No, she would as quickly repent, she was glad she had taken care of him. She only wished he would show her as much attention as he showered on the Indian woman, but she reminded herself she was the one responsible for his not being able to. She was the one who had allowed him to believe she was a nun. And now even if she did confess to him that she was not, he wouldn't believe her. He would think she was lying to him because she was jealous. So he would make love to her.

"You are quiet, Marta Carolina," Strong Bear said.

"I am thinking."

Strong Bear knew about whom. He angled his head and looked back at Will and White Blossom. He knew that Marta Carolina was attracted to the paleface, and he knew Will felt protective toward the woman black robe. Other than that, he was not sure of Will's feelings toward her. Aware of the celibacy of the Roman Catholic ministry, Strong Bear said, "Sometimes we find our chosen paths easy to walk, Marta Carolina; other times they are extremely difficult. Perhaps this is one of your most difficult."

"Yes," Marta Carolina whispered, feeling an affinity for this Indian warrior who was so understanding.

His words of wisdom made her think of her beloved Tía Karolina and Sister Angelica. She missed them so, but surprisingly she was not as distraught as she had been immediately after Tía Karolina's death. Her feelings for Will must be put behind her, Marta Carolina thought with resolve. She must get to Mexico and to her *repartimiento* where she would start a new life for herself.

With her promise she lifted her face and looked at the autumn beauty which surrounded her. She was interested in every face of nature. All of them were beautiful to her; all of them offered her new plants and roots for medicines in her cabinet, remedies for sickness. If only Sister Angelica could see her now! How strange the holy woman would find the situation. Here Marta Carolina was trudging along with Indians as if she were one of them.

Strong Bear touched her shoulder and pointed into the forest. "Come with me," he said, "I'll show you some of our plants." He called to White Blossom. "I will take the shaman another pathway. We wish to collect some roots and herbs. We will meet you at the gate to the city."

White Blossom shot her father a venomous glance, and Will turned so fast pain shot up his leg and he emitted a low grunt. Although he had been enjoying his journey and visit with White Blossom, he was reluctant to see Marta Carolina leave with Strong Bear. He was surprised he felt this way, but he couldn't get thoughts of her out of his mind. His lust for her was increasing rather than decreasing. In his mind's eye he never saw her dressed in the nun's habit.

Now with sinking heart he watched her and the Indian disappear into the forest together. Although Strong Bear was White Blossom's father, he was a handsome man, a virile one—masterful and forceful. And he was quite interested in Marta Carolina. Will had seen it yesterday when Strong Bear and his braves had entered their camp. He saw the interest growing.

Will told himself that his concern came from his protectiveness for Marta Carolina. After all, she was his responsibility now—whether he wanted it or not. She was young, he told himself for the hundredth time, and passionate . . . Dear God, yes, she was passionate.

Will also knew that Marta Carolina was an innocent,

reared away from the wordly flow of society. He remembered her innocent flirtation with him. Because he respected her, because he respected her dedication to God, he hadn't taken advantage of her, but would Strong Bear respect the church robes of a people whom he hated? Or would he take the woman whom he desired with no thought of the consequences?

White Blossom issued a command in Chicoran, and one of her braves headed up the party, leading them through the forest to Chicora. White Blossom stayed behind with Will to keep him company, but he was so preoccupied with Marta Carolina that he could not concentrate on what White Blossom was saying. He would look over his shoulders, his eyes peering into the forest as he looked for some sign of them. Every so often he would hear the melodious tinkle of laughter, and he would feel the terrible tentacles of jealousy as they wrapped around his heart, suffocating him.

Using Strong Bear's blanket as a basket, Marta Carolina gathered plants and herbs. One time when she looked up she saw a small mountain in the distance; the next time she caught an iridescent reflection. She moved from beneath the trees, shaded her eyes with her hand, and gazed toward the rainbow of color.

"What is that?" she asked Strong Bear, straining to see more clearly.

"What is what?" He moved to stand behind her and looked in the direction of which she pointed.

"The building next to that mountain."

Strong Bear chuckled. "The small mountain was built by our people many years ago. On the summit is located our Upper Village—where the queen and the most important members of the city live. The shining, colorful building is the Temple, the most magnificent building in all Chicora."

"I can hardly wait to see it," Marta Carolina breathed. "Even from here it is beautiful."

"You may admire it from afar only," Strong Bear replied. "Only tribe members are permitted near it; only they can enter." He paused, then spoke, his voice growing reflective as he said, "Long ago we permitted the people of the black robes to visit our temples, but they robbed our treasures and desecrated our dead. Now we protect them from outsiders."

"How awful!" Marta Carolina was horrified that her people would commit such atrocities.

By the time she and Strong Bear met up with the other party, they were at the gate of the city.

"This is Chicora," Strong Bear proudly announced, "the capital city of our kingdom."

Will wasn't looking at Chicora. He was glaring at Marta Carolina. She, however, was oblivious to his displeasure. She was stunned by the paradisiacal beauty that greeted them. Laughing her pleasure, she moved beside Strong Bear as they walked down the main street of the town, a broad avenue, fifteen or twenty feet wide and marked out by posts buried in the ground. She gazed in awe about herself as she walked.

An Indian met the returning warriors. "Strong Bear, White Blossom, we welcome your safe return."

"We are glad to be home, Running Deer," Strong Bear said.

"The council is waiting in the ceremonial house to hear your report. I shall escort our guests to the queen."

"No," Strong Bear declared, "I will escort them. I shall give my report to the council later."

White Blossom was stunned. She could not believe the words issuing from her father's lips. Both she and Running Deer cast disapproving glances at Strong Bear, who flaunted Chicoran custom.

White Blossom said, "Do what you wish, Strong Bear." Her words were contemptuous. "My braves and I will meet with the council." She shoved past her father and motioned her braves to follow. Running Deer tarried only momentarily before he, too, left.

"Come," Strong Bear said, "we must go meet the queen." Again he and Marta Carolina led the way, Will and Kee-lee following.

The Scupperongac noticed Will's preoccupation. "What is troubling you, my friend?" he asked, then answered before Will could. "The tenderness which Strong Bear has for the shaman."

That definitely bothered Will, but he wouldn't admit it to himself much less anyone else. She's a little fool, he inwardly seethed. Doesn't she know this isn't a religious cloister and Strong Bear is not celibate! When he glanced around to see Kee-lee waiting for his answer, Will shrugged. "We're being treated as if we were guests, Kee-lee, but I'm wondering what our true status is."

"That we will not know until we have talked with the queen," Kee-lee responded easily, shifting his shoulders beneath the weight of his burden-basket.

"Look," Marta Carolina cried, interrupting Will and Kee-lee's discussion. "What is that?" she asked, pointing at the green stalks.

"Maize," Strong Bear replied, "our chief food." He gestured to the gardens. "We also grow beans, squash, pumpkins, onions, and potatoes."

They walked farther, and Marta Carolina saw the

homes built around the public square. They were constructed of logs or poles, plastered within and without with clay or mud. Some of the roofs were gable-built; others were shaped like bowls. All were covered with either thatch or split canes placed so as to shed water.

"With a small door," Strong Bear explained, "the house is easily heated with an inside fire, and in winter the people are able to sleep at night without cover and heavy clothing. The inside walls are ornamented with hanging tapestries. And that," he pointed to a smaller building around which several adobes cloistered, "is the kitchen. We keep the heat out of our homes in the summer and keep down the threat of fire—our most deadly enemy"

"What kind of trees are those?" Marta Carolina asked, looking at a large grove that surrounded the village.

"Mulberry," he replied, and pointed to an orchard between the corn field and the gardens. "Those are plum." His hand swept to the tall, stately trees under which the houses nestled. "Those are walnut. From their fruit we make meal for bread and hickory milk, an oil with which we season our food."

Marta Carolina could not believe all she was seeing. Although the Indian culture was different from that to which she was accustomed, simpler and more primitive, it was grand and eloquent.

The city was planned; the streets, all outlined and marked with posts, opened to the public square. The houses circled a communal kitchen. The lawns around the houses were manicured and terraced. Then they passed a wooden house, raised aloft on four posts, with a floor of cane hurdles.

"What is that?" Marta Carolina cried in delight. Her curiosity could not be contained.

Strong Bear smiled. He liked the woman black robe. She was different from the others with whom he had come in contact. "That is a *barbacoa*, a corncrib. When the crop is harvested, we store it in the crib, and it is distributed by the chief of the members of the tribe as each has need and as the limited supply will allow."

Suddenly Marta Carolina stopped. She saw the corral and the horses. She couldn't believe her eyes. Neither could Kee-lee. He had never beheld such an animal in his entire life.

"What is it?" he asked Will in Scupperongac as Marta Carolina raced across the lawn to the fence.

"A horse," Will answered. As they followed Marta Carolina, he explained their uses and purposes.

"Oh, Will, look," Marta Carolina cried. "Aren't they beautiful?"

"Remarkable beasts," Will agreed.

When one of them pranced to the fence and nuzzled Marta Carolina's hand, she asked Strong Bear, "Who owns them?"

"They belong to the queen. We recently took them from the soldiers of the black robes."

"Does the queen ride?" Marta Carolina asked as she ran her hand down the neck and shoulder of the horse.

"No one rides them."

"Then who takes care of them?" Marta Carolina whirled around indignantly. "Who exercises them?"

"We have no knowledge of the animals," Strong Bear replied, "but we would learn."

"If I had time, I could teach you," Marta Carolina said. "I am most knowledgeable about horses." She nuzzled the horse's nose. "This one reminds me of mine at home."

"Perhaps you will be allowed to ride before you depart," Strong Bear said. "But now we have more important matters to attend."

He ushered them to the avenue where they resumed their journey to the queen's lodging. They walked through the large public square, or marketplace, where the Chicorans were bustling to and fro, preparing for the feast in honor of their guests. The street ended, and they paused at the foot of a pyramid, the base of which was about a thousand feet in circumference, the height about seventy feet. The summit was crowned with a large terrace, huge cedar trees, and beautiful houses constructed of a white cement mixture.

"This is where the Great *Mico* of all the Chicorans lives," Strong Bear said, pointing to the top of the pyramid that contained twelve houses for the queen, her family, and all her retinue.

Leaving Will and Kee-lee to follow, Strong Bear guided Marta Carolina up the beamed steps that spiraled the pyramid and were shaded by small flowered bushes that grew on each side of the stairway. Again she was lost in the beauty of the wilderness paradise. When they reached the summit, Marta Carolina sucked in her breath.

A group of low, rambling houses were built around a large court. Some of them had verandas, under which were benches and couches made of cane. Groves of trees shaded the entire area, and terraced gardens decorated it. They walked across the courtyard into the most stately residence.

The interior of the house was warm and filled with

sunshine. The furniture was simple, couches and benches set about and a long, squat table in the center of the room. The windows had reed shutters which were flung open in the day to allow sunshine to flood the room. The walls were adorned with beautiful cloth tapestries, the designs in bold, vivid colors. The floor, Marta Carolina observed, was covered with cane mats which resembled the rush carpets of the moor. The ceiling of the house was so beautiful, she gasped. Plumes of diverse colors were suspended from the roof in a way to create rainbow-colored clouds. At the far end of the room was an arched door, two braves standing on either side.

"Wait here," Strong Bear commanded, long strides carrying him into the adjoining room.

Strong Bear had no sooner disappeared than Will's hand banded around Marta Carolina's upper arm. In an undertone he grated, "What do you think you're doing?" He pulled her into a corner away from Kee-lee.

Jerking free from his grasp, Marta Carolina rubbed her arm where he had held her so tightly. "I don't know what you're talking about." She was clearly puzzled by his anger.

"Don't you have any respect for the church which you serve?" he raged. "Behaving like a whore with Strong Bear!"

As if he'd slapped her, Marta Carolina backed away. At first she was hurt that he made such base accusations. But then, her indignation died, quickly giving place to anger, anger which she no longer repressed.

"How dare you accuse me of behaving like a whore," she spat. "I've behaved more honorably than you. You had better thank God that he saw fit to attach your eyes to your head somehow, Will Dare, else you would have

150

lost them—the way you've been ogling the naked female warrior."

"I, ogling the female!" Will retaliated. "Who went off unchaperoned with a man in the forest?"

A smile suddeny radiated Marta Carolina's face. Will Dare was jealous. "Strong Bear is old enough to be my father," she quietly retorted.

"He wasn't casting fatherly glances at you," Will scathed.

"Are you jealous?" Marta Carolina taunted.

"Hell, no!" he growled, his face coloring when he realized he had raised his voice. "I'm worried about you."

"Worried?" Again Marta Carolina was puzzled.

"Strong Bear is a Chicoran Indian chief. He has no respect for the robe which you wear, and at times I wonder if you do either."

"Will—" Marta Carolina laid her hand on Will's lower arm. She wanted to confess to him that she wasn't a nun. She couldn't bear to have him think she would desecrate an office of the church.

Will felt the heat rush from her hands throughout his body. Balancing his weight on his crutch, he grabbed her hand and pulled it off his arm. "Now stop that!" he admonished. Bringing his frustration under control, he said, "If you'll trust me, Sister Marta Carolina, and if you'll quit flirting with every man you meet, I'll get you to St. Augustine, your virtue intact. What you do after that is your responsibility. I wash my hands of you."

Marta Carolina had no time to reply. Strong Bear reentered the room. His gaze, centered on her, was warm and tender.

"Come, little shaman." He caught her hands in his and

spoke gently. "The queen would see you." He turned to Will and Kee-lee. Offhandedly he included them. "And the two of you." He walked between them. "She would know why you are traveling through the kingdom of Chicora, and she would listen to your tales of valor."

Again Marta Carolina was filled with awe as she moved through the arched doorway into the large room. Holding long-handled, plumed fans, two women, dressed in cloth brassieres and short aprons, stood on either end of the couch on which reclined an elderly woman.

Her face was ageless, bearing the wisdom of many years, but it was also stern, a result of many years of responsibility for the well-being of her people. Her black hair, belying her sixty-eight years, was parted in the center and hung in long plaits over her shoulders. Around her forehead she wore a gold diadem set in pearls. She wore a sleeveless sack dress in colors as bright and vivid as the tapestries on her wall. Over her shoulder hung a vermilion mantle, clasped around her neck with a gold pin.

When she pushed up to a sitting position, her moccasined feet touched the floor, and she shoved the mantle aside. Marta Carolina saw the bands of gold that spiraled her upper arms. She held a gold scepter in her hand, plumes attached to one end by strands of pearls.

"Come closer, woman black robe." She also spoke Spanish fluently. "I would see you clearly."

Marta Carolina advanced until she stood in front of the queen. "I have seen many male black robes, but you are the first woman. What are you doing in the kingdom of Chicora?"

"I did not mean to invade your kingdom," Marta Carolina began, and in a clear voice she told the queen of her land grant in Mexico, of the shipwreck, and of Will's rescuing her and promising to take her to the Spanish garrison of St. Augustine. "I mean your people no harm," she finished. "My only desire is to reach my countrymen."

"Strong Bear tells me that you have knowledge of the horse." Marta Carolina nodded. "You will teach us to use the animal."

"I would gladly teach you, if I had time," Marta Carolina replied, "but I must reach St. Augustine."

"You have time," the queen pronounced quietly. "You will teach us." Dismissing Marta Carolina, the queen looked at Kee-lee. Her hands began to move in the silent language. "From what tribe do you come?"

"I am Kee-lee, chief of the Scupperongacs," Kee-lee signed in reply. "I come as a friend from the Kingdom of Scupperong which lies to the north of Chicora. I am traveling with the paleface warrior to the Southland."

"Welcome to Chicora," the queen answered.

"I bring gifts," he informed her, "and I have goods to barter."

The queen smiled. "My people will enjoy your visit, Kee-lee, *Werowance* of the Scupperongac." She clapped her hands and a young boy dashed into the room. Speaking in Chicoran, she said, "Take the warrior to his lodging. The apartment on which *Tonatico*, the sun, first looks each morning."

The queen now lifted her hand and beckoned. "Come," she said. When Will stood in front of her, she addressed him in Spanish, "Are you a soldier of the black robe?"

"No."

"What are you doing in the land of the Chicora?"

"I am traveling to the Southland to scout out the Spanish forts. My people, the English, live in the Northland Forest, close to the kingdom of Scupperong. For many years we and the people of the black robes have been at war."

The queen smiled. "What are you called?"

"In English I am called Will Dare. By the Scupperongacs I am called Ca-leb-a-dam-a, the Bold One."

"You are a warrior?"

"I am a warrior."

The queen lowered her voice and asked seriously, but her eyes were full of mockery, "And you, one man, one warrior, are on your way to war against the many soldiers of the black robes at St. Augustine?"

Will chuckled at the absurdity. "No, great *Mico*, I'm not so foolish to think I can war with the soldiers of the black robes by myself. However, I am wise enough to learn their strength, so I can lead my braves back later to defeat them if it is necessary."

"You are as wise as you are valiant," the queen granted. "I also have a feeling, Will Dare, that you can be quite arrogant."

Will grinned. "I should like to think not, Queen of all Chicoras."

"We have another guest with us—a black robe also."

"May I see him?" Will asked, eager to question the man.

"He is ill, señor," the queen replied. "His head is filled with evil spirits, but the shaman has been treating him. He is better, but he still speaks strangely."

"Perhaps he is not a black robe," Will suggested. "He could be one of my scouts. That would account for his

154

speaking strangely. His native tongue is English, not Spanish."

The queen nodded her head. "I will let you visit with him, but not now. You need to bathe and rest. Tonight we will have a feast in your honor."

She looked at Marta Carolina. "You are a black robe. Do you wish a lodging by yourself?"

Before Marta Carolina could nod her head, Will shoved in front of her. "She is mine, Your Majesty," he answered, addressing the queen as if she were European royalty. "I want her to share my lodging."

Marta Carolina was so dumbfounded by Will's outburst that she said nothing.

"I fought to the death for her," Will declared. "She is mine."

"She wears the black robe," the queen reminded him. "Black robes do not marry."

Will laughed derisively. "I don't intend to marry her, my *Mico*. The black robes are my enemy."

"No," Marta Carolina cried, grabbing Will's arm, "you can't mean that! I belong to the Church."

"You belong to me!" Will's words thundered through the room.

"You may have the black robe," the queen said, dismissing Will and Marta Carolina. She spoke to Strong Bear in Chicoran. "See to the preparations for the feast tonight. Take the black robe and Will Dare to their lodgings."

Chapter VII

"I refuse to go with you!" Marta Carolina raised her voice in anger. She had no intention of staying alone with Will Dare.

"You will!" he grated as he clamped his hand on her upper arm. Unnoticed, the crutch dropped to the floor.

Refusing to move, her feet dragging across the floor as Will forcibly propelled her, Marta Carolina yanked her arm, but Will's grasp was like an iron vise. When she saw the blatant grins on the faces of the Chicoran onlookers, she hissed, "Do you wish to make a spectacle of us?"

"You, *Sister,* are the one making the spectacle of yourself," Will returned, anger so strong he forgot his injured foot, his strides never slackening. "To the Chicorans you are nothing but chattel. By the law of the forest you belong to me."

"I belong to no one!" Marta Carolina shouted, not caring who heard her.

Will stopped, and clasping both shoulders in his hands, pulled her face up until it was only inches away from his. In a dangerously low tone that only he and

Marta Carolina could hear, he said, "I admit that I appreciate your anger. Since, however, you don't understand the seriousness of your position, I shall tell you. I am the only one who can save you. Now if you want to keep your virtue intact, if you want this black robe to protect your innocence rather than hide your sins, you'll shut your mouth and quit acting like a shrew." His black eyes raked the pale face that peered from the folds of the wimple. "Do you understand me, Sister Marta Carolina?" She nodded. "Are you going to obey me?"

"What if I choose not to?"

"Then, *dear Sister*, I would have no recourse but to knock you unconscious and haul you out of here over my shoulder—as I would a bag of manure."

"You wouldn't," she whispered disbelievingly, her descriptive words coming back to haunt her. She stood absolutely still.

"Wouldn't I?" He spoke with a calm that assured Marta Carolina he would.

With that his hand dropped and caught hers; he took a step. Marta Carolina didn't move. His head angled, and the raven-black eyes pierced into the defiant blue ones.

"Turn me loose," she said. "I'll walk with you, but I won't be dragged like baggage. Before I allow you to do that you will have to knock me unconscious."

Again he glowered at her, but Marta Carolina refused to be intimidated or to cow. She refused further compromise to her dignity. She straightened her back and squared her shoulders, never taking her eyes from his face.

Will nodded curtly and released her hand. He walked, his head straight ahead, his eyes fixed on Strong Bear who stood in the arched doorway. This time Marta Carolina walked by his side.

Strong Bear had watched the exchange between Marta Carolina and Will, and although his expression remained impassive, his dark brown eyes were filled with sadness. The little black robe had brought a touch of happiness to his life. For that short time in the forest when they had been searching for herbs, her youth and vitality had extended to him, becoming his. He had embraced her joy for living, her excitement at discovery.

But Strong Bear, steeped in discipline and custom, honored the universal law of the forest. The black robe belonged to Will Dare. Strong Bear would not take another man's possession. In time the one called Will Dare might grow tired of Marta Carolina. Then perhaps he would barter her away.

Will and Marta Carolina followed Strong Bear across the courtyard. Because they were so caught up in their own thoughts, neither saw the beauty of the gardens, aflame in autumn's vivid vesture. Finally they came to an apartment on the far side of the summit. White and rambling, like the other structures, it was surrounded by a well-manicured lawn with the terraced gardens and was canopied by large evergreen trees, their moss draped bows sweeping low.

"Your *boa*. Your home while you're in Chicora." Strong Bear swept his hand around the spacious house that was filled with golden sunlight. Looking at the forlorn Marta Carolina, he said softly, "I will have someone bring your chest to you."

"Thank you," she murmured. She looked up, smiling into Strong Bear's eyes. "You're so kind."

Strong Bear exerted all his self-discipline to keep from

158

touching the paleface woman. Many years had passed since he was so enamored with a woman. To break the tension, he pointed to the swinging bed made of netting and suspended from the ceiling by cords tied to the supports at each end.

"A *hammoc.*"

"*Ham-moc,*" Marta Carolina stammered, repeating the Chicoran word as closely as possible. She and Strong Bear laughed together.

Enjoying the lesson and using any excuse to stay near Marta Carolina, Strong Bear pointed to himself. "*Chivy,*" he said in Chicoran. Then in Spanish: "*Man.*"

Marta Carolina repeated the word several times. Then she asked, "What is woman in Chicoran, Strong Bear?"

"*Ira,*" he said. "*Ira* is soft and silver; she is *tona,* the moon; *chivy* is blazing and golden; he is *tonatico,* the sun."

"How poetic," Marta Carolina murmured. Over and over again she repeated the words as Strong Bear spoke to her in Chicoran.

Grimacing and shaking his head, Will stalked to the window and raked his fingers through his hair, too distraught to give his injured ankle more than a passing thought. This woman was going to be the death of him yet, and if not the death, she would surely drive him insane. Through her innocence he didn't know what would happen to her. She had wrung more emotions out of him in their short acquaintance than Ellen had in all the time that he'd known her. Simultaneously he was angry at Marta Carolina . . . jealous . . . then protective.

After Strong Bear had departed, Marta Carolina walked around the room, repeating the words which he had taught her. She admired the bright colors woven into

159

the wall tapestries that blended with the floor mats. She sat on one of the couches, sinking into the soft mattress. She ran her hand caressively over the yellow ticking and admired the fabric. Then she stood and crossed to the hammock.

"Hammoc," she said softly, weaving her fingers through the flax netting. Suddenly she realized this was the only bed in the room. The benches and couches were too narrow to sleep on. This was the bed she was to share with Will. Slowly she turned until she was staring into his face, all her thoughts blazing in her eyes for him to read.

Forgotten were the halcyon moments when she and Strong Bear had been exchanging cultural information. Remembered were Will's hateful words to the queen, his promises, his derision. He was English. Did this suddenly make him her enemy?

"I don't know why you told the queen that I belonged to you," she said quietly, summoning a calmness she certainly didn't feel. She emotionally withdrew and hovered behind the nun's habit. "But I want you to know, Will Dare, that I will not sleep with you. I will not be wenched and thrown aside like chattel when you're through with me. I—I—won't let you desecrate a holy office of the Church."

"You ungrateful woman," Will sneered as he moved silently across the thick carpet of mats. "Are you really so naive?" Before Marta Carolina could say anything, he said, "I didn't have to do anything underhanded to pluck your virtue or desecrate an office of the Church. You've been mine for the taking since the first moment I laid eyes on you. Had it not been for me and my principles, Sister Marta Carolina, you would be a wench at this very

160

moment." Two strides brought him within inches of Marta Carolina. "But to set your suspicious little mind at ease, rest assured my motives were pure. I told the queen you belonged to me so I could protect you."

"Protect me?" Marta Carolina exclaimed indignantly.

"As long as the Chicorans think you are my woman they will not touch you."

"They wouldn't touch me anyway," she said. "I'm— I'm—a—" She couldn't bring herself to voice the lie. She looked down at the dust-covered habit and shook her head. "Surely they wouldn't!" Her last words were a mere whisper.

"They would, Sister," Will softly affirmed. "The Chicorans hate the Spaniards."

"More than the English!" Marta Carolina jeered.

"As much if not more," Will replied quietly. "Especially Strong Bear and White Blossom." He paused but a moment before he said, "White Blossom told me a particularly interesting tale as we walked to the city. A Spaniard captured White Blossom's mother, Strong Bear's favorite wife, who happened to be with child . . . with Strong Bear's child. The Spaniard whored her and killed the baby she bore. He beat her unmercifully. When she finally escaped and returned to Chicora, she was little more than skin draped over bones. White Blossom said her entire body was covered in scars where she had been beaten. She died in Strong Bear's arms, giving birth to the Spaniard's bastard."

Marta Carolina was so horrified she was nauseous. "That—that doesn't mean that Strong Bear would—"

"That does not mean that he would not, either," Will said. He reached out, caught her by the shoulders, and dragged her to him. "Remember, Sister Marta Carolina, your safety as well as—" his tone turned sarcastic "—*your virtue* lies in my hands."

Marta Carolina twisted out of Will's grip. "From henceforth, señor, I will be responsible for both my safety and my virtue." Her eyes were a glacial blue; her voice cold and cutting.

The long sharp silence was broken by Strong Bear. "May I come in?" he asked from the door.

"You may," Will answered.

Strong Bear shoved the mat aside and entered the room, a Chicoran woman behind him, Will's crutch in hand. "I thought you might need this," he said, leaning it against the wall. Then he nodded to the woman. "This is Moon Stone," he said. "While you are a guest of the Chicorans, she will be your servant."

Marta Carolina smiled at Moon Stone, but the woman's face remained expressionless, her eyes unfriendly. "Hello," Marta Carolina said, "I'm glad to meet you. I'm Marta Carolina."

Strong Bear translated Marta Carolina's words; then he said to her, "We have many who speak your language, but we have few who will." His eyes apologized, but he said nothing. "Knowing how travel weary you must be, I have asked Moon Stone to prepared you a bath."

Moon Stone moved to one of the benches and set the basket down. Immediately behind her came a young boy, a large bark tub in his arms. Looking at neither Will nor Marta Carolina, he set the tub in front of the window in direct sunlight.

"I thought you would wish for clean clothes," Strong Bear pointed to Moon Stone who spread several aprons across one of the benches.

Marta Carolina's face flamed red when she saw the

woman place a gold brassiere similar to the one that White Blossom had worn on top of the aprons.

Strong Bear chuckled. "The women of our kingdom are rather vain, Marta Carolina. Their beauty is judged by their trim, shapely bodies and their well-rounded breasts." Visions of White Blossom rose before Marta Carolina. "In order to keep their youthful figures, our women use certain herbs to prevent childbirth."

Moon Stone now laid out fabric mantles and cloaks. Picking up a piece of tanned hide, she moved to where Marta Carolina stood. Without a change in that stone expression, she motioned for Marta Carolina to place her foot on the skin. When Marta Carolina did so, the Chicoran woman, using the point of a flint knife, drew the outline of her foot. Puzzled, Marta Carolina looked at Strong Bear.

"She's going to get you a pair of moccasins," he explained.

"How thoughtful," Marta Carolina marveled, moving to the bark tub at the same time that Will walked out the door to sit on a bench in the sunshine.

Two young boys came into the room with a large jug of water in each hand. These they proceeded to pour into the tub. As soon as they were finished, they left. By this time the young woman returned, a pair of moccasins in hand. After she laid them on the bench beside the apron and brassiere, she pulled small clay jars out of the basket and laid them on the rim of the tub. Over the rim she also draped two small bathing cloths and two drying cloths. This done, she quietly withdrew.

Pointing to the jars as he spoke, Strong Bear said, "With this oil you cleanse your body and hair. This one is a scent you put on after you have dried off." He lifted

163

the small container so Marta Carolina could smell it.

After she sniffed the fragrant musk odor, she lifted surprised and pleased eyes to him.

Returning the jar to the lip of the tub, he smiled at Marta Carolina. "I will leave you now. After you have bathed, *ira*, please do not leave your lodgings. My people do not feel kindly toward black robes. Later I will be back to escort you to the feast." Walking to the door, he said to Will, "The shaman reported the other paleface is feeling better. He is sleeping right now, but as soon as he awakens, you may visit with him."

Will stood and returned to the apartment. As Strong Bear walked out, he pulled the mat over the door. Will and Marta Carolina were alone, both of them staring at the bathtub, which bespoke an intimacy neither one of them was ready to face. Yet face it they must. Strong Bear had explicitly ordered them to remain in the room.

"You may bathe first," Will suggested, going to the hammock on the pretense of looking at the clothing which Moon Stone had brought for him. He picked up the buckskin breeches and held them up to his waistline and kicked one of the legs out to measure the length.

"No," Marta Carolina said, "you shall bathe first. Your wounds need to be cleaned and your bandage changed. Besides," she added, "you must be ready when the man awakens."

Will laid the breeches down. Except for an occasional twinge of pain when he moved the wrong way, he had quite forgotten about the deep cuts that slashed his body and the sprained ankle. He unlaced his jacket and pulled it over his head; then he slipped out of his shirt.

Beside him now, Marta Carolina untied the strips of cloth and unwrapped his chest. Directing him to the

164

window, she inspected his wounds, her eyes slowly moving over his cheek and neck, down and across his pectoral muscles. Lower her eyes moved.

As she looked at the thick mat of hair that covered his chest and stomach, that swirled into the waistband of his breeches, she sucked in her breath. She controlled the desire she had to reach out to caress the taut flesh of his stomach. With trembling hand she touched his shoulder and turned him around. She looked at the red gashes that extended from shoulder to shoulder.

She touched soft fingertips to the swollen areas around the cuts and gently moved her hands across his welted back. But she was no longer thinking of Will Dare's wounds. She was mesmerized with the beauty of his body: the proud tilt of his head; the broad expanse of shoulders; the narrow waist and hips; the—the . . .

The air around Will was charged with sexual tension; it was still, the quiet marked only by their deep breathing.

"They—" Marta Carolina cleared her throat "—the cuts seem to be healing . . . properly." With trembling hands she wadded the bandages and dropped them on the floor.

Will slowly turned around. "Are you sure you don't want to bathe first?"

Marta Carolina shook her head and separated herself from Will. At the window she said, "No, you need to bathe first. You need to be ready when Strong Bear comes back for you." She had to stall for as long as she could because she didn't trust herself in the presence of this man.

Her face to the window, her back to Will, Marta Carolina couldn't see him, but she was surrounded by the sound of him. The rustle of material as he slipped out of his clothes. The gentle splash when he stepped into the bark tub. The friction as he rubbed ointment between his hands and slicked it over his body. Then she smelled the perfume—the heady, herbal scent. She thought she was slowly going insane. She laid her hands, palms down, on the thick window casement, closed her eyes, and leaned out, inhaling deeply of the clean air.

She fought and won the urge to open her eyes, to turn her head, and to look at Will Dare. But she couldn't stop the parade of memories. She remembered him in the early light of morning, a bronzed god emerging from the river. She remembered the taste of his full, sensuous mouth on hers, the feel of his chest against her breasts.

"I'm through."

Marta Carolina breathed deeply several times before she turned to face him. He stood beside the tub, his midsection wrapped with a drying cloth. His hair was coiled into hundreds of thick little ringlets which softened the angular hardness of his face and gave him a handsome vulnerability. Even the angry red welts added to his aura of masculinity.

"You're an excellent apothecary," he said, glancing down at his feet. "I can put my weight on my ankle without its hurting too bad."

"You must be careful," Marta Carolina admonished.

"I will, little Sister." He grinned. "Your time to bathe now."

She looked around wildly. "My—my trunk," she said. "I don't have my trunk."

Will pressed both hands on his lean hips and leveled eyes on her. His grin broadened into a taunting smile.

"Strong Bear promised he'd have someone bring it to me," she said. "He must have forgotten."

"I'll go get it," Will said, knowing she wanted him out of the room while she bathed. And he wanted to be gone also. It had been difficult for him to bathe knowing she was a few strides away from him.

"What about your cuts?".

"What about them?" Will asked.

"They need to be doctored."

"We can do that later."

"Strong Bear told us not to leave the room."

"He told you not to leave the room 'little black robe,' not me." His hand went to the tuck of the drying cloth. "I'm going to dress," he told Marta Carolina, devilish glints in the black eyes. "You might want to turn your back."

The words brought swift color to her cheeks, and Will chuckled. As soon as she spun about, he flipped the tuck of the drying cloth and it skirted down his legs to land at his feet. He stood for that fraction of a moment, naked. Cautious not to put his full weight on his injured ankle, he moved to the hammock, picked up the pair of buckskin breeches Moon Stone had brought him, and slipped into them.

"I'm decent," he announced.

But I'm not, Marta Carolina thought as she turned around to watch Will don a thin fabric shirt. Her hand mentally followed his movements as he tucked it into the breeches, and she felt the heat of desire blaze through her body. Merely by looking she couldn't slack the emotions that ravaged her insides; merely by watching she couldn't appease the deep ache in her loins. She wanted to touch him intimately; she wanted to slide her hand down his stomach. Afraid that her needs were written on her face for him to see, Marta Carolina took refuge in the window, her back to him again.

About his waist Will fastened a decorated belt as he walked out the door and called over his shoulder, "I'll return shortly." Before he could pull the mat into place, he heard Marta Carolina's soft call.

"Will, I have to tell you something." No matter what the consequence, Marta Carolina determined to tell Will the truth.

"Can't it wait until later, Sister?"

"No," Marta Carolina replied, lest her nerve fail her. Will stood outside and waited.

"I'm—I'm not a nun, and I—I have never been."

Speechless, Will entered the room to stare at her in bewilderment.

"Sister Angelica had me put the habit on when the corsairs boarded the ship. She said—she said this was the only protection she could give me. I am—I am Doña Marta Carolina Lucas de Santiago."

"Evidently Sister Angelica's connection with Providence is strong," Will finally said, his voice laced with amusement. "The garment truly kept your virtue intact." He was standing behind her now, his hands on her shoulders. He twisted her around so that she faced him. "Why did you choose this time to tell me?"

Marta Carolina's cheeks colored softly, and her lips tentatively smiled.

Inhaling quickly at such an awesome sight, Will lowered his face and dropped an infinitely soft kiss on her pouting lips. "Take your bath," he said. "We'll talk about this later."

"Will—"

"Later," he said, a gorgeous smile curving his lips. "We'll have plenty of time for confessions later—a much

168

better time—a much more pleasurable time."

His mouth slanted across hers in the softest of kisses, a kiss that was meant to be a promise of passion to come, but Marta Carolina, starved for Will's possessive touch, wound her arms around his neck and pushed up on her tiptoes. As she crushed her breasts against his chest, passion hardened Will's body. His lips gently pressured hers open, and he kissed her for the longest time, first nibbling around her mouth, then stroking in the fullness of her lips with his tongue.

When her fingers tangled in the thickness of his neckline hair, when she innocently arched her hips against the protruding evidence of his arousal, Will's tongue entered the moist sweetness of her mouth. With a shudder of sheer ecstasy, she received him. But still this wasn't enough. She wanted more. Her body demanded more. She pressed closer to him, the most intimate cavity of her body warming moistly as she moved her hips.

Will's hands slipped to her buttocks, and he arched as he brought her closer to him. His lips ground into hers. His tongue explored deeply and thoroughly. As if she were a delectable morsel, he savored her body, her lips, the kiss. Finally he raised his head and gazed, bemused, into the passion-ravaged face.

Marta Carolina's eyes were glowing with awakened desire; they were dreamy with innocent love. Red, swollen, and pouting were her lips; they begged to be kissed again and again. Her breathing heightened and irregular, she laid her head against Will's chest, and her palm slid from his chest down to the knotted material at the waistband of his breeches.

"Sorely you tempt me, *querida*," Will murmured, his hand halting hers, "but this is not the right time."

169

"How do you know the right time?"

Will laughed quietly. "You ask me that, *querida*, when you are the one who was reared by the nuns. Don't tell me that even you cannot remember the words of the Wise Man, Solomon?"

Marta Carolina moved her head so that she gazed into Will's love-softened face. She watched his lips as he quoted the scripture.

"'To everything there is a season, and a time to every purpose under the heaven: a time—'"

She listened to his resonant voice that filled the room with warmth.

"'. . . a time to embrace, and a time to refrain from embracing . . .'"

Her voice joined his and they quoted together. "—time to love."

As if they had rehearsed the scene, they stopped speaking at the same time. Neither voiced the rest of the verse for fear it would be prophetic: "'a time to hate . . .'"

Will bent his head to touch the tip of her nose with a tender kiss. "This is not the time, my darling. When we make love, I want us to have all the time in the world, and I don't want to be worried with untimely interruptions." He smiled, a very special smile that was meant for Marta Carolina and for her alone. "I want your first time to be one of your most treasured memories—a good one to replace the many sorrowful ones."

Because joy was welling up in her in such proportions, Marta Carolina couldn't speak. She simply nodded and looked at Will through eyes that sparkled with liquid love. They moved out of their embrace, and he walked across the room. At the door he stopped, turned, and looked at her, his soul shining in his countenance for her to see. At the wondrous sight she caught her breath, held it prisoner, then released it with a tremor. She knew at this moment she loved Will Dare. He moved out the door and pulled the mat into place.

Smiling, Marta Carolina stripped out of her soiled habit. Her hot, sweat-moistened skin welcomed the cool air. She unfastened the wimple, pulling it off her head. After she loosened her hair from the coil, she shook her head and let the damp mane tumble down her back. Then she finger-combed it.

Moving to the center of the room, she gratefully sank beneath the surface of the water, glad for the warmth of the sunshine. Leisurely she bathed and luxuriated in the oils and scents with which the Chicoras had supplied her. Then she washed her hair.

After she dried off, she went to the hammock and selected one of the more modest of the dresses that Moon Stone had brought—one similar to that which the queen wore. Marta Carolina slipped the cool material over her head. Again she searched through the items which Moon Stone had given her. Finding what she sought, she walked to the window and stood in the sunshine, brushing her hair.

The terraced garden was so beautiful, she could stay in the house no longer. With a grin she looked down at her colorful frock. No one would mistake her for a black robe in this dress. Her hair hanging freely, she ran out the door and rounded the house. Taking her time to admire the beauty and to study the plants, she strolled through the garden.

When she heard the tinkle of laughter and the rush of water, she walked to the edge of the terrace and looked down the incline of the man-made mountain. In a garden on a lower level, White Blossom was bathing. Naked, she stood ankle deep in the stream of water. Her beautiful lips were curved into a smile.

"A beast of burden?" White Blossom spoke to someone in Spanish.

Wanting to identify the person to whom White Blossom was speaking, Marta Carolina leaned over the stone fence. She saw Will set her chest on the ground beside himself and move closer to the pond.

"Nay, *Ira*." His voice floated up to Marta Carolina.

White Blossom's delighted laughter filled the flower-scented air. "How wonderful! You've learned a few words in Chicoran."

Will's laughter mingled with hers. "The most important."

"Where are you carrying the chest?"

"To the black robe."

"You are her slave?"

Will stared at the naked woman who deliberately taunted him with her body. She was totally feminine, her willow slenderness graceful and flowing. Her breasts were large and firm, the aureoles strutted. Her waist was small, tapering into rounded hips and well-shaped legs. Indeed she was beautiful, one of the most beautiful women he had ever seen. But her beauty didn't stir his senses or excite his imagination as the cloaked and hooded Marta Carolina did.

"She's my slave," he replied.

"But she is a black robe," White Blossom reminded him. "She can have no man on her platform."

"Then I shall put her on my platform."

Still not sure of their status in Chicora, Will risked lying more than he risked Marta Carolina's integrity and

172

virtue. As he had moved through the town, he felt the open hostility the natives felt toward the Spaniards. None was directed toward him, but they spoke openly of their hatred of the Spaniards. The Chicorans were suspicious of Marta Carolina and did not like the idea of her being in the town. Uncertain of Marta Carolina's safety, Will thought it prudent to assert his claim to her.

"Any time you wish, Will Dare, you may share my platform and my lodge."

"Thank you, White Blossom, for offering," Will said. Since the Indians were not a promiscuous people. Will knew White Blossom had proposed marriage to him, the highest honor she could bestow on a paleface warrior. He would not belittle her proposal. "At this time I cannot consider joining any woman in her lodge. I have a mission I must perform. I must make a journey into the Southland."

"To learn of the people of the black robes."

"Of one in particular," he replied.

"I will make the journey with you," White Blossom declared. "I will fight the soldiers of the black robes by your side."

"Thank you again, White Blossom. Truly you are a valiant warrior."

"No, Will Dare," White Blossom returned, wading out of the water, "I am not making this offer because I am a valiant warrior and because I wish to fight the soldiers of the black robes. I am doing it because I want you by my side for the rest of my life. I wish you to be my warrior husband."

"I cannot accept," Will replied.

"Then let me give you something that will protect you as you travel through Chicora." She moved to a bench on

173

which lay her clothes and picked up a gold semicircled neck band. "Wear this always," she said, slipping it around his neck. "It is my totem. It will protect you."

She locked her hands around his neck and pressed her large breasts against his chest, the aureoles cresting as they brushed the thin material to feel the hard muscular wall beneath. When she kissed him, Will felt no excitement or arousal. He gave no response. His hands slid to her waist, and he gently set her back.

"It is the woman black robe?"

White Blossom's soft whisper was lost in the breeze, and Marta Carolina never heard it. She never saw Will's nod of affirmation. Her heart heavy, she pulled back from the fence, her palms brushing over the rough stones. Tears burning her eyes, she rushed into the house where she stood in front of the window, staring blankly into space. Her confession to Will had been for naught. He didn't love her. He lusted after every woman he saw.

"Will Dare. Woman Black Robe." Strong Bear's resonant voice carried through the apartment. "May I come in?"

"You may." Marta Carolina's voice was dull with disappointment.

The Chicoran chief slid the mat aside and stepped into the room. His eyes moved from the bathtub to the heap of soiled clothes in the middle of the room to the bare feet of the woman who stood in the splash of sunshine. Slowly his gaze ascended the slight frame to center on her eyes, then on the beautiful hair cascading down her back.

"You are beautiful, Marta Carolina," he said. "Your hair is long and healthy, indeed your glory. Your eyes are the color of the sky."

Marta Carolina's body flamed with embarrassment.

174

She had been so caught up in Will that she had forgotten how scantily attired she was. Grasping for a composure she was far from feeling, she said, "Thank you," unable to forget how beautiful White Blossom looked. When Strong Bear continued to stare at her with a gaze akin to adoration, Marta Carolina's uneasiness grew. Discomfited by the web of intimacy—whether it was intentional she did not know—Strong Bear seemed to weave around them, she asked, "What did you wish to speak to me about?"

"I came to get the paleface."

"He went to get my trunk," Marta Carolina said. "I'll tell him as soon as he returns."

Her words hardly left her mouth before Will's thundered across the room, carrying all the rage of a winter storm. "What are you doing here?" The raven-black eyes speared through Strong Bear; the words were directed to him. Will dropped the chest on the floor and stood menacingly in the door, his hands on his hips, his legs straddled. Silhouetted by the afternoon sun, his shadow lengthened across the floor, touching both the surprised woman and the Indian chief.

Will was angrier than he could remember himself having been for a long time, and he didn't bother to hide his feelings. Reason was totally obliterated by the fury that raced through his bloodstream. Walking in and finding Strong Bear with Marta Carolina had destroyed all his lovely fantasies of making love to her.

So caught up in Marta Carolina's beauty, Strong Bear hadn't heard Will enter. His face impassive, he replied, "The other paleface is awake. You may talk to him."

The softly spoken words were like the splash of cold water that doused the fire. The blaze of Will's fury

175

turned to the billowing smoke of jealousy. His gaze riveted to Marta Carolina. For the moment he forgot Strong Bear. He forgot everything but the woman who stood in front of him. Will Dare was a man dazed. None of his dreams about Marta Carolina came near reality. She was tinier than he had imagined, but she was more voluptuous. The fabric dress, sleeveless and thin, outlined her breasts and hips. For the second time since he had met her, he saw her without the headdress. The sunlight sparkled on the sable mane that hung below her buttocks.

"Are you ready?" Strong Bear's voice, the blast of a musket, shattered Will's fragile world.

"Wait for me outside," Will said. "I'll join you in a moment."

Strong Bear's expression remained apathetic, but beneath the surface of those chocolate eyes brewed hostility and anger. He, too, wanted the paleface woman; he, too, warred with the same emotions as Will. The Chicoran chief hesitated fractionally before he did Will's bidding.

Marta Carolina wasn't aware of what was going on around her. She was transfixed, her eyes cemented to the gold band that circled Will's neck. Her mind was filled with scenes of Will and White Blossom on the terrace below, but her body with a mind of its own responded to Will's closeness.

"You're . . . so . . . beautiful." His words shattered her thoughts and resolve; they drove reason away as they beckoned her to come. "So much more than I had imagined." Trancelike, she came even closer. When he bent and touched his lips to her shoulders, he felt the tremors that shook her small frame. "Marta," he mur-

176

mured. "Marta Carolina."

To his unspoken summons, Marta Carolina moved fully into his embrace. His voice, his touch dismissed her doubts and fears, pushed aside her jealousies and hurts.

His hand slipped up the base of her neck, and his fingers fanned into her hairline. With gentle movements he brought her mouth against his, his lips guiding hers open to grant his tongue entrance. He craved the sweetness which he remembered only too well.

Marta Carolina pushed up on her toes and twined her hands around his neck to mold her body to his. The warmth and friction of his chest against her breasts caused her nipples to harden, and as his hands moved in erotic patterns up and down her back, she felt desire warm and moisten her most intimate part.

Will, pulling back slightly, pushed the straps from her shoulders and lowered his head again. This time his lips claimed the creamy terrain as his. "I've tried to stop myself from wanting you," he confessed, his hot breath fanning across the rounded firmness of her breasts. "But, God help me, I can't stop the wanting, and I'm not going to try." He muttered, "You belong to me, and I'm going to take you."

He was so caught up in his passion, he didn't think of the words which he said, and neither did Marta Carolina at first. Then her fingers touched the gold band that circled his neck. The touch of the cool metal brought her back to reality. Her ardor cooled. She went slack in his arms. Then she pulled out of his arms altogether.

"No," she announced, stepping away from him and folding her arms across her chest, "I don't belong to you. I belong to no one but myself. If you want a wench for your platform, you'll have to look elsewhere." Her eyes burned on the gold band White Blossom had given him. Unconsciously Will's hand lifted, and he touched it. "Perhaps you can find one of the local maidens who would be willing to share your bed with you." She pointed to the gold circlet. "How about the one who gave you the necklace!"

Chapter VIII

When Will walked down the beamed steps beside Strong Bear, he did not even think about White Blossom, who had so recently bathed in the terraced garden; his thoughts were centered on Marta Carolina. Far from being dismayed or upset by her reaction to the gold neck band which White Blossom had given him, he was delighted. Without Marta Carolina's knowing it, she was going to help him complete his mission. He had wondered what plan he would use to gain entrance into the fort at St. Augustine—and he knew it had to be believable in order for him to gain refuge and to obtain transport to Havana; now he knew. When he returned, he would explain White Blossom's gift to Marta Carolina and clear away all misunderstandings.

Unconsciously he lifted his head, a smile spanning his face, a jaunty bounce in his steps. Marta Carolina was not a nun, and she wanted him to make love to her. Otherwise, she would never have confessed; she wouldn't have been jealous. Will enjoyed the wanton beauty a woman displayed when she was jealous; he thoroughly enjoyed manipulating a woman's emotions to that extent. It gave him a sense of exhilarating power.

What a beautiful mating he and Marta Carolina would have, he thought, basking in his daydream as he followed Strong Bear down the steps and across the public square that bustled with activity as the villagers prepared for the evening feast. What a wonderful way to spend the time between Chicora and Havana! What a way to exorcise Ellen Graystone's memories!

Finally at the outskirts of the village but still within the confines of the city, Strong Bear stopped. He pointed to a solitary building where two warriors stood, one on each side of the door.

"This is where the man is kept," he said.

"Is he a prisoner?" Will asked curiously.

"Only of himself," Strong Bear returned. "When he has the evil spirits, he yells and screams. He needs strong warriors to keep him from hurting himself or someone else."

At the entrance of the lodging, Strong Bear spoke in Chicoran to the guards who removed the mat, letting the bright, afternoon sunlight spill into the room; then the Chicoran chief and Will entered, the warriors closing the door behind them. At first Will could see nothing; his eyes had to grow accustomed to the darkened interior. When finally he could focus, his gaze swept the room— the bench, the couch, the hammock. All were empty.

Then Will heard a low shuffling noise as if someone were brushing against the mat walls. He looked from one of the shadowed corners to the other. When he saw the figure squatting, face forward, his back to the wall, he moved in that direction.

"Don't be taking another step unless you want to be disemboweled!" A quiet, gravelly voice spoke in English. "I killed óne of them son-of-a-bitch dogs, and I'll kill you, too. I ain't letting no Spaniard kill me."

Although the man's voice was low, slightly shaking, Will recognized the truth behind the threat. He stopped walking. "John," he muttered, studying the thick-bearded face. "John Cartwright, is this you?" Before the man could answer, Will said, "'Tis Will Dare, John."

"Will Dare?" the man questioned wonderingly. "'Tis you, Will?"

Accustomed to the darkness now, Will slowly advanced toward the crouching man who held a long, spiked cane in his hands. As Will neared he saw that it was indeed John Cartwright, but he saw no reciprocal recognition in John's eyes.

"You came for us?" John asked, his hands tightening on the wooden spear.

"Aye," Will replied, his voice soft and assuring.

John Cartwright straightened up and swung the cane. "Then why didn't you come sooner, man?" he screamed wildly. "Why didn't you get here in time to save the rest of them poor devils before the Spaniards butchered them." His eyes were large, his pupils dilated. "You're not really Will Dare," he accused, his straddled legs slightly bent at the knees. Holding the shank of the cane with both hands, he waved it from side to side; then he jabbed it in front of himself and forced Will back a step or two. "You're one of them come to get me." He threw his head back. "Got those man-eating dogs somewhere out there, waiting to turn them loose on me."

"John," Will said, taking another step backward,

181

"listen to me, please. I am Will Dare. I come from the colonists at Roanoak. I have a message for you from Anne."

"Anne," John whispered, a sudden spark lighting the otherwise dull eyes. "You have seen Annie?"

Will forced himself to laugh. He tried to sound natural and reassuring in order to allay John's fear and to gain the older man's trust. "Annie Cartwright said exactly this: 'Tell John Cartwright to get hisself back here to Roanoak in one piece because every bit of that old body belongs to me and I want it all'."

Tears running down his face, the old man dropped the cane and fell to his knees. "Annie," he cried. "My Annie!" He crumpled to the floor, his sobs reverberating through the small lodge.

Still Will moved cautiously, not sure if John were sane or not. As he touched John's shoulders, Strong Bear whisked up the cane spear and moved out of the wigwam, leaving the two Englishmen alone.

"Will," John cried, his huge hands contouring Will's face, his fingers searching as a blind person would. "'Tis really you, Will?"

"Aye, John," Will murmured softly, "'tis I."

"How did you find me, lad?"

As Will helped the old man to his feet, he answered his questions. By the time he had finished his tale, the two of them were sitting on separate benches, facing each other.

"Was it your idea or Ananias's to come find us?" John asked. When Will didn't reply, John reached out and laid a wrinkled hand on Will's leg. "I thank you, lad. Verily I do. I thought I was losing my mind. Being tortured by the Spaniards and then held prisoner in this hut by them

Indians." He shivered at the memories. "That medicine man puffing on that pipe and blowing that tobacco smoke in my face, mumbling and dancing over me." He shook his head and looked directly into Will's eyes. "I'll be glad to get out of this place. When are we leaving?"

"I'm not sure," Will answered as he stood and moved to one of the walls where he studied the mats. "They call us guests, but they forced us to come to Chicora. They've given us the liberty to move about the city, but not to leave yet."

"My God, man," John barked, "we're prisoners of these here Indians, and you're taking the time to study their art work! Why aren't you devising a plan of escape?"

Will chuckled as he slid his hands down the wall. "I'm not admiring or studying their art work," he denied. "But neither am I devising a plan of escape so soon, John Cartwright. I'm trying to undo some of these mats, so you can get some sunshine in the room. Found it," he grunted. He unpegged several mats and created a window. "There," he said, throwing them on the floor. He turned to the man who was a shadow of the giant he used to be. "Now let's get you some food." He walked to the door and signed to the guard to bring food for John.

Later after he had eaten, John stood, his bark cup of water in hand, and walked to the opening in the wall. He stared at the pyramid in the distance. "We were almost at St. Augustine," he said, his eyes blank. "We stopped at a friendly village, and one of the braves offered to guide us to the garrison. What we didn't know was one of them was a spy for the Spaniards. He slipped out during the night and went to tell the Spaniards that we were

183

coming. They sent out a dog patrol."

"When word came to the village that the Spaniards were coming on their horses, bringing their bloodhounds with them, the people fled in terror. In their rush they took our canoes, leaving us afoot. Following our Scupperongac guide, we backtracked, but we wasn't able to hide our trail. The hounds could sniff us out. We managed to get as far north as an old abandoned Spanish fort before we were overtaken."

John's hand trembled so, he could hardly keep from spilling the water in the cup. He stopped talking and swallowed deeply.

"They didn't kill us outright," John continued, his voice low and tight with suppressed emotion. "First, they tortured us for information, tricks they learned from the Moors and the Turks, using canes to whip the bottoms of our feet until we fair belched up every secret we be knowing. But that wasn't enough; they thought we was hiding something. So each morning they hanged one of us. Finally only me and Howling Wind was alive, and we decided to make a run for it. We had nothing to loose. We walked up the river for miles in the dark. But we could hear them dogs braying in the distance, and we knew they was after us."

John drew in a deep ragged breath. "They caught up with us, and Howling Wind climbed out of the water. He told me to stay in the river and go on up, that he had a better chance of outrunning the hounds than I did." John set the cup down and hid his face in his hands. "I saw the hounds catch him, and they ripped him to pieces and ate his flesh." John couldn't stop the shudder that racked his body. "I was about to run help him when

184

someone caught me and pulled me back. I fought, but they knocked me unconscious. I'm not real sure what happened after that. When I regained consciousness, I was here in this place, tied to a hammock."

He turned and smiled grimly at Will. "Now you're a prisoner, too. Think we'll ever get back to Roanoak, lad?"

"Aye, John," Will said, "we'll be getting back. We'll just have to wait for the Chicorans to give their permission. Now, tell me," he changed the subject, "did you learn anything about the Spanish fortifications?"

"Perhaps not enough about their fortification," John replied, "but they learned enough about ours that they aren't interested. They think us too few to be a great threat against them."

"How did you find this out?" Will asked. "Did you suddenly learn to understand Spanish?"

"I didn't have to, lad," John answered. "One of the soldiers who spoke broken English was cocky enough to tell me." He smiled, dismissing the soldiers at St. Augustine as no consequence. "Now, Will Dare, if only these Indians will let us leave. We can be on our way."

"You can leave with Kee-lee as soon as the queen allows you to," Will murmured, "but I want to go on to St. Augustine."

"You must be daft, man," John exclaimed, shuffling across the room. "There's no need for you to go there. Our orders were to discover the strength of the fort and to find out if it posed a threat." He caught Will by the shoulder and turned him around. "I've learned that, and I'm ready to return to Roanoak and make my report."

"And you shall," Will declared, "but I am going on to

185

St. Augustine."

"What for?" John's frown, as he scrutinized the young man standing in front of him, pulled his thick white brows together in a bushy point above his nose. "Not for the colony, Will'am," he drawled. "Must be something . . . or someone else."

Will nodded. "Not long after you and the others left for St. Augustine, Sir Roscoe Bennett put into harbor. He brought us good news. We defeated the Spanish Armada in our own channel."

"'Tis good news indeed, Will," John exclaimed exuberantly. His gray eyes sparkled with pride. "'Tis good news indeed. England is indeed mistress of the seas."

"Aye, but the captain also gave us more news—news which I'm afraid is not so good, John. We now have a Spaniard, Rodrigo Fernandez, on pension for us in Havana."

"Laddie—" John's voice was gentle, but his eyes were silver pools of concern "—you still sound daft. None of this sounds like bad news to me."

"Drake doesn't trust Fernandez," Will said. "Neither do I. He's the spy who was working with, or shall I say working against, with Sir James Palmer, the queen's ambassador in the Spanish Netherlands. Fernandez is the man who was there when Sir James Palmer was captured and put into prison for spying. He was in the Spanish Netherlands and is responsible for the apprehension of another of our spies."

"And what are you proposing, young Will?" John asked, raking his hand down his beard.

"I must get down to Havana," Will said. "I must find Fernandez." Will paced around the hut for a few minutes. John Cartwright waited for an explanation, Will thought, and truly he deserved one.

But on that fateful day when Will'am Dare had been declared a traitor and a murderer, he had made many promises to Sir Francis Drake: he would speak to no one of the assassination plot against the queen; he would seek anonymity with the planters who were coming to the New World; he would await instructions from Sir Francis before he began a search for the man who framed him. No such instructions had come, but Will had to get to Havana. He had to find Rodrigo Fernandez. He was the man.

"Your desire to find this man is as much personal as it is a matter of state," John quietly surmised.

"Aye," Will replied.

"Then I'll go with you, laddie." John placed a large calloused hand on Will's shoulder and squeezed.

"Nay, John Cartwright," Will returned. "This is my mission, and it is a dangerous one. As much as I would like to have your company, the planters at Roanoak need you worse. Without you or me, Ananias has no strong person on whom to depend. You must return to Roanoak with your report. Tell Ananias to move the colony from the Croatoan village as soon as possible up to the Chesapeake. Leave some kind of markings so I'll know where you are when I return."

"You being English—how are you going to get from St. Augustine to Cuba?" John asked.

Knowing he could trust the old man, Will said, "Ananias and I are only half brothers, John. My mother was Spanish. I'll trade on that."

"Ah," Cartwright drawled thoughtfully, studying Will and drawing a mental comparison between him and

Ananias, "that is why you and he are so different."

"Aye," Will replied. Although he liked and trusted the older man, Will chose not to tell John the details of his background. He smiled and shrugged. "My Spanish heritage and Marta Carolina shall be my keys to the fort." He smiled.

"Will Dare," Strong Bear called.

"Enter."

The mat slid across the opening, and Strong Bear stepped into the room. "It is time for the games to begin, and the shaman would like for your friend to rest."

Quickly Will introduced Strong Bear and John Cartwright, and asked if the Englishman could attend the games also. Strong Bear gave his permission, but when Will told John, the older man shook his head.

"Nay, lad," he said on a weary sigh. "I'm quite tired. If you don't mind, I think I shall stay here and rest." He looked at Strong Bear. "I would like to walk around outside this hut. Do you think they would mind my doing that?"

Will asked Strong Bear, then turned to John with the answer. "They don't mind," he said, "but don't stray too far. The shaman said you are still very weak."

"Aye," John concurred, sitting down on the nearby bench, "that I am, laddie. That I am." He lifted his head and smiled. "Knowing you and Kee-lee are close by, I shall rest better now." Then he said, "Ask Strong Bear when they will let me return to Roanoak."

After Will had interpreted the question, Strong Bear replied, "The queen makes that decision, but I know of no reason for her to detain your friend. I'm sure she will allow him to leave as soon as he is strong enough."

"What about our goods?" John asked, his eyes darting

from Will to Strong Bear as they discussed the question.

"Strong Bear said they found nothing. Evidently the Spaniards took everything of value and destroyed the rest."

"Aye," John murmured, "that is as I thought." Again he breathed deeply and rubbed his hand over his forehead.

Will picked up one of the blankets that lay on a bench, shook out the folds, and spread it across the hammock. "Come," he said. "Why don't you lie down and rest for a while."

After the old man was settled on the hammock, Will and Strong Bear slipped out of the wigwam. As they stepped off the side street onto the avenue, a group of braves surrounded Strong Bear and pushed Will out of the circle. Not minding the exclusion, he watched the Chicorans as they talked. He could tell they were excited; they talked rapidly; their eyes danced, and they gestured profusely. Finally Strong Bear broke the circle. The other braves trotted off, and Strong Bear turned to Will.

"When we have guests," he said, "we entertain them with a feast and games. This afternoon we will play ball in your honor." He smiled proudly. "My team has been chosen to play. I will let you watch us practice."

Without moving from the spot, Will's gaze quickly scaled the pyramid to the garden outside their lodging. Standing behind the low stone fence was Marta Carolina. His smile turned into a frown. She was dressed in her nun's habit. The autumn wind was blowing softly, the wimple brushing against her cheeks. She looked directly into his face. Then her eyes lowered to his neck. As if she had spoken an accusation, Will's hand involuntarily lifted, and he touched the gold band.

"Come!" Strong Bear barked the word.

Although Will preferred to return to talk with Marta Carolina, so he could convince her that White Blossom meant nothing to him, he knew his refusing to go with Strong Bear would be construed by the Chicoran as an insult. Still he didn't move.

"Strong Bear! Will! Please wait. I have been looking for you," White Blossom shouted.

Will heard the other woman's call, but he couldn't take his eyes off Marta Carolina. She was the one who finally broke visual contact and disappeared. He sighed and looked down when White Blossom laid her hand on his lower arm.

"Since Strong Bear will be competing in the games, I am to be your interpreter."

Will spared the terraced garden on the summit of the pyramid one last glance, but Marta Carolina was nowhere to be seen. Then he turned to walk between Strong Bear and White Blossom. He listened as they talked about the coming games, but his thoughts were on Marta Carolina. He was puzzled—no, he was troubled about his growing obsession with her. She was beginning to occupy too much of his time and his thoughts . . . especially his thoughts.

"A good player catches the ball on his shoulders, his elbows, and sometimes on his hips. Seldom does he catch it with his hands."

White Blossom's words jarred Will from his thoughts. He looked around. Strong Bear had joined the other members of his team and was in the middle of the ball field. One of the players bounced the ball on the ground—the clay was packed so hard it was like a wooden floor. Will and White Blossom stood by themselves on

espicable gold band around his neck. She stiffened her
ack and bowed her neck. She refused to let this trifler of
earts intimidate her!

"Woman black robe," the queen said, addressing
Marta Carolina in Spanish, "I would have you walk by
he litter with me. I would talk with you."

Marta Carolina nodded her acknowledgment. Follow-
g Will and White Blossom, the litter-bearers began to
alk, and Marta Carolina fell into step with them.

"Strong Bear told me that you have great magic," the
ueen said.

"I have knowledge of herbs and plants," she ack-
wledged. "With them I can cure people of some of
eir illnesses." Her answer was to the queen's question,
 her eyes and thoughts were on Will Dare and White
ossom who walked just ahead of her. Marta Carolina
ld not help but compare herself to White Blossom,
 in her reckoning she came up short.

hy wouldn't Will desire the Indian woman more
 he wanted her! Marta Carolina wondered. White
som was beautiful, and she wasn't ashamed to show
 beauty. In fact, she was quite proud of it. Marta
lina looked down at the plain robe which she wore,
ards of material obscuring her body, taking away her
inity. She reached up to push the scratchy material
 her face.

e queen—alert to everything that went on around
saw Marta Carolina's preoccupation with Will
Although it didn't surprise her; she was disap-
d. The more she knew about the woman black robe
re she liked her and wanted her for Strong Bear.
gdom could benefit from a shaman as powerful as
Carolina, the queen decided, and she would be a

the sidelines.

Although Will had seen a similar version of tennis
played at the royal palace in England, he was still
fascinated by this primitive game. The Indians were most
agile; yet they were rough. Seldom did the ball touch the
ground, but continuously one team member after the
other sprawled across the dirt.

"We will play more games," White Blossom informed
him. "And to honor the queen, you and the woman black
robe may be asked to compete also."

Will lifted his brows in surprise. This was the first he
had heard about his and Marta Carolina's having to
participate in their events. "What kind of games?" he
asked.

White Blossom shrugged as if it were of no consequence. "I don't know," she replied. "The queen will
announce what she chooses to see."

Will heard the fife and drums in the background.

"Come," White Blossom said. "We must hasten to the
public square. The feast is about to begin."

Beautifully designed reed mats were laid in a square,
following the architectural formation of the marketplace.
The only reserved seats were those at the base of the
pyramid, and these were for the queen and her retinue.
Down the center of the mats, the Chicoran women set the
large, flat serving bowls. The aroma of the freshly cooked
food filled Will's nostrils, and his mouth watered when
he saw the variety of dishes.

Impaled on sticks and basted with rich oil made from
the nuts and berries which grew around the city were
alternate chunks of venison, wild onions, mushrooms,
and potatoes being roasted to a golden brown. Various
sorts of domesticated fowl—chickens, ducks, and

geese—were being turned on spits. Filleted fish were broiling on some of the smooth, heated stones at the fire's edge. On others, the Chicoran women were baking thin patties of bread out of minced walnut meat. Buried in the fire were ears of corn, their tender morsels protected from burning by their husk. Huge cooking pots contained an array of vegetables.

White Blossom led Will to the head of the runner where the queen sat. The old woman waved her hand. "Come, Will Dare. Sit beside me and eat."

Will acknowledged her greeting and sat down to cross his legs in front of himself. He glanced around for Marta Carolina, but he didn't see her. When White Blossom saw his searching glances, she pointed.

"There comes the woman black robe."

Will was surprised when he looked up and saw Marta Carolina with Strong Bear. His eyes narrowed and his lips lined in disapproval. After having played such a strenuous game of ball all afternoon, how could the Chicoran chief look so fresh and rested. So strong! So virile! And so obviously enamored with Marta Carolina! Will looked at her, his frown deepening. Her blue eyes were twinkling with devilment, and she was laughing at something Strong Bear said; that made Will even more angry. She was obviously enamored with him!

"Come, Strong Bear," the queen said, and gestured to her left side. "You and the woman black robe will sit on this side of me."

"Thank you," Marta Carolina murmured. Out of the corner of her eyes, she stole a glance at Will, but she pretended to look at the vast assortment of food. "How nice."

Strong Bear smiled as he sat down beside her. "You are

hungry?" he asked solicitously.

"Oh, yes," Marta Carolina said, careful to kee[p] eyes off Will. She pointed to one of the dishes. "W[hat's] that, Strong Bear?"

"Squash," he replied, dipping his spoon into the [...] As he gave her nibbles of the different dishes, he s[...] name of the food, repeating the word until she [could] pronounce it correctly. "Pumpkin. Cheese."

"That was delicious!" Marta Carolina exclaime[d as] she swallowed deer cheese mixed with berries.

Strong Bear chuckled and gently laid his hand [on her] mouth to hush her words as the shaman stood to [...] evening prayer. After he took the first bite of f[ood the] Chicorans began their feast. Marta Carolina enj[oyed the] meal immensely, tasting everything Strong Be[ar put in] front of her, but Will was so furious he had no [idea what] he ate or what he and White Blossom talked abo[ut during] the meal.

Finally the women gathered the bowls and [...] carried them to the kitchens. The shaman sto[od, pipe] in hand. He inhaled, then blew tobacco smok[e to the] heavens. As soon as the smoke dissipated, h[e lifted] his hands upward and started chanting a[s the] musicians picked up their instruments, [moved to the] center of the square, and began to play. Th[e shaman ...] and in a loud clear voice called four nam[es, among] them Strong Bear.

"I must leave now," Strong Bear sai[d, rising to his] feet. "We will play ball."

Marta Carolina watched Strong Be[ar as he strode] across the square and joined the other p[layers. Then her] gaze shifted to Will. She saw his anger [...] and she was pleased; then her eyes [...]

the sidelines.

Although Will had seen a similar version of tennis played at the royal palace in England, he was still fascinated by this primitive game. The Indians were most agile; yet they were rough. Seldom did the ball touch the ground, but continuously one team member after the other sprawled across the dirt.

"We will play more games," White Blossom informed him. "And to honor the queen, you and the woman black robe may be asked to compete also."

Will lifted his brows in surprise. This was the first he had heard about his and Marta Carolina's having to participate in their events. "What kind of games?" he asked.

White Blossom shrugged as if it were of no consequence. "I don't know," she replied. "The queen will announce what she chooses to see."

Will heard the fife and drums in the background.

"Come," White Blossom said. "We must hasten to the public square. The feast is about to begin."

Beautifully designed reed mats were laid in a square, following the architectural formation of the marketplace. The only reserved seats were those at the base of the pyramid, and these were for the queen and her retinue. Down the center of the mats, the Chicoran women set the large, flat serving bowls. The aroma of the freshly cooked food filled Will's nostrils, and his mouth watered when he saw the variety of dishes.

Impaled on sticks and basted with rich oil made from the nuts and berries which grew around the city were alternate chunks of venison, wild onions, mushrooms, and potatoes being roasted to a golden brown. Various sorts of domesticated fowl—chickens, ducks, and

191

geese—were being turned on spits. Filleted fish were broiling on some of the smooth, heated stones at the fire's edge. On others, the Chicoran women were baking thin patties of bread out of minced walnut meat. Buried in the fire were ears of corn, their tender morsels protected from burning by their husk. Huge cooking pots contained an array of vegetables.

White Blossom led Will to the head of the runner where the queen sat. The old woman waved her hand. "Come, Will Dare. Sit beside me and eat."

Will acknowledged her greeting and sat down to cross his legs in front of himself. He glanced around for Marta Carolina, but he didn't see her. When White Blossom saw his searching glances, she pointed.

"There comes the woman black robe."

Will was surprised when he looked up and saw Marta Carolina with Strong Bear. His eyes narrowed and his lips lined in disapproval. After having played such a strenuous game of ball all afternoon, how could the Chicoran chief look so fresh and rested. So strong! So virile! And so obviously enamored with Marta Carolina! Will looked at her, his frown deepening. Her blue eyes were twinkling with devilment, and she was laughing at something Strong Bear said; that made Will even more angry. She was obviously enamored with him!

"Come, Strong Bear," the queen said, and gestured to her left side. "You and the woman black robe will sit on this side of me."

"Thank you," Marta Carolina murmured. Out of the corner of her eyes, she stole a glance at Will, but she pretended to look at the vast assortment of food. "How nice."

Strong Bear smiled as he sat down beside her. "You are

192

hungry?" he asked solicitously.

"Oh, yes," Marta Carolina said, careful to keep her eyes off Will. She pointed to one of the dishes. "What is that, Strong Bear?"

"Squash," he replied, dipping his spoon into the bowl. As he gave her nibbles of the different dishes, he said the name of the food, repeating the word until she could pronounce it correctly. "Pumpkin. Cheese."

"That was delicious!" Marta Carolina exclaimed after she swallowed deer cheese mixed with berries.

Strong Bear chuckled and gently laid his hand over her mouth to hush her words as the shaman stood to offer the evening prayer. After he took the first bite of food, the Chicorans began their feast. Marta Carolina enjoyed her meal immensely, tasting everything Strong Bear set in front of her, but Will was so furious he had no idea what he ate or what he and White Blossom talked about during the meal.

Finally the women gathered the bowls and spoons and carried them to the kitchens. The shaman stood, his pipe in hand. He inhaled, then blew tobacco smoke toward the heavens. As soon as the smoke dissipated, he lifted both his hands upward and started chanting a prayer. The musicians picked up their instruments, moved to the center of the square, and began to play. The queen stood and in a loud clear voice called four names, one among them Strong Bear.

"I must leave now," Strong Bear said, rising to his feet. "We will play ball."

Marta Carolina watched Strong Bear as he trotted across the square and joined the other players. Then her gaze shifted to Will. She saw his anger and displeasure, and she was pleased; then her eyes lowered to that despicable gold band around his neck. She stiffened her back and bowed her neck. She refused to let this trifler of hearts intimidate her!

"Woman black robe," the queen said, addressing Marta Carolina in Spanish, "I would have you walk by the litter with me. I would talk with you."

Marta Carolina nodded her acknowledgment. Following Will and White Blossom, the litter-bearers began to walk, and Marta Carolina fell into step with them.

"Strong Bear told me that you have great magic," the queen said.

"I have knowledge of herbs and plants," she acknowledged. "With them I can cure people of some of their illnesses." Her answer was to the queen's question, but her eyes and thoughts were on Will Dare and White Blossom who walked just ahead of her. Marta Carolina could not help but compare herself to White Blossom, and in her reckoning she came up short.

Why wouldn't Will desire the Indian woman more than he wanted her! Marta Carolina wondered. White Blossom was beautiful, and she wasn't ashamed to show her beauty. In fact, she was quite proud of it. Marta Carolina looked down at the plain robe which she wore, the yards of material obscuring her body, taking away her femininity. She reached up to push the scratchy material from her face.

The queen—alert to everything that went on around her—saw Marta Carolina's preoccupation with Will Dare. Although it didn't surprise her; she was disappointed. The more she knew about the woman black robe the more she liked her and wanted her for Strong Bear. The kingdom could benefit from a shaman as powerful as Marta Carolina, the queen decided, and she would be a

194

good wife for Night Star's favorite Chicoran chief. Also this woman black robe knew how to ride the horse, and the Chicoran queen wanted her warriors to master this art. She wanted to steal more horses from the Spaniards.

Besides, Night Star thought, her gaze moving back to Will, she would like to see the paleface warrior married to White Blossom. She was a headstrong woman who needed a man like him. He was indeed a warrior; one who would equal her in strength and prowess; one strong enough that he would not be dominated by an equally strong woman; and he would love enough that he considered his mate his equal.

"I want you to teach Strong Bear and White Blossom how to ride the horse," Night Star said.

"I would love to teach them," Marta Carolina returned, "but I don't have time, great *Mico*." When she saw Night Star's countenance hardened with resolve, she cast the Chicoran queen an imploring look. "Really I must reach my people as quickly as possible."

"When the time comes," Night Star responded, her eyes on the ball field, "I will let my warriors escort you to the Spanish fort. Until then you will share your magic and knowledge with us." Night Star smiled. "Now let us enjoy the game. Strong Bear is one of my most valiant warriors and my favorite."

Marta Carolina sat beside Night Star, and although she enjoyed the game, she couldn't get involved in it. Her eyes kept straying to Will . . . to White Blossom. Marta Carolina watched the Chicoran woman occasionally reach out to lay her hand on Will's arm; she saw the brilliant smiles; she heard the husky trills of laughter. Marta Carolina felt like a rocking chair. Her emotions continually rocked back and forth from fury to jealousy.

Her body hungered for his caresses; she wanted to be the one sitting next to him, touching, smiling and laughing with him.

At dusk Strong Bear and his partner were declared the winners amidst the boisterous roar of the celebrating audience. After the religious ceremony that ended the game, Strong Bear and the other three braves raced to the river where they bathed. By the time Night Star's litter reached the public square, the music of drums, fifes, and rattles could be heard above the happy roar of the gathering villagers. The ceremonial fire blazed high, the flames hungrily lapping into the coming darkness.

Night Star clapped her hands and yelled, "Let us dance our victory tonight."

The volume of the music increased; the rhythm accelerated, and the villagers sat down, lining the square. Out of the darkness Strong Bear trotted into the empty plaza. Slowly he began to dance around the fire, chanting his victory song. After he had circled the fire several times, his partner joined him, the two of them dancing. Finally the tempo of the music slowed, the volume lowered.

His eyes on Marta Carolina, Strong Bear steadily moved toward her. She was so mesmerized by the music and the hypnotic sway of his body that she didn't contemplate breaking the spellbinding gaze. However, when he held his hands out to her, beckoning her to join him, Marta Carolina could only stare.

Then she heard the "Ha . . . ya!" and a heavy thud as someone bounded to his feet.

Having discarded his shirt and belt and clad only in the buckskin breeches that rode low on his hips, Will stood in the plaza. His legs were straddled, his hands to his sides. His hair was polished to a high sheen by the flickering firelight, an errant lock falling across his forehead. Golden shadows played across his bronzed physique, contrasting him with the Chicoran *cacique*. Strong Bear dropped his hands and turned, but neither warrior spoke; neither had to; each understood what the other was saying and doing. The challenge had been issued.

Will moved gracefully and fluidly, with all the smoothness of a man in excellent physical condition. His eyes were like shining black glass; they glittered with purpose; they were rife with determination.

Marta Carolina's breath lodged in her chest. She couldn't take her eyes off Will. She saw the bear marks that gashed his chest; the slightly pink and swollen welts winding sinuously through the tuft of thick black hair. As he moved to the beat of the drums, he seemed oblivious to his wounds, and so was she. Her gaze lowered to the hair that swirled around his navel, that lazily dipped below the drawstring at the waistband. Nothing detracted from the animal magnetism she felt for this man—an animal magnetism it was, she decided.

"The black robe woman belongs to me," Will declared as his hands moved in the universal language of the forest. "No one but me will have her. I bought her through the blood of another, great chief of the Chicoras, and I will not hesitate to kill again for her."

Strong Bear's expression never changed; not one muscle twitched on his face, but anger and resentment and hatred brewed in his eyes. They spoke to Will Dare; they answered the challenge. Will never flinched. Although Strong Bear was the bigger man, Will reckoned he was the stronger, the more agile. But if he weren't, he wouldn't let Strong Bear have Marta Carolina without a struggle. He would die before he gave her to the Chicoran chief.

Marta Carolina could not understand what the two were saying, but she knew Will and Strong Bear were fighting over her. Anxiously she looked from one to the other. She glanced at White Blossom who sat statue still. Every feature of her face seemed to be carved out of stone.

The drums never stopped their beating, but Marta Carolina could not hear them for the pounding of her heart. When Will extended his hands to her, she placed hers in them. She rose to her feet, lifted her head, and stared into the fathomless black depths. At the moment her entire world was Will Dare.

He reached out, his fingers moving into the limp folds of the wimple. Never had he been so nervous before; yet he appeared to be the calm before the storm. His eyes never left Marta Carolina's face. His fingers groped with the fasteners. Finally they were unhooked. He withdrew the material, slowly revealing her neck and the coil of thick black hair on the nape of her neck. He dropped the wimple to the ground.

Marta Carolina felt the cool night air as it touched her bare skin; she trembled as she felt Will's fingers brush against her shoulders and neck. The pins and combs fell to her feet; then her hair tumbled down her back.

Will slipped the ring off his little finger; then he reached for Marta Carolina's hand. He began to speak in Spanish and to sign, "This woman is mine. From this day forward she will wear my token. She will no longer wear the black robe."

Tears of joy sparkled in Marta Carolina's eyes. Will

198

loved her. In front of all these people he had declared his love for her; he had given her a token of that love. She lifted her hand and stared at the ring: an embossed five-pointed star.

"Come," Will said softly, an enigmatic smile lingering on his lips. "It's time for you and me to return to our lodgings, Marta Carolina."

Chapter IX

"You may not go, Will Dare!" Although she spoke in Spanish, Night Star's authoritative tone caught the attention of everyone. "Before we are visited by Younger Sister, the Dawn, I must choose the champions who will participate in the festivities on the coming sun."

Will and Marta Carolina turned.

"You shall be one," the Chicoran queen continued in Spanish, her finger pointed directly at Will. "When Elder Brother, the Sun, is overhead, you will face Strong Bear in a wrestling contest."

Will heard Marta Carolina's gasp of dismay, and when he felt the slight tremble of fear that raced through her body, his hand tightened on her shoulder. She glanced up, but his face was unreadable, his stance resolute. Somewhere in the distance Marta Carolina heard the queen speak in Chicoran. Then she heard the murmured acceptance of the people.

Will was acutely aware of Marta Carolina's fear, and he wanted to take her into the protective circle of his arms, to hold her warmly, securely. He wanted to assure her

200

that everything would be all right, but he couldn't. Marta Carolina's survival—his survival—all depended on him. Therefore, his attention never wavered from the queen as he made reply.

"What is the prize?" He was glad that he had lived in the town of Scupperong long enough to understand Indian custom.

"The champion will receive the woman black robe for his own," Night Star replied, still speaking Spanish. Her gaze was defiant; she dared Will to challenge authority.

"That is a prize for Strong Bear, my wise *Mico.*" Will was careful in his reply, but he stood firm and resolute. "But it is no prize for me. I already own the woman black robe. What shall I receive if I win?"

Night Star did not immediately answer Will. Rather, she lay back, propped up on pillows, and studied the paleface who stood so arrogantly in her presence. Her face was so shadowed by night that Will could not read her expression.

Eventually she asked, "What would you have, Will Dare?"

"I want you to release the Englishman, John Cartwright, so he may return home with *Werowance* Keelee and the Scupperongac warriors." Night Star nodded. "And," Will continued, "I want you to have several of your braves escort Marta Carolina and me to St. Augustine."

Another long period of silence followed Will's demand. Finally Night Star nodded her head. "You have spoken, Will Dare. So be it." She flung her hand up and shouted in Chicoran. "Now my people rejoice with song and dance."

White Blossom, hidden in the shadows, glared first at

her father then at Will Dare. She hated both of them for loving the woman black robe. But most of all she hated the woman black robe; she hated all that Marta Carolina symbolized.

Exhilaration pounding through his bloodstream, Strong Bear raced to the center of the ceremonial square and with a victory whoop leaped into the air. Other braves followed and soon the entire village was chanting and dancing its victory over the Englishman.

Will draped his arm around Marta Carolina's shoulder and led her to their upstairs apartment. They were silent until they neared the summit.

Then Marta Carolina said, "Strong Bear is a strong warrior."

"Yes," Will replied.

"He's much larger than you."

Again Will muttered only the monosyllable "Yes."

In the central courtyard now, she faced him. "You can't fight him, Guillermo." The agonized whisper was louder than a shout.

"I must," Will quietly returned. "I have no alternative, little one."

"Why?" In the generous spill of moonlight, Marta Carolina saw his smile. She heard the amusement in his voice.

"Night Star is determined that Strong Bear shall have you, and White Blossom shall have me."

"Is—is that what you wish?" Marta Carolina asked.

Will caught Marta Carolina's hands in his and lifted them. Placing them against his mouth, he said, "If that is what I wished, *querida,* I wouldn't have challenged Strong Bear in the first place. I would not have pulled the sacred cloth from your head, and I would not have given

202

you my token to wear. I am determined to have you."

Although it was night, sunshine splashed brightly in Marta Carolina's heart, lighting every corner and chasing all the shadows of fear away. "This afternoon when— when—" she faltered over the words. "—I—I thought you wanted White Blossom."

"No, little one," Will replied, gentle amusement still on his face, "I did not want White Blossom. Since I laid eyes on you, I have wanted no other woman."

Marta Carolina heard Will's confession, but she was so innocent she inadvertently misinterpreted it. Mentally she erroneously substituted love for want. She pushed up on her toes, pulled her hands from Will's, and cupped his face. The moonlight mirrored the happiness on her face. She enjoyed the rasp of his beard stubble on her palms; she felt the accelerating beat of his pulse on her fingers. She lightly rubbed her thumbs over the fullness of his lips.

"And I think I have wanted you from the first moment I saw you, Will Dare."

With gusty laughter, Will scooped Marta Carolina into his arms, carried her into the apartment, and set her down in front of the window—both of them caught in the silvery web of the moon. When he went to undress her, however, she lifted restraining hands.

"No," she whispered, "let me. You wouldn't know where to begin with the unfastening of such a gown."

Will didn't argue. His hands slowly lowered, and he stepped back into the shadows. He knelt and picked up one of her tiny feet. "But I can unfasten your shoes."

One, then the other came off, and Will tossed them across the room. He reached under her skirts and caught her garters, pulling her stocking down. These he

203

deposited on the nearby bench.

He didn't move from her, however; rather he balanced on his knees and leaned back on his toes to watch her hands as they darted in and out the folds until the gown lay bundled around her feet and she stood in her undergarments. Although Will had seen her naked before, he couldn't quell his anticipation of seeing her nude again. Astonishingly she made him feel so innocent; she made each experience so new. His breathing heightened; his pulse accelerated. Tonight he would taste the wonderful sweetness of her body; and tomorrow he would face no recriminations . . . neither would she.

As if she were suspended in a world beyond Chicora, Marta Carolina slowly pivoted, her lips curling into a provocative smile, her hair gloriously swirling about her shoulders. She unhooked the front of her chemise and stood for that moment, her hands to her side, letting the soft white material drape open to reveal the creamy swell of her breasts. Then she lifted her arms, crossed them, and shoved the straps from each shoulder. The chemise slithered to the floor, leaving her naked.

She remained where she was, but Will swayed toward her. She looked down into eyes rendered fuliginous by the moon but were burning with passion; she looked into the face that was filled with adoration. With the tips of her fingers, she touched the shadowed lines of eyebrows, nose, cheek, and mouth. She felt him tremble beneath her whisper-soft strokes. Feeling his desire gave her daring; it instilled in her a sense of power.

"You are indeed a handsome man, Will Dare," she said, using the English version of his name. "And I would imagine many a maiden has told you so."

Her hand rested on his mouth, and she felt his hot breath when he said, "Many a maiden has said as much, but I'm not so vain as to believe them, lass. I'll never tire of hearing you say the words to me."

Still kneeling in front of her, he caught her wrist gently and held it against his lips as he kissed each tip. His nipping mouth moved down her index finger to her palm, where he planted more hot, moist kisses in an effort to cultivate a roaring blaze of passion deep within her. When Marta Carolina sucked in her breath, his lips traveled to her inner wrist. He brushed his chin around and around the sensitive skin until he knew she could stand the torment no longer. Yet his mouth would not be stilled. He blazed a path across her stomach as he moved for the other arm, kissing the elbow, down the forearm to the wrist, finally to the palm.

When Will felt Marta Carolina's tentative quiver beneath his touch, exhilaration winged through his body, and his hands moved to circle her body, his fingers cupping her buttocks. He pulled her so close that his chest brushed against the creamy smoothness of her thighs and his cheek rested on the warm, sensitive skin of her stomach; his breath fanned into the dark pubic hair.

Marta Carolina was gripped by such overwhelming emotions she didn't know what to do. Forgotten were the teachings of the nuns; unheeded were the faint warnings of her heart. Her body, totally disregarding propriety, totally responding to Will's guiding touch, grew warm and moist. When his hand glided from her ankle . . . up her calf . . . behind her kneecap . . . to her inner thigh, Marta Carolina was so weak she squinted her eyes and swayed against him. When his fingers touched the moist portal, she convulsed with desire. When they slid into the velvety corridor, she tensed and drew back.

Will knew he had proceeded too fast for Marta Carolina. Reared in the Church, she would not . . . she could not accept making love outside wedlock. He withdrew his hand and lifted his head.

"You're beautiful," he murmured, rising to his feet. He caught her hand in his and lifted it to his lips to kiss the ring. He deliberately said, "And you belong to me."

Although Will didn't say the words, he knew his actions implied love; more, they implied marriage. They were the assurance Marta Carolina needed. He sensed her surrender. Now his hands spanned her waist. When they slipped up her abdomen to cup the fullness of her breasts, to tilt her aureoles, Marta Carolina gasped. He bent to take them into his mouth, his tongue laving the sensitive peak until it became a throbbing pleasure point.

Will lifted the unresisting woman into his arms and carried her to the far side of the room where he laid her on the couch and knelt beside her. For the first time that evening, his lips touched hers. The kisses began softly, but the longer he kissed her, the deeper they became and the more his hand roamed her body.

Marta Carolina reciprocated his love. She lifted her hand and caught the back of his head, forwarding his lips to her. Under his tutelage she opened her mouth and received him, delighting in the sensuous exploration of his tongue. She even whimpered when his love strokes kindled anew the fire in her groin that could not be quenched without their physically coming together.

His lips on hers, his tongue teased and stroked her mouth. His hand again strayed to the soft mat of hair between her thighs; gently he spread her legs apart, and his fingers tentatively moved in sensual designs on the sensitive arch of inner flesh.

Marta Carolina instinctively rotated her hips, this time welcoming the probing fingers into the moist cavity. She moved with him, groaning softly as her passion mounted and her hips thrust against his hand. When he withdrew his fingers, she opened her eyes. She tensed. She was lost, forsaken, alone . . .

"I'll be back," he reassured her and stood. "I'm going to take my breeches off."

Marta Carolina watched as he untied the drawstring and pushed the offending material over his hips. She heard it swish as it slid down the length of sinewy legs to pool at his feet, but her eyes were on the dark thatch of hair at his thighs from which his engorged muscle sprang. She looked at the trim hips and waist, the flat, taut stomach. Higher she looked at the pectoral muscles, also dark with a mat of crisp black curls. She watched as he sat down beside her.

"I want to make love to you," he said. "I want to teach you all the joy and fulfillment to be found in love."

Marta Carolina lifted her hands to cup his face. "I want you to," she whispered. "I want to make your body as happy as you make mine."

Will groaned, and his lips settled on hers in a long, lingering kiss. But even then he could not take her; he had to give her one more chance; he had to warn her. "We can stop now, my darling, but if we go any further—"

Marta Carolina shook her head. "Perhaps you can—" her hand reached for his, and she guided it to her most intimate part "—but I can't. I want you to make love to me."

As Will's lips captured hers, he stretched out and let

his hand work magic on her. Again he heightened her desires and prepared the way for his entry. When he felt her moistness and heard her low whimper, he knew she was ready. He angled himself over her.

"I'll be gentle, *querida*," he murmured.

When his shaft sank into the warm cavity and he penetrated the small membrane of virginity, he felt her stiffen. Then, once he was fully sheathed, he waited; he murmured endearments in her ear, his hands spoke love to her.

"No more pain, *querida*," he promised. "From now on it's all pleasure."

His lips caught hers, and she gave herself to the kiss, relaxing as he began to move within her and to stir up the cauldron of desire. Passion created such a blaze in Marta Carolina that her emotions spilled over, inundating every inch of her body. Her every thought and action was for Will Dare. Two people, yet they were one. She was a part of him; he a part of her. When he tensed, she felt his muscles flex beneath her hands.

Deeper went his stroke; harder were his thrusts. Marta Carolina, her arms locked around his back, rose to meet him. She sheathed him in the velvety warmth of her body. Then, daringly, her hands slipped down the incline of his spine, over the dimples of his lower back. She cupped his hips in her hands; she kneaded and drew erotic designs on them. She felt him quiver as her finger traced the sensitive indention of his buttocks.

His gasp of pleasure, his hand stimulating her breast, his deep thrust—combined, these cast all coherent thought from Marta Carolina's mind. She was lost in the wonderful bliss of love. She had thoughts but knew no thoughts; she had no feelings but was all feeling.

Then she exploded. She was a million tiny pieces. She was everywhere; she was everything. And Will was with her! He was an indelible part of her . . . whatever she was . . . wherever she was.

Her joy complete, she relaxed and breathed deeply. Then she felt Will tense; he lunged deeply into her; he gasped and shuddered convulsively. Instinctively she knew what she must do to ensure his having the same happiness that he had given to her. Her hips arched to meet and to sheath him; they held him, then rotated to caress him as he moved to that pinnacle of ultimate pleasure—pleasure that only one who truly loves can give.

Later, embracing, they lay quietly as their breathing normalized. Marta Carolina was afraid to speak for fear of breaking the delicate thread of love which twined her and Will together. Had he wanted to, Will couldn't have spoken. He was too confused, too bemused.

His lovemaking experiences were varied and wide, and he had bedded many a maiden and many a whore who had given him what he thought was the ultimate pleasure. But now—this night—with Marta Carolina, a Spaniard and his enemy, he had experienced the ultimate pleasure. Every sexual encounter before this had been nothing but a wonderful release—the partner soon forgotten, her face blending into one of many. In the wake of this discovery, a discovery so new Will couldn't even put a name to it, his feelings for Ellen Graystone paled into nothing. He knew that no matter how many lovers he might have in the years to come, he would never forget Marta Carolina.

Consciously he recognized that his feelings were more than lust—he even admitted to being infatuated with her, but he truly wasn't aware of his falling in love with Marta Carolina. Subconsciously both Will and Marta Carolina knew without their planning or even conceiving it they had become a part of each other. From this moment on their souls were irrevocably bound together for the duration of time . . . beyond the limits of time! Love patiently awaits recognition. Such a tiny thread yet so strong—invisible at first but there nonetheless.

For the first time in his twenty-six years, Will'am Dare was frightened. The kind of coupling which he and Marta Carolina shared brought with it a spiritual binding which demanded commitment. Commitment demanded responsibility. And for the moment his only responsibility, his only commitment was saving his queen and redeeming his name. He could not become involved with Marta Carolina. He could not! He must not!

Like a kitten, Marta Carolina sighed her contentment and stretched, brushing her palm up Will's chest. "I have never been so happy in my entire life. I think perhaps I have been looking for you to complete me, *querido.*" Her hands brushed up his whisker-shadowed jaws to cup his cheeks. "Have I made you happy?"

"Yes, my darling—" like the smooth pull of silk, the husky tones flowed over her "—you have made me extremely happy."

"Even if—"

Their souls blended together so perfectly, Will knew what she was trying to say. "Even if you were inexperienced."

He propped on one arm and looked down at her. In the brilliance of the autumn moonlight, her features were clearly visible. An enchanting contrast to the white mattress ticking, her black hair fanned from her face. Her eyes, the color obscured by night shadows, sparkled with the fire of passion; her lips were a radiant smile of love.

He ran a finger gently down the arch of her neck and the collarbone; he smoothed his hand over her breast, down her midriff to the small waist. His fingers skipped erotically over her stomach, their fanciful flight stopping only when they touched the thick triangle of curly hair.

"What happens now, Guillermo?" Marta Carolina whispered.

"Now, my precious," he whispered in return, a wonderful smile curling his lips, "we're going to bathe."

"Bathe!" Marta Carolina's whisper escalated into an exclamation as Will scooped her into his arms, strode across the room, and kicked the mat away from the door opening.

Draped only in the silver glow of the moon, they descended the back steps into the small terraced garden below. The ceremonial fire of the Chicorans burned brightly, and the music reached its crescendo, but Will and Marta Carolina were oblivious to both. In the quietness of the world which they created they stood in the shallows of the manmade pool where they bathed each other and shivered . . . they made love to each other and burned up.

Afterward, wrapped in warm mantles, they walked back to the apartment where they dried off; then each wiped sweet-smelling herbs over the other. That done, Will lifted her into his arms, carried her across the room, and deposited her in the hammock.

"I'm afraid, love, that you're going to be sore on the morrow."

"Perhaps," Marta Carolina murmured, squirming against the soft fabric blanket as delicious memories warmed her body, "but it was worth it."

Will laughed, the exuberant laugh of a lover who is pleased and who has pleased. "The words are a balm to my soul, my darling girl."

He climbed into the hammock with her, and the two of them lay there in peaceful quietude, looking out the window.

Marta Carolina was the first to break the beautiful silence that engulfed them. "When I think of you as Guillermo, I feel that we have a future," she said, her eyes on the moon-dappled trees. "But then I remember you are Will Dare, an Englishman. I remember that we are sworn enemies." She twined her fingers through his. "Can Will Dare and Marta Carolina Lucas de Santiago have a future together?"

"The same thoughts plague me, sweetheart," Will said and pulled her into the circle of his arms. "I have nothing to offer you but—"

"Your love is enough," Marta Carolina naively interrupted.

Although his conscience bothered him, Will didn't correct Marta Carolina. He understood how important his love was to her, and at the moment he couldn't tell her differently. He wanted to. Dear God, he wanted to, but he couldn't. So much . . . so very much was at stake.

"My name is sullied," he softly confessed. "I cannot even give that to you with the sanction and blessing of the Church."

"Your love is more than enough, more than I ever dreamed of finding," she insisted and snuggled closer, enjoying the feel of his naked body against hers.

212

She ran the bottom of her feet up and down his corded legs. "And whose name, *querido,* hasn't been sullied at one time or another."

Will was quiet for a long time, fearing all that he had found would be stripped from him. He held Marta Carolina tightly. Eventually he said, "I have never met another woman who compares to you, Marta Carolina."

"Not even Ellen Graystone?" The words slipped out unbidden.

Will's lazy chuckle filled her heart with warmth. "Nay, love, not even Ellen Graystone."

"I love you, Will Dare," she whispered, her lips touching his in fiery kisses. "I can hardly wait for us to arrive in St. Augustine. We can be married there by the bishop himself."

Marta Carolina was playing directly into Will's hands; had he written the script himself, he couldn't have planned it better. But he hadn't—really hadn't—planned on using their emotions as a tool of manipulation. He hadn't meant for her to fall in love with him. He didn't feel good about what he was doing. Yet he must! He had to find Rodrigo Fernandez; he had to clear his name; he had to save the queen. Oh, God, so much he had to do!

And marriage . . . well, marriage to Marta Carolina would not be bad. She need never know that he didn't love her with the intensity that she loved him. She would make him a wonderful lady-wife. They would have healthy sons and daughters. The thought appeased his conscience and made his task a little easier.

"You're forgetting, love," he murmured, his lips nuzzling her throat. "I'm English. The Spaniards won't welcome me to St. Augustine."

"But your mother was Spanish," she said. "You could

use her name and pretend you were traveling on the ship with me. No one would know the difference. The corsairs set the ship on fire so the roster burned up with it. Sister Maria Theresa and I watched it burn. No one escaped but her and me, my darling, we can go to Mexico and claim my *repartimiento*."

Will never answered. His mouth found its way to the tip of her breast, and for a long while talk became whispered endearments and moans of love. After the perfection of their coming together, they lapsed into silence.

Marta Carolina was almost asleep when she remembered. "Will?" she called softly, but he didn't answer. Again, this time louder: "Will!"

"Hmm." He was almost asleep, too.

"Do you—do you love me as much as you loved Ellen?" Marta Carolina voiced her greatest fear.

"Have I not answered that?"

"No," she whispered, wanting to be reassured. "You compared my lovemaking to hers. You said nothing about how much you love me in comparison to her."

Will chuckled softly, his breath warmly touching Marta Carolina's forehead. "Ah, love, that confession was the rambling of a foolish man. Tonight bore witness that I only imagined myself in love with Ellen." He planted tender kisses on her forehead.

"Will—" Marta Carolina rubbed her hands over his chest "—tell me something about yourself." Immediately she felt Will's withdrawal—mentally and physically. "I know so little about you—where you came from, what your family is like, what you're doing here in America."

Only the celebration of the Chicorans could be

214

heard—the whooping, the fife, the accelerated drum-beats. Her palm pressed flat against Will's chest, Marta Carolina felt the steady, rhythmic cadence of his heart. Then she heard the sigh that seemed to come from the very depth of his inner being to ripple anguish through his hard, muscular frame.

"I was born in a small village close to Dover. My father was John Dare, an Englishman, my mother Dona Maria Arabella, a young Spanish girl."

Will's memories were priceless possessions packed and stowed and had been for many years. Before he could share them with Marta Carolina, he had to look at each one of them, to touch it, to savor it. Therefore, he paused for a long time before he spoke.

"Maria Arabella, a young girl visiting relatives in Santo Domingo, was en route home when her ship was captured by an English privateer. Taken captive, she fell in love with one of the young sailors, Matthew Forrester. So great was her love for this Englishman that she gave up all—her home, her family, her heritage—to marry him and return to England to live with him."

Will was resurrecting memories that had long been hidden in the coffers of his heart, shared with no one, not even viewed by the owner himself. Escaping the vulnerability that was descending on him, he swung his legs over the edge of the hammock and walked to the window where he stood, illuminated in the brilliant glow of the moonlight. He lifted his left hand and pressed his palm against the wall to stare at the shadowed garden which lay beyond.

His monotone, a parody of his deep resonant voice, carried above the frenzied noise of the Chicorans below. "Not long afterward, Matthew was killed, and the young

Maria Arabella was devastated. Her English in-laws disinherited her; she had nothing and could not return home because her family had also disinherited her. Although born a lady, her only recourse now was to earn her living in this new land. She became a servant in the household of my father, who at this time was an old man with a twelve-year-old son, Ananias. Because he was lonely and wanted a mother for his son, John proposed marriage to Maria Arabella. She accepted, and a little over a year later, I was born."

Marta Carolina sensed the sensitivity Will suffered as a result of his confession. She slipped off the hammock and moved across the room to stand behind him. Reassuringly, comfortingly, she pressed herself against his back and laid her cheek on his shoulder.

"My father, English in every way, forbade my mother to speak Spanish and to teach it to me. He didn't want her to share any of her heritage with me. In all things but this, my mother obeyed my father. She was a small, quiet woman, but she was strong, and she had her philosophy in regards to sharing her birthright with me."

Marta Carolina heard the amused pride in his voice as he spoke of his mother.

"Because I was the center of her life, she taught me Spanish, and she taught me to love my Spanish heritage. Unknown to my father and Ananias, I was tutored by a Jesuit priest, who lived in our village, disguised as a teaching master. When I was ten, my father, discovering what my mother had done, vented his fury on her. In his rage he struck her, the blow so powerful it knocked her to the floor. She hit the back of her head on the fireplace and died instantly."

Will drew a deep breath, unmindful of the tears that

coursed down his cheeks—tears that had been bottled up for sixteen years.

"My father, the same rod in his hand that killed my mother, turned on me. He beat me until I was unconscious. When I came to, Ananias had hidden me and was tending to my wounds. When I was stronger, my brother saved my life the only way he knew how. He carried me to the Jesuit priest who in turn transported me to the Netherlands and enrolled me in a monastic school. I was educated there. But neither life in the monastery nor the priesthood appealed to me. On leaving, I returned home. My father was dead, and Ananias was head of the household. He welcomed me back with open arms. We spoke of the past only once; then we put it behind us."

Will maneuvered so that Marta Carolina slipped into the warm circle of his arms. As she moved, she looked up to see the tears sparkling on his cheeks. Cupping his face in her hands, she guided it down. At the same time she pushed up on her toes and kissed his eyes; then her lips softly followed the trail of tears. Finally she laid her mouth over his.

"I love you," she whispered.

He held her tightly, unable to voice words without crying.

After a long time in which they held on to each other, she asked, "Why did you and Ananias decide to come to America?"

Will hesitated to answer this time because he couldn't tell the truth, yet he wanted to. He wanted to share every little detail of his life with Marta Carolina, but he couldn't. For the first time in his twenty-six years love hedged Will into a corner. Because he cared for Marta Carolina—truly cared for her—he wanted her to know little about his political intrigues. The less she knew the safer she would be, especially when they reached Florida.

Nor could Will betray Ananias. That his half brother had bought the hand of the woman he loved, Eleanor White, by promising to finance her father's colonizing venture in America was a secret Will would carry to his grave. Although Ananias had been too weak to stand up to their father, to stop the murder of his stepmother and the beating of his younger brother, Will would never forget that Ananias was the one who saved and cared for him, and once Ananias was the head of the household, he opened the door of his home as well as his heart to his younger brother.

Bemused, Marta Carolina pulled away from Will and stared at him. She gazed into the raven-black eyes that were deepened by the night light; yet, awash with tears they sparkled tenderly. Love softened the craggy hardness of his face.

Disappointment dulled her voice. "Is the reason for your coming to America another secret you cannot share with me, *querido?*" She waited a moment longer before she affirmed in a louder tone, "I know you're not a planter, Will Dare, and I have begun strongly to suspect you are a soldier."

"You're right, my darling. I am a soldier not a planter." Deciding on the truth—perhaps not the full tale—Will spoke slowly and chose his words carefully. Ananias came to America because he wanted to be a part of the colonizing venture. I had to come to America because I was framed for a murder I didn't commit, and the only way I could save my life at the time was to leave England."

"Couldn't you have bought your freedom?" Marta

Carolina asked, fully cognizant of the power of wealth.

"No," Will replied with a rueful shake of his head. "The victim was too important." His voice lowered to a whisper. "Just a lowly tavern keeper, but the man was too important." Again he paused; then seeing questions aswirl in her eyes, he said, "Sir James Palmer, the queen's ambassador in the Netherlands, was an English spy who was apprehended by the Spaniards. While in prison awaiting his trial he was killed. The same person who killed the ambassador then killed the queen's specially chosen courier—a tavern keeper who lived in the seaport town of Dover. As a result the queen failed to receive important documents which Sir James had dispatched to her."

"Why were you framed for the murder?" Marta Carolina asked.

This was the difficult question! And Will had known it was coming.

"I was a courier for Sir Francis Drake," he replied, again relying on selective truth.

"Sir Francis Drake," Marta Carolina murmured in a daze. *El Draque*, the scourge of Spain. Spain's most deadly enemy. Feared and hated by all Spaniards. This was the man to whom Will pledged allegiance. Yet somehow now that she could associate someone she loved with the man, Drake didn't seem so horrible—he couldn't be or Will wouldn't have been his courier.

"Sir Francis Drake," Will repeated and waited a few minutes for the impact of his words to subside. "Because I know the Netherlands and can speak both Spanish and Dutch fluently, I was chosen to rescue Sir James Palmer for the queen. I failed." Thinking of Rodrigo Fernandez, Will's voice hardened. "The man whom I was to contact in Brussels was a traitor. He murdered Sir James and the tavern keeper, then blamed both the murders on me." The confession hung heavily between them, and Will felt uncomfortable. He tried to shrug the gravity of the situation aside. "'Tis nothing to worry about, love."

"Yes, love," Marta Carolina softly contradicted, "'tis something to be concerned about. Although I was reared in a convent, I haven't kept myself hidden from the world. I do know what's going on about me, and I understand more about political machinations than you would believe . . . especially charges of treason." She quietly added, "My aunt and uncle were executed as traitors."

"I'm sorry," Will whispered—the expression so trite and ineffective—and pulled her into the safety of his arms.

"My tía Karolina," Marta Carolina murmured, her words muffled against Will's chest, "said the word traitor was relative. She was the same woman, yet she was viewed differently by three nations. The English saw her as a business associate; the Dutch as a patriot; the Spanish as a traitor." Suddenly Marta Carolina spun out of Will's arms. Her uplifted face was glowing with anticipation. "You were in the Low Country in the Netherlands," she said, "working with Sir James Palmer. Perhaps you heard of my aunt, Dona Karolina Lucas De Santiago."

"No—" Will shook his head "—I didn't know her."

Marta Carolina compressed her lips together and blinked back the tears. She crossed the room to kneel in front of her chest. The straps she unfastened so she could lift the lid; then she extracted the leather satchel. She rummaged through until she found the lone chess piece.

"This," she cried bitterly, holding the exquisite white marble and gold figurine, "is all I have left of my aunt. Just the queen's piece."

Marta Carolina's exclamation had the impact of a slap. Will couldn't have been more startled or more frightened. In a few long strides he was kneeling beside her; he was studying the tiny figurine. Dona Karolina Lucas de Santiago he did not know, but this chess piece he recognized. In his possession was the black queen's piece, the matching piece given to him by Santica—the code name of Queen Elizabeth's spy in Brussels.

"Where did your aunt and uncle live?" Will asked.

"Brussels." Marta Carolina returned the answer that Will feared. "She and my uncle were kept prisoners for over a year before they were executed as traitors and their property confiscated by the state. After their death I was so alone. I had no one but the good sisters at the convent, and they belonged more to God and the Church than they did to me." Sadness clouded Marta Carolina's eyes. "You must prove your innocence, *querido*. I cannot bear to lose yet another loved one."

"I am trying, sweetheart," Will replied, so lost in the labyrinth of confusion he was hardly aware of speaking. "That is one of the reasons why I am traveling to St. Augustine. I have reason to believe the man whom I seek is living in Havana."

"Together we will find this man," she whispered, her eyes lighting up. "Nothing will stop us, Will Dare. I promise."

As she spoke she pressed her softness against Will, but even the wonderful promise of her desire could not dispel the gloom that descended over him. Marta Carolina must never learn his true identity.

221

Chapter X

"Ca-leb!"

In the grayness that precedes the golden rush of dawn, Kee-lee's voice rang out, shattering the peaceful sleep that hovered over both Will and Marta Carolina.

"You must be up. I have been sent to get you. Strong Bear met with the tribal council today and petitioned for the purification rites which last for eleven suns; the contest will take place on the twelfth. Today, when Elder Brother, the Sun, is directly overhead, you are to be taken to the warrior's camp where you will stay until you and Strong Bear meet at the wrestling contest."

The Scupperongac's words penetrated the outer periphery of the sleeping man's consciousness, but Will didn't allow them full entrance nor did he dwell on them. At the moment he was sated with love and in no way wanted to be roused from his dreams or his lover. He certainly didn't want to think about being confined to a training camp for eleven days with warriors as his only companions. He turned in the hammock and gathered Marta Carolina's slight form even closer, cupping her body with his and unconsciously rubbing against the soft roundness of her buttocks.

"Ca-leb."

Neither Marta Carolina nor Will responded to Keelee's second summons. Marta Carolina burrowed further into the warm curve of Will's body. When she felt him harden against her, wonderful memories stirred the smoldering passion within, and her lips involuntarily curled into a smile. She sighed her pleasure and turned in his arms, her hand provocatively sweeping up his chest to his face. Slowly her lids lifted, and she lightly scraped her fingertips over the black shadow of his whiskered cheek.

"I've never seen a man when he first awakens," she murmured, her lips touching his. With the daring of newly awakened passion, Marta Carolina explored in minute detail the texture and the taste of his lips, nipping, nibbling . . . each corner, then the indentation at the curve of his upper lip.

Because Marta Carolina's caress in its tentative innocence was slow and erotic, like nothing Will had ever experienced before, a shudder of anticipation ran through his body. Her hand slipped around his arm, her fingers caressing his thick biceps as his lips firmed against hers. At first the kiss was tender, hesitant, almost excruciating in its slowness. But suddenly Will became the aggressor. His mouth fully covered hers, his tongue parted her lips, exploring the sweet recesses of her mouth, as he once again branded her with the possessiveness of his love.

When he finally lifted his head, he said, "I better be the only man you wake up with, woman."

Marta Carolina laughed joyously, the sound echoing happily through the room, and she lifted her hand to push the errant locks from Will's forehead. Will answered her erotic communication. His hand brushed up her midriff to cup her breast; she quivered her delight when his fingers gently kneaded the nipple into an erection.

Again her body responded with a mind of its own. The bottom of her feet slid down the smooth blanket, her legs straightened, and she arched so that she filled Will's hand with the roundness of her bosom; she breathed deeply to valve the fast billowing fire of desire and laid her hand over Will's guiding his hand into a rougher, more urgent caress.

Speaking in Scupperongac, Kee-lee said, "Will Dare, I am not going to stand outside your wigwam and yell any longer. If you do not answer, I will push the mat aside and enter."

"Do not come in, my friend. I'm awake, and I hear you." Will's answer was muffled because his mouth lowered and circled one of the pert nipples.

Marta Carolina stilled her movements. "What does he want?" she asked, her ragged breathing and husky voice betraying her heady emotions.

Now was not the time to tell her the contest would follow an eleven-day purification ceremony, so he murmured, "He's come to get me so I can prepare to meet Strong Bear." His love quest never ceased; he nibbled his way to the curve of her outer ear. "Said something about taking me to a training camp."

"Strong Bear!" Marta Carolina repeated the name dully, the events of the previous night tumbling in on her. She mentally withdrew from Will. "I'd forgotten." After a long pause, she said, "I wish the world would go away and leave us alone."

Will determined to bring her back to him as surely as he determined to bring her to an even more wonderful pinnacle of fulfillment than she had known the night before. His lips moved down her throat and across her collarbone. When they nestled in the tiny hollow at the base of her neck and his warm breath spread across the swell of her bosom, Marta Carolina shivered. Somewhere in a distant part of her brain she heard the scrape of the pegs, and she knew Kee-lee was coming in.

"Tell him to go away," she said.

Eager to comply with her request, Will said in Scupperongac, "Replace the peg, my friend. I'll be out later. At the moment I'm finding great pleasure in the arms of my woman."

Marta Carolina's face turned a delicious shade of red at Will's comment.

Kee-lee's chuckle softly penetrated the mat. "Don't be too long in coming out, Will Dare. You will find great pain in the arms of the Chicoran champion unless you learn something of Chicoran rules and procedures."

So noiselessly did the Scupperongac war chief walk, Marta Carolina didn't know when he left. After a few seconds of silence, she whispered, "Is he gone?"

"Umhum," Will droned dismissively, his lips and hands ably rekindling the fires of pleasure for both of them.

Marta Carolina's lips brushed against his. "What did you tell him?"

"To go away—that I'm going to make love to you."

"You what!" She was so embarrassed she straightened and tensed like a board.

"I did just what you told me to do." His even teeth flashed white against the deep tan of his face. He threw

225

his legs over the side of the hammock and stood.

And then embarrassment was forgotten. Marta Carolina's eyes, wide with wonder, centered on his arousal. She looked away only when he caught her hands—and then only to lift her eyes to his face. He pulled her toward him, and she felt him as he moved between her spread legs. Her arms slipped over his shoulders, and her hands locked at the base of his neck. His hands clasped her hips as he urged her forward, drawing the warm center of her femininity against his lower body. When he surged hard into her softness, filling her swiftly, fully, she gasped. When intuitively her legs curved around him, her ankles crossed at his buttocks, and she encased him more completely, a primal groan vibrated from Will's throat.

Caught in the urgency of the moment, his caresses were swift and combustible, spreading like a forest fire in a drought. At the same time, his movements were slow, erotic torture that drove her to the brink of insanity. Coherent thought gone, she cried out as the force of his lovemaking pushed her to that highest point of pleasure—today all pleasure—no pain. Today all joyous, eager anticipation because she knew what to expect rather than anxiety over the unknown.

Marta Carolina felt the muscles in Will's body tense; she heard his low guttural gasp; then she felt him fill her with the issue of his body. She held him tightly against her as he whispered her name. Still inside her, he pulled back slightly, and she gazed into the awesome beauty of his passion-glazed face. A hand she lifted to brush the lopping wave from his forehead; then she wiped the perspiration from his face.

"I love you," she said. Her beautiful lips, red and pouting from their lovemaking, twitched into a beguiling smile. "And I love the feel of you inside me."

"And I love the feel of me inside you."

Marta Carolina noticed that he didn't make a direct confession of love, but she ignored the omission. At the moment she thought his actions spoke louder than mere words.

The radiant glow dimmed in Will's eyes when he said, "I only wish we could spend the entire day hidden from the rest of the world so I could teach you all the intricacies of making love, my darling." He slowly pulled away from her and moved to the door where the water jug was pegged. "But I have other matters to which I must attend."

By silent agreement neither mentioned the contest by name. Rather they savored the beauty of the moment by thinking only of their caring for each other, of their coming together physically, of their being together. Marta Carolina watched as he bathed and dressed, putting on his leather breeches, shirt, and knee-high moccasins. She looked at the gold band on the couch.

"Will—" she called when he picked up the buckskin jacket and lifted it above his head.

His movements stopped, and he turned his head toward her.

"What about White Blossom's neck band?"

"Because of the way you felt, I wasn't going to wear it," he quietly returned.

"I don't mind," Marta Carolina said, joy singing through her body. Then she hastened to explain when Will cocked an eyebrow disbelievingly. "I was jealous yesterday because I didn't know how you really felt about me." She watched as he dropped the buckskin jacket over his head. "Will it hurt her feelings if you don't wear it?"

As his head emerged through the neck hole, he said, "According to Indian custom, you dishonor the giver when you refuse to accept or utilize a gift."

"Yet you would do this for me?" Marta Carolina exclaimed softly.

"I would."

"You must wear it," Marta Carolina insisted.

"No," Will replied, "I won't wear it. I'll keep and cherish her gift, but I won't be branded with her token."

To know that Will cared enough about her to make such a sacrifice filled Marta Carolina to overflowing with love; her joy knew no bounds.

"When we leave Chicora, Night Star will give both of us a personal token that will guarantee us a safe journey through her kingdom," Will continued.

Not understanding the Indian customs, Marta Carolina wondered about this. "Won't she be angry if you defeat her champion?"

"She will be unhappy and disappointed if Strong Bear doesn't win," Will explained, "but she will be proud of me. She will respect my ability as a warrior and will honor her word."

"Have you ever wrestled Indian-style before?"

"No."

"Are you afraid?"

Will's grin was a quick flash of pure devilment across his face. "Actually I'm quite excited about it. If their wrestling matches are anything like the ones I've seen in Scupperong, it'll be rough, but—" he turned to her as he laced the jacket "—I'm a tough man, darling. It'll take more that Strong Bear to wrest my woman from me."

He returned to the hammock and planted a kiss on the tip of her nose. "Now I'm going to find Kee-lee. I'll probably have to meet with the Chicoran shaman and go through some sort of purification ritual like Strong Bear." He straightened and prepared to tell her the bad news. "Although I'm not thoroughly versed in Indian custom, I have all ideas I won't be allowed to see you again before the wrestling match which Kee-lee says will be twelve days from today."

"Twelve days!" Marta Carolina exclaimed. "I won't see you for twelve whole days—" her voice dropped to a mere whisper "—or nights."

"It won't be as long as it sounds," Will assured her, already missing her himself. He caught her hand in his, the one on which she wore his ring, and raised it. "Every time you look at my ring think of me."

Fear rounded Marta Carolina's eyes. "Guillermo," she said, lapsing into the Spanish pronunciation of his name, "what if—" she began, but he hushed her words with the touch of his finger over her mouth.

"The Chicorans will send someone to stay and take care of you while I'm gone and to escort you to the game. For me, wear the most beautiful dress you have—bright and colorful." He skimmed a finger over her lips. "And smile, my darling. Smile!"

"I'll try," she promised, tears not far away.

He brushed his finger over the ring. "I've given you my token of love. And I'm no longer wearing White Blossom's. Have you one to give me?"

Marta Carolina thought only a second before she leapt out of the hammock, pushed past Will, and raced to her trunk. In her haste she fumbled with the strap, but she finally opened the lid. Through the leather satchel she delved until she found the chess piece.

"This, *querido*," she said, returning to Will. "This is

all I have to give you, and it is truly my most treasured possession."

With a leadened hand Will reached for the miniature figurine. He forced himself to smile. "How shall I wear it?" he asked.

"On this." A gold chain dangled from Marta Carolina's extended finger. "As soon as I returned to Spain after having visited with Tía Karolina, I had the jeweler fix it so I could wear it around my neck. Since it was the only tangible memory I had of her, I wanted it with me always." As she spoke she opened the clasp on the chain and looped it through the queen's piece. "Now," she said, "bend over and I'll secure it around your neck." She smiled softly, her blue eyes glistening. "Every time you see it or even feel it, think of me and my love."

"I will, sweetheart," Will murmured, lowering his head while she fastened the chain.

The black figurine was a tangible symbol of Will's conscience which mocked him as it swung to and fro like a pendulum. How heavy was the punishment fate was meeting out to him. Not only must he keep his past secret from Marta Carolina, he must wear a constant reminder that he was indirectly guilty of Dona Karolina's apprehension by the Spanish government and her subsequent execution. Were Marta Carolina to learn this she would judge him guilty of murder. He must constantly be reminded that he was using Marta Carolina, that he had deliberately made her fall in love with him and was now manipulating her actions through that love. Guilt weighed heavily on him.

"What does the star stand for?" Marta Carolina asked as she gazed at the ring he had given to her. She wanted to know, but she also wanted to keep him with her a little longer.

Will hesitated only momentarily before he replied. "My mother's family crest. She was Dona Arabella Lucero."

"The morning star," Marta Carolina whispered, remembering the peculiarity of her aunt's words: "Your destiny lies with the morning star."

"Or Lucifer." Will grinned. "Some would prefer this definition to the morning star." And at the moment he thought Lucifer was the most apt description.

Marta Carolina chuckled. "You can be quite a devil sometimes, Will Dare."

"As long as I have you, Sister Marta Carolina, to pray for me, I'm not worried." He watched Marta Carolina as she ran her fingertips over the embossed star. "When my mother married a commoner and an Englishman at that she was disinherited." Marta Carolina heard the thread of sadness in Will's words. "This ring was all she had left of her life as Dona Arabella Lucero. Because Ananias knew how much my having this ring meant to my mother, he found and hid it immediately after my mother's death and before my father pilfered her belongings. When I returned to England at age sixteen, Ananias gave it to me."

He lifted his face to Marta Carolina's. Before she could voice her next question, Will answered. "It has not been gone from my hand one time during the past ten years. No one but my mother and me has worn this ring—she on her index finger, I on my little one."

"I shall wear this ring as long as I live," Marta Carolina promised solemnly, love sparkling in her blue eyes. "If only my jewels had not been stolen," she said.

Will lifted her hand in his and pressed it over his heart

where the chess piece hung. "I need no more, my darling. I have this token of your love, but far greater than this, I have you and the memory of your love."

He caught her in his arms one last time, and she slipped up on her toes and brushed her hands up his chest. Her face angled to meet his, their lips coming together in a deep kiss that lacked in passion but promised fidelity and everlasting love. Desperately they clung together, loath to part. In the deepest part of their hearts they wondered if they would ever see each other again. Finally each withdrew and stepped back. For a moment that stretched into forever, they looked at each other; they studied each other, the one memorizing every detail of the other's face.

Will would never forget the vision of loveliness which Marta Carolina presented. Naked, her entire body was haloed by the soft, golden rays of morning sun. Her hair, sable rich, hung in a thick curtain down her back, tendrils wisping around her face, silken strands falling over the beautiful swell of her breasts.

Will backed out of the room. At the door he said, "No matter what happens, my darling, remember always that I—that I—love you." The lie was hard for him; the word would hardly roll off his tongue. He hated lying and deceit, and he epitomized both. Yet somewhere in his heart of hearts Will Dare unconsciously recognized that he was falling in love with Marta Carolina.

How cruel fate is, Marta Carolina thought as she struggled to keep the tears at bay. Always taking away those whom I love. She swallowed the bitter thoughts; she blinked back the tears and smiled brightly.

"I love you."

Marta Carolina's soft words followed Will as he

descended the stairs and made his way to the crowd that gathered in the market square at the base of the pyramid.

Kee-lee detached himself from the group as soon as he saw Will approach. The obsidian eyes, purposefully blank, ran Will's tall, lean frame. Speaking in a low voice, the Scupperongac repeated in greater detail the message he'd given Will earlier. "We are to go to the warrior's training camp and remain there until the contest. Although you do not have the same beliefs as the Chicorans, Strong Bear has requested that you undergo the cleansing rites also, and he has insisted that the contest be stayed until the time of purification is complete. He wants your magic to be strong, so the two of you will be equally matched and he can honestly win Marta Carolina."

Will nodded, his eyes skimming the crowd. He was surprised when White Blossóm broke from the others and walked toward him, another brave following behind her. Because the day was cool, she wore a complete suit of buckskins, the yellow color a splendid foil for the thick black braids, the brown eyes, and the cinnamon complexion.

"You are in Brown Beaver's custody until the contest, Will Dare." She spoke in Spanish, her tone cold, almost hostile. Her hand swept to the Chicoran who stood next to her. "He will take you to the Chicoran training camp."

"What about Marta Carolina?" Will asked.

White Blossom heard the question, but her thoughts were not on Marta Carolina. Her gaze was fixed on the base of Will's throat, which was bare except for a thin gold chain.

Will saw a small flicker in the depth of White Blossom's expressionless eyes when they lighted on his

233

throat. Otherwise, not a muscle gave away White Blossom's thoughts. She said, "Night Star has placed the woman black robe in the custody of Morning Dew."

"Will she be kind to Marta Carolina?"

"I do not know, and I do not care," White Blossom replied frankly. "I do not like the woman black robe. She is creating trouble in Chicora. I do not want her to become my father's woman."

"If I win the contest, she shall remain my woman," Will softly said.

"I do not wish her to be your woman either, Will Dare." White Blossom waited a moment, then said, "No matter who wins the contest, I am the loser. Already you shame me by not wearing my gift."

"I mean you no shame or dishonor," Will apologized sincerely, "but I cannot wear your token. I shall always keep the neck band as a cherished gift from a friend."

"I would be more than a friend."

"Marta Carolina is my woman."

"For now."

"She's young," Will reminded White Blossom, "and innocent. Unlike you, she's unable to take care of herself. She needs someone to provide for her."

Inside, White Blossom flinched as if she had been struck a physical blow. Anger and resentment roiled within. She alternated between despising the woman black robe, Will Dare, and her father, then all three. Never in her nineteen winters had she regretted the path she had chosen to walk. She had always been proud of being a warrior; she had gloried in her strength and prowess. Now her hurt urged her to walk the path of a woman. This was a new and foreign feeling for White Blossom, and she did not yet know how to deal with it.

234

But today, under the unrelenting gaze of this paleface, she wanted to be feminine and soft. More than anything in the world she wanted a protector like Will Dare; she wanted him to be her lover, her husband, a warrior *mico* to fight beside her. Just his look, his very presence awakened desire in her.

"What about Marta Carolina?" Will persisted. He refused to leave before he knew what would happen to her.

"Morning Dew is Night Star's niece by marriage, and she's one of our elders. She will treat Marta Carolina courteously," White Blossom replied.

"Thank you."

"None of us is doing this for you or the woman black robe, Will Dare. Night Star commanded it." All the bitterness of White Blossom's soul was wrung out in her confession. "We are treating the woman black robe politely because Night Star has warned us that if anything happens to her we must answer both to Strong Bear and to her. I do nothing to harm the woman black robe," she continued, her brown eyes burning Will with their intensity, "because I have much to lose if I do. Strong Bear is Night Star's great-nephew. I am her great-great niece. I am one of the chieftains whom the council is considering for their next *mico*. I want nothing—absolutely nothing—not even the woman black robe—to keep me from becoming queen." Ashamed of her weakness, ashamed that she had betrayed her emotions to this paleface, she said, "Now go. I will see you at the contest."

White Blossom turned and walked away, her graceful strides taking her to the steps at the bottom of the pyramid. Without a backward glance she ascended, soon lost on the spiral staircase. When she reached the upper village, she crossed the courtyard to enter the royal kitchen.

"Morning Dew," she spoke in Chicoran to the white-haired woman who supervised the cooking of the morning meal, "Night Star wants you to take charge of the woman black robe."

Morning Dew acknowledged with a slight nod of her head, her hands busy with her mortar and pestle.

"You are to address her in Spanish."

"It is not my native language, and I do not speak it well," the old woman replied.

"Night Star has spoken."

"Night Star has the power to command, but she does not possess the magic to make others perform miracles. I do not know if I remember how to speak Spanish. It has been many years since I have spoken it."

"You will remember," White Blossom promised her in a tone that brooked no further argument. "Come with me."

"Although you are a warrior chieftain, White Blossom, and are being considered by the council for our next queen, you do not have the authority to speak to me in such a tone."

White Blossom's eyes flashed angrily. "Be careful how you speak to me, old woman."

"No," Morning Dew returned, her voice flint hard, "you be careful how you speak to me. Remember, two others stand between you and the queenship. The council may choose either one of them."

A cruel smile curled White Blossom's lips. "You hope foolishly, if you think your son will one day become king of Chicora. Torch Light has been gone from Chicora for eight winters, and during this time you have received no word from him. He is not coming back!"

"Hope is never foolish," Morning Dew replied, "and my son will return. Even if he is not selected as the successor for the queen, you are forgetting Night Star's daughter and granddaughter."

White Blossom snorted. "There is even less chance she will come to Chicora than Torch Light will. How many times through the years has Night Star sent messengers in search of her daughter and granddaughter. They are not to be found because they do not want to be found. They want nothing to do with Night Star or Chicora. They prefer to stay in the fort with the soldiers of the black robes." White Blossom tossed her head arrogantly, and her lips curled disdainfully. "From now on, you had better treat me with respect, Morning Dew." The warning hung in the air.

"I shall treat you exactly as your behavior demands," the older woman returned. "Like a spoiled child. But you—" she said, "you will speak to me with respect whether you respect me or not. If you do not, I shall take the matter up with the tribal council. Think what your chances of becoming queen will be then. And do not doubt that I have the power, the motivation, or the inclination. I am a member of the town council as well as the tribal. My word is respected and honored as truth. Never speak to me in such a tone again, do you hear me?" When White Blossom did not immediately answer, Morning Dew looked at her and spoke sharply. "Did you hear me?"

"I heard you, my aunt," White Blossom responded sardonically, using a title of respect.

A kind woman, one who was aware of White Blossom's

237

hatred of the Spaniards and one who understood this hatred, Morning Dew's visage softened. "I understand the emotions which you are feeling, my child. I, too, wonder at the wisdom of Strong Bear." She smiled assuringly. "All will work out as the Creator directs. Now wait a moment, and I'll come with you."

Morning Dew laid the pestle aside and emptied the corn meal into a large bark basket that was lined with leaves. Then she set the mortar down. Rising, she said to a young woman who labored over the fire pits, "You, Blue Water, will be in charge of the kitchen while I am gone. Make sure the meals are prepared and served on time."

Although White Blossom was seething inside because Morning Dew had openly rebuked her, she said no more, but neither did she hide her feelings. She was further irritated because the older woman deliberately procrastinated. Morning Dew continued to give detailed instructions on the managing of the kitchen to Blue Water.

Finally the older woman said to White Blossom, "I'm ready now. You may lead the way to the woman black robe's lodging." Then she proceeded to follow the huffy White Blossom across the courtyard into the guest quarters. Knowing she had riled the warrior chieftain, Morning Dew chuckled softly.

When they stopped at the door to Marta Carolina's apartment, Morning Dew saw her first glimpse of the petite woman. Clad in the soft, skin dress which the Chicorans had tanned, worked, and dyed themselves, her back to them, Marta Carolina stood in front of the window looking at the garden.

"Marta Carolina," White Blossom called from the

doorway, "may we enter."

Marta Carolina turned around, the sky-blue dress with its fringes swirling around her ankles. "Yes."

White Blossom entered first, Morning Dew following behind. Her words cold and clipped, the Chicoran chief said, "I have brought one of our Elders, Morning Dew, who is going to stay with you until the wrestling contest is over."

"What then?" Marta Carolina asked, her blue eyes steady on the dark brown ones. She took a step forward, her moccasined feet making no sound as they sank into the cushioned, rush carpets.

White Blossom studied the woman who stood so defiantly in front of her. Young and innocent you might be, the Chicoran thought, but you are quite capable of taking care of yourself no matter what Will Dare may think. White Blossom visually delved into Marta Carolina. In those blue eyes, the Chicoran chief looked for telltale emotions, but she found none. If you fear, she concluded, you hide it behind an inscrutable face and blank eyes. I could do no better myself. Although White Blossom disliked Marta Carolina, the warrior/woman gave grudging respect.

"What happens to you then will be determined by the champion of the contest. If it is Will Dare, you will remain his woman, and the fate of both of you rests with Night Star. If Strong Bear is the champion, you will become his woman—his property to do with as he wishes."

"I have no wish to remain in Chicora or to become Strong Bear's woman," Marta Carolina said.

"Your wishes don't matter, woman black robe," White Blossom taunted. "Haven't you learned that yet?"

She stepped toward the door. "I am leaving now."

"Wait a minute," Marta Carolina called.

Her hand on the door frame, White Blossom paused and looked over her shoulder.

"Am I free to walk around the town, or am I a prisoner to remain in the upper village?"

"Night Star said you are free to do as you like," White Blossom replied, "as long as you make no attempt to leave Chicora." Her eyes sparkling with curiosity, she asked, "Is there any place in particular you would like to go?"

Marta Carolina nodded. "Strong Bear told me about your shaman. I would like to visit with him to discuss his recipes and medicines." White Blossom nodded her approval. "Also I would like to ride one of the horses."

"The animals that we captured from the soldiers of the black robes?" The Chicoran chief sounded doubtful even in question. "They belong to Night Star. You must seek her permission." White Blossom then turned to Morning Dew. "With your permission, my aunt—" though she again used the title of respect, her tone was sarcastic "—I shall leave."

"Will I see you at the feast?" Morning Dew asked.

White Blossom replied, "Yes. Night Star has asked me to select the twelve messengers who will carry word of the contest throughout the kingdom. We shall dispatch them as soon as we have eaten the evening meal."

"You will inform all your people of the wrestling match between Will and Strong Bear?" Marta Carolina questioned incredulously.

"Invite them to the celebration," White Blossom informed her. "To make sure we cover the territory in the quickest time, Night Star sends twelve of us. Three to the face of each wind: the East, West, South, and North."

Before Marta Carolina could say more, White Blossom walked away, leaving the two of them alone. The silence was unbearable. Marta Carolina was intimidated by the older woman; she was nervous, wondering what to say, wondering if the Chicoran really could converse in Spanish.

Although Morning Dew experienced some of the same emotions, she coped with them differently. Disciplined through the years to let no one read her expressions or her features, her face was immobile and blank. Her eyes swept around the lodge then focused on a distant point.

Marta Carolina, thinking Morning Dew was deliberately ignoring her and determined to get a response, moved to the middle of the room to stand near her chaperone. "Hello, I'm Marta Carolina."

Morning Dew said nothing. She was having great difficulty translating the Spanish words. She found it even more difficult to think in the language . . . so she could speak it.

"I'm—I'm glad that you're going to be with me and that you speak Spanish." Marta Carolina laughed nervously. "I—I wondered if I would be kept in my apartment like a prisoner."

Still Morning Dew made no comment.

Taking a deep breath, Marta Carolina tried again to converse with the Chicoran woman. "How did you come to learn Spanish?"

Morning Dew lifted her head so that she was looking directly into Marta Carolina's brilliantly blue eyes. Marta Carolina gasped when she saw eyes that were as startling blue as her own.

241

"I . . . am . . . French," Morning Dew said in faltering Spanish.

"French?" Marta Carolina gasped. "How do you come to be living in Chicora?"

The older woman smiled, the first friendly gesture Marta Carolina had witnessed since White Blossom had introduced the two of them. "I am Madeleine de Coligny—" she still spoke falteringly, but as her tongue grew accustomed to forming the words, she found herself once again thinking in Spanish "—by marriage a distant relative of Gaspard de Coligny, who was admiral of the French fleet. I am part of the plantation which he settled here in the New World in 1562."

"Where is this French settlement?" Marta Carolina questioned in wonderment. "And why do you speak such perfect Spanish?"

Madeleine's smile saddened. "To answer your first question: the French settlement does not exist any longer, child, and had it not been for the friendly and hospitable Indians in Chicora, none of us settlers would have survived at all. And for the second, I was selected to accompany my husband on this journey because I was fluent in languages. Since we were settling in territory claimed by Spain, Gaspard thought it was necessary that we have amongst us at least one who spoke the language."

"Come." Marta Carolina motioned to one of the couches. "Sit down and tell me all about yourself and your village."

Once they were seated, Madeleine began her story, her eyes sad and faraway with memories. "I was a widow by the time we arrived in the New World. Henri, my husband, died on the way over. From that point on, conditions deteriorated. Our captain, Jean Ribault, left in June to return to France for supplies and more settlers. When we despaired that relief would reach us from France, the men who were left constructed a crude sloop. None of them were skilled in shipbuilding, but necessity taught us many things. They caulked the seams with moss and pitched them with rosin from the pine trees of the forest. They made sails of their own shirts and sheets. Our Indian friends supplied cordage of their own manufacture. In this frail makeshift of a vessel, the Frenchmen who were left attempted the perilous voyage across the Atlantic."

"All but one," Marta Carolina softly added.

"All but two," Madeleine softly corrected. "Guillaume Rufin, a young lad of seventeen, and I chose to remain with our Indian friends rather than attempt the journey in such a frail craft."

Marta Carolina noticed the sudden sparkle in the depth of Madeleine's beautiful blue eyes. "Was that the only reason you chose to remain behind?"

"No—" Madeleine smiled "—I had fallen in love with the war chief of Chicora who had traveled south during the trading truce to barter with Audusta, one of our dearest friends and a neighboring Indian chief, and his four allies. The chaplain married the two of us before he and my countrymen departed. I returned to Chicora with my husband, Heb-hel, where a year later I gave birth to our son." Her eyes were misty. "And I have been here ever since."

"Do you ever long for home?" Marta Carolina asked.

Madeleine didn't answer Marta Carolina immediately. Instead she rose and crossed the room to peer out the window. "Sometimes I wish to see the France I used to know," she eventually said, "but I have no desire to return there to live permanently. This is my home; these are my people."

So thrilled to have one of her own people with whom to talk, Marta Carolina was bubbling with curiosity. "Do you and your family live in the Upper Village?"

"Since my husband died five years ago, I have lived with his father's sister, Night Star," Madeleine replied.

"What about your children?"

"I have a son."

Marta Carolina noticed the pause; she heard the sadness.

"He has chosen to walk another path."

Madeleine's eyes darkened with unexplained sorrow. Then she lifted her face and lowered a veil on her expressions. In the twinkling of an eye, Marta Carolina saw her change from Madeleine de Coligny to Morning Dew.

"Enough about me," Morning Dew said. "Now let's discuss you. You told White Blossom that you wished to visit with the shaman and to ride the horses?"

"Yes." Marta Carolina nodded. "I am an apothecary," she announced proudly, "and I'm most interested in learning about their medicines."

"Although Knowledge-of-the Forest would welcome your visit, today is not the right time," Madeleine slowly drawled. "The medicine men and women will be preparing for the purification ceremony. I suggest we start with the horses Strong Bear captured for Night Star—but first we must get Night Star's permission."

As the two women moved through the courtyard to the queen's lodgings, Marta Carolina asked, "When may I see Will again?"

"You won't be allowed to see him until he and Strong Bear meet on the contest field."

"Where will he stay?"

"In the Great House at the warrior's training village. Come," she answered, gently tugging Marta Carolina's arm and guiding her across the courtyard. "I will show you." She walked to the edge of the garden that surrounded Night Star's home and pointed. "See that clearing."

Following the invisible line marked by Madeleine's finger to a distant point at the bottom of the pyramid, Marta Carolina saw three huge round houses that were some three-hundred feet in length with walls—made by pulling together at the top two rows of pine trees—fifteen to thirty feet apart. The walls and top were filled in with thatch and other timbers.

"Each Great House has room for two hundred of our warriors," Madeleine explained. "At times our warriors occupy all the houses in four or more such training villages. However, since this is only a purification ceremony, only a few select braves will move to the training camp with Strong Bear and Will Dare. All but the two of them can return to Chicora for the festivities that take place before the contest."

Her eyes fixed on the training camp, Marta Carolina asked, "Will women be staying in the Great House?"

"Yes," Madeleine softly replied, knowing she spoke of White Blossom, "if she is a warrior, she can."

"How long will White Blossom be gone?"

"She won't be gone," Morning Dew replied; then she said, "She chooses the runners and dispatches them; she doesn't go herself. Come. Let's speak to Night Star about your riding the horse."

Entr'acte

At dusk four men walked around the deserted fort that until recently had been the site of the Roanoak Colony. The wind, as if hunting for the lost inhabitants, whined through the empty buildings, and at finding no one, angrily banged shutters and doors against the walls.

"This here ain't what I stole the ship from the Spaniards fer, Captain Turner," one of the men whimpered, his beady eyes darting furtively about as he ran to keep up with the others. "This ain't no place fer sailors." He loosened the soiled linen cloth at his neck and wiped the sheen of perspiration from his face—a moisture caused by fear rather than heat. "There ain't no treasure on this here godforsaken piece of land. Ain't nothing here but death."

"Shut up, Barkley!" The captain's voice cracked with authority, but he didn't look back at his crewman. His steely gray eyes were scouring the countryside in front of him, and his ears were alert to the sounds around him. "We'll do this my way or no way at all. That was our agreement, remember."

"Aye," the man muttered morosely, dogging the motley group.

A sudden gust of cold, winter wind caught and lifted Captain Timothy Turner's cloak, billowing it away from his body. Although he had walked the entire area two or three times, he refused to accept the evidence he found. This could not be the end of his search for Will Dare. He reached into his doublet, and his fingers closed over the ring he had bought for Betsy. They tightened until the gold cut into his flesh. The Roanoak colony couldn't have disappeared without a trace. It couldn't have! Would he chase apparitions all his life?

"Captain, sir—" one of the other men spoke "—I don't be telling you what to do, but I have to agree with Barkley. We ain't finding no information about Spanish gold on this deserted island. Everybody's gone. Probably killed by them savages! All's we be finding is a few weapons, trunks, and stuff they seen fit to leave behind. All's we gonna find is trouble, sir."

"Aye, Captain, sir," the third one spoke up, drawing his jerkin closer, "we best be getting back to the ship before nightfall."

Timothy stopped walking and looked at the sky, drooping with heavy, black storm clouds. Amidst the winter chill that was settling upon him, he felt the heat of penetrating eyes on his back. They were being watched.

"Aye, lads," he called extra loudly; his hand moving to the hilt of his sword. He lifted his face to the sky, letting the wind whip through his golden brown beard. "We best be getting back to the ship. Storm's a-brewing." Under his breath he added, "Stand ready, lads, and be careful. We're being watched. Act naturally as we turn back toward the ship."

Before one of them could move more than a hand, Indians ran out of the surrounding forest, yelling at the top of their lungs. Their hair was shaved to the scalp on both sides; a cockscomb ran the center of their head, heightened with a greased deer roach that was painted brilliant red. Their faces were also smeared in different colors, making their scowls even more ferocious. Some had arrows nocked in their bows; others brandished primitive war clubs. A more fierce sight none of Timothy Turner's crew could imagine.

When the sailors were disarmed, a man emerged from the forest where he had been waiting. As he walked, Timothy observed his leather breeches, tucked into knee-high boots, the white cambric shirt, the jerkin. His hair was trimmed in a European cut. One of the colonists, Turner thought, a partial smile playing his lips. But when the man drew nearer, the captain saw the obsidian eyes, the chiseled features, and the immobile countenance.

"Who are you?" the Indian asked in English.

"My Gawd," one of the sailors exclaimed, his eyes raking over the tall, muscular man, "this here savage speaks English, Captain!"

Ignoring the exclamation, Timothy said, "I'm Captain Timothy Turner, sir, recently from England, on my way to the Spanish Main. I stopped by here to bring news of the defeat of the Invincible Armada. I'm searching for the Roanoak colonists. And who might you be?"

"I'm Manteo," the Hatteras chieftain replied.

"An Indian?"

"I am."

"Are you acquainted with the colonists?"

"I am."

Timothy's palms were moist with apprehension. His senses were honed to the highest degree. Danger was the game he loved most. "Did you learn to speak English from them?"

"No, I lived in England for several years as a ward of Sir Walter Raleigh. I was taught by one of Master Harriot's most able students, Catherine Graystone. Perhaps you know her."

"No," Timothy said, "can't say that I do."

As another blast of icy cold wind howled down the empty, forlorn street, Timothy hunched his shoulders and pulled his cloak closer about himself. His gray eyes scanned the deserted settlement. "Where are the planters?"

"They have moved inland," Manteo replied. "Several months ago we sighted a Spanish ship cruising our shores. We sent a small group to scout out the Spanish garrisons, but we have heard nothing from them. Only weeks ago a seond one came closer. Fearful of attack the colonists decided to wait no longer to move to the Chesapeake, the destination of their permanent sight."

"May I see them, please?" Timothy asked, his heart pumping so fast he was heady. "I would share news of the homeland with them."

Manteo spoke to one of his braves. "Go tell Ananias that we bring friends to the village. Have the women prepare supper for them."

Timothy could not understand what the Indian was saying, but he did understand one word. "Ananias—" Timothy savored the moment. He found such sweet pleasure in exacting his revenge, and now he was one step closer to his goal. "Ananias Dare?"

"Yes," Manteo replied, his head quickly swinging toward the captain, "do you know him?"

Timothy shook his head and laughed. "Nay, but I've heard of him. The lads and I were in Plymouth recently, and a tavern wench there talked a great deal about the man." Timothy winked at Manteo. "Said she couldn't imagine why a beautiful woman such as his wife is would marry an old man like him."

Manteo's eyes narrowed, and his mouth thinned in disapproval. He didn't respect Ananias, and he, too, had many times wondered the same thing, but he refused to listen to those who voiced these sentiments. Because he loved Eleanor Dare and little Virginia, her baby girl, Manteo promised friendship and protection for all of them—Ananias included.

Timothy felt more than saw Manteo's displeasure, but he couldn't stop once he had begun. He had to play his last card. He had to know if he had gambled to win or lose. Were Will and Ananias Dare one and the same? If not, were they related? Was Will Dare indeed a member of this wretched colony.

"The wench couldn't figure why such a comely woman wouldn't have been attracted to Will rather than to Ananias."

"Do you know Will Dare?" Manteo asked.

"Well, no, sir," Timothy said, maintaining the boisterous, friendly facade of a traveler in need of familiar companionship, "I don't rightly know him, either."

"I would advise you then, Captain Turner, to keep your tavern talk to yourself." Manteo was so displeased his words were clipped, hinting at his Indian heritage.

250

"Mistress Eleanor is married to Ananias Dare, and she's a good, faithful wife to him. She has no interest in his young brother at all, nor does Will Dare have an interest in his brother's wife. And right now both of them are worried about Will. He's one of them who went to scout out the Spanish forts in Florida."

"I'm so sorry," Timothy apologized profusely—and truly he was; he meant no harm to any of the settlers. Will Dare was the only one with whom he had business. He wanted only the younger brother!

"Come," Manteo said, cutting him short, "we'll go to the mainland, and you can speak with the colonists."

The sailors fell in step behind Manteo, his braves behind them. Barkley sidled up to the captain and whispered, "How do you know we can trust this Indian?"

"We don't." Timothy chuckled. He hadn't felt this exhilarated in a long time.

"And why do we have to visit with these settlers?" Barkley persisted.

"Because, my good man," Timothy returned airily, "without them we could not find the treasure which I seek."

The words mollified Barkley, and he slid back to follow the captain.

Later that evening after they had feasted with the Indians, Timothy and the Roanoak colonists moved into a large wigwam so they could visit together. With rapt silence they listened as each of the sailors talked—about the defeat of the armada, about the places they had been, the people they had seen. Eventually, of the colonists only Ananias and Manteo remained, and all the sailors were asleep but Timothy who lifted a hand to stifle a yawn.

"Ah, good captain," Ananias apologized, standing to reach for the sputtering torch, "we have wearied you with our questions."

"Nay," Timothy denied. "I enjoyed visiting with you and your settlers, Governor Dare. Verily I did." The shadowed light hid the gleam of satisfaction in his eyes. "But I must be to bed, for on the morrow my men and I must be leaving."

"Where are you headed from here?" Ananias asked.

"To rob the Spaniards," Timothy returned, "but first I want to visit St. Augustine and destroy it the way Drake did in '86. I want to repay them for their kindness to me during my imprisonment in the galley."

"Robbing the Spaniards should be less dangerous now," Ananias said. "According to Sir Roscoe, the queen has an agent on pension in Havana." Ananias thought for a minute, then looked at Manteo. "What did Bennett say his name was?"

Chapter XI

Although she was lonely without Will, time in Chicora passed quickly for Marta Carolina. She spent the earlier part of the day at the corral working with the horses and teaching White Blossom and a select number of Chicoran braves to ride. The afternoon Marta Carolina and Morning Dew spent walking through the forest together, gathering herbs. Much to Marta Carolina's surprise, Morning Dew had a wonderful knowledge of the plants which she willingly shared. Through the days, as Marta Carolina's medicine pouch bulged and her recipes increased, White Blossom's horsemanship improved.

Today—the eve of the great event—Marta Carolina was left to her own devices. Morning Dew was called upon to supervise the preparations for the feast which would initiate the contest between Will and Strong Bear, and since visitors from all corners of the kingdom had been steadily pouring into the city for the past ten days, a large meal was to be prepared.

Lessons over for the day and the horses taken care of, Marta Carolina didn't immediately leave for the forest to

253

gather her plants; rather she headed toward the kitchen where Morning Dew was. She moved briskly up the broad avenue through the crowd. The children were running to and fro, playing their games; the adults, when not laying their wagers, were sitting together. The women exchanged their cooking recipes and housekeeping techniques; the braves discussed the hunt.

The vibrant colors of early autumn had given way to the muted browns that announced the coming winter as did the storm clouds that gathered overhead and the wind that swirled around Marta Carolina, whipping the large mantle around her legs with every step she took up the stairs to the upper village. But she didn't feel the cold. She was dressed warmly in a long leather dress beneath which she wore leggings and moccasins, both interlined with moss for additional insulation.

Tendrils of black hair defied the severe braids that hung over her shoulders and wisped across her face. Her blue eyes, always keenly attuned to the world around her, were focused on a distant point. Today they weren't so alert; they were shaded with concern. Tomorrow Will met with Strong Bear, and she was worried for him. Although Will was a strong man, a soldier of high merit according to European standards, Marta Carolina wasn't so sure about his fighting Strong Bear. She wasn't sure that he had mastered the wrestling techniques of the native Americans.

Since the spectators had begun arriving, she had seen groups of men participating in different sports, one of which was wrestling. The game was rough; the Indians highly skilled. And Marta Carolina knew their proficiency came from years of practice and conditioning. She worried about Will, especially with his newly healed

254

wounds. The way the warriors threw their opponents over, using their legs as levers and backs as springing boards, she knew Will's ankle could easily be wrenched again. This would give the Chicoran chief a decided advantage.

Pushing the mat aside, she entered the kitchen, glad for the warmth provided by the blazing fire pits. Morning Dew, dropping portions of hickory-nut bread dough into a large clay cauldron, sat in front of a fire, her legs gracefully tucked to one side of her body. The older woman looked up and smiled, her movements never stilling.

"Are you through for the day?" she asked.

"Umhum," Marta Carolina said as she sat down. She leaned over the pot, sniffing the delicious aroma. "Stew?" she asked.

"Squirrel dumplings," Morning Dew replied, reaching for the wooden spoon with which she stirred the thick broth. "Are you hungry?" Out of the corner of her eyes she saw Marta Carolina nod her head, but even before that, Morning Dew reached for a bark bowl which she set in front of Marta Carolina.

"Honey," she said. Then she reached for a piece of fried cornbread that lay on the large flat stones that circled the fire pit. She tore a small portion off the fritter and dipped it into the thick golden honey. "Eat," she instructed. "It's delicious."

Marta Carolina didn't have to be told the second time. Without ceremony she ate the corn fritter and the honey.

"How is White Blossom doing with her riding lessons?"

Marta Carolina nodded her head and swallowed her

bite of food. "Excellent," she replied. "I have never seen someone adapt to the horse as quickly as she has." She hesitated, then said, "It's as if she and the animal communicate, Morning Dew."

"They do," the older woman replied. "Indians cherish nature in a way that we Europeans do not."

"Umhum," Marta Carolina murmured, her mouth full. Between bites she said, "White Blossom didn't come for her lesson today. Do you know where she is?"

"At the town hall." Morning Dew dropped seasoning herbs into the pot of dumplings. "Three of the runners returned early this morning and gave their report to the city council. Since she's a member of the council she had to be present."

Marta Carolina licked the honey from the tips of her fingers. "I didn't hear you leave."

Morning Dew chuckled softly. "You were deep in sleep, my child, probably having wonderful dreams about Will Dare."

Marta Carolina set the bowl of honey down and shook her head. "No," she replied, "I haven't dreamed of him at all." She was silent for a few seconds before she said, "I'm worried about him, Morning Dew. He's not ready to meet with Strong Bear. He hasn't recovered from his fight with the bear."

Morning Dew could understand Marta Carolina's anxieties, but she couldn't let the girl dwell on them. "His body is young and healthy; it will heal quickly," she said. "Besides, he has had eleven days in which to regain his strength."

The same sermon I've been preaching to myself, Marta Carolina thought; yet, it brought little consolation.

A brave entered the kitchen. "We have built arbors

256

Unwelcome came the thought of Strong Bear. What was he doing? Will wondered. Where was he at this moment? Will knew the Chicoran chief had been taken to a training village, but he wondered if the queen had conferred special favor on Strong Bear and had allowed him to attend the feast.

Such thoughts pierced Will's heart like the finest stiletto, but the pain was even greater and lingering. Although he never doubted Marta Carolina's fidelity—a privilege he was claiming for himself with no conscious thought of giving to her—he didn't like the thought of Strong Bear's being able to visit with her, to sit next to her, even to look at her. Will couldn't abide the thought of Strong Bear's touching her. Denied these privileges himself, Will did not want the Chicoran chief to have them.

For the first time in his life, Will Dare felt the suffocating and strangling touch of jealousy as it wrapped its tentacles one by one around his entire being and squeezed . . . and squeezed. Unbeknown to him, love was making inroads, slowly moving him toward commitment. A man bemused, as if he were manipulated by a force stronger than himself, Will pushed away from the wigwam and put his full weight on his feet. When he did, he stumbled. Only by throwing out his hand and bracing himself on the side of the building did he keep from falling down.

He cursed his stupidity. Only this morning he had twisted his foot, reinjuring his ankle. Already it was swollen and fevered. As long as he didn't put his full weight on it, he was able to hobble about. He was worried about meeting Strong Bear tomorrow. He wouldn't have time to be careful during a wrestling match and his injury

261

would give the Chicoran a decided advantage.

Brown Beaver, who had been posted as guard, lounged close to the fire at the center of the village. He watched Will limp away, but he said nothing; he did nothing. He had no interest in the paleface; he cared not that Will violated the purification ritual. To do so would be to his own detriment. The less magic the paleface possessed the greater the advantage for Strong Bear. Brown Beaver's eyes gleamed maliciously, and his lips eased into a smirk

Slightly winded, White Blossom trotted into camp, her eyes eagerly scanning the deserted square for a sign of Will. When she saw him limping toward Chicora, she stopped. Her eyes narrowed and thought creased her brow as she gazed hard at the man whom she desired so much for her own. Unwittingly she pulled the bearskin robe closer around her shoulders to ward off the evening chill that came quickly when the sun started its descent in the western sky.

She moved to the fire and spoke to Brown Beaver. "Why is Will Dare limping?"

"He twisted his leg this morning when he was practicing," he replied indifferently. "He asked for the woman black robe, but Night Star refused to let her come. She sent a shaman."

"The woman black robe has great magic," White Blossom murmured, more to herself than to Brown Beaver. "With her medicine she could heal Will Dare's leg."

Brown Beaver shrugged.

Sudden inspiration brought a speculative gleam to the depths of White Blossom's eyes. If, she thought, I can only discredit the woman black robe, Night Star will send her away from Chicora in disgrace. Then she will no longer be a threat to me. Neither Strong Bear nor Will Dare would receive her for his woman. Besides, if Will Dare and the woman black robe break the purification ritual, their magic will be less than mine and Strong Bear's. Sprinting ahead, White Blossom was soon walking beside Will.

"Brown Beaver tells me that you have injured your ankle again. Is it painful?"

"No," Will replied, not wanting her to know how badly it hurt. "What are you doing here?" he asked to change the subject. "I would have thought you'd be in Chicora celebrating?"

"Not until later tonight," she answered.

"It's turning into quite an affair, isn't it?" He hobbled a little bit faster, but White Blossom easily fell into step with him. Farther into the thick forest they went.

"But it will be no contest if you are injured before the game begins. Night Star will postpone the game until you are completely healed."

"No one will know unless you tell," he said.

White Blossom chose to ignore his barb. "The woman black robe has great medicine. She could heal you."

Disinclined to discuss Marta Carolina with White Blossom, Will didn't reply, and when his gait lengthened so did White Blossom's.

"You can see her if you wish."

Again Will said nothing.

"I know a secret way into the town," she finally informed him; she tempted him. "I know a way for you and the woman black robe to meet without others

263

knowing it. You can see her, and she'll bring medicine for your ankle."

Will stopped walking, turned, and fixed a penetrating gaze on White Blossom's face, clearly illumined in the brilliance of the moonlight. "Why would you go against your customs to do this?"

White Blossom said, "You are not Chicoran, nor is the woman black robe, so neither of you is bound by our tradition or our religion. Furthermore, if I let you meet with her, according to our beliefs, your magic will be weaker. Thus, Strong Bear will easily defeat you in the contest tomorrow . . . and I want the contest to end tomorrow."

"If he wins, he gets the woman black robe."

"I would rather he had the woman black robe than you. If you lose, you become my property."

Simple reasoning, Will thought, his speculative gaze remaining on the woman who stood in front of him. He wanted to see Marta Carolina, but he didn't know if he trusted White Blossom or not. Yet he could understand the Indian's reasoning; she wasn't doing this for either him or Marta Carolina but for her own selfish reasons. He lifted his hand and placed it over his chest, pressing the queen piece against his flesh. Sweet memories rushed warmly over him; he could feel Marta Carolina next to his naked body; he could hear her melodious voice, husky with passion.

"What would you do? Take me to her?" he eventually asked.

"No, it will be easier for me to slip her in and out of Chicora than you. I will take you to the river where you will wait for us."

"Not the river," Will absently murmured, other memories returning. "She is frightened of water, terribly frightened."

Like a message of impending doom, the black clouds hung so low, Marta Carolina felt as if she could reach up with her hands and touch them; lightning flashed periodically through the sky; thunder clapped, its ominous boom drowning out the crescendo of the drums and fife. Marta Carolina felt as if she were slowly walking to the brink of insanity. She was weary of watching the Chicoran and Scupperongac dancers as they stomped and changed around the ceremonial fire hour after hour, competing with the flames to see who could become one with the streaks of lightning. She was tired of hearing them boast the prowess of their champion, and she was sick of the endless feasts. Most of all, she was disgusted with their laying wagers on the outcome of the match. And she was worried about Will.

She leaned over and whispered to Morning Dew. "May I go to my room?"

"You are tired?"

Marta Carolina nodded, brushing tendrils of hair beneath her hood.

"We will go then."

"I don't want to take you away from the festival," Marta Carolina apologized. "I can find my way alone."

"I don't mind," Morning Dew assured her. "I would rather you didn't go by yourself. I want no harm to befall you while you're in my charge."

Marta Carolina gently laughed the woman's concern

aside. "Nothing is going to happen, Morning Dew. I shall go directly to my room and to bed."

"Nonetheless," the older woman replied decisively, "I shall come with you."

She rose, walked to one of the large columns, and untied a burning torch. With this to light the way, the two of them ascended the stairs.

Halfway up, Marta Carolina said, "The contest does not begin until late in the afternoon."

"That's right," Morning Dew replied. "The festival will last until it is nearly time for Elder Brother, the Sun, to rise, and the people will sleep until he is overhead. Then they will prepare for the game."

"A game," Marta Carolina sighed, Chicoran reasoning totally escaping her. "So much is at stake and these people treat life as if it were a game. Can't they ever get serious?"

"They are more serious than one suspects," Morning Dew defended. "But they have adopted a wonderful philosophy to life which enables them to endure. Why be sad and worry when you can be happy; why mourn when you can rejoice. Your soul is attached to the Creator by a very thin thread—which the Chicorans call the breath of life. The Creator gives you all the things which are necessary to your life and well-being—your body and the Great Forest. He also endows you with the knowledge, wisdom, and strength to use these blessings. But one day the Creator will cut the thread that binds you with your body and the Great Forest. He will pull you home to heaven. Nothing to dread," Morning Dew reflected. "A wonderful fact of their life. Therefore, they face both life and death with dignity."

"But to challenge Will because he wants me," Marta

Carolina said. "This I do not understand."

"It was not so different in France when I left," Morning Dew quietly insisted. "And I'm sure England and Spain are much the same as France. Men all over the world fight for their lady-loves. Why should the Indian be any different?" She looked directly into Marta Carolina's face. "Feel honored that they care enough to fight for your love." She laughed quietly. "And it is not as if they are fighting-to-the-knife."

"Fighting-to-the-knife!" Marta Carolina exclaimed.

"Either one of the men could have issued a challenge to fight to the death. As it is, both have agreed to fight until one surrenders or until an umpire passes judgment."

"And if Will should lose?"

"According to Chicoran custom you become Strong Bear's woman."

"Will won't let that happen," Marta Carolina said.

"No," Morning Dew replied, "I don't think he would allow that to happen . . . willingly." She hesitated, drew in a deep breath, and said, "Her-hel taught me that at one point in our life we are allowed to choose the river on which we wish to travel. But once we have chosen we are at the mercy of our decision. The tributaries of that river do not necessarily take us where we wish to go."

"Are you telling me that Will has no choice?" Marta Carolina voiced her fears.

"No," Morning Dew returned, "we always have a choice, but that choice sometimes comes at great cost." She laid her arm across Marta Carolina's shoulders. "Come," she admonished, "let us think of happier things. God has a way of working all things out for the best to all who are concerned."

The two women lapsed into silence as they climbed the last round of stairs. Morning Dew walked into the apartment and attached her torch-light to the rafter in the ceiling; then she knelt and quickly built a fire to warm the room. Although it was cold, the wind blowing, drops of rain falling every now and then, Marta Carolina tarried in the courtyard to admire the beauty. In the brilliant streaks of lightning that continued to flash, she thought she saw movement in the surrounding grove of trees, but she couldn't be sure. In the darkness anyone could blend into obscurity. She took a step, then stopped. A shadow lenghthened to emerge as a form.

Marta Carolina wasn't frightened, but she was wary. Who was hiding here? she wondered. Why? Her thoughts were interrupted by a whispered greeting.

"It is I, woman black robe, White Blossom." The Chicoran chief was near Marta Carolina now, but her voice was softer. "I bring you a message."

"From Will?" Marta Carolina knew without asking.

"He has injured his ankle again."

"I know," Marta Carolina whispered, the wrestling scene flashing before her eyes.

"You must come with me." She couldn't see it, but White Blossom could imagine the narrowing of Marta Carolina's eyes and the contemplative caution in the shadowed depths. "He would like for you to come with your medicine, so his leg will he healed enough for him to wrestle with Strong Bear tomorrow." White Blossom lied.

Marta Carolina knew Will was hurt; she had seen him limping from the practice bout. But she did not trust White Blossom. "How do I know Will sent you?"

"He would have sent you a gold chain with a small

statue on it, but he said he could not part with it because it was your token. Instead he let me study it so that I might describe it to you." Another lie. She was still angry because Will refused to wear her neck band, choosing rather to wear Marta Carolina's chain and totem.

As White Blossom described in minute detail the chain and the chess piece, Marta Carolina listened. She didn't know whether to trust the Chicoran woman or not, but her heart and body didn't want to quibble about such trivial matters. If he were hurt—and he was hurt, she knew that—she must be with him. White Blossom had no sooner completed her description than Marta Carolina ran into the the lodging.

"What is it?" Morning Dew asked.

"I must go to Will," she said. "He has been hurt and needs my medicine."

"One of our shamen will take care of him," Morning Dew said.

"No," Marta Carolina said, "I must go to him tonight. I must see him." Her mind made up, she rushed to the far side of the room, opened her chest, and pulled out her medicine bag. "I need to tend to his ankle." She slipped it beneath her cloak and draped the strap over her shoulder. She turned pleading eyes on the older woman. "I have to go, Morning Dew."

"According to Chicoran custom, you will ruin his magic if you cause him to break the purification rites." Morning Dew was torn between cultures. For twenty-six years she had abided by Chicoran custom, but she also knew what Marta Carolina was feeling. She wanted to let the girl go to him.

"Neither Will nor I believe in Chicoran custom,"

Marta Carolina countered.

"You don't know how to get to the training village," Morning Dew pointed out. "It is too dangerous for you to go wandering around the Great Forest alone—especially with a rainstorm coming. One such as this is called—"

"Winter's Rage," Marta Carolina softly interrupted.

"Yes, the river will swell—"

Marta Carolina wasn't listening. "I'll get someone to show me the way."

White Blossom, who had been hovering in the darkness outside the apartment, saw her opportunity. She moved through the opened door. "If you give your permission, Morning Dew, I will escort the woman black robe to the training camp."

Morning Dew turned her attention to the warrior/ woman. "You brought the news of Will's injury to her?"

White Blossom returned Morning Dew's direct gaze. "I brought the news."

"Not altogether," Marta Carolina hastened to add. "I—I saw him injure his ankle this afternoon." When both of the Chicoran women turned puzzled eyes on her, Marta Carolina told them what happened earlier, concluding with "He didn't see me, though." She lifted her head to encounter White Blossom's steely gaze but didn't flinch under the overt hostility and hatred.

"But you, White Blossom, are guilty of encouraging her to go to him," Morning Dew quietly charged. "You know what the consequences can be. You know the danger."

White Blossom replied in Chicoran to keep Marta Carolina from understanding her answer. "Neither Will Dare nor the woman black robe can be hurt by their seeing each other. Her magic is strong; she can heal him.

Besides, if he is crippled tomorrow, Strong Bear will ask Night Star to postpone the contest until Will Dare is well. None of us wish this, especially Will Dare and the woman black robe."

"Why are you willing to take her?" Morning Dew asked, refusing to talk Chicoran in front of Marta Carolina.

"Because I want the man." White Blossom was glad when she saw the stricken look on Marta Carolina's face. "I want his magic ruined, so Strong Bear can defeat him. And I would have Strong Bear defeat him on the rising of the new sun." Now her gaze riveted to Marta Carolina. "I do not wish her to be my father's woman, but I would much rather she be his than Will Dare's."

Feeling White Blossom's hatred for the young Spanish woman, Morning Dew slowly shook her head. "I am afraid for you to go."

"Will needs me, so I have no choice."

"I will wait at the edge of the courtyard for you," White Blossom said as she bent over the wood box. She picked up two small splinters of kindling and measured them so they were the same length. Then she walked to the torch-light and lit them. The first she laid on one of the round rocks that circled the fire pit; the other she held. "When this has burned out, I will leave. You have that long to make your decision." She walked out of the room, across the courtyard into the grove of trees. As she blended into the shadows, lost in the rain that had begun in earnest, only the flickering blaze of the kindling protected by her hand could be seen.

Marta Carolina turned to Morning Dew, her blue eyes pleading. "Please understand."

Morning Dew stood silently as she contemplated Marta

Carolina's request. Eventually she said, "I will go with you."

When Marta Carolina and Morning Dew stood in front of White Blossom and told her their decision, the Chicoran chief shook her head. "I can slip one of you out of the town and into the village easier than two of you," she said, "If three of us go, we will surely be caught. Also one needs to stay in the apartment to answer in case someone calls for either of you. No one must know that the woman black robe is gone."

"That is true," Morning Dew acknowledged; still she was loath to let Marta Carolina out of her sight. Her distrust of White Blossom was increasing.

"I will see that she gets back to her apartment before Elder Sister, the Moon, has lifted her veil of darkness from the earth."

Morning Dew reluctantly gave her permission. What else could she do? Marta Carolina was determined to see Will Dare. As night cloaked the two women, she returned to the apartment and doused the torch-light. She lay in her hammock and listened to the rain as it beat against the roof of the wigwam. Sleep did not come to her troubled mind.

Quickly White Blossom led Marta Carolina down the stairs until they reached the first terrace. Here, they darted into the grove of fruit trees and cautiously picked their way until they were at the base of the pyramid on the opposite side of the public square where the festivities were going on.

Unaccustomed to the fast pace set by White Blossom and blinded by the rain, Marta Carolina was winded, but she was determined to stay right behind the Chicoran. Although she was angry and muttered imprecations under her breath when White Blossom turned branches loose that slapped her in the face, Marta Carolina resolutely moved forward. The longer she followed, the wetter and colder she became. Finally she heard a familiar sound: the river. Her palms beaded with perspiration and her chest constricted. But she refused to let the Chicoran chief see her fear of water.

"We must cross the river," White Blossom said when they reached the bank.

Marta Carolina shivered and jumped when a sudden clap of thunder reverberated through the air.

"This is the quickest way to reach the training camp," White Blossom lied.

"How—" The word was nothing but a grating noise. Marta Carolina cleared her throat. "How are we going to cross?"

"On a tree trunk that bridges the river." White Blossom had deliberately brought Marta Carolina this way because it was a dangerous crossing. The fungus-covered tree that connected the two banks was old and slippery. With the rain it would be even more dangerous. The river itself was wide and exceptionally deep; the undercurrent was swift—even swifter when Winter's Rage came—and many an experienced swimmer had drowned in this very spot.

Marta Carolina followed White Blossom to the log. In an explosion of light she saw the agile Indian leap onto the narrow bridge. Blood raged through Marta Carolina's bloodstream with such force she was dizzy.

"The water is very deep," White Blossom screamed, her voice barely carrying above the howling wind, "and the river is wide. If you should slip and fall in, swim toward this shore." She pointed to the distant mark and said, "If you're careful, you have nothing to fear."

Marta Carolina was glad for the rain which hid her fear. At least, White Blossom couldn't see the perspiration on her brow. She ran her finger above her lips. She glanced over her shoulder to the beckoning glow of the ceremonial fire—safe beneath its arbor—that lit the distant sky, and she listened to the hypnotic lap of the water against the bank.

Emotionally she was torn in two. She wanted to reach Will; at the same time she wanted to turn around and run away from the river as fast as she could. She was in agony as fear tightened in her stomach, but calling on hidden resources of strength, she scolded herself.

White Blossom balanced on the log in the middle of the river. "If you're frightened," she taunted, "we'll take the long way."

Marta Carolina knew White Blossom had issued a challenge. Somehow the Chicoran knew about her fear of water, Marta Carolina thought, and she had deliberately led her in this direction. Now she dared her to cross the bridge. Marta Carolina stared at the water.

You know how to swim, she told herself, so you have nothing to fear but your fear. She looked at the log that spanned the watery width; the longer she looked the narrower it seemed to become. Move slowly, she admonished silently, and you can make it.

"Are you coming?" White Blossom softly challenged.

"I'm coming," Marta Carolina replied as she placed her right foot on the tree trunk. Nothing—no one—would stop her. She would walk through the flames of hell itself in order to save Will.

One step. Two. She extended her arms on either side and slowly lowered and raised the one or other for balance. Her breathing was almost suspended, and her heart seemed to beat at the base of her throat and make breathing difficult. Several more steps. Then her foot landed on a patch of slippery fungus; her moccasin slipped forward, and she teetered. She caught her breath and held it as she waved her arms. Finally she regained her balance. Carefully—so very carefully—she lifted her foot, and she looked up. White Blossom stood immediately in front of her.

Marta Carolina's breath rushed out her lungs in relief. "I—I thought you were on the other side."

"No," White Blossom replied quietly, "I'm right here."

Standing on the huge oak tree in the middle of the river, the two measured each other in the brilliant blast of lightning that shimmered and hung suspended in the sky.

"Although I tempted him with your presence, Will wouldn't send for you," White Blossom said. "He cares too much about you. But I knew you would come."

"You deliberately lied to me? Why?"

"Because I want you out of my life, woman black robe, and I want you out of my father's life, out of Will Dare's life."

"What are you going to do?" Fear had grown to gargantuan proportions.

White Blossom didn't answer the question; instead she said, "You and your people have caused us nothing but trouble since you came to our land. A soldier of the black robes shamed my mother and killed Strong Bear's child which she bore. He beat her until her body was bent and scarred. When she finally did escape to return to Chicora she carried the soldier's child. Much to our grief

275

Lovely Spring died giving birth to a child of the black robes."

"I can see you have reason to hate, White Blossom," she said with compassion, "but I am not a soldier of the black robes." Her clothes were dripping wet; they clung to her body and offered no protection to the icy blasts of wind. "And not all Spaniards are like the ones who shamed your mother."

"Did you really think I would stand idly by and let you ruin Strong Bear's life," White Blossom grunted, jerking Marta Carolina's cloak from her body. "I will kill you first." She grabbed the strap of Marta Carolina's medicine satchel and yanked it off her shoulder.

Marta Carolina staggered back, but she didn't fall off. "Even if you kill me, you'll have to deal with Will and Strong Bear," she cried, slowly moving backward and unable to see where she was placing her feet. "You'll have to answer to them because Morning Dew knows I left with you."

"But no one will know that I helped you find your death," White Blossom said, advancing a step with each one that Marta Carolina took back. "They will think your death an accident. Remember you begged me to take you to Will. You insisted."

"No," Marta Carolina croaked. She lifted her hands and brushed wet hair from her face. "What about Will?" She refused to think of the watery grave that lay below her. One false step and she would be lost in the swirling death below.

"His foot is not so bad that I cannot care for him," White Blossom said. "My magic is strong enough to cure him. The shaman will help me."

"I'm not worried about his foot," Marta Carolina

screamed. "What are you going to tell him about me?"

"I will tell him that although I insisted on taking you the safer route, you insisted on coming this way. You lost your footing on the way over and fell in. I tried to save you, but the current was too strong for even me. You drowned." Pleased with her plan, White Blossom threw back her head and laughed.

Marta Carolina took advantage of the Chicoran's negligence. She quickly turned around and headed for the shore, but White Blossom was faster than she. She lunged toward Marta Carolina, knocking both of them into the water. They sank beneath the surface. White Blossom was the first to rise. Using all her strength and ability, she defied the current and swam to shore.

"With you dead," she cried, her words lost in the raging storm, "Will Dare and Strong Bear will have no need to fight each other, and it will only be a matter of time before Will turns to me for comfort and eventually for love." A strange smile played across her face as she strained to see if Marta Carolina surfaced. When she didn't, White Blossom smiled. The woman was dead; a watery grave had claimed her.

Marta Carolina's entire life passed in front of her as she sank to the bottom of the river. Her fear passed, and a lethargy settled over her limbs. She rose in a dreamy almost euphoric state and broke water. With a splutter and gasp, air painfully swelled her lungs, making her feel as they would burst, and she realized what was happening. She flailed her arms, but she had enough presence of mind not to scream. She mustn't alert anyone to her being here—that would be a sure death also. Out of the corner of her eye, she saw a thoroughly soaked White Blossom standing on the shore.

She saw the Chicoran chief with a surprising clarity. She noted every detail of her clothing and her jewelry. She smiled when she saw her medicine satchel over White Blossom's shoulder. At least that wasn't lost with her.

She sank the second time. Down, down she went. You can swim, Marta Carolina! a voice kept screaming inside her. You're a fool to let yourself drown. You're a strong woman, and you were an excellent swimmer. Are you going to let that woman win? Are you going to let her have Will without a struggle? What about Will? Doesn't he deserve more from you? He loves you. He needs you.

When Marta Carolina broke the surface the second time, she drew in another deep, painful gasp of air. Then she eased into the turtle position, the fetal position, and floated with the current. Forcing herself to be calm and no longer fighting, she let the water buoy her and carry her to a safer part of the river. A branch, sweeping down the river with debris, slapped her in the face. Never had such physical pain been more welcome, so reassuring. The pain of life.

Rain pelting into her eyes and running down her face, she clasped the branch and slowly pulled herself to shore. Inch by inch she crawled up the bank. Then she saw the two moccasined feet firmly planted on the banks and lifted her face. Before she could do anything about it, White Blossom kicked her in the chin to send her splashing back into the murky water. Marta Carolina fought the dizziness; she fought unconsciousness, and she clawed at the riverbank to no avail. Both hands fisted tightly, mud squashing through her fingers, she slid into the water. Under she went.

Oblivious to the storm that raged around her, White

Blossom stood on the shore for a long time after Marta Carolina sank beneath the rushing tide. Finally satisfied that the woman black robe was dead, she patted the medicine satchel which hung to her side and headed for the training village. Immediately on her arrival, she entered the Great House where Will was.

"Will Dare, it is I, White Blossom," the Chicoran identified herself. "May I come in?"

Surprised, Will turned to look at her, water still dripping from her clothes. He hadn't expected her to return. He saw Marta Carolina's medicine satchel, and his surprise turned to perplexity. "What are you doing with that?"

White Blossom sat down next to him. "The woman black robe insisted on coming to see you," she softly explained.

"Insisted on coming to see me," he repeated. "In this storm?" His preplexity increased.

White Blossom nodded. "She saw you injure your ankle this morning when you were practicing. When she learned that I had seen you, she asked about you, and I— I—" She centered compassionate eyes on Will. "I'm so sorry, Will. I didn't know she would insist on coming to you." She shrugged the strap from her shoulder and handed the pouch to Will.

"She would not come the long way even though it was raining. I explained about Winter's Rage, but still she insisted on coming by the river—even though she was afraid. She fell in and drowned. I jumped in after her, but I was not strong enough to save her."

Will was so stunned he couldn't say a word. Like a man in a trance, he sat on the couch, staring into space, and gripped the leather medicine bag.

"As soon as I arrived in camp, I sent Brown Beaver with the news to Chicora and to Strong Bear's training camp." She knelt beside him and touched his swollen ankle. "You are unable to walk. I'll have you carried to Chicora on a litter."

"I can walk," Will grated, jerking his foot from her hands. His life had just ended—without Marta Carolina he had no purpose or reason for living. Ironically, with her death came the realization that he loved her. He loved her . . . and hadn't told her. She couldn't be dead! She was so beautiful, so alive. How could her Spanish-blue eyes be closed in death? No, it could not be!

"She was afraid of the water," he kept muttering. Then he turned on White Blossom. "Why did you take her by the river?" he growled. "I told you she was afraid of the water. Why did you bring her out in weather like this? She didn't know any better. You did."

"I wouldn't have," White Blossom replied so kindly, so patiently, "but she insisted. She wanted to get to you as quickly as possible. She loved you so much that she was willing to make any sacrifice to reach you." She reached out and ran her fingers down Marta Carolina's medicine bag. "When she fell into the water, she slung this onto the shore."

Will unfastened the belt and opened the bag to extract each object singularly and to set each on the couch beside himself—vials of medicine; jars of salves; herbs and roots.

Tears burned down his cheeks. So much he hadn't told her. So much they hadn't done or shared. He forgot his ankle and jumped to his feet. The minute his weight hit his injured foot, he groaned and buckled under the pain. He cursed his injury; he cursed his stupidity; he cursed death. Limping, he crossed the room to stand in front of the window and to gaze into the blackness of the forest—an exact reflection of his heart, he thought. Occasionally a streak of lightning illuminated the sky, but Will saw no such moments of brightness for him.

Without Marta Carolina he would be emotionally blind; he would live in darkness the rest of his life.

Chapter XII

Although White Blossom urged Will to be transported to Chicora by litter, he refused to go. A man obsessed, he charged out of the Great House into the raging storm and made his way to the river, soon to be joined in the hunt for Marta Carolina by the Scupperongacs and Strong Bear. Carefully they moved through the downpour up and down both the river banks, and though unable to see because of the darkness, the strongest of swimmers, White Blossom among them, dove to try to find Marta Carolina's body, to see if it were ensnared by roots or underwater debris.

The rain slackened during the wee hours of the morning, and the search intensified. However, by noon the next day neither the body nor any sign of Marta Carolina's having survived had been found. One by one the Indians abandoned the search, but not Will or Strong Bear.

Haggard, his eyes bloodshot from his numerous dives, his face shadowed with a day's growth of whiskers, Will kept insisting that they find Marta Carolina. Strong Bear agreed. White Blossom, because of her loyalty to her father and her love for Will, remained with them, willing to continue until both of them called the hunt off.

She regretted the effect Marta Carolina's drowning was having on her father and Will; but getting rid of the black robe had been necessary—for all of them. White Blossom smiled to herself. So well did she play her game of deceit that none knew her treachery. And if it were this easy to dispose of Marta Carolina could she not do the same with any who would stand in the way of what she wanted? No one would keep her from becoming queen of the Chicoras! And her husband/warrior would be Will Dare. This she promised herself.

"The current is swift, my friend, and the rain caused the river to swell," Kee-lee finally told Will. "It would have swept Marta Carolina's body far away by the time you arrived last night. Though I grieve her death and I feel your sorrow, you need your rest. Otherwise, you will follow the path of Marta Carolina."

Although White Blossom couldn't understand what Kee-lee was saying to Will because he spoke Scupperongac, she guessed his argument. She, too, was thoroughly exhausted and ready for the search to end. Her eyes were as tired and red as Will's. She laid her hand on Will's arm. "We must quit, Will. Many experienced swimmers have drowned in this spot, and we have never found their bodies. You are too tired to continue your diving. The river will sweep you away."

Obstinate in his determination to find Marta Carolina, Will jerked his hand away, moved to the river, and dove yet another time. By late afternoon, however, sheer exhaustion forced Will to abandon the search. Followed by the Scupperongacs and White Blossom, a dirty and bedraggled Will Dare and Strong Bear silently led the way to the city. Without a word they parted at the courtyard, Strong Bear and White Blossom going in one direction, Will in the other. His throbbing ankle was swollen and discolored, but the pain was nothing compared to that which he felt in his heart.

He limped into the lodging he had shared with Marta Carolina and stood, leaning against the door, for the longest time and stared at her baggage. He reached up and wrapped his fist around the tiny chess piece that hung from the chain, clutching so tightly that it cut into his fingers and the chain sliced into his neck. He looked at the battered chest that set in the corner of the room. These were the only mementoes he had left of Marta Carolina . . . these and his memories. They would have to last him a lifetime. He would always remember shining blue eyes that looked at the world—at him in particular—with trust and confidence.

Unable to bottle up his grief any longer, he collapsed on the nearby couch and laid his face in his hands, unashamedly letting the tears rack his body. He remembered every word they had spoken, every promise they had made to each other. He remembered her sweet innocence; her smiles; her touches.

He remembered all that he had left undone and unsaid. For this he grieved most of all.

He thought of the joy she had brought into his life, and he was grateful for the brushstroke of her love on his heart, no matter how short-lived the experience. Because of her, he would never be the same again; he would never look at things in the same light. He was a new man, a complete man—a man who had learned that to love you must give love—even if that love is taken away from you.

And afterward you must continue to give love . . . if only he had told her. If only he had confessed to her that he loved her.

When his tears subsided, his grief seemed a little more bearable. He moved to the trunk, sat down, and opened the lid. Slowly he went through all her belongings. He took her clothes out lovingly to fold and repack them; he read her recipe books and her letters from her aunt; he looked at her medicines and herbs. Tears again burning his eyes, he replaced them, rose, and limped to the hammock where he lay down.

Time, like his emotions, seemed nonexistent. He was numb all over. His life had no purpose; he had no course to follow.

"Will Dare!"

White Blossom's voice echoed through the silent room some hours later. When he didn't answer, she quietly entered the apartment, and not sure if he were asleep, tiptoed to the hammock. He lay on his back, his hand on his chest, wrapped around the figurine on his chain. He stared at White Blossom, almost unblinkingly, no recognition in his eyes.

"Night Star has called a town meeting on the rising of the new sun. She wanted me to let you know so that you would be present."

Will heard the words, but they didn't penetrate his consciousness. He couldn't have cared less about a town meeting. He couldn't care less about violating Chicoran custom.

"You must be there, Will." She waited for a response, and when none was forthcoming, she asked, "Did you hear me, Will Dare?"

"I hear."

White Blossom was worried about Will. He looked so gaunt; his eyes hollow, his voice emotionless. "You must eat something."

"I'm not hungry."

"You can't stop living because the woman black robe is dead." White Blossom spoke more sharply than she intended, but Will's grieving for Marta Carolina crushed her. She had expected some remorse but not this.

"I wish to God dying were that easy. Can you imagine how Marta Carolina must have suffered? She was so frightened of the water." His voice hushed to an anguished whisper. "So frightened of water."

"You cannot blame yourself," White Blossom quietly admonished on a deep breath. She must be patient; it would take time for him to recover from Marta Carolina's death, but she would be there when he did. "Is there anything I can do for you?" she asked. "Anything to heal the sorrow of your soul?"

"No."

"I—I will leave now."

Will never spoke; he never moved. His thoughts centered on Marta Carolina, he gazed into space. Not once during the long night did he sleep, nor did he turn the chess piece loose . . . nor did he see the coming of day as dawn clothed his room with gentle color.

"Are you awake, my friend?" Kee-lee called several times before Will replied.

"Yes."

"May I enter?"

"The mat is not over the door." Will referred to the Scupperongac custom. "You may enter without asking permission."

"You must get up." Kee-lee strode into the room. "The council will be meeting soon."

"I know. I'm not going," Will returned dully. "I have nothing to say to the Chicoran council; they have nothing to say that I wish to hear."

Before Kee-lee could answer, Morning Dew appeared at the door and asked in Spanish, "May I come in?"

Will turned his head and looked at the older woman, a stranger to him. "You may," he finally replied.

"I am Morning Dew," she said, moving through the open door. "I stayed with Marta Carolina while you were in the training camp." Near him now, she smiled. "You are Will Dare."

Emotionally and physically exhausted, Will made no response.

Morning Dew took no umbrage. Having lost the man she loved through death, she understood all he was going through. "Put the tub over here," she instructed the three young girls who followed her into the apartment.

Kee-lee moved to the other side of the room and sat on one of the couches where he watched one of the maids set the large bark container in the middle of the floor; the other two filled it with water. Morning Dew laid the towels and clean clothes on the couch; then she walked to the hammock and looked at the grieving man.

"Have Blue Water bring Will a bowl of corn mush," she instructed, waving the girls out of the room.

"I'm not hungry," Will muttered.

"I didn't ask if you were hungry," Morning Dew replied quietly. "I'm sorry about Marta Carolina. I loved her, too, but we can do nothing about her death now, Will Dare. For some reason the Creator left you and me

287

here. We must make the best of it. Marta Carolina wouldn't want us to live the rest of our lives grieving her."

Will's eyes filled afresh with tears, but he made no comment.

"You must take your bath and eat the morning meal," she urged. "White Blossom told me that you have had nothing to eat in two days."

"I'm not hungry."

"No, I'm sure you're not," Morning Dew said, "but you must eat." When Blue Water brought the bowl of mush to her, Morning Dew took it and dismissed the girl. "Either you eat it, Will Dare, or I shall feed you as one feeds a baby, spoon by spoon."

Kee-lee, leaning against the wall, observed the older woman's ministrations with a glint of amusement in his eyes. She could do more with his stubborn friend than he could.

Evidently Will thought so, too. He sat up in the hammock and ate several spoonfuls of the warm cornmeal mush. However, after Morning Dew left, he lay down and made no effort to take a bath.

"Come, Will," Kee-lee coaxed.

"I'm not going," Will adamantly refused.

"How can you be so selfish!" Kee-lee charged.

"Selfish!" Will growled, coming out of the hammock careful to rest his weight on his good foot. "How can you accuse me of being selfish?"

"You are thinking only of yourself and your grief," the Scupperongac pointed out. "You haven't given one thought to John Cartwright, who is still a prisoner of the Chicorans, nor have you given any thought to the paleface settlers who are waiting for you to return with word of the Spanish forts."

"Marta Carolina is dead," Will shouted. "Can you understand: The woman I love is dead! I don't care about anything else."

"Not too many days ago, she was the woman whom you intended to use to get into the Spanish fort." Kee-lee wasn't a harsh man, nor did he speak impulsively. He understood that grief was as deadly as drowning. And at the moment, Will'am Dare was emotionally dying. The Scupperongac would do whatever was necessary to save his friend—even to the point of being cruel.

"Don't ever speak of Marta Carolina in those terms again!" Will gritted, inwardly cringing at the thought of his deceitfulness.

Friendship closed Kee-lee's ears to Will's anger. "What about the man who framed you for murder, Will Dare? What about the man who has branded you a traitor to your people? The man who is keeping you from returning to the country you love?" Kee-lee waited only long enough for the words to penetrate the numbness that cocooned Will. "What will happen to your queen, if you do not find this man?"

Because of his grief, Will was angry at Kee-lee for having dug into his private life, at his having resurrected more painful memories, for having reminded him that he had a purpose and reason for living when all he wanted to do was die. For the fraction of a second, he felt that his load was heavier than he could bear; he felt as if he would buckle under the weight.

"Perhaps you will never find a love like Marta Carolina," Kee-lee told Will, his voice much softer now, "but you cannot give up on living because she is dead. You must thank the Creator for giving you an opportunity to see Elder Brother the Sun rise again; you must be glad for all your blessings. Think on the good things of life, Will Dare; they far exceed the bad."

"What do you know about grief?" Will asked. "Have you ever suffered the death of someone whom you dearly love?"

"No."

"Then how can you accuse me?"

"I don't fault you for having and showing your grief," Kee-lee said, "but I will fault you if you don't carry it with dignity like the strong warrior you are . . . more important, Will Dare, you will fault yourself. In time you will come to hate yourself. I will forgive you, but you will never forgive yourself if you behave shamefully now."

Will stared at Kee-lee for a long time; finally he smiled—the gesture a mixture of gratitude and apology. No words were necessary between friends. Will simply nodded his head. Then he bathed and dressed in the clean clothes which Morning Dew had brought to him. Afterward he and Kee-lee walked across the courtyard, descended the stairs, and entered the Town House.

The Chicoran meeting house was filled to capacity. Sitting in the center of an elevated platform that ran the length of the building was Night Star; the tribal council was to her right, the village to her left. Directly in front of the tribal council, on a lower level, John Cartwright and the Scupperongac warriors sat. Chieftains and dignitaries of Chicora and other villages in the kingdom sat on the same level to the left. All other villagers, grouped according to clans, sat in a large semicircle, facing the queen.

Will and Kee-lee pushed through the crowd and climbed the bleachers until they were sitting beside John

Cartwright and the Scupperongac braves.

"Ah, laddie," John breathed a sigh of relief as he laid his big, calloused hand on Will's thigh, "right glad I am to be seeing you."

Will laid his hand over John's. "It's good to see you, John."

"'Tis a large crowd," the planter said, his head rotating from side to side. "And the city itself is full," he marveled. "Where do they all come from, Will?"

"From all over the kingdom of Chicora," Will answered bitterly, his mouth quirked in a humorless smile. "They came to watch the wrestling match between Strong Bear and me."

"Ahh," John drawled, running his hand through his thick beard. "A tournament of sorts?"

"Of sorts," Will replied dryly, "The outcome was to determine Marta Carolina's fate."

"Aye," John murmured, "and where is the lass?"

Will hesitated, not wanting to utter the words aloud as if saying them made Marta Carolina's death a fact. Finally he said, "She drowned night before last during the storm." Then he succinctly told John what had transpired over the past twelve days.

"Ah, laddie, it's sorry that I am," John replied and would have said more but a sudden hush fell over the building.

Knowledge-of-the-Forest, the oldest and most respected shaman in Chicora, entered the building and walked to the center of the building toward the ceremonial fire. Scooping a coal on a piece of bark, he lit his pipe and extended it directly in front of himself, both arms stiffly outstretched. He mumbled a prayer, inhaled deeply, then exhaled. This he did twelve times until he had completely rounded the circular building.

"That's the medicine man," John whispered, "but why does he blow that smoke all over the place." He grimaced as he whiffed the pungent odor of the burning tobacco. "He used to do that when he'd come visit me."

All of this had been explained to Will while he was in the training camp. "The Chicorans' magic number is twelve. Knowledge-of-the-Forest is honoring all twelve clans and asking a blessing from the Creator for each. It takes a long time because the prayer must travel through the twelve heavens before it reaches the Creator."

When he was through, Knowledge-of-the-Forest set his pipe on one of the stones that banked the fire, moved to the east door, and lifted both his arms and his head to pray.

When he sat down, Night Star, dressed in a long buckskin dress, rose and held out her scepter. "At our town meetings we hear the grievances of our people," she began.

She spoke her native language, relying on one of her braves to sign the interpretation to the guests. Since John neither spoke Chicoran nor understood the sign language, Will leaned closer to the older man in order to translate.

"Today, however, we have more pressing matters to discuss. First, we will hear from the runners who have returned from the far reaches of the kingdom."

"Prepare for a long sit," Will said. "Twelve runners were sent out, and we're going to listen to a report from the eleven who have returned.

One by one the runners rose and moved to the center of the wigwam, each waiting to be blessed before he began to speak. Although their stories were quite similar in tone and content, none strove for brevity. Late afternoon after the eleventh one had concluded his report, Night Star stood.

"Wise Owl, who was sent toward the South Wind, has not returned yet. When he arrives, you will hear his report. We will call another meeting." With hardly a pause, she said, "Now we will hear White Blossom's report on the horses."

White Blossom rose and stepped down the platform until she stood in the center of the building. She was beautiful. Her long hair, brushed until it gleamed blue-black, was hanging loosely down her back, contrasting with her fawn-colored buckskin skirt and jacket. As she moved, the ankle-length skirt swirled around her leggings. She waited while Knowledge-of-the-Forest blessed over her. When he sat down, she began to speak in Chicoran. Clearly, precisely she gave her report, giving Marta Carolina praise for having taught them to ride the beasts of the Spanish soldiers; then she moved toward the platform to return to her seat.

Before she could take more than two steps, Night Star stayed White Blossom with a motion of the hand. "Yesterday was to have been a festive occasion for Chicora," she said, "but the death of the woman black robe has interfered with our celebration and has raised many questions. I have already agreed to let Kee-lee, Chief of the Scupperongacs, leave as soon as he has completed his bartering. But now we must decide what we are going to do with our paleface guests, John Cartwright and Will Dare?"

A murmur ran the building, but ceased as soon as Night Star raised her hand.

"Before we make a decision, the Tribal Council has

asked that we investigate the death of the woman black robe. Though most of our elders feel no sympathy for the people of the black robes, they want to know all the facts surrounding Marta Carolina's death."

Again the building buzzed as the people whispered one to the other, the older ones nodding their heads in agreement.

"First, we shall hear White Blossom speak. She was the last person to see the woman black robe alive."

White Blossom was not surprised at the queen's request, and she was prepared for the questioning. Again she spoke, her voice loud and clear. "I wanted the paleface to be my warrior," she said, offering no apology for her actions and beginning with the truth. "Although I knew it was wrong, I agreed to lead the woman black robe to the training camp, so she could tend to his injured foot. I wanted to weaken his magic, so Strong Bear would win the contest." The half-truth rolled easily off her tongue.

Now her lie began, but White Blossom was not afraid to voice it. No one witnessed Marta Carolina's death; therefore, she could never be caught. "Without anyone's knowing it I slipped the woman black robe out of Chicora," White Blossom deliberately let her brown eyes linger on Morning Dew as if she dared the older woman to refute the statement "Because she had seen Will Dare injure his foot earlier in the day—" White Blossom adroitly blended truth with lie to produce a believable story "—she was eager to reach him, so I did not have to encourage her, and despite her fear of water and the danger of the storm, she insisted on crossing at the log."

White Blossom waited a moment, then she continued.

"I explained the danger of crossing at this spot, but her love for the paleface was so great, she insisted. I walked over first; she came immediately behind. We were holding hands, but when she slipped, she panicked and turned loose. As soon as she fell into the water, I jumped in after her, but she struggled with me. I tried to hold onto her, but I couldn't. The current pulled her away from me and carried both of us down the river. The rain blinded me. When I finally swam ashore, I could not find the woman black robe." After she concluded her statement, White Blossom remained in the center of the building.

Night Star spoke. "You have shamed your position and your people, my daughter. By breaking the purification ritual you have transgressed our customs. You have broken our laws."

"Yes, my queen," White Blossom admitted, "I have shamed my people and my position. I apologize to you, to the Village Council, and to the Tribal Council. I let my emotions rule my judgment."

"That speaks badly of the one who is being considered as my successor," Night Star softly said.

"It speaks badly of me as a person, a chief, and a future *mico* also, my queen," White Blossom agreed, "but it has also taught me a valuable lesson. I am a much stronger woman and leader now. I will always be aware that one cannot make sound judgments based on emotions alone; I shall never be at emotion's mercy again. Always my judgment shall be based on reason tempered with emotions."

Pleased with White Blossom's answer, Night Star smiled. Many of the council members nodded their heads. They, too, were pleased with the wisdom of her answer. Surely she would make Chicora a wise and strong queen.

"And you, Morning Dew," Night Star said, "do you have anything which you wish to say?"

Morning Dew, one of the few who doubted White Blossom's qualifications to be queen of the kingdom, rose and descended the platform. Knowing she had scored high with the elders of the tribe as well as the village, White Blossom looked smugly into Morning Dew's face as the two of them passed each other.

Once she had been blessed, Morning Dew said, "I have one thing to add, my queen. The woman black robe would not have considered going to the training camp in the storm had White Blossom not encouraged her with tales of Will's injury."

"What did you do to stop the girl from going?" Night Star barked the question.

"I did nothing," Morning Dew replied. "I knew that Marta Carolina and Will Dare were not bound by our cultural and religious beliefs; therefore, I saw no harm in their meeting with one another." Her voice thickened with tears. "I would not have permitted her to go had I known she would die. I did not know of her fear of the water.

"Did White Blossom force the woman black robe to go?" one of the council members asked.

"No," Morning Dew replied. "She offered to take her, but she did not force her to go."

"Was it raining when the woman black robe made her decision to go to the paleface warrior?" He persisted in the questioning.

When Morning Dew replied, "Yes," he smiled and

nodded his head, satisfied with the answer.

"Tell us about the woman black robe as you knew her," Night Star commanded.

Will thought the council meeting would never end. In minute detail Morning Dew recounted all the time she had spent with Marta Carolina. When they had concluded their discussion of Marta Carolina to their satisfaction, the council asked Kee-lee to speak, and after him each of the other Scupperongac braves who traveled with them. Then they called for John Cartwright.

"Time for you to speak," Will said, and stood to accompany the older man to the center of the wigwam. "Don't be afraid."

"Nay, lad," John said, slowly rising and stepping down the platform, "I don't be afraid. These Indians are a tame lot beside the Spaniards."

Night Star and members of both councils questioned the Roanoak planter. In less than an hour John had given them a detailed description of his life from the time he had landed in the New World until now. With Will's help he thoroughly answered all questions put to him.

"If we free you," Strong Bear asked, "where will you go?"

"I shall return to my people who now live in Roanoak," John replied after Will had translated the words. "Like your runners, I shall give my people a report of all I have seen."

"Will your people come back to fight with the soldiers of the black robes?"

John chuckled when Will's translation died out. "I can think of nothing the men in our settlement would enjoy more," he replied, "but, alas, great *mico*, our number is much too small."

After the queen dismissed John and Will, they returned to their seats and the council deliberated. Finally, after an extremely long debate, Gray Rabbit, chief of the village council, stood and proclaimed their decision.

"One-called-John Cartwright, you are free to return to your people to report all you have seen. You may leave with Chief Kee-lee of the Scupperongacs and his braves when they depart. Our braves will escort you to the borders of Chicora that lie toward the North Wind."

John rose, thanked the queen for her generosity, and sat back down. Night Star then addressed Will. He stood and returned to the center of the room. As Knowledge-of-the Forest went through the blessing, Will glanced around the building which had two doors. The one facing the east, Brown Beaver had told him on the day that the purification ceremony began, honors the east wind and the rising of the sun and was the entrance; the one facing west—the home of the west wind and the place where Elder Brother the Sun rested—was the exit.

The meeting house was so filled with people, Will could hardly see the doors, but as soon as Knowledge-of-the-Forest concluded his prayer, people quietly shuffled out of the doorway to let two scantily dressed braves trot in. The one was dressed like the Chicorans; the other was not.

"Our last messenger has returned," Night Star announced.

Will faced the *mico,* but out of the corner of his eyes he observed the two warriors move to an empty section on the platform and sit down.

"As soon as Will Dare has spoken, we will hear Wise Owl," Night Star said.

Will forgot the two warriors; his full attention was on Night Star. She was going to decide his fate.

"Because the soldiers of the black robes are your enemies, you have asked permission to travel south through Chicora," the queen said. "You wish to observe their fort and discover their strength?"

"I do," Will answered.

"Are you satisfied with the facts surrounding the death of the woman black robe?"

"I am grieved that she is dead," Will replied, "but I hold none of you guilty." His gaze never leaving the queen's immobile countenance, he said, "Morning Dew cannot be faulted at all for her actions, but I do blame White Blossom for encouraging Marta Carolina to come to meet me. I blame her for encouraging Marta Carolina to come out during the storm and to cross the river at that place." He paused. "Still, from what I've heard, I cannot blame her for Marta Carolina's death. All decisions ultimately belonged to Marta Carolina."

Night Star curtly inclined her head, then turned to Strong Bear. "You challenged the paleface for ownership of the woman black robe; however, when she died, the village council and I voted to cancel the contest. Have you anything to say?"

Strong Bear stood but did not move from the platform. "I no longer have a reason to challenge the paleface. I say we furnish him with a guide who speaks his language and allow him to travel to the southland."

"What do you say in regards to the wrestling match, Will Dare?" Night Star turned to him.

"I wish to wrestle him," Will declared, his resonant voice easily carrying through the building. "I want it forever established that Marta Carolina was my woman."

His eyes trained on Night Star, he said, "Please designate the time."

Night Star's eyes glinted with admiration and respect. "So be it, Will Dare, you and Strong Bear will meet at the next rising of Elder Brother the Sun. No matter whether you win or lose, you will be allowed to travel unharmed through Chicora, and I will furnish you a guide. I will give you one of my most valiant warriors." She pointed to her village chieftains. "White Blossom."

"I accept," Will replied. That Night Star had selected White Blossom as his guide mattered little. He considered her only a guide, nothing more.

A satisfied smile lit White Blossom's face. The queen had played right into her hands. The Chicoran chief could not have planned this any better herself.

After Will had taken his seat, Night Star motioned for Wise Owl to come forward. The blessing bestowed, Knowledge-of-the-Forest seated, Wise Owl began to speak.

"I was sent to the villages which lie toward the South Wind," he began, "to tell them of our celebration."

Again Will watched the flowing hands of the interpreter to hear the minute details of Wise Owl's journey which he quietly interpreted for John.

Then Wise Owl said, "At the request of the Council for all the Chicoras, I also traveled into the Land-of-the-Sun to the capital city of the kingdom of Timucuan. I was welcomed by our brothers to the south. Silver Bow who returned with me brings us a message from the soldiers of the black robes."

The room was quiet. Will saw the tall, tawny-colored brave rise. His black hair was tied and coiled atop his head with bands of reeds. Around his neck hung many strings of shell and pearls and on his arm were bracelets of polished fish teeth. His only piece of clothing was a girdle made of silver-colored balls and brass ornaments that tinkled like bells when he walked. His entire body was tattooed in red, black, yellow, and blue designs.

Kee-lee moved his head so that his mouth was close to Will's ear. "He is a Timucuan chief from the Southland."

"How do you know he's a chief?" Will asked. "Wise Owl introduced him as a scout."

"Only the royalty can be tattooed," Kee-lee answered. "And for a chief to deliver it, the message must be important."

Will studied Silver Bow's body which was covered in the most intricate geometric designs he had ever seen. "How do they do that?" he asked curiously.

"With a thorn" came the soft reply.

Silver Bow spoke. "My brothers, the Chicorans, I Silver Bow, Chief of the Timucuans, have come from the Southland, the Land-of-the-Sun, to bring you a message. The Spanish soldiers have learned that you have a woman black robe in your city. They are angry and wish to have her returned because she is a holy woman. They have sent word that if you do not bring the woman black robe to them, they will march through Chicora with their man-eating dogs."

A gasp of fear ran the room.

Silver Bow concluded, "They give you one moon in which to deliver her."

War Chief of the Chicorans, Strong Bear rose and looked at the queen for permission to speak. When she nodded, he said, "Just as we have eyes and ears among the soldiers of the black robes, so do they among us.

Someone has seen the woman and reported her presence to the Spaniards. Was the one who betrayed us found?"

"No," Silver Bow answered. "As soon as any of our villages have news, they will send a runner immediately."

"Have they sent you to escort the woman black robe to their fort?" Strong Bear asked.

"The Spaniards do not tell Silver Bow, Chief of the Timucuans, what he must do," Silver Bow replied with great dignity. "I came because you are my brothers and we are at peace with you. I do not wish to see the bloodhounds loosed."

"You are friends with the Spaniards," Night Star said.

"We are your friends; we only live in peace with the Spaniards," Silver Bow replied. "That is why I came to bring the message, Great *Mico* Night Star. I guarantee a safe journey for the woman black robe through the kingdom of Timucuan. I also guarantee that no Spaniard with his dog will enter the kingdom of Chicora."

"We are grateful that you have made the journey yourself, Silver Bow," Night Star said. "But we do not have good news for you to carry back to the Spaniards. The woman black robe is dead."

An old man, a respected Elder of the Chicorans, Gray Rabbit rose and spoke. "My queen, what are we going to do?" His words were more rhetorical than questioning. "Although we are not responsible for the death of the woman black robe, her people will not believe our innocence."

"Hear! Hear!" The people acknowledged the truth of Gray Rabbit's words.

Gray Rabbit pointed to his head. "I have the white hair of sixty winters, Chicoras. My memory is not that long,

302

but I can remember when I was only twelve winters. The soldiers of the black robes with their horses and their dogs came through our kingdom."

"Hear! Hear!" All had heard; they nodded their heads. The younger ones had memorized the stories; the older ones remembered the events.

"We promised we would never allow them to penetrate our kingdom again, my queen. Never again would the Spaniards march through our main cities and certainly not our capital city of Chicora."

"You have spoken the truth. I, too, remember," Night Star said.

"I also say, my queen, that we give these palefaces to the soldiers of the black robes." Gray Rabbit pointed an accusing finger at Will and John. "Let Silver Bow, Chief of the Timucuans, take them back to St. Augustine. Perhaps this will pacify their anger and turn their wrath from our people."

"Hear! Hear!" The people shouted their agreement.

"No!" White Blossom leapt to her feet. "We will not give Will Dare to the soldiers of the black robes!"

Her exclamation still echoed through the building when she felt the heated gaze of censure coming from everyone in the building.

"Were you given permission to speak?" Gray Rabbit's quiet voice finally broke the heavy silence.

"No" came White Blossom's answer, her body flaming with embarrassment.

"If you cannot control yourself," Gray Rabbit continued, "we will ask you to leave the meeting. You are shaming yourself, my daughter, your clan, and your father with your behavior."

"I apologize," White Blossom murmured.

As soon as she sat down, Night Star answered Gray Rabbit's question as if there had been no interruption. "I cannot go back on my word, Gray Rabbit. I have given John Cartwright permission to return to his settlement, and —"

Will stood. "I would speak, *Mico* Night Star." The queen nodded. "You and your people have received me as friends. You have shared your food and your homes with me. I would not bring trouble to you."

"You have not brought the trouble, Will Dare," Night Star said. "The soldiers of the black robes have been in our land for many winters—long before you and your people came. Our fear," she continued, "is not unwarranted, nor are we cowards. Against their dogs and horses we have no chance. We are more afraid of ten Spaniards with the dog than of one hundred without him. Gray Rabbit's mother was torn to bits in front of his eyes when he was no more than twelve winters. That is why he speaks as he does." She smiled. "I am grateful for your concern, but we must handle this our own way."

"I would speak." Will was adamant.

Gray Rabbit spoke. "Hear him, *Mico* Night Star."

When the queen nodded, Will said, "I wish to travel to the Southland so that I might see the Spanish garrison for myself, and you have already agreed to give me a guide so that my journey will be quicker."

Night Star again gave an affirmative shake of her head.

"It matters not to me, my queen, whether I'm escorted as a prisoner or not, but for your people it matters a great deal. After you have allowed John to leave, send word to the Spaniards that you are honoring their request. You are bringing me to them. Let Silver Bow, Chief of the Timucuans, take me to St. Augustine."

"You are either an extremely brave man, Will Dare, or an extremely foolish one." Her words had no sooner vanished into quietness before she softly added, "Or a man with no purpose for living."

"Whichever, Great *Mico* of all Chicoras," Silver Bow said, "he is a wise man. He gives you the answer. Will you hear him?"

"I have heard all that Will Dare said, Silver Bow," Night Star replied as Will crossed the room and stepped up the platform to return to his seat. "I have heard all that has been said by everyone, but I cannot make a decision without weighing these words. I am dismissing the town meeting so that I may speak with the Council for All Chicoras. I will give my answer after they and I have met."

As soon as Knowledge-of-the-Forest gave the benediction, the meeting was formally dismissed, and the people prepared to leave. Above the shuffle a feminine cry was heard.

"My queen! I would speak."

The congregation seemed to melt into their seats, so quiet did they become. Their heads turned to the eastern door from where the sound came, and their eyes riveted to the woman who walked into the meeting house. She looked like a goddess coming from heaven. Her back was straight; her shoulders squared; her head held high. Behind her was a sudden burst of sunlight, holding her entire body in golden shadows. The Chicorans thought they were seeing a ghost.

Will whispered disbelievingly, "Marta Carolina!"

White Blossom visibly shrank into the bench on which she was sitting, and she blanched. She curled her hands around the edge of the bench to keep them from trembling. So carefully had she planned and schemed. So sure she was that the woman black robe had drowned. She had sacrificed all she held dear in order to get this woman out of the life of the paleface warrior.

Will Dare had eyes for no one else. His heart was lighter than he could remember its having been; joy was from his soul. Marta Carolina was truly the most lovely woman he had ever seen. She eclipsed everyone whom he had ever known or admired. She was wearing a long buckskin dress, embroidered in bright, vivid colors. The bodice accented her firm bustline and tiny waist; the skirt flared from her hips, the fullness swirling around her knee-high moccasins as she walked. Her hair, brushed to a brilliant sheen, was pulled back from her face and coiled at the base of her neck, and curling tendrils wisped about her cheeks. A royal blue band was wrapped around her head, and pearl-decorated tassels hung down her back.

But her loveliness wasn't in her physical appearance. Will saw a deeper beauty than he'd seen before. Gone was the childish innocence that came from her having lived such a sheltered life; gone forever was the woman/child. In her place was a mature woman—serene, calm, in total control of the situation. Her eyes, the color enhanced by the headband, sparkled with resolve; they glinted with purpose. She had a task to perform, and she wouldn't be deterred until it was complete.

Tears moistened Will's eyes, and he softly murmured her name. Yet it wasn't so soft that his beloved didn't hear. At the sound of the familiar husky tones, her heart quickened. She turned her head and looked at him. When she saw the ravage of grief on his face, she wanted to run to him, fling herself into his arms, and assure him

306

that she was most assuredly alive, but at the moment she could do none of these things. All she could do was smile.

Will's eyes filled with tears, and a smile trembled on his lips.

Then Marta Carolina looked straight ahead, her eyes on Night Star. "My queen, I would speak."

Chapter XIII

"We are happy to see you again, woman black robe" came Night Star's heartfelt greeting. "For the past two suns we have been searching for your body in the river. White Blossom thought you had drowned."

"Verily she did," Marta Carolina replied dryly, and she let her gaze shift from the queen to the young Chicoran chief. "I did, too."

Only White Blossom knew Marta Carolina's words were double-edged; only she felt their sting. She clutched the seat of the bench even tighter. Yet she maintained her aplomb; her expression never conceded fear; her posture remained arrogant.

"You must learn to swim."

White Blossom was glad Night Star had spoken. The words forced Marta Carolina to break the solemn stare and return her full attention to the queen.

"I knew how to swim, Great *Mico*," Marta Carolina replied. "However, I was afraid of the water—unusually afraid—because I had almost drowned when I was a small child."

White Blossom wanted to hear everything Marta Carolina would say; likewise, she wanted the meeting to adjourn. She needed to get outside where she could have fresh air. Because she was guilty she felt as if everyone were looking at her, pointing an accusing finger. Her head never moved, but her eyes darted about surreptitiously, skimming the crowd. No one was looking at her; all eyes centered on Marta Carolina. White Blossom relaxed. Then she felt a heated, fixed gaze on her. Again she flicked her eyes over the building, to her side, to the Tribal Council. Morning Dew was looking directly at her. Morning Dew knew! Unable to return the steady, knowing gaze, White Blossom quickly dropped black lashes over her eyes and turned her head to stare straight ahead. Her world could so easily tumble in on top of her.

She heard Marta Carolina say, "Instead of conquering my fear, I let it grow until it was large enough to destroy me. I realized the other night how easily someone could use this fear to hurt me."

White Blossom never moved, but her entire body burned with guilt.

"Fear didn't kill you," Night Star said. "Fear is a gift given us by the Creator, but he also gives us the wisdom to control this fear. Properly used it motivates us to reason and to move cautiously in all situations. Improperly used, we are no longer in control, and it destroys us from within because it produces panic. Panic is dangerous; that is what almost killed you, my child."

"That may be, my queen," Marta Carolina murmured.

"Now, my child, tell us what happened."

Marta Carolina was in no hurry to tell her story. During the eleven days of feasting, she had learned that Indians enjoyed hearing tales of bravery and courage.

They wanted to know the most minute details, they wanted to experience every emotion, so they would listen until they had memorized the story and could retell it word for word.

"On the eleventh day I wandered into the woods outside the walls of the city. Standing on a large boulder near the river, I saw Will as he practiced wrestling." Her voice never wavered as she told Night Star all that had happened.

Hardly daring to breathe, Will listened and love swelled inside him, a new kind of love for him—one that encompassed but far surpassed mere passion and desire. As if they had gone back in time, he was there with her on that night. He saw as she saw; he felt what she felt.

"I willingly violated the Chicoran purification ceremony," Marta Carolina confessed. "When White Blossom told me that Will was hurt, I never considered not going to him. Nothing would have stopped me. Not the Winter's Rage! Not the flames of hell!" Marta Carolina paused, turned her head, and leveled a measuring gaze on the Chicoran chieftain. Only the two of them understood all Marta Carolina was saying. "I wanted Will to win the contest so much I was willing to break any law. I wanted to give him the medicine that would help his ankle."

As Marta Carolina's tale unraveled, she vindicated Morning Dew and accepted the full responsibility for her actions. She told the truth, but she carefully worded her statements when she spoke of White Blossom's involvement. She had no evidence with which to substantiate her accusations; she had no witnesses to prove that White Blossom had tried to murder her. Thus, she decided to keep her counsel where the warrior/woman was concerned.

"When White Blossom led me to the river, I was so frightened I couldn't move. In the flashes of lightning I could see the water, and I could hear it. Then I saw the log over which I must cross."

"You behaved foolishly, Marta Carolina," Night Star quietly interjected as if she were admonishing a child. "You allowed your emotions to overrule your reasoning—a trait that is prevalent with you palefaces. Why did you insist on going the shortest route? Will Dare was not injured so badly that you couldn't have waited a little longer! Surely White Blossom pointed out the danger of crossing on the log?"

Oh, yes! White Blossom pointed the danger out! But she lied by telling her that this was the only crossing to the training camp! Marta Carolina drew a ragged breath. If only she could show proof that White Blossom had tried to murder her!

"Yes," Marta Carolina finally replied, "White Blossom pointed out the dangers of crossing the river at that place, but I—I insisted."

Will was watching Marta Carolina closely. He could see the humorless smile that curved her lips. Although she appeared to be at ease, he could see her tenseness—he could see her calculated alertness. She measured each word before she spoke as if . . . as if she were keeping something back. So attuned to her, he felt her bitterness and silent anger.

"White Blossom crossed first," he heard Marta Carolina say, "and I followed. I slipped."

Marta Carolina's palms beaded with perspiration as she thought about that night. She could still feel the rain pelting against her shivering body; she could feel the river swirling around her, taking her down, down, down.

311

She shuddered.

Disregarding Chicoran custom, forgetting his sprained ankle, Will bounded to his feet. As pain shot up his leg, he sucked in his breath and repositioned his weight so that the most of it fell on his uninjured foot, but he didn't stop his descent. Aware of Will's purpose, Kee-lee reached out to restrain him, but Will easily evaded his friend's grip. Down the platform he went to the center of the wigwam to stand beside Marta Carolina. He hadn't been there when she almost drowned, but he was here with her now.

He caught her tiny body in his arms, and he held her, the embrace a physical symbol of his receiving her fully into his heart and life.

"Don't be afraid, *querida*," he whispered. "I'm here with you, and I'll never leave you."

Marta Carolina's cheek brushed up his chest. She heard the steady thump of his heart; she felt the strength of those arms which banded her.

Through the winter buckskin which he wore he felt the warmth of her touch. She tilted her head and smiled, and that was Will's undoing. No one but Marta Carolina existed at that moment. Everyone around them seemed miles away. He lowered his head, his lips so softly touching hers, not passionately seeking, not lustfully asking, but tenderly assuring, promising. Against her mouth, he whispered, "You are indeed my lady-wife, Mistress Marta Carolina Dare."

"Yes," she whispered, glad for the haven of Will's love, "I'm your lady-wife, and you are my lord-husband."

The intimate scene caused White Blossom to seethe, and she didn't bother to hide her emotions. Her beautiful

312

face contorted with hatred; she balled her hands so tightly her nails dug into her palms. She had failed to kill the woman black robe, but that didn't mean she wouldn't try again. She would get Marta Carolina out of her life altogether, away from Will, away from Strong Bear.

Sitting beside his daughter, Strong Bear was unaware of the depth of her hatred or the measures to which she would stoop to be rid of Marta Carolina. His eyes misted with tears as he beheld the tender embrace between Will and the woman black robe; he was happy for the love which the two of them had found, and he grieved his loss. But he blinked the tears away. A highly disciplined warrior and war chief, he didn't give public expression to his emotions. When he glanced sideways at his daughter, he inwardly shuddered. So caught up in her hatred and in her scheming, all her emotions were written on her face; at the moment she was controlled by them. He was worried. She had changed so much since she'd met Will Dare—and the change had been for the worse.

"Marta Carolina," Night Star called, "we are waiting to hear the rest of your story." The queen chuckled. "We are curious and wish to find out how you saved yourself, how you returned to Chicora and why you waited so long to present yourself to the council and the people."

Will's presence and the strength of his love caused Marta Carolina's fears to abate; she wiped the tears from her eyes and smiled shakily at the queen, but she didn't move out of the circle of Will's arms. She wanted to feel their warmth against her body; she wanted and needed the physicality of his strength.

"I grabbed a tree that had been swept into the water," Marta Carolina replied, "and was able to climb on it. I straddled it and rode it down the rapids into a calm spot in the river. By that time the storm was over, and I managed to paddle ashore. I was so weak, I lay down to rest but went to sleep instead. When I awoke the following morning, I traveled the river until I reached the city. I—I returned to Chicora and the upper village the same way I exited with White Blossom, and no one saw me." Now she smiled and shrugged. "But it would have made no difference had I come through the main gate. The town was empty. When I asked one of the women who was tending the fires where everyone was, she told me you were gathered here at the town hall. I was so dirty that I went to our apartment first to bathe and change clothes before I presented myself."

She looked up at Will and whispered, "I remembered my promise to you." Tears washed her eyes until they sparkled like blue diamonds. "I wore the brightest dress I could find, and I smiled."

Will's embrace tightened, and he wished he and Marta Carolina were not standing in the middle of a public meeting house in front of so many people. So much he had to tell her; so badly he wanted to love her.

"You may be seated," Night Star said, an understanding smile in the depth of her obsidian eyes. Then: "Will anyone else speak?"

Although both John Cartwright and Kee-lee smiled at Marta Carolina when Will led her to the platform, neither spoke. They were listening to Strong Bear who had moved to the speaker's position.

"I am Strong Bear, War Chief of all Chicorans. My totem and my clan is the same: the bear."

Situated beside Marta Carolina, his arm wrapped around her, Will heard Strong Bear recount his finding them in the woods; he told of Will's and Marta Carolina's battle with the bear which ended in its death; he extolled Will's prowess as a warrior and Marta Carolina's magic of healing; he thanked them publicly for giving him the bear.

"She has great knowledge of the horse," he continued, "which she has willingly shared with us, teaching our warriors to care for them and to ride them. I wanted the woman black robe for my own," he admitted, making a complete turn in the circle and gazing at the grouped clans each in turn. "I challenged the paleface warrior for her." He spoke to Will, his countenance closed and unreadable, and his voice rang out as he said, "I still challenge him." The two men stared at each other for endless seconds; then the Chicoran's stern features relaxed into a smile. "With Marta Carolina's having returned to us, I invite the return of our festival spirit."

"Hear! Hear!" The people shouted and clapped their delight.

Strong Bear raised his hands for silence. "The prize has changed this time. By her own choosing, the woman black robe belongs to Will Dare. I respect her choice." He moved so that he faced Night Star. "If I win the wrestling match, my queen, I should like for you to give me one of the horses which we took from the soldiers of the black robes."

Night Star's eyes laughed. Her great-nephew had placed her in a difficult position. She could hardly refuse his request without incurring the displeasure of her people. The laughter softly erupted. She really didn't mind giving him one of the beasts; they looked like they would be more trouble than they were worth. Let him be the one to get all battered and bruised learning to ride them.

Night Star raised her scepter. "One of the beasts you shall have if you win the wrestling match, Strong Bear. Be it so; I have spoken." Her eyes still twinkling, she asked, "What about the paleface soldier? Does he receive the horse if he wins?"

Strong Bear walked the length of the platform and stood before the Englishman. "Will Dare, do you accept the challenge?"

Life strongly surged through Will, and the anticipation of such a contest exhilarated him even more. His black eyes, so lackluster before, were shining with anticipation; his body vibrated with the excitement that permeated the air.

"I accept."

"What do you claim as your reward if you should win?" Since Strong Bear had denounced his claim to Marta Carolina in front of the entire tribe, both councils and the queen, Will knew the Chicoran chief planned no deceit. "If I win, Night Star—" Will faced the queen and spoke directly to her "—you will send word to the Spaniards that Silver Bow, Chief of the Timucuans, is bringing the woman black robe and a paleface brave to them."

He saw the almost imperceptible change in Night Star's features; she was irritated with him for having introduced this subject again. He didn't see White Blossom scoot to the edge of the bench, her face pale.

"We will be in no danger, *Mico* Night Star," Will softly explained. "Marta Carolina is in no danger of the Spaniards; they are her people."

"And you, Will Dare?"

"Like your grandchildren, my queen, I, too, belong to

two peoples. My father was English; my mother was Spanish. I was reared to be both." He waited, but Night Star didn't answer. "From this moment on, Wise *Mico* of all Chicorans, I am Guillermo Lucero."

Marta Carolina smiled. Here was yet another title for this complicated man whom she loved. He had moved from Indian savage to Englishman—now to Spaniard. What would he be next? she wondered on a soft chuckle.

Time had moved slow for Will before, but this was one of the few times that it seemed to stand still.

Finally came the answer. "Be it so. I have spoken." Night Star's voice rang through the meeting house. "Now, my people, you may go. Wise Owl, you will remain to give a detailed report of your journey through the kingdom to the council. The rest of you enjoy the celebration. I know we're looking forward to the contest between Will Dare and Strong Bear which will be—" the people eagerly, almost breathlessly, awaited the queen's announcement "—on the new sun when Elder Brother is directly overhead and we have no shadow. Tonight we feast and dance."

As soon as Knowledge-of-the-Forest gave the second benediction, pandemonium broke out in the Town House. Everyone was talking at once; they were pushing and shoving to get out of the building, eager to lay their wagers once again.

To get away from the congestion so they could talk, Will guided Marta Carolina out the west door of the wigwam. Closely behind was White Blossom who glowered her hatred. The other Scupperongac braves milled with the crowd, making their wagers, but John and Kee-lee followed Will across the public square, up

317

the pyramid to the garden outside their apartment.

"Ah, laddie," John said, when he reached the spot where Marta Carolina and Will stood, holding hands and looking into each other's eyes, "this is the lassie you told me about."

"This is the lassie," Will said in English. "This, John Cartwright, is Mistress Marta Carolina Lucas de Santiago."

"Right pleased I am, mistress, to make your acquaintance," John said, waiting for Will to translate.

Marta Carolina extended her hand. "And I am pleased to meet you, John Cartwright."

"I will not stay with you long, lad," John said. "Now that I've met the little lady, I'll be on my way." He grinned and winked at Will. "Think maybe I'll make me a wager or two."

When Kee-lee saw John walk away, he laid his hand on the old man's shoulder and detained him, but he spoke to Will. "I have been away from my village and my people long enough, my friend. Now that you have a guide and escort to the Spanish garrison, it is time for me and my braves to travel home."

Although Will hated to see his friends leave, he knew they must.

Kee-lee knelt and, with his index finger, marked in the soft dirt. "Tell John that we will be leaving before Elder Brother the Sun rises this time," he said, pointing to the second mark. "I will come to his wigwam and get him. Tell him to be ready."

"You will be leaving the day after tomorrow before sunrise," Will translated to John. "Kee-lee will come by to get you, so have everything packed that you intend to take with you."

John nodded. "You'll be going on to the Spanish garrison?"

Will drew a deep breath and nodded, but Marta Carolina's close encounter with death had altered his way of thinking; it had shuffled his priorities, and revenge was now at the bottom of the list. Loving Marta Carolina and savoring that love was first.

"The little lady will help you get in and out of the garrison safely." John unconsciously lowered his voice as if she understood English and might overhear their conversation. "She seems to think mighty highly of you, young Dare."

"Aye, John," Will drawled, the old man's unwitting remarks slapping him in the face, "she thinks mighty highly of me. That she does."

John clapped Will on the back. "I'll be seeing you later, lad, to tell you good-bye. Let me get to the square and lay some wages. Annie would love to have some of these fabric garments which the Indians make."

After John and Kee-lee left, Will hungrily pulled her into his arms, and she as hungrily went. She had much she wished to discuss with Will, but talk would wait. As starved for his touch as he was hers, Marta Carolina readily gave her lips to his kiss, and the two of them melted as if boneless onto the nearby couch.

"I have missed your touches, *querido*," Marta Carolina murmured between deep, leisurely kisses.

"And I yours," Will replied, his grip tightening. "I thought I would never hold you in my arms again. I thought I would never have the opportunity to tell you how much I love you." He pushed up on his elbow and leaned over her. "I do love you, *querida*."

Happiness glowed on Marta Carolina's face. "And I love you," she replied, lifting her hand to map his face with her fingers. The thick black eyebrows, the arrogant nose, the full sensuous lips. "I'm so glad we're finally alone," she confessed. "I didn't want to share you with anyone."

"Aye, love." He took her finger into his mouth. "Just you and me," he murmured, "and at this moment that's all I want is you and me."

His tongue, tracing exotic designs on the tip of her finger, sent an involuntary shiver through Marta Carolina's tiny frame. She laid her head on his chest, and the tears she had not shed during the past twenty-four hours welled in her eyes to spill warmly on him. His lips spread kisses across the exposed skin, pulling at the curling hair and stirring to life the ever-glowing embers of desire. As starved as she was for the taste of Will Dare, this was not enough for Marta Carolina. She lifted her head to reach for his lips.

As her mouth came down, Will stared into her face, scratched and bruised from her near drowning, but to him she was beautiful. She was everything to him . . . everything. This beauty of body and soul shattered his heart into a million pieces, miraculously to put it together again without any scars. Will was so over-powered by the depth of his love that he was weakened by it. He wanted to kiss her, to make love to her, and to possess her in all the ways a man possesses a woman, but a far greater want filled his heart—a want to take care of her, to protect her, and to cherish her. He had unconsciously moved from infatuation to love; heady was his discovery.

Her lips softly landed on his, and she whispered, "I love you, *querido*," the words merging into the essence of their kiss. Her warm lips parted his to send desire coursing through Will's veins. Her hands moved to his waist, gathered the material of his shirt, and tugged it from his breeches. Then up his warm flesh her hands crept. She felt Will's muscles flinch uncontrollably beneath the surface of his skin.

Will wrenched his mouth from hers and shifted slightly so that she was beneath him. He said, his voice thick, his breathing heavy, "I love you, and I've never wanted to make love to you any more than I want to at the moment, *querida*, but I love you too much to do it now. This is not the time."

"Why?" Marta Carolina asked softly—a little disappointed—lifting a hand to touch the dark crescent of fatigue and worry beneath his eyes.

"You have been through too much, my darling," he answered. "No matter how much both of us may want this, the body can only take so much. Both of us have suffered too much the last two days. Now we need to rest." He settled on the blanket and tugged her body until she curved against him. "Let's sleep now."

"What about making love?" she asked, her voice already growing drowsy.

"After the feast we will make love all night long."

Her giggle was interrupted by a yawn. "You have the wrestling match with Strong Bear on the morrow."

"So I do," he murmured.

"Will, there are so many things we need to talk about," Marta Carolina began. He needed to know that White Blossom had tried to kill her.

"Not now, *querida*," he said on a yawn, dropping his

321

arm over her and curling his hand against her breast. "We'll talk later." He squirmed toward her and tucked the gentle curves into the warmth and security of his hard frame. Proprietary was the gesture, but also wonderful and loving.

Both fell into peaceful slumber.

Chapte XIV

The day was growing late and the sun was steadily lowering on the western horizon. It cast beautiful spindles of golden light into the apartment Marta Carolina and Will shared. Rested from their afternoon nap and dressed for the coming festivities, she agitatedly paced back and forth, he sat on one of the couches.

"You're not listening to me," she declared not for the first time. "White Blossom did try to kill me!"

Will sighed, pushed to his feet, and walked to where she stood glowering at him. He pulled her into his arms. "I'm sure you thought so," he said, "but you panicked, *querida*. You were fighting her.

"I panicked," Marta Carolina admitted testily, jerking out of his embrace, "but I did not struggle with her, and I do know what I'm talking about. I've told you she deceived me about your wanting me to come tend your ankle and about my having to cross the river at the log. She deliberately took me that way, Will. She knew I was afraid of the water."

"Yes," Will murmured, memory flashing through his

mind, "I told her so myself!"

"White Blossom waited until I was in the middle of the river, then she pushed me," she reiterated.

Will brushed his hand through his hair and sighed. "She probably did deceive you, but I don't think she deliberately tried to push you in. Perhaps she meant only to frighten you, and you panicked."

"She did deceive me; she did frighten me; she did push me in. And I panicked!"

"All right," Will conceded, "she deceived you, and she was wrong for doing that. But she couldn't afford to murder you, Marta Carolina. To do so under the circumstances would ruin her chances of becoming queen of the Chicoras. As you admitted, you panicked when you fell and—"

"Under what circumstances?" Marta Carolina demanded. "The Chicorans have no liking for me! Didn't Gray Rabbit prove what they all think when he spoke at the meeting today?"

"No, they have no liking for any of us," Will agreed, "but none of them would do us any physical harm. Strong Bear had challenged for you, and you had been promised as the prize for the winner of the contest. No one could touch you without fear of punishment."

"No one was to know," Marta Carolina contended heatedly, quite upset because Will was defending White Blossom. "I am the only witness, and I would be dead."

"*Querida*—" he spoke mollifyingly "—you must not speak of this to anyone."

"Do you believe me?" Marta Carolina asked.

Will gazed into her eyes for a long time before he nodded his head. "I believe you."

"So—" Her face brightened.

"But you must never speak your accusations to anyone, sweetheart."

"Do you think I do not know that!" Marta Carolina snapped. "Many things I may be, Will Dare, but a fool I am not. Why do you think I did not make any accusations at the council meeting today? I knew no one would believe me. But we cannot let White Blossom be our guide to St. Augustine."

Will silently agreed with Marta Carolina. "We have no choice, sweetheart."

Marta Carolina swung around, her hands on her hips. Her countenance was stern and fixed. "I will not travel in the same company with her, Will Dare! I would be a fool. She tried to kill me one time; she'll try again."

Will saw reasoning was lost on Marta Carolina presently, the conversation closed. "Come," he said resignedly. "We must go to the feast. We'll discuss this another time."

"We'll go to the feast," Marta Carolina said, "but the subject of White Blossom's going to St. Augustine is closed. I have said all I intend to say."

Deep in thought, the two of them were silent as they walked across the courtyard to the stairs. When they stepped into the square and stood beneath one of the massive columns, filled with torches ready to be lit at dark, Morning Dew greeted them with a warm smile.

"I'm glad to see you are not hurt any worse than you are," she said, her eyes moving over the cuts and scratches on Marta Carolina's face.

From behind them came a voice, and White Blossom materialized. "Welcome to the celebration feast." Although she addressed her greeting to both of them, the Chicoran chief singled Marta Carolina out. "I'm glad you

325

did not drown. I would have blamed myself if you had." White Blossom's face was warm with friendliness and concern.

"I would have blamed you also," Morning Dew returned evenly, the statement as sharp and cutting as her gaze.

"And you," White Blossom asked, her wounded eyes on Will, "would you have blamed me, also?"

Marta Carolina's anger was so great, a convulsive tremor ran through her body. Will slipped his arm around her shoulder and drew her closer. His fingers gently dug into the soft flesh, a nonverbal command for her to keep silent.

"I blame you for having chosen the river route by which to bring her to the training camp," he said, "but I could not blame you for her death."

"Of course not," Marta Carolina drawled sarcastically. "A Chicoran chief is above reproach."

White Blossom smiled. "It will do you well to remember that."

"It will do you well, Chicoran chief, to remember that I have an excellent memory!"

The air hung heavy and still around them.

"Will Dare!" Strong Bear's voice rang out. "Marta Carolina! Come with me. Night Star wishes you to sit with her during the feast."

"I will speak with you later, Will Dare," White Blossom said, "to find out when we are leaving for the Spanish garrison." As if the Chicoran chieftain could read Marta Carolina's thoughts, she smiled. "We will be in each other's company for many suns. We will learn one another much better."

Before Marta Carolina could make reply, Will's fingers

326

dug into her shoulders, and using his body, he guided her so that they followed Strong Bear to the queen's litter.

When they stood in front of Night Star, she said, "You have much magic, Marta Carolina."

Marta Carolina was surprised. This was the first time the queen had addressed her by name.

"Chief Kee-lee of the Scupperongacs told me all that has happened to you since you left your home in the land-across-the-sea. Twice you have been at the mercy of the water and could have drowned; twice you survived."

"That is true."

"Strong Bear told me of your valor when you and Will Dare fought the bear."

Marta Carolina chuckled softly. "More Will Dare's valor than mine, *Mico* Night Star. He is the one who killed the beast, not I."

"And you have taught my young braves-to-be how to care for and ride the horse. They say you can talk to this creature. Because your magic is so strong," Night Star said, "I have a request to make. But, first, let us go to the Temple." She clapped her hands, and two braves picked up the shafts.

The Temple! Marta Carolina was stunned. She was going to see the Temple up close! In awe she walked between Will and the queen's litter, her eyes never leaving the magnificent building that loomed larger and larger.

The walls were high, and the roof, extremely sloped for better water drainage, was covered in intricate designs of shells, their mother-of-pearl interiors exposed to catch and reflect the sunlight. Hanging across the entire length of the roof from ridge to cornice were festoons of pearls, their luster joining the vivid brightness of the shells to produce a most beautiful effect in the sunshine.

"I can't believe Night Star is taking us to the Temple," Marta Carolina whispered to Will. "Morning Dew told me all about it. They don't worship in this building; they bury their dead here." Then she urgently tugged his arm and pointed to the siding of thin cane mats which the Indians wove. "Aren't they beautiful?" She still spoke in the awed whisper. "They look like the rush carpets of the Moors that we use at home."

She was so caught up in the beauty of the building, Marta Carolina lagged a step or two behind Will, and she wasn't noticing where she walked. At the entrance to the Temple she bumped into someone and turned to apologize. When she saw the giant statue, so ferocious and menacing, their sightless eyes staring at nothing but seeing all, she caught her breath and her hands flew to her chest.

"Do not be frightened," Night Star said. "These will not hurt you." The braves stopped and set the litter on the ground. "Open the windows," she instructed as she rose and waved her scepter toward the twelve wooden statues, six of which stood on either side of the ornate doors. "These armed giants were put here to defend the entrance of the Temple."

Night Star laughed softly. "Although they can harm no one, intruders harm themselves when they see the giants. Never forget Marta Carolina: fear is like a double-edged knife. It can be a weapon to those who know how to instill it in others; it can be deadly when it's instilled in you." As they walked through the entry corridor to the massive interior doors, Night Star pointed at the braves who stood guard. "These are the ones to fear. They are the ones who can do you harm."

A nod from the queen was the only command the guards needed. Immediately they opened both doors to allow Night Star entrance into the Temple. Will and Marta Carolina followed. Both appreciated the honor the queen had bestowed in allowing them to enter the temple; they marveled as they beheld the beauty of the inner room. The ceiling was bright and vivid with colored plumes and festoons of lustrous pearls. Warmth and sunlight poured in from the twelve open windows.

High around the four sides of the temple were two rows of statues, one of men and the other of women, each shelved above the other. Carved in perfect proportion to the inhabitants of Chicora, each had his niche joining another's. All the men were holding arms in their hands from which hung numerous rows of strands of pearls, bright colored tassels at the end. At the base of these walls were beautiful hand-carved benches on which rested equally elaborate coffins.

"These are the lords of the entire province of Chicora and their families," Night Star said as she slowly strolled through the huge building. She pointed to a third row of statues, two feet above the coffins and niched into the wall.

"These represent the persons so naturally that you can tell how they looked at the time of their death."

She stopped in the middle of the temple and stood in front of three rows of reed chests, stacked in such a way that the largest chest served as a base to the medium size, and these for the smaller.

Night Star spoke in Chicoran to one of her male attendants. "Open one of the larger chests." Then she said in Spanish with a great sweep of her hand, "All these are filled with pearls. The smaller the chest the smaller

329

the size of the pearl."

The brave easily hoisted the chests from the stack and laid them aside as he dug. When finally he reached the bottom, he swung open the lid and stepped aside.

Marta Carolina gasped. Although she had been reared in wealth and affluence, she had never beheld so many pearls in her life. While astonished, Will controlled his reaction much better. Having lived in Scupperong in an Indian society, he understood Night Star's motivations. In order to ask Marta Carolina for a favor, she must present her with a gift.

Night Star walked the breadth and length of the building—more than a hundred steps long and more than forty steps wide—opening the lids of chests. Marta Carolina followed. Finally the old woman knelt in front of a chest and dipped her hands into the pearls, fanning it back and forth in the sea of jewels. She motioned for Marta Carolina to join her.

"Are they not beautiful?" the Chicoran queen asked. She brought a handful of pearls up; then using her fist as a funnel dropped them into the chest.

"Yes," Marta Carolina murmured, playing with the jewels also.

Night Star leaned over, and when she had untied a package that laid nearby, she held beautiful chamois skins in the air. Marta Carolina forgot her interest in the pearls and looked at the skins. She took one and rubbed it against her cheek.

"So soft," she said. "Oh, Will, wouldn't this make the most lovely gauntlet gloves!"

Pleased with Marta Carolina's interest in the chamois, Night Star opened other packages of skins, each bundle dyed a different color.

Quickly Marta Carolina delved into each of the bundles, pulling out the different colored skins. "These are dressed and dyed as best I've ever seen," Marta Carolina exclaimed, "as good as those which come from Germany and Russia."

"Indeed they are beautiful," the queen replied without conceit. "And we have many more." She stood. "Come. I'll show you."

Night Star led Will and Marta Carolina to a stairwell which they climbed. The entire second floor of the building was a magazine divided into eight halls of exactly the same size. These halls were filled with arms, overlaid with gold, painted in bright colors, and embellished with pearls.

"Are you not afraid to have such wealth in this—this mosque?" Marta Carolina asked.

"We do not fear our people taking them," Night Star replied. "The Chicorans take pride in their Temple. All the chiefs of our country, and principally these of our province, want our grandeur to consist in the magnificence of our temples."

"You have more than one?" Marta Carolina asked.

"Each village has one," Night Star answered. "Because Chicora is the capital city of the kingdom, this one is the most magnificent."

As they retraced their steps through the magazine and descended the stairs, Night Star said, "I do have one fear, Marta Carolina. I fear the soldiers of the black robes. I fear their coming to take our wealth. We have found them to be greedy. They do not want to take the tools which the Creator has given them and work the ground for their food, clothes, and shelter. They want to take our gold, pearls, and virgins. The gold and pearls they wish to

331

keep; when the women are no longer virgins, the soldiers discard them."

Standing in front of the pearl chests, Marta Carolina said, "I am a woman black robe. Are you not afraid that I will steal your wealth?"

Night Star shook her head.

"Why have you shown me your temple?"

"I have a favor to ask you." Night Star reached for one of the smaller chests of pearls which she held out to Marta Carolina. "This I give to you."

Not understanding the Indian custom, Marta Carolina looked at Will beseechingly.

"If you will hear her request, take the chest."

"I will hear your request, my queen," Marta Carolina said, "but I will not accept the pearls."

"You must take the gift before she can ask," Will said.

Only when the chest was in Marta Carolina's hands, did Night Star speak. "Forty-eight winters ago when I was a young chieftain like White Blossom, a soldier of the black robes called De Soto marched through our kingdom. I was chief of the town of Cofitachequi on the banks of the river which the soldiers of the black robes call Santa Elena, by us called the Savannah. My people and I were frightened of these strangers, but I received and welcomed them into our country. My attendants carried my litter to the water's side where I entered the royal canoe. Three canoes, each carrying two of my ambassadors, preceded my bark. Behind me came canoes filled with my warriors. I talked through an interpreter, Juan Ortiz. Seeing that this man, De Soto, prized them, I presented him with my necklace of pearls which was so long it encircled my neck three times and each loop extended down to my waist. I opened my people's

332

granaries to the soldiers."

"He repaid goodness with evil. He robbed our temple, took me captive and forced me to guide his men toward the mountains where we found our gold. My subjects became burden bearers; I was forced to become his woman. In the villages through which we marched, I was made to order food and burden bearers for the army to replace those who had been beaten to death or who had died from fatigue. He also demanded Indian women and maidens to do the bidding of his men. These captives were marched with iron collars about their necks and chained together. Packs of bloodhounds were used to chase fugitives and execute summary punishment upon delinquents by tearing them to pieces."

"After many days my maids and I escaped, taking with us the pearls and gold which De Soto had stolen. When I became queen of all Chicorans and came to live in Chicora, I made a vow that no soldier of the black robes would ever ransack our capital city. We do not allow them to penetrate this far into our kingdom."

If Marta Carolina had learned anything during her stay in Chicora, she had learned that although an Indian loved to talk, he always spoke economically. Every word he spoke was direct and for a purpose. Patiently awaiting Night Star's revelation, Marta Carolina set the heavy chest on the floor.

"Because De Soto bound me in one of the iron collars and kept me by his side, I could not gather and take the herb which keeps a woman from conceiving a child." She paused, then said, "When I returned to Cofitachequi, I was with child. Seven months later I bore a daughter. Although I reared her to be an Indian, she chose to be a woman of the black robes. She journeyed to their village in the Southland and lived with one of the soldiers until she died."

"When I asked Silver Bow about my daughter, he told me that many years ago he had heard a rumor of such a person living among the Spaniards. He also heard that she died giving birth to a daughter. Nothing has been heard of her since." Night Star looked at Marta Carolina. "I would see her before I die."

"What are you going to do with us?" Marta Carolina asked sadly, touched by Night Star's story.

"I have given my word. If Will Dare wins the contest with Strong Bear, you and he will travel to the Southland with Silver Bow."

"And if he should lose?" Marta Carolina asked.

Night Star's eyes were twinkling. "Word had already been sent that Silver Bow is bringing you and Will Dare to the Spanish fort."

"You are going to let us go either way?" Marta Carolina quickly looked at Will and smiled.

"That is your heart's desire, is it not?"

"Yes. Do you wish to travel to St. Augustine with us?"

"I am too old to travel that far," the queen returned. "Furthermore, I cannot leave my people without a leader." She looked at Marta Carolina. "Since you are a woman black robe, my granddaughter will listen to you. She worships your god who lies on the sticks. Tell her that I, Night Star, her grandmother, would like to see her one time before I die. I will send White Owl with you, and he can bring her back to Chicora if she agrees."

"What about White Blossom?" Marta Carolina asked.

"She cannot go with you," Night Star answered. "The tribal council has reprimanded her; therefore, she must

334

remain in Chicora to begin her purification. Her behavior has been less than that of a warrior, less than that of a chieftain." She was silent for a moment, then she asked, "Will you search for my granddaughter, Marta Carolina, and give her my message?"

"Yes," Marta Carolina said, relief flowing through her. She was elated that White Blossom would not be accompanying her and Will to the garrison. "I will do this for you."

"I will give you another chest of pearls," Night Star said, "to show you my gratitude."

"I do not want your pearls," Marta Carolina replied. "I do this because I want to, because I respect you, Night Star, wise *Mico* of the Chicorans."

Night Star stared deeply into the blue eyes and nodded her head. "You cannot refuse a love gift, Marta Carolina. If you do not take them with you, I shall keep them for you. They will be here for your asking." She lifted her hands and took off two of her pearl-and-gold necklaces. One she looped over Marta Carolina's head, the other over Will's. "Please wear these. They will keep you safe as long as you are in my country. They are my tokens, bearing my sign." She pointed to the etching in the gold disc. "This is a star of the night—the symbol of Night Star, Queen of Chicora."

Again Marta Carolina was reminded of the words of her aunt. Your destiny lies with the morning star! Was the night star and the morning star one and the same?

"Come now," Night Star commanded. "We must return to the feast."

Amid laughter and talk, the queen's company arrived at the public square and moved into the ceremonial hall where they would eat. Night Star stood and opened the feast with a prayer. Afterward she waved her hand to the food-laden mats.

"Let us eat now."

Marta Carolina did not have to be urged. After her ordeal, she was famished. Still she deliberately tantalized her taste buds by sniffing deeply the aroma of the succulent feast that was spread before them. Unlike the Indians who ate only enough to fill themselves, Marta Carolina gorged herself.

She sighed contentedly as she wiped the honey bowl with the last bit of her corn fritter and popped the succulent morsel into her mouth.

"Would you like to have another bowl?" Will asked with amused tolerance.

"Umhum," she droned, "but I don't have anyplace to put it." She rested her hand on her stomach and grinned. "I'm too full."

"Finished just in time," Will said, their soiled dishes disappearing as an Indian woman gathered and stacked them. "The music and the dancing is about to begin."

Marta Carolina lifted her hands and licked the honey from each finger.

"Some right here," Will murmured, touching the corner of her mouth with the tip of his finger.

Marta Carolina turned to look at him, and the expression in his eyes awed her. She forgot the drop of honey on her face; she forgot everything but Will Dare. She had the distinct impression that all others had moved a long way off, as if they sat not an arm's length on either side of her and Will but sat miles away. Despite their proximity, their figures seemed small and inconsequential. Only Will's face filled her vision; only he mattered at this moment.

Marta Carolina flicked her tongue, but she couldn't quite reach the sticky sweetness.

"Here, let me," Will whispered, his head slanting closer to hers. His lips touched her cheek, and his tongue softly wisped against the corner of her mouth. He heard the swift intake of breath.

"It's time for us to bid our host a good-night," Will drawled huskily. "I have other plans for us tonight that don't include music and dancing."

As if she were outside herself, Marta Carolina was aware of their standing, taking their leave, and moving toward their lodging. The farther they went the softer the frenzied music became. She felt Will's arm about her, his hand curving warmly around her waist. She heard and cherished all the beautiful endearments he murmured to her as they walked.

Tightly embraced, they stood in the privacy of their room, shut off from every world but theirs. Marta Carolina pushed up on her toes and tilted her head to brush a kiss across Will's lips. As she did, she pulled his shirt from his breeches and ran her hand beneath it, her fingers spreading lightly across his bare chest, the fingertips touching his nipple. She smiled deliberately; she lightly traced circles over the sensitive area until it peaked.

Will guided her to the cushioned couch where they lay down. He kissed her lightly all over the face, and his hand slipped up her skirt to trace the shape of her ankle and the smooth slender leg that curved close to her body.

Marta Carolina luxuriated in the feel of his hand, warm and protective and caressing, against her bare skin. She closed her eyes and squirmed closer. She opened her mouth for the fullness of his possession, but he continued to torment her with a sprinkle of peppering kisses across her brows, down the line of her nose, in the hollow at the top of her mouth.

All the while his hand followed the course of her leg upward to her hip, across her belly. She was naked beneath the material. He had known it, but something about discovering it through touch exhilarated him. His hand stopped its moving and rested on her abdomen. Marta Carolina laid her hand against his face and when she would have deepened the kiss, he pulled away, turning his lips to her fingers.

He nibbled the tip. "You taste good," he said, his face cast in silver relief against the shadowed room. Beneath her skirt his hand drifted down, over the supple lines of her hips, down the outer edge of her thigh.

Involuntarily she sucked in her breath.

Will's knuckles lightly grazed the inner curve of her thighs. An uncontrollable shudder of sheer ecstatic anticipation racked her body. She reached for the drawstring on his breeches.

"No, *querida*," he said, his voice thick with passion, commanding, completely spellbinding, "I shall make love to you tonight." He stood and shed his clothes. "I will give to you."

"What shall I give you?" she whispered when he returned to the couch and undressed her.

The buckskin slithered to the floor. "Your taking me shall be your giving," he replied as he ran his tongue along the exposed surface of her inner arm.

Marta Carolina melted into his quiet, masterful touch. Beneath her skirt his hand massaged the tightening muscles of her belly, pushing gently against the pressures of anticipation that were beginning to build inside her.

His hand drifted down, brushing with the gentlest of caresses against the apex of her thighs. He laid his head on her breast where he listened to the heavy thudding of her heart and felt her shallow, contained breathing.

Marta Carolina arched her back and lifted a hand to curve it around Will's neck. She was drifting on a tide of wonder, loving him, needing him, completely inundated by him. In such a short period of time, he had become her entire life. The Indians thought she had great magic, but she knew differently. Will possessed magic, and she was helplessly bound in the spell he wove so artfully about her.

Although she was inexperienced, Marta Carolina felt the natural responses of her body to Will's loving ministrations. Eyes open, propped so that he was leaning over her, he looked into her face. Her hand drifted up his neck to his cheek to his lips. His mouth opened and took the tip of her finger, as his finger slid into the dewy, moist lower cavity of her body.

As he caressed her, his lips and his tongue played with her finger. She caught her breath. He took the second finger into his mouth, sucking, teasing; the second entered her lower body, withdrew, entered again slowly, deliberately. So gentle was his caress that she opened to him. The twisting knot of need within her tightened to a painful intensity.

He removed his hand, lifted himself above her, and slowly entered. She let him guide her to the rhythm he created, to bring her to the trembling edge of fulfillment and hold her there for one brief shimmering moment before he stilled her and let the tide recede only to build it again, each time more powerful than before. She let him guide her to his rhythm until her body could endure the torment no longer, until it clamored for complete fulfillment.

Her hands circled his shoulders, and her fingers dug into the tensed muscle. She arched and begged for his heated thrusts. Then she drew in her breath, clutched him tightly, and gasped as she exploded into a million fragments, only to be put back together unscarred when she felt him tense and release himself in her.

Entr'acte

His golden hair cut short, his beard trimmed, Captain Ignacio Tello moved through the bustling port city of Havana, Cuba. His gray eyes were the color of sunlight sparkling on the blade of a sharp, superbly crafted sword. They were as alert and ready for action; they were as deadly. His lips curved into a smile that did little to erase the harsh and chiseled facial features. The tilt of his head suggested self-assurance, arrogance . . . even defiance.

Though dressed fashionably in a rich blend of honeys and grays, he refused the padding and whale bone that restricted natural movement. He chose rather to let his splendid phsyique, honed and muscled from long days at sea, complement his clothing. He wore small neck and sleeve ruffs, but they didn't diminish his masculinity; rather their softness accented his hardness. His dark cloak swirled from his broad shoulders around long, lean legs, that were all muscle and covered in thigh-high boots, polished to a high shine.

He stopped in front of a large two-story house, constructed of a white cement-looking mixture. This was the place, he thought. He lifted the black metal bar, slid it open, and walked through the ornate iron gate up the walkway to the veranda. His hands, covered in elegant and expensive gauntlet gloves, balled into a tight fist, and he knocked on the door soon to be partially opened by an Indian slave, a man whom the captain judged to be in his late sixties.

"Is this the residence of Rodrigo Fernandez?" Tello asked.

The slave nodded, but he didn't open the door or invite the stranger in. In silence he waited.

"Would you please announce Ignacio Tello recently arrived in Havana aboard the *San Pablo?*"

The old man opened the door and gestured the captain into the receiving room. "Wait here, please." Then he disappeared through a door to the left. When he returned, the stranger was standing in front of a large portrait of a beautiful woman that hung on the wall above the fireplace.

"Señor Rodrigo will see you now."

Tello nodded his acknowledgment, but he didn't move his gaze from the painting. "She's beautiful," he murmured.

"Yes, sir—" the old man shuffled nearer, and love softened his voice, "she is indeed beautiful." He chuckled indulgently. "But she is a spitfire, that one."

"Yes," Tello muttered, looking at the fiery black hair and the equally black eyes, so alive, so vital, "she would have to be." He studied her image longer before he asked, "Who is she?"

"El Señor's young sister," the slave answered.

"Does el señor's young sister have a name?" Tello asked.

"Yes, sir, she has a name!" The soft, husky answer—definitely feminine in gender—came from behind.

Tello spun so quickly, his cloak rustled as it swirled about. His gaze was deliberately caught and held by ebony eyes, eyes in which devilment and audacity blatantly romped.

"Alejandra." The full lips curved into a provocative smile. "And does the befuddled man standing in front of el señor's young sister have a name?"

Tello stared at her for a long time, as blatant as she in his perusal, and made no secret of his appreciation of her beauty. So decorously dressed, he thought. Outwardly so cold and formal, so subdued. The mass of thick black waves was combed in a bouffant upsweep of curls, cast about with strands of pearls and lacework. She was covered from neck to toe in black velvet and elegant white ruffs.

Yet he could see that she was all fire and spirit. Her hands, escaping the long-sleeved dress and resting against the somber background of the dark skirt, were a beautiful contrast; they were smooth and white, her fingers slender. Two curls defied the pins and combs to wisp her temples. The black bodice, as if on purpose, accented, rather than hid, the shape of her breasts and her tiny waist.

Finally Tello returned her smile, a slow, devastating smile. "The man is not befuddled, madam. He is dazzled by your beauty. And yes, he does have a name." With a flourish he bowed low, the courtier, the aristocrat. "Ignacio Tello at your service."

He took her hand in his and grazed his lips over the top knuckles; the gesture was totally within the bounds of propriety but the added pleasure of his tongue rasping across her flesh was sensual wantonness. He chuckled to himself when he heard the soft intake of breath and felt her slight tremble.

"At my sister's service, sir?" came the blazing rebuke from Rodrigo Fernandez who stood in the door between his office and the receiving salon.

Tello straightened, but he didn't immediately release Alejandra's hand. He held it a moment longer than decorum allowed. More was necessary to chastise Ignacio Tello than the outrage of a brother.

Bowing her head modestly, lowering thick sultry lashes over laughing eyes, Alejandra withdrew her hand. "Pray excuse me, Captain Tello, I have duties to which I must attend."

Tello watched her walk into another room; he heard the swish of material as she moved; he smelled the elusive scent of her perfume—a wild, heady fragrance that belonged entirely to her.

When the door closed behind her, Tello turned to her brother. Without appearing to do so, he studied the other man, a good ten years older than himself, he judged. Black, close-cropped hair and a rare stiletto beard, not a spade beard as so many men sported. Eyes as black as his beard.

"Rodrigo Fernandez?"

"Yes. What may I do for you, sir?"

Tello motioned toward the room from which his host had entered the salon. "May we talk in private?"

Rodrigo nodded and led the way into a large pleasant room with two windows, their shutters flung open to allow the afternoon sunshine to warm and brighten the study. The walls were paneled with an expensive, imported wood.

"Won't you be seated," Rodrigo invited, his hand indicating the two chairs that set in front of a large, darkened fireplace. He didn't stop moving himself until he stood in front of the table on the far side of the room. He poured two glasses of wine. The one he carried to Tello, the other he sipped.

"Ignacio Tello? You wished to see me?" the slight inflection of his voice created the question more than what he said.

"Excellent wine, sir," Tello replied, lowering his glass.

"Thank you, Captain." Rodrigo smiled, no emotion in the gesture. "But I'm sure you didn't come all the way to Havana to discuss the merits of my wine cellar."

"No, sir," Tello replied, "I did not."

"If you do not mind my asking," Rodrigo said, "I should like to see your papers, Captain."

"By all means." Tello reached into his doublet and withdrew the small case.

Rodrigo watched the captain as he untied the leather strings, opened the case, and extracted the papers. He set his glass on the nearby table, reached for the documents, and taking them, he rose. He unfolded them as he walked to the window where he read them; then he studied them.

"They seem to be authentic to me," he finally murmured. "I can detect no forgery."

"No, they are not forged," Tello said, "and they are most authentic."

Rodrigo returned the documents to the captain. Still he was puzzled. Tello was not what he seemed to be.

"You have an accent," he said. "Where did you learn to speak Spanish?"

"In England."

"How came you to be in England?" Rodrigo asked. He

had been involved in political intrigue long enough to detect the facades behind which people hid. Generally he could expose them if given time. Hadn't he exposed the renowned El Desafiador?

"Because, sir, that is where my mother decided to give birth to me. I had no voice in the matter. In fear of the Englishmen, my parents anglicized our name and reared me to be English. Later I joined Sir Anthony Chadwick and became a privateer in the service of England. But, alas, we met a better seaman than he was, sir, and we were captured by the Spaniards."

Rodrigo's eyes crinkled with laughter.

"For eighteen months I served as a galley slave on a ship belonging to Don Pedro Avilar. When he learned the true nature of my background, sir, he made me to see the error of my ways. I returned to my family name, and he taught me Spanish—both to read and write—and he it is who helped me get fitted out in my own ship."

Through narrowed eyes, Rodrigo studied for a long minute. The gray eyes were open, no deceit or guile to be found in them; the hand steady—no guilty conscience; the explanation so farfetched as to be real. It would take time, but the story could also be authenticated.

"Then, sir," he finally said, "you have me at a disadvantage. I cannot begin to guess why you wished to speak privately to me."

"I solicit your help, sir."

Rodrigo shrugged his shoulders and lifted his hands in a helplessness. "Tell me your need, sir, and if I can be of help, then so be it."

"Since the winter of 1586, I have been hunting a man."

Perspiration beaded in Rodrigo's hand, but he held it

steady as he reached for his wine. A master at disguise and deceit, he lifted the glass to his lips. He sipped the tasteless liquid; he swallowed.

"This man killed my betrothed and her father."

Rodrigo set the glass down. "Where did this murder take place, Captain?"

"At the Boar's Head Tavern in Dover, England. The man was Henry Smyth, the young woman was Betsy, his daughter."

"Why were the man and his daughter murdered?" Rodrigo asked. Nothing about his demeanor betrayed his inner turmoil. He looked directly into Tello's eyes; his hands were steady; his voice calm, assured.

"I do not know," Tello replied as he watched Rodrigo rise. "But I do know who killed them."

Rodrigo stood behind his desk now. He felt safer. He could reach for his sword or the knife that lay in the opened drawer. "Pray, sir, finish your story. Tell me who murdered the good man and his daughter."

"El Desafiador."

"Do you know who this El Desafiador is?"

"I do."

His game of intrigue was over. A line of sweat broke out over his upper lip. "Need I ask who, Captain?"

Tello's hand rested on the hilt of his sword. "I don't mind telling you." He paused for a poignant moment. "'Tis Will'am Dare."

Rodrigo's aplomb broke. He reached up and nervously wiped the sweat from his upper lips, blinking in surprise. "Will'am Dare," he repeated unnecessarily. What kind of game was this man playing?

Tello moved to the desk to face Rodrigo. "I am going to lay my life in your hands." He reached into his doublet, withdrew the leather case, and dropped it on the desk. "I am Timothy Turner of England. I captured the *San Pablo*, killed the crew, stole the papers, and am impersonating the officer, Captain Ignacio Tello."

"Why?" Rodrigo's voice cracked at the edge. Never had he played the game with one such as Timothy Turner—so cold; no emotion but hatred. Rodrigo wasn't sure where he stood; he wasn't even sure what game they were playing.

"I want the son of a bitch who killed Betsy," Timothy's gray eyes were steely and full of hate. "I want to kill him with my own bare hands."

Rodrigo looked at Timothy's calloused hands; they were strong and powerful. He felt them bind his throat and cut off his air.

"I know where El Desafiador is, and I know where you can capture him."

"El Desafiador is Spanish," Rodrigo said. "Why—" he cleared his throat "—why would I wish to go against one of my own?"

"I have heard that you are a pensionary for the queen of England." Rodrigo said nothing. "If you are, the capture of such a one as El Desafiador would bring you a handsome sum from Her Majesty."

Timothy turned from Rodrigo and walked to the table to pour himself a second glass of wine. With an indolent ease which Rodrigo Fernandez was coming to despise, the Englishman raised the glass to his lips and drained the glass. Only then did he turn around.

"You have the documents which give me my identity, sir. Do with them what you will. As for me, I'm leaving." Only the clip of his boots on the wooden floor broke the silence in the room. His hand caught the door handle.

Before he could exit, however, Rodrigo spoke. "Señor Turner, please return and get your documents of identification. As long as you stay in Havana, you will need your papers. Only Spaniards are allowed port in this corridor." He added, "I will be most happy to assist you in the capture of the Spanish spy. Sit down and tell me what you know about him."

Rodrigo smiled to himself. Had he planned the capture of El Desafiador himself, he couldn't have planned it this well. An Englishman would commit the murder. Afterward he, Rodrigo Fernandez, would capture Timothy Turner and his crew and have them executed as pirates, and no one would be the wiser. He could continue his double role. The world would know only what he wanted it to know: El Desfiador, the Spanish spy, the English traitor, was killed by one of his own countrymen.

As Turner had pointed out, the capture of this man would bring him a handsome sum from the English treasury and the complete trust of the queen herself. No one would doubt his loyalty to the English throne. He would be more important to Elizabeth than her beloved, the deceased Sir James Palmer. Oh, yes! Sir James Palmer was forever dead, and what a death he had died! That, too, had been planned and executed by Rodrigo Fernandez! What a stroke of genius!

Now with Will'am Dare finally dead, Rodrigo would be in a position to carry out the assassination plot that had been staged for nearly two years—every little detail planned to the smallest degree. The Invincible Armada had not been invincible after all. It had failed, but he would not. That stupid woman would not long be on the throne. By his ingenuity she would cease to be a thorn in Phillip's side. Then he—Rodrigo Fernandez—would be rewarded for services rendered the Crown. Riches. Titles. Land Grants. Who knew? He might be of service to the new monarch in England!

The capture of this man would also give him a peace of mind he hadn't had for the past two years. With Will'am Dare dead, he could quit looking over his shoulder; he could stop jumping at every shadow. He would be a free man.

After Timothy left the Fernandez residence, Rodrigo sat down at his desk, picked up quill and paper, and began to write. When he finished his letters, he lifted the papers and fanned them through the air until the ink was dry. A strange smile hovering on his lips, he folded each and sealed it.

"Rodrigo—"

He turned at his sister's voice.

"Who was our visitor?"

Careful never to let Alejandra know the double life he lived, Rodrigo smiled. "A mere captain, my dear, who has some goods to deliver to us from Spain."

"He is handsome," she murmured.

"And most certainly not the man for a beautiful young woman such as you," Rodrigo returned. "He is a married man."

"No," she cried, remembering the touch of his lips on her hand. "No, he is not."

Rodrigo lifted the leather packet. "Here are his papers, little one. You may look at them yourself. Your Captain Ignacio Tello is indeed a married man." At her crestfallen expression, he softly soothed. "I'm sorry."

"I am, too," she murmured. "I thought perhaps I should have fun in Havana after all."

"You shall, my young beauty," Rodrigo promised.

350

"You shall. Now run along while I attend business."

As soon as Alejandra left the room, Rodrigo called his house slave. "Julio."

The door opened, and the old man entered.

Rodrigo handed him a letter. "Deliver this one to Don Diego, and wait for a reply. This one—" he held up the second letter "—is to be dispatched to St. Augustine on the next ship to sail." He smiled at Julio and flipped him a coin. "You shall have another when you return with the reply from Don Diego and the receipt from the ship's pilot."

Chapter XV

Despite winter's approach, the climate in the South-land was enjoyable. Coats were used only at night when, without the warmth of the sun, the temperatures plunged. A large burden basket on her back, secured with shoulders straps and a trump line across her forehead, Marta Carolina was exhausted by the time Silver Bow raised his hand to indicate they were stopping for the night. As was his custom, he and his braves scouted ahead while Wise Owl and the Chicorans set up camp. Feeling as if she couldn't pick up one foot to put in front of the other, Marta Carolina stumbled to the river, shrugged out of the binding straps, and set her basket on the ground.

"I think you should have kept that horse," she muttered wearily to Will as she brushed hair out of her eyes. "You won him fair."

"Aye, love," he said, lowering his basket to the ground and sprawling beneath the shade of a tree. A grin lit his face when he remembered the wrestling match with Strong Bear. "So I did. But now we have won the everlasting friendship of the Chicorans, Strong Bear is indebted to us, and if we had entered St. Augustine with a horse, think how much more explaining we would be doing. We have enough half-truths and lies to remember as it is without having to hide something. And speaking of that, sweetheart," Will said, squirming out of the blaze of the afternoon sunlight into the shade, "from now on you should call me Guillermo. I don't want you to make a mistake in front of the Spaniards." Having gained his second wind, Will was on his feet again and off into the woods. Over his shoulder he said, "Wise Owl, I'm going to gather the firewood. Watch Marta Carolina." To her he added, "Don't you stray from the camp."

He didn't have to worry about her going anywhere, Marta Carolina thought as she greedily lapped the cool river water from her hand. She had a camp to set up. She cupped her hands and dipped the cool, refreshing water in her hands to wash her face; then she sprinkled it on her neck and shoulders. Afterward she moved to the center of the clearing and began to prepare the evening meal. By the time she had located enough stones to circle the cooking pit, Will returned, his arms loaded with wood. Kneeling beside her, he helped build the fire.

"Did Silver Bow say how much longer before we reach the fort?" she asked.

"Tomorrow morning."

"Tomorrow morning!" Marta Carolina exclaimed, her head jerking up as she cast accusing eyes on Will. "If we're that close, why did we stop tonight? Why not go on to the fort?"

"Silver Bow said the fort is patrolled by soldiers with bloodhounds. He felt that it would be safer for us to arrive in the morning; the Spaniards would be less skittish and less likely to release the dogs on us. Also Silver Bow has sent word to them that we're arriving on the morrow. This way they will have time to prepare for your coming." The fire blazing, he leaned back and looked at Marta Carolina, a smile pulling his lips as he reached over to pick a twig out of her hair and wipe a smear of dirt from her face. "And I think you need time to prepare for them."

Marta Carolina lifted her hand and laid it over Will's, pressing his calloused palm against the softness of her cheek. As always the most innocent of touches, generated by the most innocent of motives, turned into intimate caresses where Will and Marta Carolina were concerned. Since they had left Chicora their lovemaking had become urgent, almost desperate, as if each feared this would be the last time for them. At night Marta Carolina would stay sleep after they made love, so she could savor a few more waking minutes with Will. They didn't necessarily talk; they simply held each other.

"I love you." The amusement in his eyes was replaced with an emotion so intense, Marta Carolina was overwhelmed. She inhaled sharply. "Remember that," he whispered, swaying toward her, "I love you."

His hands caught her shoulders and drew her against his chest. His mouth came down on hers in a deep, leisurely kiss, the mere touch flashing through her to ignite the embers of desire into flames that licked her insides until she blazed with all the fury of a fire out of control. The kiss turned into kisses, and soon their hands joined in the sensual plunder, igniting brushfires of passion all over their bodies. She had never felt such heat before; she was burning up.

Marta Carolina was lying on her back, Will leaning

over her, braced on both palms, a hand on either side of her head. Her arms wrapped around his waist, and she pressed a kiss to the pulse that beat in his throat. Her tongue lingered to lick the moisture from his skin. The whisper-soft touch sent a shudder through him and drew a low, hungry groan.

Exhilarated, Marta Carolina laughed softly. Her hands traveled over him warmly, like the gentle touch of sunshine on a cold winter day. Fleetingly she touched the strong, sinewy muscles of his chest, the firm curve of his buttocks, the rock-hard strength of his thighs. Her mouth feathered along the chiseled line of his jaw and traced the sensual curve of his mouth with agonizing slowness as her hand pulled his shirt from his breeches and touched the sensitive area around his navel. The tight muscles of his abdomen jumped beneath her fingers.

Everywhere she touched him, Will burned. Like a slow moving blaze, she seared him with her sweetness and passion, until he thought he would die from wanting her. When her hands slipped into his breeches and closed around him gently, the fire in him almost raged out of control. He sucked in his breath and caught her hand in his.

"Nay, *querida*," he rasped in a thick voice. "Although the Indians are an open-minded people, love, and have no inhibitions about married couples making love in public, I have no inclination to do so in front of them."

Marta Carolina grinned and turned her head to look at the Chicoran braves who set up camp and who seemed totally oblivious to her and Will. They acted as if the two of them did not exist.

"And do you have an inclination to make love to me?"

she whispered, her eyes returning to his face.

He nodded. "I have that inclination, my darling—not just at this moment but all the time. I never have enough of you."

She extracted her hand from his and touched his face, enjoying the feel of the late afternoon whisker bristle beneath the soft pads of her fingers. "Then, Guillermo Lucero, make love to me."

The way she could make the mere sound of his name a caress thrilled Will; the feel of her hands on his face delighted him. In fact, he could think of nothing he didn't enjoy about her. But he was also extremely worried and had been ever since they left Chicora. Ever since her shipwreck, Marta Carolina had been living in a new environment, one that was at variance with the staid conformity of her upbringing. He did not doubt the sincerity of her feelings, but he wondered if she were not in love with the idea of love.

He was the hero who had rescued her from the hostile Indians who first captured her; he had challenged and fought Strong Bear for her. He was the first man to push aside the veil of childhood and touch the woman beneath. He was the first to make her aware of her womanhood; he was her first lover. He was her only link with civilization as she knew it.

How would she feel about him once they reached her people in St. Augustine? He lowered his face, his lips softly brushing hers. How puny had been his feelings for Ellen, compared to what he felt for Marta Carolina. For him she was the love of a lifetime, his first, his last love. But what was he to her? Would civilization reveal to her how primitive he really was? How much like the American natives he was?

"Too much is between us," Marta Carolina softly complained.

As if she had struck him, Will pushed up. His wounded soul showing in his eyes, he stared at her.

Unaware of his thoughts, her eyes on his chest, Marta Carolina giggled, her hands busy with the laces on his buckskin shirt. "We need to take off these clothes."

Will didn't realize he had been holding his breath until he released it. He feared that somehow she had read his mind; that somehow she had answered his fears. So much was between them—that he didn't dare tell her—that she had a right to know.

"And since you do not wish to make love to me in front of the Indians, we need to find a private place." She levered up on her elbows to plant tiny, fiery kisses on the small triangle of hair-matted chest that she had revealed with the unlacing of his shirt. Her face reddened as she added on a lower note, "Even though they know what we're doing."

Will laughed and stood, holding his hands down to her. "Then, *querida*, let us find some privacy." Easily he swung her to her feet and stood looking at her. "We shall make love, and afterward bathe while we still have sunshine for warmth."

"How do you know the sun will still be shining when we get through making love?" Marta Carolina parried. "How do you know what I'm going to do for you—" her eyes turned midnight-blue "—to you."

Again her innocent teasing caught Will off guard. "I don't," he finally replied, a warmth slowly oozing throughout his entire body, taking residence in his groin.

A basket over his shoulders with their clean clothes, blanket, and washing paraphernalia, Will searched for a

357

secluded spot on the river, one that was exposed to the warmth of the sun but was hidden from man's peering eyes. While Marta Carolina spread the blanket, Will carried the basket to the water's edge and set it down.

Their gazes locked, they began to undress, slowly at first, then more quickly as their desire mounted. Clothes fell at their feet. When they were naked, Marta Carolina ran to Will and threw herself into his arms, both of them splashing into the river. They gasped as the cold water swallowed them, but soon they were so caught up in the fervor of their love they failed to notice the temperature. Under they swirled, their mouths together in a hot, sensuous kiss, their arms wrapped around each other.

Down, down they went, and neither wanted to ever surface again, but somehow without either knowing it, they burst through the sparkling film of water. Their kiss broke at the same time; they gulped in the air, laughed, choked, and gasped again. Treading water, Will held onto her.

"You are no longer afraid of the water, *querida?*"

Marta Carolina shook her head. "That night White Blossom pushed me into the river, I conquered my fear once and for all. Besides," she added, "how can I be afraid when you're here to hold me?"

"I'll be here to hold you the rest of my life," he promised as they exchanged a gaze of pure, blatant desire.

Will's heart was thundering. Marta Carolina made him feel new. His feelings for her completely eradicated reasoning; they gave him faith in the future. For so long he'd cared for nothing but revenge and retribution. Now his thoughts turned to home, to a family.

He slipped beneath the water, his hands moving over her breasts down to her hips, his lips tracing a blazing path from her abdomen to her navel. His tongue tormented her, and he delighted in the convulsive shudder of her stomach muscles. Then he left her. His head emerged, and he drew in a deep gulp of air. Using his powerful legs, he propelled both of them to the shallows.

Once there, in water that barely covered them, Will began to make love to her in earnest. His lips on hers, his tongue gently caressed and his hands tenderly mapped the sensitive planes and curves of her body. The terrain explored, he set out to possess. Tentative softness turned into urgency. He plundered her mouth as his hands plundered and ravaged her body, but still he didn't claim her. Although she begged for the final touch, she begged for his entry, he stalled the ultimate moment. With his hands, his tongue, he worked her up to the brink of insanity, to that moment of desire when she thought she would burst into a million fragments, but he would always stop short of fulfillment.

Sweetly again; softly again. He lapped at her; the water lapped at her, both lulling her into an euphoric state where nothing mattered but her and Will. When he was gone from between her legs, she felt the rise and fall of the water, cold at times, warm at others, but brushing against the part of her that was on fire for Will, tempting her, tormenting her, but never putting out the fire his touch generated.

Then Marta Carolina could stand no more; she wanted him. She ached for him. She was almost nauseous with wanting. Her hand slipped down the wet sleekness of his body to find the protuberant muscle. Her fingers closed around it, and she measured out loving torment in kind. She stroked him to the point of total surrender. She listened as he begged her hands and mouth to love him to completeness, but she refused the request. Again and again she pushed him to the same brink of insanity. And then she spread her legs, her inner self moist and ready. She moved so that she was over him; she lowered herself and took him in her body, slowly, fully.

"Oh, God," Will murmured deliriously, his hands cupping her buttocks, but he was so weak, so debilitated he could hardly hold onto her.

Marta Carolina was an aggressive lover; she was beyond the point of tender forays. Now she wanted that complete satisfaction that comes with an urgency that nears desperation, a hurt that is wonderful because its the pain of need and want about to be quenched. Sure in her ability to carry both of them to a climax, she moved herself with powerful swift strokes, taking all of him.

Marta Carolina felt him tremble. Then she felt his hands dig into her buttocks as he pulled her down on him and thrust upward. She heard his deep intake of air, then the primeval groan of release. His body jerked convulsively against hers, and he pressed his face into her shoulder. He held her locked into timeless suspension as he released all his body issue into her.

Knowing she had not reached the summit for which she labored, Will adroitly turned so that he was on top, and his bigness still throbbing inside her, he began to move. His head lowered, his mouth captured one of her breasts, and he sucked. Bolts of desire streaked through Marta Carolina's body, flashing from her breasts to the seat of her femininity.

His hands caressed her buttocks, tracing the fine line, pushing her up higher and higher. He felt her tense; he heard that first moan of ecstasy. His lips left her breast and settled on *her* lips. His tongue filled her mouth as he made that final deep lunge that carried her to the consummate fulfillment. She moaned and pulled him against her, spiritually locking them together for all time.

Later they bathed each other; they washed each other's hair. They dried off, but they didn't immediately re-dress. They lay on one blanket and snuggled under another to ward off the late afternoon chill. This was a time neither of them would ever forget. No matter what the future held, this night would stay forever in their memories.

"What shall I wear tomorrow?" she murmured, not really caring.

Will chuckled. How like a woman to think of what she would wear when they had so many important matters which they needed to discuss. "One of your dresses," he replied.

Oddly the answer jarred him from the warm cocoon which he and Marta Carolina shared. He knew they had just closed the door on one of the most beautiful parts of their lives, one of the most idyllic. At the same time they had opened the door to another. He was unaware of himself in this world; he didn't know what her reaction would be to the Will'am Dare of civilization. Could she love him as much as she loved the primitive?

"All I have are Sister Maria Theresa's habits," she replied. "When the pirates put us overboard, they thought both of us to be nuns and they allowed us only one chest. So I have only habits in the chest and my medicine cabinet and recipes." She sighed. "How I would long to wear a beautiful gown again."

"I would love to see you attired in such, sweetheart," he said, "but I am also a selfish man. I would love to hide your beauty from the soldiers at St. Augustine." His arms tightened about her to communicate his inner fear—his fear of losing her once they reached the fort.

"It's going to be different, isn't it?" Marta Carolina asked in a small voice.

"Yes, my darling," he replied, "it's going to be different. Also it will be difficult." Will had lived in a world of intrigue that was held together with lies and deceit for so long he had mastered it. He had never grown accustomed to his role, nor had he even liked it most of the time, but for his country, for his queen no sacrifice had been too great.

"You will have to be on edge continually, weighing everything you say. Tell the truth as much as possible, but once you've told a lie, you must remember it. Always think of us as living in a viper's nest, for in one nest you will find hundreds of vipers ready to sting you to death. Each lie we tell spawns another, and at any time they may turn on you, release their venom, and kill you. You must repeat your story about me until you have it memorized, until you can say it backward as well as forward. Most of all, my darling, you must learn to discipline your expressions and control your spontaneous reactions to other people's remarks. These will give you away quicker than your deceitful words."

"I do not fear for myself," Marta Carolina told him. "I fear for you, my love. I don't know what I should do if the Spaniards should learn that you were English."

"If they should find out," Will said, sitting up, the blanket sliding down his shoulders, "you must pretend ignorance." He solemnly gazed into her face. "If they should learn that you know who I am, your life will be in jeopardy, my love."

"But we're—aren't we going to tell them that you

escaped from the ship with me?"

Will shook his head. "Nay, lass, I think not. I have been mulling that over since we left Chicora. I think it would be prudent to tell the Spaniards a tale that is as nearly true as possible. We shall tell them that I, a shipwrecked countryman had escaped from the Indians who were holding me captive, and was making my way to St. Augustine, when I rescued you. Because you had no alternative, you were forced to travel with me."

"I have never practiced deceit," Marta Carolina said, "and I don't enjoy it now. Telling lies to save your life is a necessity I gladly bear. But this story makes me less than honorable." Her blue eyes were dull with pain. "I can share none of the blame."

Will's hand tightened on her shoulder, his fingers biting into her tender flesh. Her love was the only unblemished thing in his life. From the moment he had rescued her, he had planned to use her and had schemed to get her cooperation. Ironically he had not had to rely on any deceit or trickery. She had fallen in love with him and had willingly given him what he wanted before he ever asked it of her—her life, her love, her safety . . . everything of value.

"I could not bear it, sweetheart—" his voice was an anguished whisper "—if anything happened to you because of me. I can't have the added burden of worrying about your safety as well as mine."

"You have no cause to be worried," she soothed, turning so that she was looking directly into the ruggedly handsome face that was only inches above her. "Even should you tell them your story, they would not be harsh with you, Guillermo. You are Spanish, and—"

"No, *querida,* only half Spanish and that by accident of

363

birth," he interrupted her. "I speak Spanish, and I was educated by a Jesuit priest and spent many of my formative years in the Netherlands, but my allegiance is to England and to my queen. As such I am considered a threat to the Crown of Spain."

"There is so much about yourself that you have not told me," she said.

"So much," he agreed. "And for your safety I shall keep it to myself."

Her palm touched his cheek; her fingers spread into his temples. "You love me that much."

Tears sparkled in his eyes. He turned his head so that his lips brushed against her hand. "I love you so much more than that, little one. Simply stated, you are my life. When I thought you were dead, I realized that I had no reason for living. None whatsoever."

Marta Carolina lifted the blanket and dropped it over both of them. Then she wrapped her arms protectively around Will and pulled him into the warmth of her love.

Afterward, without eating any supper, they fell into a deep, sated sleep. For the moment their anxieties were pushed aside. Tomorrow would come soon enough. For now they could hold on to each other.

Will felt the light touch on his shoulder, and he heard the soft call, so low at first he couldn't recognize the voice. Again he heard, "Guillermo," and he knew it was Silver Bow. Will was instantly awake and alert; his eyes opened. He was amazed at how quietly the Indian could move through the forest, his girdle making no sound whatsoever unless he wished it to do so.

"I would talk with you."

Will gently untangled his arms and legs from Marta Carolina and slipped from beneath the blanket. Hurriedly he put on his clothes, adding a jacket to ward off the night chill, and followed the tall warrior to the fire which still blazed.

"Soon the dawn comes," Silver Bow said, his face on the bluish gray lines that broke the black mural of night. "Our journey will be over. Before the sun reaches the top of the sky, we shall be at the Spanish fort."

"Have you slept at all?" Will asked.

Silver Bow shook his head. "I traveled many miles, my paleface friend, retracing our trail. We were followed; of that I'm sure, but I don't know why or who." His head swiveled and he stared across the fire at Will. "Whoever follows our path is an excellent scout; he has hidden his trail well."

"Or her perhaps," Will suggested, thinking of White Blossom.

"A warrior of great skill," Silver Bow answered.

Although Silver Bow never showed his exhaustion, Will could hear it in his voice. "Lie down and sleep awhile," he suggested. "I'll keep watch until the camp awakens."

Silver Bow nodded, rose, and moved away from the fire. As soon as he spread his blanket, he lay down and rolled up, asleep almost immediately.

Will stoked the fire, then moved into the shadows of the forest where he could see all the travelers. Every once in a while he would look at the horizon and the coming of the new day. A new day that was going to bring irrevocable changes into his life.

He was a step closer to apprehending Rodrigo Fernandez, a day closer to stopping the assassination plot on Her Majesty's life. So close was revenge, so near was retribution! He could smell its fragrant blossom. Soon he would taste its sweetness.

But ironically the closer he came to Rodrigo Fernandez, the closer he was to losing Marta Carolina. He had to be so careful when he explained his part in the death of her aunt. Not that he was guilty, but because he had trusted Rodrigo Fernandez, Dona Karolina Lucas de Santiago—also known as Santica—had been apprehended and executed. Will wished he could confess everything to Marta Carolina now, but he couldn't take the risk of her saying something that would give him away. He couldn't risk her knowing too much about him. He wouldn't risk her coming to hate him. Ensnared in deceit, he could do nothing but keep his silence and hope his confession did not come too late.

When morning's light came, he returned to the fire and began the morning meal. By the time the camp first stirred, he had the leftover bowl of cornmeal mush warming and filleted fish cooking on the heated stones. As if everyone understood the importance of this day, silence prevailed. Without being told, each assumed his responsibility. Time came to leave. Following Silver Bow, the small group began the last phase of their journey. They marched over the last incline into the valley.

Silver Bow pointed. "There is the fort."

Marta Carolina, wearing one of the loose, flax dresses of the Chicorans, stared in the direction the Timucuan chief pointed. St. Augustine—the settlement that was to have been the first port of call for her trip to Mexico. How much she had changed since that fateful day when she was washed ashore in the New World.

Will brushed her shoulder as he moved to her side, and

together they watched the soldiers, mounted on their horses, move out of the garrison. Beside them loped packs of bloodhounds on leashes.

"They are taking no chances," Marta Carolina murmured, fear chasing goose bumps over her body.

Closer came the soldiers, and the tension grew. Finally the presiding officer halted his steed in front of them. His eyes narrowed, and he studied the group.

"I have brought you the woman black robe and the paleface soldier," Silver Bow said in his fluent Spanish. "You have brought the knives and tomahawks which you promised my people."

Marta Carolina stiffened. She did not understand the ways of the Indians. She felt as though she and Will had been betrayed by this strange man.

The officer nodded his head and waved his arm. A soldier rode forward, bringing a pack horse with him.

"Those are yours, Chief Silver Bow. You may examine them. If they meet with your approval, take them and leave. I relieve you of your duty; I will escort my guests into St. Augustine."

The officer dismounted, but he didn't watch as Silver Bow went through the weapons and implements. Rather he stared at Marta Carolina, then Will. Both of them were a surprise to him. The woman certainly didn't look like a nun; and the man didn't look like one of those whimpering Englishmen they had been chasing up the coastline.

When the Timucuan was through with his inspection, he nodded to the Spanish officer. "You have kept your word. I accept them." He spoke in the Timucuan dialect, and his braves, single-file, moved out behind him. Soon they were lost in the thick forest.

Only then did the lieutenant walk to Marta Carolina He bowed low and reached for the hand which she extended. His lips, cold and distant, brushed over her skin.

"I am so glad that you have arrived, good Sister. Since we learned of your captivity, we have been concerned about your safety."

"Thank you, kind sir," Marta Carolina murmured, wishing she could wipe his touch from her hand. "Although you could not know it, your concern was misplaced. The Indians who have given me shelter were most hospitable." She motioned toward Wise Owl, wishing he understood Spanish. "The village chief gave these to me as my personal slaves. Do you mind their traveling to St. Augustine with me?"

"Not at all," the presiding officer answered. Then he said, "How remiss of me. Let me introduce myself. I am Lieutenant Emilio Domingo Bustamante, commander of St. Augustine in the absence of our governor. I'm at your service. I have sent word to the bishop at Havana. As soon as possible, we will transport you directly to him."

"And I, sir, am Dona Marta Carolina Lucas de Santiago."

The lieutenant looked puzzled. "You are not from a convent?"

"I am," Marta Carolina replied, "but I am not a nun."

"But you are wearing the clothing of a holy order," Emilio pointed out.

"That was a necessity," Marta Carolina answered. "Posing as a nun was the only way I could save my life when the corsairs boarded our ship." The lieutenant nodded his head, but Marta Carolina could see many more questions in his eyes. She laughed. "I shall tell you all about my journey. It is a long story indeed." She turned to Will. "Had it not been for him, sir, I would not be alive today."

Emilio's attention turned to Will. "And who are you, sir?"

"I am Guillermo Lucero," Will replied in the finest Castilian accent anyone could boast of. Not a trace of English to give him away.

"You're not going to tell me that you, too, escaped the burning ship, disguised as a nun," the lieutenant said dryly.

"Would you believe me?" Will parried, his eyes never leaving the almost feminine-shaped face.

"No, sir, I would not." No softness in the tone.

"Then, sir, I shall tell you the truth. I was not aboard the ship Mistress Marta Carolina traveled on. I have been in the New World for a long time."

Emilio reached up to stroke his finely pointed beard. "I'm glad you decided on the truth, sir. You see—" he reached into his doublet and extracted a sheet of paper "—when I first heard the rumor that a nun was stranded on the coast of the New World, I doubted the tale. But also I was haunted by the message; therefore, I sent word to His Holiness. In turn, he sent me some information which he had obtained from one of the port officials in Cuba." The paper crackled as he unfolded it. "This is a roster of the people who traveled aboard your ship, madam. Your name, sir, is not on the list."

"How did you get the roster?" Marta Carolina asked, excitement quivering in her voice.

Emilio smiled indulgently. "We captured the corsairs."

"Then you have all my belongings!" she exclaimed.

Now Emilio laughed. "I do not have them, but I'm sure the port officials in Havana do. I shall dispatch a letter as soon as we return to the fort to make an inquiry into your belongings. Before I do so, however, I must have a detailed list and description of all that was taken."

"Yes," Marta Carolina sighed, her face beaming, "I have such a list. Sister Angelica refused to let me travel before I made one."

"Good," the lieutenant replied, rubbing his hands together. "Now let us proceed to St. Augustine. We shall talk over the midday meal; then you shall retire to your rooms for a siesta." He waved his hand through the air, and one of his men led two mounts forward. "I assumed that both of you ride," Emilio said.

The ensign, a fat slovenly man who brought the horses forward, stared at Night Star's pearl and gold necklace that hung around Marta Carolina's neck. He admired its beauty and craftsmanship. Then his gaze swept to an identical necklace around Will's neck. He had heard of the riches of the New World, and many of his friends had tasted it, but not he. Yet, here was evidence that riches did abound even in the land of Florida.

Chapter XVI

"While these are far inferior to your quarters at home," Emilio said as they rode down the muddy street toward church and the second largest building in the small settlement, "these are the best we have to offer you, Mistress Marta Carolina."

"I'm sure they will do fine," Marta Carolina replied dully. She was quite disappointed with St. Augustine. She wasn't sure what she expected, but not this crude, primitive version of Chicora. The flat-roofed buildings were made of tabby—a mixture of lime and mud over wood. Like the Chicorans, the Spaniards had large outdoor, dome-shaped ovens in which they baked.

They dismounted in front of a large rectangular-shaped building. "My residence," Emilio announced when he invited Marta Carolina and Will inside. The soldiers he dismissed to the barracks. As they walked into the long receiving room, a young Indian woman came running.

She was beautiful, Marta Carolina thought. Like Strong Bow, the Timucuan warrior, this woman was tall and tawny-colored. Her thick black hair was coiled into a chignon on the top of her head, but instead of its being held in place by reeds, it was secured with mother-of-pearl combs. She wore European clothing with the exception of cumbersome farthingales and stiff petticoats.

"Provide each of our guests with a woman servant," the lieutenant ordered. "Have their clothes carried to their rooms and unpacked. Also have a warm bath waiting when they arrive. See that Mistress Marta Carolina's Indians are cared for and have a place to stay."

"Yes, sir," the young woman replied. "Anything else?"

Emilio shook his head. "Please serve the midday meal in my study, Anita, and do not let anyone or anything disturb me. I want to enjoy my visit with my guests."

As soon as they were shut up in the study behind the heavy doors, the lieutenant said, "Señorita, I would like for you to give me a detailed recounting of your plight since you left Spain." He poured three glasses of wine, giving one to each of them, and he listened attentively as Marta Carolina told her story, every word the truth, every word having the ring of truth to it.

"And you sailed on board the *El Salvador*," Emilio murmured, rubbing his mustache with his finger.

Marta Carolina nodded, her eyes momentarily shading with sorrow. "Our Savior," she repeated. "Sister Angelica and Sister Maria Theresa thought that was a good omen. Little good it did us when the corsairs boarded our ships and killed everyone."

"You are indeed fortunate," Emilio pronounced, "that Sister Angelica was farsighted enough to have you dress as a nun. Otherwise you would be dead, señorita."

372

Marta Carolina still felt shivers dance across her arms when she thought of her close encounter with death aboard the ship. "What have you done with the corsairs, sir?"

"They have been questioned and hanged," he answered coolly. "English dogs! They deserved to die. Plundering our ships. Taking our wealth and killing our citizens."

"And you think it is possible that my belongings have been salvaged from their vessel?" she asked again, not quite believing her stroke of good fortune.

His eyes twinkling, Emilio said, "I have all ideas you are in for a pleasant surprise. Now let's eat. Afterward, Mistress Marta Carolina, you shall retire to bathe and take your siesta, and your friend and I shall stay and talk." Fear, disappointment—the lieutenant wasn't sure which, but he saw an emotion flicker through those expressive blue eyes. He smiled. "Gentlemen's talk, my dear. Nothing that should interest you."

Later, they gathered for lunch around the small reading table in front of the open window. Marta Carolina could hardly swallow her food. Would she see Will before supper? Would she have time to learn what he had told the lieutenant? Less than two hours at St. Augustine and already the subterfuge was on her nerves! Yet, she remembered Will's advice. They could read her actions and her expressions. She must keep them hidden at all costs.

"The food is marvelous," Marta Carolina said, forcing down bite after bite, forcing herself to indulge in senseless prattle. "I haven't had salt since I've been in the New World."

"A luxury that we have little of," Emilio replied,

running the tip of his fingers through the salt crystals in the small container. "A luxury the Indians do not want," he scoffed. He refilled his glass with wine. "And this," he said, picking up the glass and holding it up so that the light filtered through the rose-colored liquid, "the Indians do not like. They much prefer their water."

Marta Carolina leveled her beautiful eyes on the commander of the garrison and spoke tongue-in-cheek. "The Indians are a primitive people. They do not appreciate the height of civilization from which we come." Even as she uttered the words, Marta Carolina hoped that Night Star would forgive her for telling such a lie. She smiled, her even white teeth dazzling. "May I propose a toast?"

"You may." Emilio was totally enthralled with his guest. All through the meal the two of them talked, she sharing information of the homeland, he drinking it up as thirstily as he drank the wine. "Our governor has petitioned to the king for me, asking that I be allowed to return to Spain to make a report directly to His Majesty. I'm expecting an answer shortly." His voice lowered. "I am so homesick to see Spain, to hear familiar voices, and to be surrounded by friends and family rather than hostile Indians who would just as soon slit your throat or stick you in the back with a knife."

During the entire exchange between the lieutenant and Marta Carolina, Will said nothing. He ate heartily, but he drank sparingly. However, Emilio did not know this. He was so thoroughly immersed in Marta Carolina that he did not see Will pour the wine out the open window directly behind him.

As if he were a snake, Will shed two years of his life as soon as he rode into St. Augustine, sooner than that, as soon as he felt the steed under his body. He was no longer Ca-leb-a-dam-a of the Scupperongacs. He was once again Will'am Dare, special courier of Sir Francis Drake. He was once again the man of many names and faces. He was El Desafiador! He was Guillermo Lucero!

But Will didn't allow himself the luxury of being lost in thought. On guard, ever alert, he listened to all that the presiding officer of St. Augustine was saying to Marta Carolina; he studied the man; he analyzed him. He judged him to be an astute man, a tough, disciplined soldier. Emilio had served in Florida for years. He had pressed the case of Spain with energy and skill. For the greater part of his life he had patrolled the coast of Virginia to the southern tip of the peninsula of Florida. He wrote a description of the entire coast, and used every means at his command to defend the Spanish settlements.

"As you can see, the presidio at St. Augustine and the presidio at Santa Elena are my principal points of defense. I must keep the English and French from settling on our shores. I must keep the corsairs from using our harbors for their ships of plunder." Then as if he rememberd himself, he smiled apologetically. "I'm sorry that I have spent the entire time talking, Mistress Marta Carolina. It is so long since I have had such a lovely audience that I fear I wore you down."

"No," Marta Carolina denied, "all you have told me is so interesting, that I could listen for hours." Inwardly Marta Carolina winced. She was glad Sister Angelica could not hear her giving voice to such lies.

When Emilio lifted the crystal bell and tinkled it twice, the door immediately opened and Anita, a beautiful, young Timucuan Indian, entered the room. "Escort

Mistress Marta Carolina to her room," he ordered.

Anita smiled and nodded as she cast a long, assessing glance at Marta Carolina.

Knowing she could stay no longer, Marta Carolina rose. Graciously she smiled. "What time is supper?"

"At eight o'clock," Emilio informed her.

"I shall see you then."

Bustamante moved around the table and took her hand in his. Again bowing low, his lips grazed hers perfunctorily. His smile was also perfunctory. "Indeed, mistress, you shall see me."

As soon as the double doors closed on the two men, Emilio turned to Will. "Another glass of wine?"

"Please," Will replied. "It has been a long time since I've tasted such wine, sir."

"How long exactly?" the officer asked, his eyes fixed on the red wine that splashed into the glass.

"Two years," Will replied.

"And the vessel on which you were sailing," Bustamante asked, "what was she christened?"

"The *Santa Maria*," Will replied easily.

He knew in a few months that Emilio could have this information checked out, but Will felt no pressure. Every other vessel that sailed from a Spanish port was named after the Virgin; therefore, in 1586 when his ship was supposed to have wrecked, he was relatively sure several had sailed for the New World. By the time Emilio could have his story authenticated, Will would have accomplished his mission.

Subtly the lieutenant questioned him, and openly Will answered. He described his home town; he talked about the Church; he discussed monastic school and theology. He followed any path of questioning which Emilio chose to pursue. He talked about the voyage to the New World, his subsequent shipwreck, his capture by the Indians. In talking about the Scupperongacs he went into minute detail.

"Why has it taken you so long to get to St. Augustine?" Emilio sat in a high-backed chair and gazed out the window.

"The Indians did not wish to let me go," Will answered. "I did not live with them out of love, sir. I stayed with them because I was a prisoner. Only recently did they consent to let me search my own people out."

"And you rescued Mistress Marta Carolina?"

"Yes," Will answered, rising. "I rescued her, and we journeyed but a short ways before we were captured again. Had your messenger not arrived in the village where we were being held prisoners, I do not know what would have happened to us." He sipped his wine, slowly moved about the room, looking at the few possessions that stamped it Spanish. "How did you hear about us, sir?"

"I didn't hear about you," Emilio admitted. "I only heard about Mistress Marta Carolina." He waited a moment, then said, "From a Timucuan runner actually."

"Silver Bow?"

"Hardly. And I would never tell him that one of his braves was the messenger. He would have the man's tongue ripped from his mouth; then I should be without a great source of information." He shrugged. "A knife here and there; a tomahawk or two. Very little, really, when you consider the invaluable service this man renders to me." Abruptly he asked, "Where were you headed, sir, when your ship wrecked?"

"I was going to visit my relatives in Mexico," Will

377

replied, again glad that he could rely on the truth. "My mother's brother, Esteban Lucero, has a *repartimiento* there, sir."

"Ironic, that both you and Mistress Marta Carolina were sailing to the same port!"

"Life does play odd jests on us mortals. Surely you must agree with that!" He smiled companionably. "Now, sir, if you have no further questions, I would like to take a bath and rest before supper."

"Of course," Emilio replied. He reached for the bell and rang it twice. The door opened. "Anita, please escort Señor Lucero to his rooms."

"Thank you," Will murmured. At the door, he turned. "Do you have any idea when we will embark for Havana?"

"If it were at all possible," Emilio answered, "I would take you immediately, but I have important business to which I must attend presently. We are looking for an escaped prisoner." He paused, the silence pregnant with meaning. "An Englishman. We fear that infidel woman who sits on the throne in England has attempted to plant a colony in Virginia. Although we think we have nothing to fear from the English, we must rid our coast of them and their influence."

"It will be a while then?"

"Yes," Emilio answered, "I regret to say, but it will be quite a while before I can send a ship to Havana."

"This is your room," Anita said, leading Marta Carolina into one of the small apartments that set on the outskirts of the town. She nodded to the young Indian girl who poured water into the large copper tub and said,

378

"While you're here in St. Augustine, Consuelo will be your slave. She has unpacked your clothes and will help you bathe and dress for supper. I will send someone to get you for supper." Anita walked out of the room, closing the door.

After Marta Carolina greeted the young woman, she slowly walked around the room, looking at the wall niches in which rested the small religious statues and several candles. She stopped at the side of the bed and stared at her leather pouch that was lying on the small table nearby. Sitting down, she unfastened the strings and went through the contents which had been rearranged. For the next hour she read every letter every recipe. Finally, when she was satisfied that no one had tampered with her belongings, she returned them to the case, closed, and fastened it.

She moved to her chest, knelt down, and unlocked it. When she lifted the lid, she found it empty. "My clothes," she exclaimed, turning to look at Consuelo. "Where are my clothes?"

"They are being washed and ironed," the girl timidly replied. "All of them were dirty. La señora took them," she explained, pointing to Emilio's residence.

"Yes," Marta Carolina answered, embarrassed over her outburst. Already she was feeling the strain of living a lie. She was suspicious of everyone and everything. What if the lieutenant sent for her and questioned her about Will? She didn't know what the two of them had talked about? She could so easily make a blunder that would result in Will's death!

"La señora," Consuelo said in reference to Anita, "is going to bring you a dress to wear to supper tonight." The Indian woman smiled. "Come. You have allowed your

379

water to get cold. You must take your bath, or la señora will be angry with me." She smiled enticingly. "Get into the tub, and I will scrub you."

Hastily Marta Carolina discarded her clothing and had no sooner sank beneath the water than Consuelo's hands began to relieve Marta Carolina's journey-tired muscles. She washed Marta Carolina's hair, wrapped it in a large drying cloth, and twisted it into a Moorish turban atop her head. Then she washed her body.

Half asleep Marta Carolina leaned her head against the side of the tub. "Here," Consuelo said, nudging her shoulder with a pewter cup, "dring this and follow me. I shall show you how to relax."

Marta Carolina reached for the cup, but she didn't immediately drink the pungent beverage. "I've already drunk enough wine to relax me," she said. She sniffed the drink. "What is this?" she asked, crinkling her nose.

"Sassafras," Consuelo replied. "Come. We must hurry. Already you are late."

"For what?" Marta Carolina asked as she slowly rose in the tub.

Rather than answer, Consuelo commanded, "Lift your arms," and when Marta Carolina did so, immediately wrapped a large towel around Marta Carolina's body. "Now follow me. We must finish your bath."

Without any argument or hesitation, Marta Carolina did as she was told and scurried out the building after the girl, holding her cup of sloshing sassafras tea with both hands in an attempt to keep from spilling it. She ran into the shelter of trees to a small wooden-framed building with a thatch roof and followed Consuelo inside.

"Do not step off the platform," Consuelo ordered, pointing out the walkway around the entire room. "The center is filled with hot stones, and you will burn your feet." She moved to the platform that circled the entire building and the small shelf above it. "Drink your tea; then lie down here."

Again Marta Carolina followed the girl's instructions without question. Curiously she watched as Consuelo lifted handled jugs from pegs on the walls and poured water on the stones. Heat rose up to fill the building, the vapor so thick Marta Carolina could not see Consuelo clearly.

"Turn on your stomach," the girl said, "and I will rub you."

The diaphoretic agent working, the wine having taken its effects, Marta Carolina sleepily rolled onto her stomach. Consuelo's hands reached for Marta Carolina's shoulders, but strong fingers biting into her shoulder stopped her movement. She peered up into the face of the nude stranger.

"I should like to do this chore for you."

"Will," Marta Carolina mumbled, "is that you?"

"Aye, love," Will replied softly, "it is I, Guillermo."

Marta Carolina giggled. "Ah, yes, love. Guillermo."

"Sir," Consuelo implored, "I cannot leave my mistress. La señora will be most unhappy with me; she will have me punished."

Will pressed an hourglass in her hand. "Take this and go anyplace you wish," he instructed, showing her how to gauge time. "When all the sand has fallen to the bottom, come get your mistress. You may keep the hourglass for your own."

Consuelo wanted to obey the stranger's bidding because she wanted the hourglass. Also she wanted the free time so she could meet with the Chicoran braves who had come to the garrison with Mistress Marta Carolina. They were so different from the Timucuan warriors, and she had heard so many tales about Chicora.

"I will not let la señora punish you," Will softly assured her.

Consuelo saw the promise in his eyes. Only then did she open the door and disappear into the forest, headed for the nearby Indian village where Wise Owl and the other Chicoran braves were lodging.

Will sat on the bench beside Marta Carolina, his sweat-slicked body rubbing against hers. When she went to move, he said, "Just lie there and relax, darling. I'll massage you."

He reached for the jars of oil which Consuelo had set on the small shelf to the left of Marta Carolina and filled his hand with the spicy ointment. He rubbed them together, then slid his palms down her back from shoulders to buttocks. Again and again his hands worked magic with her body, kneading and tapping and sliding. As he worked, he repeated his entire conversation with Emilio.

"Do you understand what I've just told you?" he asked when he was through.

Marta Carolina chuckled. "I do."

"Repeat it."

She did. Then she turned over under his hands, his palms naturally covering her breasts. "Do you understand what my body is telling you?"

He lifted one of the jars of oil and poured the thick liquid between her breasts. "I do, love," he murmured. His hands slowly spread the mixture over her breasts, down her midriff, below her navel . . .

*　　　*　　　*

Quite alone and deep in thought, Emilio paced back and forth in his study, the door shut. Marta Carolina had been telling the truth, he thought, but the man he could not be so sure about. Guillermo Lucero. Certainly a Castilian name, and the man spoke perfect Castilian. He was at ease; had the right answers . . . Perhaps that is what worries me about him, Emilio thought. He had all the right answers. No hesitance on his part. He hadn't had to stop and think.

He returned to his desk and thumbed through his correspondence. Finally he found the letter. He started to unfold it but his nail caught under the glob of sealing wax. Most meticulous, he spent a second scraping the residue from the paper; then he looked at the stain. He looked at the bold handwriting of Rodrigo Fernandez.

He reread the letter several times and paced the room more. Was this man the one whom Fernandez told him to expect? Was this in fact El Desafiador, the one who discovered the English spies in the Netherlands and revealed them before they could send vital information to the queen of England concerning the Invincible Armada? What was he doing here? Emilio wondered.

Was it some deficiency on his part? he wondered. Had Phillip dispatched this El Desafiador to spy on the governor's operation in Florida? The thoughts plagued Emilio, but he could do nothing about it. Unless Lucero admitted to being El Desafiador, he dared not mention it. Fernandez had warned him to keep his silence, and that order had come directly from His Majesty. Emilio did not wish to anger His Majesty.

But, Emilio thought, there was nothing to stop him from writing to the bishop in Cuba to inform him of Marta Carolina's arrival. And for a long time the only sound in the room was the scratch of the quill on the paper. When he was through, he stood and walked to a table on the opposite wall. He poured himself a glass of wine and sipped it as he gazed at the beautiful sunset. He could hardly await dinner tonight. He would enjoy entertaining his guests.

He returned to his desk and lit the candle; then he picked up his letter to the bishop and folded it. An enigmatic smile curving his rough features, he tipped the candle and let the tallow splatter on the paper. Then he pressed his ring into the glob of wax. Satisfied with his seal, he wrote His Holiness's name on the square and stood it on edge.

And he would write a letter to Rodrigo Fernandez. Being one of the port officials, he would know if Mistress Marta Carolina's belongings had been aboard the corsairs's ship. With her list of the stolen goods and a description of them, Fernandez could easily find out. Once again the room was filled only with the scratch of the quill across the paper. When the letter was finished, he left it on his desk to await Marta Carolina's list. He would dispatch all of these at one time.

A soft coded tap on the door announced Anita. Emilio looked up as she entered the room. He drank his fill of her beauty. More than a house servant and mistress, she was his love. Never in a thousand years, he thought, would he grow tired of her. Perhaps that was one reason why he hadn't insisted on a transfer to Spain. He didn't want to lose Anita.

"The preparations for supper have begun, my lord. Everything to your specifications."

Emilio smiled and opened his arms to the dimunitive woman. Eagerly she went into his embrace, lifting her mouth for his kisses. She cared not that her master could not marry her, that she would never be more than his mistress. She loved him, and in his own way he loved her. When he was here in Florida, he belonged to her and to no one else. As long as she took the herb and never conceived, he would not grow tired of her.

"My darling girl," he breathed, his hands plunging into the neckline of her dress to cup her breast, "I have given the better part of my life to Florida, and up to now, you are the only wonderful thing she has given me. But perhaps she is about to reward me for such faithful service."

In his haste he ripped the gown, and Anita did not mind. He was a violent, hot-tempered man, which she liked, but he was not cruel to her. She enjoyed the vehemence with which Emilio took her; the urgency that always verged on violence. His head lowered, and his mouth closed around the already taut nipple. His mustache and beard caressed her hot skin.

As if her very presence stimulated him, he released the nipple, and picked her up to carry her to the couch. Quickly he divested himself of his clothes, she of hers. Roughly they came together, needing no forays, their total enjoyment coming from their fierce and heated coupling. When finally they had reached the highest pinnacle of sexual experience, they lay on the couch, drawing in deep ragged breaths.

"What is Florida going to give you, love?" she finally asked, her fingers tracing designs on his hairy, sinewy thigh.

"The recognition and the wealth which I have always sought," he answered. He sat up on the couch and leaned against the wall. "Did you notice the necklaces which our guests wear?"

"Yes."

"Those, my darling child, are very precious where I come from. They are made of pearls and gold." His eyes took on a faraway look.

"You would like to have these pearls and gold," Anita asked, sometimes puzzled with the Spaniards.

"Yes, I would," Emilio replied. "Do you know where they came from?"

"I think from the land of Chicora," Anita replied. "A kingdom that lies on the other side of the Savannah River. A rich kingdom, my lord. My brother has a couch which the great *mico* of Chicora sent him, and the men who delivered it were old. You could tell by the color of their hair and the wrinkles in their faces, but they were messengers for the queen. They did what only young men in our tribe could do. The Chicorans live to be very old, and they are as strong and healthy as the young are."

"Are they wealthy?" he asked.

"Do they have a lot of the pearls and gold?" Anita asked, not sure what he meant by wealthy.

"Yes."

"I've heard that they have many, many chests full in their capital city of Chicora, but I have never traveled that far north, my lord. I do not know."

"Come—" Emilio patted her buttocks fondly "—time for us to get up, bathe, and dress for supper. I will question our guests tonight. Perhaps they can lead us to this capital city." He smiled. "If not they, then perhaps Mistress Marta Carolina's Indians can."

Her arms locked around Will's neck, Marta Carolina snuggled closer to his hard frame. She was glad that he was carrying her; she was relaxed to the point that she felt boneless, absolutely too weak to stand on her own two feet. Her mind was so numbed she never thought about the consequences of their running through the woods naked.

"Where are you taking me?" she asked.

"Wait and see." Will's eyes twinkled with pure devilment. "After a steam bath such as we've been through, there's only one thing left for us to do."

"Make love again," Marta Carolina whispered.

"No, this," he said, stepping smoothly from the bank into a small crystal clear pool.

He heard her gasp as the icy cold water slapped their warm bodies. Immediately all lethargy was gone; numbness was replaced with the sting of returning life. Marta Carolina gasped, spluttered, and splashed to the bank, but she was shaking so she couldn't climb ashore. Moving behind her, Will caught her by the waist and hoisted her out of the water. A hand on the bank, he jumped out beside her.

"How—how—could—could—you—" she chattered.

"You'll thank me for it later," he said, scooping her into his arms a second time and racing to her apartment. Once inside the room, he dried her off with a large, fluffy towel. Then he tucked her into the bed, pulling the cover beneath her chin.

"I would take a nap with you," he said, "but I have a strong suspicion that I should be in my apartment in case Lieutenant Bustamante sends for me."

"What makes you think he hasn't already?" she murmured, already sinking into the sweet oblivion of sleep.

He kissed her on the cheek. "I didn't come until I was

sure that he was otherwise engaged."

Marta Carolina giggled. "With whom?"

"La señora." He straightened, his loving gaze not leaving her until she was breathing softly in sleep. Then he tiptoed out of the room.

Later Consuelo returned, the hourglass in hand. She sat it on the table opposite the bed. Then she quietly straightened the room so not to awaken Marta Carolina. When she heard the soft knock, she opened the door.

"Give this to Mistress Marta Carolina to wear tonight," Anita said, handing Consuelo a beautiful gown complete with ruffs, petticoats, farthingale, and shoes.

Consuelo laid the ivory satin-and-lace garment across the foot of the bed; the petticoats and farthingale she hung on wall pegs. Quietly moving to the head of the bed, she laid her hand on Marta Carolina's shoulder and shook her.

"Mistress, it is time for you to awaken and dress for supper."

Chapter XVII

Marta Carolina had not felt so pampered in her entire life. The gown, though a slight bit too large, was beautiful. The ivory satin and lace complemented her smooth, creamy skin and defined the color of her hair and eyes. She sparkled as she pirouetted around the room for Consuelo's approval.

"How do I look?" she demanded.

"Pretty," Consuelo said, clapping her hands together. "Very pretty." She reached out to adjust one of the combs that held Marta Carolina's chignon of curls in place atop her head. "Señor Lucero will be proud of you tonight."

"Yes." Marta Carolina's joy seemed to swell from her soul to flood through her body. "He's never seen me in a gown like this before." As if she couldn't believe it herself, she ran her hands down her sides, pressing out the wrinkles in the gown. She didn't have a full-length mirror and could not see herself, but she felt beautiful. "What are you going to do tonight?" she asked Consuelo.

The Indian girl's dark eyes were just as animated as her

own were. "We are having a feast in honor of our guests. Tonight they will tell us their stories of valor. We will hear more about Chicora. Afterward we will celebrate with song and dance."

A knock interrupted the conversation. When Consuelo answered, she saw a uniformed soldier standing outside the door. "The lieutenant sent me to escort Mistress Marta Carolina to supper."

"Thank you," Marta Carolina said, grandly sweeping out of the room, laying her hand lightly on the bent arm of the soldier. The one, she noticed, who had brought their horses to them this morning, and who, now in a clean uniform, still looked unkempt and dirty. They walked stiffly for a few seconds before Marta Carolina said, "The nights are beautiful here, so cool."

"Yes," he replied.

"And do you like it here in Florida?"

"I am ready to return to my home and family, mistress," he replied. "I have been over here thirty years. That is too long to be separated from loved ones."

"And what are you called?" she asked.

"Manuel Pena."

As they moved down the crude walkway of logs, Marta Carolina continued to ask questions to which Manuel replied. Then they were standing in front of the commander's residence. The door swung open, and candlelight spilled from the long receiving hall onto the small veranda, sparkling on the necklace Night Star had given Marta Carolina and again catching the attention of Manuel Pena.

"Thank you for bringing Mistress Marta Carolina," Emilio said, extending his arm for her hand."

"A pleasure, sir," Manuel murmured, bowing low, his

gaze never leaving the brilliant glint of gold and the shimmer of hundreds of pearls that looped six times around Marta Carolina's neck.

Then Marta Carolina found herself inside the parlor. "Señor Lucero has not yet arrived," she heard Emilio say as he handed her a glass of wine. "But you, my dear, are looking absolutely ravishing." His smile set her at ease. "Also I could not help but notice the necklace which you wear. May I see it closer, please?"

Although reluctant to take her necklace off, Marta Carolina was also reluctant to upset Emilio by refusing his request. She reached up and lifted the necklace off, loop by loop.

"Such exquisite work," Emilio murmured as he inspected the necklace. He delicately rolled the pearls through his thumb and index fingers. "They are strung in graduated sizes," he commented, "each section closed off by a gold medallion. This one," he said, touching the large star at the center of the necklace, "what does it stand for?"

"The chief who gave it to us said it would guarantee us safety through her kingdom. I do not understand their picture language—" she shrugged "—therefore, I cannot interpret the words for you."

Emilio moved closer to an ornate candelabrum and held the necklace up to the light. "Could you lead us to these natives?" he finally asked.

Marta Carolina shook her head and said truthfully, her voice lowered a regretful octave. "Nay, my lord. I have no idea where we have been." Then she added thoughtfully, "I have the distinct feeling that the Indians led us in circles for hours before we were taken to the village, as if they deliberately were disorienting us."

The lieutenant nodded his head. "Probably so." For a moment longer, he held the pearls in his fist and looked at them. Almost reluctantly he returned them to Marta Carolina. "Do you know what tribe they are from?"

Marta Carolina's throat suddenly went dry. She couldn't force a word past her lips. Mutely she shook her head and raised the glass to her lips.

"No," Emilio mumbled, "they wouldn't have told you that, either. But never mind, Anita told me the Indians are Chicoran."

Marta Carolina could hardly swallow her wine. Her hands were clammy, and she wished Will were here to lead the conversation, to give her strength. She felt as if any moment she were going to say the wrong thing.

"Their kingdom is on the north side of the Savannah River," he said, remembering all Anita had told him earlier. "I understand they are a more advanced people than the Indians I've encountered so far."

Marta Carolina set the base of the glass in her palm; the other hand lightly held the stem. "The Indians with whom I stayed were highly civilized, and they were kind. They received and welcomed Señor Lucero and me into their village."

"Did you see evidence of more pearls and gold?" Emilio persisted. "Did you see evidence of mining?"

Will arrived outside the window in time to hear the lieutenant's question. Without giving himself away he stopped to listen to Marta Carolina's answer.

"I saw no evidence of mining," she replied, "and yes, I did see evidence of great wealth."

Will unconsciously balled his hand into a fist. Was civilization changing Marta Carolina? Was she going to betray Night Star and her people?

"But the Indians define wealth differently from us, sir. They do not measure the wealth of a man through the amount of pearls and gold which he possesses. They measure wealth through an individual's personal qualities and through the bounty of nature given freely to all men to share."

Will smiled. Marta Carolina was doing quite well for herself. He moved out of the light that filtered through the open window so Emilio and Marta Carolina could not see him and stared into the parlor. When he beheld Marta Carolina he couldn't believe his eyes. This was the first time he had seen her in European clothing, and she was breathtakingly beautiful. He watched her bow her head as Emilio looped the pearls around her neck.

Then Will was gone, moving to the front door. When Anita answered, she immediately led him into the parlor.

"Good evening," Will greeted. "I'm sorry I'm late, but I had to go through several trunks before I found clothes that would fit me." He smiled at the commanding officer. "And you, sir, I must be thanking for your thoughtfulness. You don't know how it feels to be dressed in such—" Will's face moved a fraction of an inch, and his twinkling gaze rested squarely on Marta Carolina "—in such finery. I feel as if I were a courtier, sir, ready to greet the king himself."

Marta Carolina sat in rapt silence. She had fantasized about seeing Will Dare dressed as such, but no thought prepared her for the reality. He was dressed fashionably in a rich blend of grays and blacks. She smiled when she saw the small neck and sleeve ruffs which he wore, but they did not emasculate him in the least. The snowy white gauze of the ruffle contrasted with his day's growth of beard and cast him in relief. It accented his primitiveness; it set him apart from any of the soldiers whom she'd seen in the compound.

She was glad that Will had chosen not to wear the exaggerated doublet that was thickly padded to hang over the waistline and which tended to distort the masculine physique. He needed none of the artificial devices, she thought, admiring his broad shoulders from which swirled a purple velvet cloak. His long and muscular legs were sheathed in gray knee-high boots.

When Marta Carolina's gaze again encountered Will's, his eyes were alight with laughter. Do I measure up? they seemed to say. A smile trembled on her lips and she nodded her head, the gesture so caressive Will felt as if she'd touched him.

"A glass of wine?" Emilio asked.

"Yes, thank you."

"I was just asking Mistress Marta Carolina about the Indians who captured you," he said, his gnawing desires for wealth propelling him about the room. "I would like to know more about them. Since they are a part of my *repartimiento* I would like to take priests to them for conversion to Christianity, and I would like to exact tribute from them."

"A worthy ambition," Will returned dryly, "but I'm afraid, sir, that I will do you no good. The Indians were quite secretive about the passageways in and out of their kingdom."

"So Mistress Marta Carolina said," Emilio quietly commented. "But I was thinking of her slaves, sir. They are Chicoran; they will lead me to Chicora."

Marta Carolina's hand flew to her breast. "But those are—are my slaves," she argued, almost stumbling over the words. "They were given to me." She desperately

394

searched for reasons to lend weight to her argument. "They are a part of my *repartimiento*, sir, and—and—" she looked at Will who had walked to the altar and was looking at the small religious statue "—and I'm planning to take them to Havana with me so they can be educated in the Faith." Once deceit is practiced, Marta Carolina wildly thought, how freely the lies flow. "Then—then I shall take them to Mexico."

Despite himself, Will—who knew Marta Carolina was fabricating to save the Chicoran braves—smiled as did the Spanish officer who thought her to be telling the truth.

"I understand your feelings, Mistress Marta Carolina," he said, "and I quite agree with you. I can understand your outrage and anger if I were to confiscate your property, but I was not planning to do that. I will give you four of my slaves in exchange for yours. According to your wishes, the Chicoran braves shall be instructed in the Faith, and they shall be of further benefit to the Crown and Church. They shall aid in the conversion of all their people." The argument ended, he smiled. "Now shall we adjourn to supper. Anita has assured me that she's prepared an excellent meal for you."

Marta Carolina would have argued further, but a slight shake from Will stopped her protest. She tried to wipe the bitter taste from her mouth with the wine, but she wasn't succeeding. When Emilio reached for her glass, she handed it to him. Then she rose, tucked her hand on his proffered arm, and the three of them walked into the dining hall.

Remembering the role she was playing, Marta Carolina again forced herself to eat, to laugh, and to talk. During a moment when Will was carrying the brunt of the conversation, Marta Carolina realized that she had changed so much since she had left Spain. This was her civilization; these were her people. Yet she felt as if she were an outsider. Her thoughts were so different from theirs. She had only claimed the Chicorans as her slaves because she wanted to protect them. The thought of owning another person as one owns chattel repulsed her. What was she going to do? How could she get Wise Owl and his braves out of St. Augustine?

When the meal was over, Emilio led them into his study. "I feel more comfortable here," he said, stretching his feet as he sat down. "I spend more of my time in this room when I'm in St. Augustine than any other room in the house."

Marta Carolina's gaze swept around the sparsely furnished office. When she spied the chess set, she asked, "Do you play?"

"I used to," he replied with a reminiscent sadness. "but that was one of the pleasures I had to give up. I have had no opponent who could equal me in skill."

"How about me?" Marta Carolina asked, her steps quickening across the room. "I am a highly skilled player, sir."

Emilio's eyes glittered; he was instantly out of one chair into another. "I always welcome a challenge, mistress."

"Since the two of you are engaged in such a game of wit and require all your concentration," Will said, "I shall bid you good night. Before I go to bed, however, I should like to walk around the garrison, sir. Is that permitted?"

"Of course," Emilio answered, arranging his men on the checkered square of marble. "However, do not stray beyond the walls of the city. Else they will turn the hounds loose."

"Good night, sir." Will's boots clicked as he moved to the table around which Marta Carolina and the lieutenant sat. "And good night to you, mistress." Marta Carolina extended her hand, and Will enfolded it with his. He lifted it to his mouth, and he kissed her, his lips tarrying longer than propriety demanded. When he raised up, he smiled at her and winked. Then he was gone.

Will meandered around the city to acquaint himself with the lay of the streets and the placement of the buildings. With careful strides, he measured the distance between milestones and finally located the barns and corral. As he leaned across the fence, he felt something hard and sharp pressed into his back—a knife? a sword?"

A guard spoke. "What are you doing out here, sir?"

"Your commanding officer has given me permission to walk about the fort," he said. "Naturally, being a horse lover and having been denied the use of one for so many years during my captivity, I sought the corral."

The guard relaxed and lowered his sword. For a long time he and Will chatted about the horses. He allowed him into the barn, even lit the candles so he could see better. For several more hours Will wandered the fort, his steps taking him to the nearby Indian village. From afar he watched the celebration, the entire village glowing from the huge blaze in the center of the town. He had no difficulty in finding Wise Owl and the Chicoran braves; their braids were so at odds with the pompadoured hairdos of the local Indians.

"Hello, Will Dare."

Will heard the soft, husky tones and turned. "White Blossom!" She had been following them! "What are you doing here? I thought you were in purification."

She stepped out of the shadows. "I have finished my purification," she answered, the lies coming easier the more she told. "I came because I was worried about you and the Chicoran braves who traveled with you."

Will noticed that she made no reference to Marta Carolina.

"The tribal council wondered why Silver Bow, a *mico* of the Timucuans, would come such a distance with a message when he has runners to perform such tasks."

Many times the thought had passed through Will's mind also.

"Since I am her fastest runner, Night Star sent me to find out," White Blossom said.

Will doubted this, but only said, "Silver Bow knew you were following us."

"I kept up with all his movements."

"You are a most skillful warrior," Will said, knowing Night Star had not sent the warrior/woman. If she had, White Blossom would have made her presence known rather than lurking behind.

"I am," White Blossom agreed without conceit. "I have been trained to become the next *mico*. I have learned many things since you have been at the fort, Will Dare. The woman who lives with the *mico* of the soldiers is Silver Bow's sister."

"How do you know this?" Will asked.

White Blossom moved closer, so that she was in the light of the fire. "Dressed as a Timucuan with my hair twisted up in these reeds, I can move about the fort freely without worry of detection," she told him. "I speak Spanish as they do, and to them one Indian looks very much like another."

Will was worried. White Blossom looked so much like a Timucuan she could easily pass for one. What, he wondered, was her purpose for coming? He didn't know when she spoke the truth, but he did know she was lying about the purification ritual. They had been followed from the day they left Chicora. There was no way White Blossom could have gone through the ceremony.

"You did not learn that Anita was Silver Bow's sister from the soldiers," Will countered.

"No," White Blossom answered, "even they do not know. I captured one of the women from Silver Bow's village and questioned her. She didn't want to talk at first, but by the time I was through she told me all I wished to hear."

Will winced at the callousness in her voice. He could imagine the duress under which the woman talked.

"Is Night Star's granddaughter alive?" White Blossom asked. "Does she live in the fort?"

"We have not been here long enough to find out," he replied, his gaze shifting to Wise Owl who sat next to Consuelo.

"The Chicorans have been in the village all day. They will have learned," White Blossom said matter-of-factly. "I shall question Wise Owl later." Then she said with a smile, "I have never seen you dressed so elegantly, Will Dare. You look much better than the other soldiers of the black robes."

"Thank you," he replied absently, his thoughts centered on White Blossom, on her reason for being here. The answer he kept coming up with worried him even more. Marta Carolina was out of White Blossom and Strong Bear's life, so surely the Chicoran chieftain hadn't followed them to complete the task she had not finished in Chicora. No, he thought, that couldn't be it altogether. Something else had prompted this visit! Something else had prompted her flagrant disregard of the purification ceremony.

As if they had been locked up in a deep, dark dungeon for centuries and were suddenly freed, the words careened through his mind: "I shall be *mico*. Nothing can stop me. No one shall come between me and my desire."

Night Star's granddaughter! Will thought with a start. White Blossom was not above killing her. She had tried to kill Marta Carolina; what would stop her from killing another?

"Are you staying in the village tonight?" Will asked, the uneasy thoughts swirling through his brain.

"No," White Blossom replied, "I would be easily recognized in the Indian village. I am safe only as long as I blend in and out of the fort and stay around the soldiers."

"Did any of your braves come with you?"

"They are waiting for me beyond the wall of the fort. I was on my way out when I saw you and the woman black robe eating with the soldier."

Will heard the bitterness in White Blossom's voice.

"I thought perhaps she would put her black robes on once she reached her people."

"No," Will replied quietly, "she will never put them on again."

"She is your woman."

"Yes," Will replied, "she is my woman."

"She is going to let the soldier make slaves out of Wise Owl and his braves?"

"No," Will replied, realizing that White Blossom had overheard their entire conversation, "she only said that so she could protect them. Emilio wants to find Chicora so he can—"

"—so he can make slaves of our people and steal our pearls and gold," she spat contemptuously. "I will kill anyone who tries to enslave my people," she promised, meaning every word she said. "I will go now." She turned and took several steps, her voice floating over her shoulder. "I shall see you again on the new sun, Will Dare. My braves and I are outside the walls of the fort if you need us. Please let Wise Owl know that we are out there to help him if he needs it."

After White Blossom disappeared, Will walked into the village. As soon as Wise Owl saw him, he moved from the ring of dancers. "What brings you here, my brother?"

"Have you located the queen's granddaughter?" he asked.

"I think perhaps Silver Bow has been misinformed," Wise Owl said. "I find no such person living here. The Indians know nothing about a Chicoran princess who lives in St. Augustine."

"Do you think he was misinformed?" Will asked, remembering White Blossom's words. "Or do you think perhaps he lied to us?"

"Why do you ask that?"

"White Blossom is in the fort."

Wise Owl was not surprised. "I knew she was following us."

"She said Silver Bow is the brother to Emilio's house slave, Anita."

"That may be true," Wise Owl conceded, "but I cannot see that that would make Silver Bow speak with a forked tongue or have ulterior motives for coming to our city."

"Why would a chief deliver a message to Chicora?" Will asked, again using White Blossom's line of reasoning, "when he has runners for that purpose?"

"That I do not know," Wise Owl replied. "I, too, have wondered about it."

"The lieutenant knows you are from Chicora," Will said. "I think perhaps it is time for you and your braves to leave the fort. He intends to make slaves out of you, and use you to guide him to Chicora."

"What our people feared," Wise Owl murmured. "I will gather my braves, but I do not know how we will leave tonight. The soldiers guard the fort with their dogs."

Looking at the Timucuan warriors, Will chuckled. "Get Consuelo to twist your hair on top of your head and fasten it with those reed ornaments. At first light of day you may slip, undetected, out of the fort."

"How shall I hear from you?" Wise Owl asked.

"I don't know," Will replied, "but I will find a way." As he watched the Chicoran move into the crowd of Indians around the huge ceremonial fire, Will murmured, "I shall find a way."

When he returned to the settlement, he walked by the lieutenant's residence and leaned against the tabby wall of the building across the street. He was so engrossed in watching Marta Carolina that he did not hear anyone approach.

"Are you unable to sleep also?"

Will turned to look at Anita and smiled. "Yes, my siesta was wonderful this afternoon, but now I find that I'm wide awake. And you, are you also unable to sleep?"

Anita's gaze strayed to the open window. "I had chores

402

to complete," she replied absently, wondering if Emilio were becoming infatuated with the Spanish woman. "I just finished cleaning the oven so that it is ready for when we break fast." She heard Will's quiet sigh, and she looked at him, his features distinguishable in the bright glow of the moon. "Are you and I thinking the same thoughts tonight?"

"What would that be?" he asked, turning to her.

"I am wondering if Emilio is infatuated with Mistress Marta Carolina. Are you wondering if she is infatuated with him?"

Although similar thoughts had been running through Will's mind, he hadn't used such strong wording. He didn't fear Marta Carolina's becoming infatuated with Emilio as much as he feared her becoming infatuated with a way of life that he could not share with her. So many things which they shared in common, and perhaps one difference—one important difference—would keep them apart for life.

"Well," Anita prodded, "I'm waiting your answer."

Will shrugged and softly said, "Yes, I am wondering the same thing."

"I have asked him to teach me the game, but he will not. The Spanish fear us too much. If we should become too educated in their ways, they are afraid that we would treat them as they treat us."

"You love him?"

"I love him."

"Does your brother know?"

"My brother?" Anita looked up at him in surprise.

"Silver Bow."

"No," she whispered, then asked, "How did you know he was my brother?"

"I have ears and eyes all through the Great Forest," he said. "Why does no one know that Silver Bow is your brother?"

"Emilio visited our city five winters ago. He found me most desirable. As a token of friendship Silver Bow, our village chief, offered me to him in marriage, but Emilio would not take me because he did not wish to bring shame to me or my family. He explained to Silver Bow, who he did not know was my brother, that he could not take me for his wife because his religion forbade his loving more than one wife."

Anita closed her eyes as she remembered the first time she saw Emilio.

"I wanted him too. I fell in love with him the first time that I saw him. I went to my brother and asked if I could become the Spaniard's woman." She paused. "At first Silver Bow was angry, but I told him that I would take the herbs and that would keep me from having a baby. I would never betray my people's secrets to Emilio nor would I ever let him know that I was Silver Bow's sister."

"He agreed after you made these promises?" Will prompted.

"He agreed after I promised to spy on the Spaniards for him. When I, Graceful Walker, came to live with Emilio, he gave me a new name. He called me Anita."

"Now you're caught in the middle?" Will murmured.

"In a way," she admitted, "I am caught in the middle, but I am not ashamed of my actions. I have betrayed neither Silver Bow nor Emilio. Rather, I have kept the peace between them for many years now. I tell my brother only what he needs to know to protect our people, Emilio only what he needs to know to protect himself."

"You knew the Indians who traveled with Mistress Marta Carolina and me were Chicorans?"

"Yes."

"You also know that the lieutenant is going to place them in slavery and use them to guide him to Chicora?"

Again only the whispered word, "Yes."

"Will you help me get them out of the fort?"

"The lieutenant would kill me if he found out that I had helped you," she murmured.

"You must. How can you not?"

"And once I've done this deed for you, sir, what else will you ask of me?"

"I have only two more favors to ask."

"What are they?" Friendliness was gone from her voice. Now she was cool and detached.

"I would like you to help me keep in touch with Wise Owl once he's outside the fort."

"That will not be difficult," she replied. "I'm allowed freedom to go and come from the fort."

"Also I would like to know if the granddaughter of Night Star, queen of all the Chicoras, lives here in the fort."

Anita was a long time in answering. Finally she said, "Among our people there is the story that the queen's granddaughter lives, but I do not know who she is. Some think she lives in St. Augustine, but none knows for sure."

"Silver Bow told Night Star that her granddaughter lives with a Spanish soldier as his concubine."

Anita's voice was derisive when she spoke. "All the Indians who live with the soldiers are concubines, sir. The soldiers can only bed us; they cannot marry us because they have a wife in the land-across-the-water.

She could be any one of the concubines. I have no way of knowing, because whoever she is, she does not profess to be Chicoran."

"Will you help me find her?" Will asked.

"Why?"

"Night Star is an old woman. She wishes to see her granddaughter before she dies."

Anita nodded. "I will help in all that you ask. Now I must go before Emilio misses me."

Will stood in the cool of the night for a few more minutes before he slowly walked to his lodging—the room so lonely and dark without Marta Carolina.

Chapter XVIII

"Gone," Marta Carolina murmured the next morning as she sat in the lieutenant's office. "The Chicorans are gone!" Although she was relieved, she shook her head because she was totally unprepared for their being gone. She had lain awake for hours last night pondering their fate. "I can't believe it!"

"You know nothing about their leaving?" Emilio demanded, his voice hard and unyielding. His inscrutable gaze never left Marta Carolina's countenance.

"No," Marta Carolina replied, "I haven't seen them since we arrived. Are you sure they are gone?"

"My men have searched the fort carefully," the lieutenant replied, his hand clenching into a fist. "When I sent my man for them this morning he found their house empty. The Timucuans whom he questioned reported they had not seen the Chicorans since the celebration last night."

"I am speechless, my lord," Marta Carolina said. "Even if I were not, I would not know what to say."

"Ah, yes," Emilio drawled sadly, his gaze inadvertently going to Marta Carolina's necklace, "'tis a sad lot, indeed. To have my hopes built so high only to be dashed so low." He paused, then asked, "Are you sure, my dear, that you cannot find your way back to Chicora?"

"No, Lieutenant," Marta Carolina asserted, truth firmly supporting her words, "I cannot find Chicora." She said with a smile and a shrug, "I'm afraid that a mile or two from the fort, I would find myself quite lost."

"As I feared," Emilio said with a rueful shake of the head. Disappointed, he said, "Come. I will show you around St. Augustine."

Although she wore the ivory gown from the evening before, Marta Carolina was lovely. One hand on the lieutenant's arm, the other holding a beautiful ivory and gold fan which Anita had given her, she walked beside him through the small fort. He was careful to go only where his men had constructed log walkways, lest she ruin her gown.

"In 1586 *el Draque* looted and razed the city," Emilio related. "We had only a handful of men and were unable to stop the attack. The rebuilding has been slow."

On and on he talked about St. Augustine and Florida, but Marta Carolina scarcely heard a word he said. When she was not watching the expression of the Indian women whom she passed to see if they recognized the necklace she wore, she was looking for some sign of Will.

When they neared the corrals, Emilio stopped to talk with the blacksmith. While he visited, Marta Carolina slipped into the stable and moved down the center aisle, looking into the stalls. As her eyes adjusted from the outside brilliance to the dim interior, she thought she saw a movement at the back of the building, but she couldn't be sure. Later, when her vision had adjusted, she saw no one. Just her imagination, she decided, but she didn't tarry in the stable. She hastened to the door.

"There you are," Emilio said. "I was looking for you." And so they continued their jaunt.

"That," he said, pointing to his left at a long, rectangular structure with a thatched roof, "is the infirmary. We had some black slaves who were good at nursing the sick when *el Draque* attacked. He stole them. Since then we have had no physicians or nurses."

Marta Carolina turned in that direction, but Emilio pulled her back. "You don't want to go in there. It is quite depressing to look at the ill and those who are dying."

"But I do wish to look inside," she said. "I'm an apothecary, and I was reared in a convent where the good sisters nursed the sick and infirm. Perhaps I can be of help to you while I'm here in St. Augustine."

Reluctantly the lieutenant followed her into the long, narrow room, and they slowly moved from one couch to the other as she looked at the patients, lying on soiled linen. Disregarding her dress, really forgetting what she wore, she immediately went to work. In a matter of seconds she became the commanding officer, Emilio the soldier.

"I need some workers," Marta Carolina announced, pacing from one end of the room to the other, her eyes viewing the dirty surfaces, her hands itching to get to work, "then I can begin to clean this place up."

"In that?" Emilio exclaimed, looking at her dress.

Marta Carolina chuckled. "No, I shall go change. This restricts me too much." She walked to the door. "I am going to my room to change, Lieutenant. By the time I return, I should like to have four men and four women

409

waiting here for me, so we can go to work immediately."

Marta Carolina moved as quickly as she could over the log sidewalks, but not as quickly as she wished. When she reached her apartment, she opened the door and yelled, "Come, Consuelo. Help me undress. We have work to do."

Her gown on the foot of the bed, her petticoats and farthingale askew on a wall peg, Marta Carolina quickly donned one of the dresses the Chicoran women had given her—a dress that afforded her freedom of movement. Then she grabbed her medicine cabinet and her leather satchel. The entire time she talked nonstop with Consuelo, outlining the work they would be doing in the hospital.

By the time they reached the infirmary, a large number of Indians had gathered. In her rush to assess the work to be done, Marta Carolina gave them a cursory glance and hastened inside the building. Yet something about one of the Indians nagged at Marta Carolina. The woman had seemed so familiar. So troublesome were her thoughts, Marta Carolina studied each of the eight when she delegated chores, but recognized none. Again she dismissed her suspicions and feelings as an overly active imagination, and she sent two of the men into the woods to find her herbs and roots. The others she put to work, cleaning up the room.

Now, she thought, she would have a reason to mix more freely with the Indians without arousing the lieutenant's suspicion who—with his desire for riches— must never learn that he had Chicoran Indians living in the fort. Marta Carolina would always wear the necklace in hopes that the queen's granddaughter would acknowledge it.

410

That afternoon, exhausted after a half day of mopping and scrubbing the entire building from the ceiling to the floor, Marta Carolina welcomed her bath and siesta. As she and Consuelo returned to their room, she asked, "Have you seen Señor Lucero today?"

Consuelo nodded her head. "As he rode out with the soldiers this morning to look for the Chicorans."

Fear gripping her, Marta Carolina stopped. "You don't think they will find them, do you?"

Consuelo smiled, a secret glittering in the depth of her dark eyes. "Not unless they wish to be found."

In the passing weeks, the days took on a certain pattern. Until midday Marta Carolina worked in the infirmary, and Will rode with the soldiers as they patroled the area. Everyone rested during the heat of the afternoon; and at night they dined with the lieutenant who seemed to be in no hurry to get them to Havana. Although both Marta Carolina and Will were eager to be gone, neither gave any indication.

As the days turned into weeks, Marta Carolina gave up hope of finding Night Star's granddaughter. Although the Indians admired the necklace, none of them recognized it as being Night Star's totem—or if they did, none of them acknowledged it as such. One afternoon when Will was on patrol with the lieutenant and she was in the woods, gathering roots, she saw a group of children playing ball.

Leaning back, wiping the perspiration from her forehead, Marta Carolina began to watch them as they tried to put the ball through a loop at the top of the small tree. She became so interested in the game she forgot about digging for her roots. At some point the ball rolled away from the clearing, and one of the children, a young girl no older than thirteen, Marta Carolina judged, ran to retrieve it. Marta Carolina followed her movements, then stopped. Sitting on the sidelines of the ball field was a frail boy, a crutch similar to the one she had made for Will Daré by his side. He lifted his hand to his mouth and coughed, the dry, hacking sound hurting Marta Carolina's ears.

Immediately she stood and wiped her hands down the side of her skirt. She tucked tendrils of hair that fanned her cheeks into the coil on the top of her head, and she looped her satchel over her head. Her eyes never leaving the boy, she moved directly to him.

"Hello," she said, smiling into his thin, emaciated face. "I'm Marta Carolina."

The child's eyes grew round with fear, and he shrank from her. The young girl who had chased the stray ball ran to the boy, placing herself directly between the two of them.

"What do you want?" she asked.

"I nurse the infirm," Marta Carolina told her. "I heard the boy coughing, and I would like to take him to the infirmary where I can take care of him. I have some medicine which will help him feel better."

The girl said nothing.

"May I?"

"I cannot give you permission," the girl finally said, sad, resigned eyes—eyes so familiar that Marta Carolina couldn't help but stare—lighting on the boy. "We must ask my mother."

"Who are you?" Marta Carolina asked, unable to tear her gaze away from the girl.

"I am Concepción. That is my brother, Justo."

Marta Carolina's heart was beating so fast, she was almost breathless. Intuitively she knew she had found Night Star's granddaughter, but this wasn't the granddaughter for whom Night Star searched. This was only a child; Night Star's granddaughter was a grown woman. This child must be . . . Marta Carolina's gaze slowly pivoted from Concepción to Justo. These children must be—yes, they had to be Night Star's great-grandchildren. She smiled.

"Come," she said when she found her voice, "let us go ask your mother." She saw Justo struggle with his crutch to rise to his feet. "May I help you?" she asked.

Discouraging her help, the boy neither answered nor looked at her. He lagged behind, following at a distance as Concepción led the way to one of the larger, tabby-constructed homes in the settlement.

"Wait here," Concepción said when they entered the parlor. "I will get my mother." The girl disappeared through a door which she closed behind herself.

Justo finally limped onto the veranda, but he didn't come into the house. He leaned against the wall, careful not to put his weight on his crippled leg. Marta Carolina walked onto the porch and knelt beside the boy.

"I'm not going to hurt you," she softly assured, reaching out to touch Justo's leg. She waited a moment to see what his reaction would be. When he didn't resist her touch, she said, "I want to see how badly your leg is damaged." She gently kneaded the muscle from the calf to his ankle.

Behind, she heard a door open and shut. Then: "What are you doing with my son?" The voice was cold, bitterly so.

413

Marta Carolina glanced over her shoulder to see a beautiful woman whom she judged to be in her late twenties. She could have been Indian, but Marta Carolina thought she looked more Spanish. Her black hair was pulled severely away from her face and was coiled into a thick bun on the nape of her neck. The austerity of her black dress was broken only by the white ruffles at neck and wrist.

"I am an apothecary," Marta Carolina said, rising. "I've been working in the infirmary for the past two months. I saw your son limping and heard his cough. I thought perhaps I could give him some medicine that would help him."

The black eyes, as brilliant as polished glass, as cold, stared through Marta Carolina without seeing her. "There is nothing that you or anyone else can do," she said. "We must let God's will be done with Justo's life."

"But God gave us knowledge to heal the sick," Marta Carolina said, barely constraining the anger that rose in her. "He gave us the wisdom to nurse ourselves."

"Thank you for your concern," the woman replied stiffly, "but I will take care of Justo. I do not want him in the infirmary."

"I—I could treat him here," Marta Carolina offered. "He needs some medicine for his cough. He—"

"You are a guest of the lieutenant," the woman said, "and I do not wish to be rude, but please go and leave us alone. We do not need or want your help."

Marta Carolina straightened her pouch on her shoulder, but she never took her eyes off the woman. So sure this woman was Night Star's granddaughter, so sure that Justo was Night Star's great-grandson, she lifted the pearls and held them out, saying daringly, "Does this

414

necklace mean anything to you?"

The woman looked at it and shook her head. No emotion played over her countenance. "Nothing."

Not to be outdone, Marta Carolina pulled it over her head and shoved it into the woman's hands. "Look at it," she insisted. "Look at it closely, and tell me that you don't know whose totem this is."

The woman held the golden star in the palm of her hand and stared at it for an extremely long time. Thinking she saw a softening in the obsidian eyes, Marta Carolina said, "Your grandmother would like for you to return to Chicora with your children for a visit."

The woman lifted her face, now full of emotion— hostility and anger. "I do not know what you're talking about," she maintained. "I am Spanish not Indian." With her declaration, she pushed the necklace toward Marta Carolina.

"No," Marta Carolina said, "you keep it. Perhaps it will jar your memory." She turned and walked away, disappointment pelting tears against the back of her eyes. Momentarily she was blinded and bumped into a Timucuan woman who was walking by. "I'm sorry," she murmured, lifting her hand to wipe her tears away.

Marta Carolina was sure the woman was Night Star's granddaughter. She was sure! She ceased walking, turned her head, and called over her shoulder, "If—if you should happen to remember, contact me."

"Are you to be my guide? The one who will take me to my grandmother?" the woman asked.

All the Indians who milled around faded into nothing for Marta Carolina. She felt the first tingle of hope since she had confronted the woman. She spun around. "No, but your grandmother has sent some of her braves to escort you and your children. I have only to get word to them that you are willing to go, and they will do the rest."

"Good day," the woman said, her cold words deflating Marta Carolina completely.

In a dull voice she asked, "You will think about all I've said?" Disappointed, Marta Carolina turned and walked away.

Teodora clenched her fist so tightly the points of the star cut into her palm. She despised Marta Carolina for bringing her the necklace, for reminding her of what she'd spent all her adult life trying to forget and trying to convince herself that she was not—one-half Indian. Shame rushed through her in such proportions she thought she would faint. Tears, unbidden, crept from between tightly clenched lids to roll down her cheeks.

"Mama," Concepción called, "Manuel is coming."

Teodora automatically lifted her hand to wipe her cheeks, the pearls swinging into her face. Hastily she crammed them into her pocket and brushed her sleeve over her eyes. "Return to the village," she bade the children. "Be gone before Manuel sees you. You know how angry he gets when you are here."

Hardly had Concepción and Justo disappeared around the house before the obese man ambled into sight. From puckered lips in a bewhiskered face he emitted a happy whistle. He walked up the dusty pathway into the house.

"Good news," he shouted, throwing his hat onto the entry table. He unfastened his cloak and slung it over the back of a high-backed chair at the head of the draw-table. "The lieutenant has received word that I am to be returned home." He patted his stomach which more than amply padded his doublet. "How wonderful!" he sighed. "I will see my homeland once more."

416

Teodora could hardly contain her happiness. The news she had been waiting for so long. To reach Spain had been her lifelong goal, her mother's first, now hers. When she had agreed to become Manuel's concubine, he had promised her that he would take her to Spain should he ever be returned. Now after fourteen years of enduring his sexual drives, obscenity rather than lovemaking, after fourteen years of verbal and physical abuse, Teodora was finally going to Spain!

Her eyes shone with excitement, and her hands would have trembled had she not twined them together. "When are we leaving?" she asked.

Manuel flopped down, the chair creaking beneath his weight, and flung his booted leg to her. "Us!" he exclaimed. "Us! No, Teodora, us is not going." He poked his chest with a short, pudgy finger. "I am going to Spain. I am. Me alone."

"No," Teodora whispered, "you cannot mean that. You have been promising me that you would take me with you."

"Do you think I'm loco, woman! I have a wife and children. Even grandchildren."

Teodora saw her last chance slipping through her fingers. "Please, Manuel," she begged, pushing pride aside until she had none left. "Please, don't leave me behind. You promised me!"

"Get away, whore!" he yelled. His hand flattened against her chest, he shoved her down. "Get out of my sight!"

She slid down his legs and wrapped her arms around his ankles. "No, Manuel!" She pressed her face against his legs. "You cannot treat me like this after all I've done for you."

"After all you've done for me, you slut!" He jerked his foot loose, pulled it back, and thrashed her in the face, the blow sending her across the room. "You've done nothing but supply me with sex and a sorry job you've done of that."

He was blindly angry now. A weak man, he vented his faults and inadequacies on someone even weaker. When Teodora, sliding her palm up the wall and using it as support, stood to her feet, Manuel lunged at her, an animalistic growl emitting from his parting lips. His hand caught her full across the side of the face, the slap of his hand and the crack of her neck sounding through the room. Blood trickled down the corner of her mouth, and combs and pins slipped from her hair, the knot coming uncoiled. The short, puffy hand slapped her time and again, first one cheek then the other, and all the time he yelled at her.

"Don't tell me what I can or cannot do. I am the master of this house, not you—you slut! You Indian slut!"

He caught her shoulders with both hands and flung her across the room. She landed against the wall, her head and shoulder both hitting the cement mixture with such force that the necklace Marta Carolina had given her earlier fell from her pocket to slither across the floor.

"What's that?" Manuel murmured. He stooped to pick up the necklace, rolling the pearls through his grimy fingers. He felt of the gold, then put it to his mouth and bit into it.

Teodora brushed her arm across her mouth to wipe the blood off and swept the hair out of her face. Still reeling from the blows, she closed her eyes and leaned her head against the wall. She hurt so badly she wasn't aware that the necklace had fallen from her pocket; she wasn't aware that Manuel had it.

"I said what's this," Manuel shouted, moving closer to her and shoving the necklace into her face.

Teodora opened eyes that were quickly swelling. "A—a necklace," she murmured through bruised lips.

"I know it's a necklace," Manuel snarled. "Whose is it? Where did you get it?" He grabbed a handful of hair and jerked her head. "How did you get it?"

"The woman who nurses the ill at the infirmary," Teodora explained disjointedly, licking the corner of her mouth. "She brought it to me earlier today."

"Why?" When she didn't answer soon enough, Manuel jerked her hair so hard pain shot through Teodora's head and she moaned. "Tell me," he demanded.

"She—she thought—I was someone else."

"This is something that one of your Indian relatives sent you," Manuel guessed. "All this picture writing on this gold star. What does it mean?" Again she didn't answer as quickly as he wanted, so he banged her head against the wall. "What does it mean?"

"My grandmother wishes to see me and the children," she admitted. "She sent her token by the woman who visits with the lieutenant."

Manuel's dull, watery eyes began to glint. "Is your grandmother wealthy?" he asked.

"It is said that Chicora is a wealthy kingdom." Teodora remembered the stories her mother had told her when she was but a child. "There is a temple in each major city where the people accumulate their treasures. They have chests full of pearls."

"Then by all means, my dear, we shall go visit your grandmother."

When Teodora saw the greedy gleam in his eyes, she saw the solution to her problem. She couldn't use her body to persuade Manuel to take her to Spain, but he could be motivated and manipulated by riches. The answer was so simple. Why hadn't she thought of it sooner?

"I don't know where my grandmother lives," she answered truthfully.

Manuel pulled his hand back to strike her again, but this time Teodora did not flinch.

Instead she laughed softly. "You had better be careful," she taunted. "If you kill me, you will never find out how to get to my grandmother's city."

Manuel's face contorted with fury. "The woman knows the way!"

"No," Teodora returned. "She has someone outside the fort whom she can contact who will lead me to Chicora, but even she does not know the way." Teodora's laughter grew louder. "I am the only way you will find the riches, Manuel, and to do that I must be alive and willing." As Teodora watched Manuel lower his hand, she pushed away from the wall and twisted her hair up again. "I will see that you get the riches you want, but you must make me a promise."

Manuel raked a hand across his whiskered face. He watched Teodora—a new Teodora, self-assured, confident—walk into the other room to return with a sheet of paper, the ink, and the quill. These she set on the table.

"The promise I want in writing," she said with dignity that defied her swollen and discolored face. "Sit down, and I will tell you what to write."

A man in a daze, the pearls hanging from his hand, Manuel walked to the chair and sat down. He laid the necklace on the table and picked up the quill which he dipped in the ink. She dictated; he wrote. He agreed to take her to Spain as his ward and to be responsible for her total welfare until she made a suitable marriage. He dated and signed it.

Teodora lit the candle and tilted it, her eyes glowing as she watched the splatters of tallow accumulate. She sat the candle down, picked up Manuel's fat, puffy hand, and sank his ring into the warm wax. Then she picked up the paper and danced around the room, her laughter ringing out through the quietness.

"I will be back later," Teodora said as she folded the paper and slipped it into the bosom of her dress. The necklace she held in fisted hand. "I must go to la señorita and tell her that I'm ready to go see my grandmother."

Not once did Teodora think about her bruises or cuts as she walked to Marta Carolina's room. She smiled and spoke to those whom she passed, but she saw none of them really. At one time she thought Manuel was following her, but when she glanced over her shoulder, she saw only a Timucuan woman disappear behind a house.

She laughed at herself and continued to walk. She was too happy to dwell on past sorrows or create new suspicions. She had the letter in Manuel's own hand-writing that declared her his ward and gave her the legitimacy she needed in Spain. Whether he was dead or alive, she now had the guarantee of passage to the mother country. The jewels she got from Chicora would more than finance her and would be dowry enough for a most suitable marriage once she arrived in Spain.

So caught up in her daydreams, she did not see the shadow flit behind the house. She knocked on the door and waited until Consuelo answered. Teodora handed her the necklace and said in a small, defeated voice, "Give this to your mistress and tell her that I'm here to see her."

Consuelo didn't have to relay the message. Marta Carolina recognized Teodora's voice and rushed across the room to pull open the door. She gasped when she saw the woman's bruised and swollen face.

"What happened?" she asked, and in the same breath said to Consuelo, "Bring me the basin and a washcloth." She led Teodora to the chair near the window and sat her down.

"He—he beat me up," Teodora sniffed, watching Marta Carolina dip the cloth in the water and wring it out. "Manuel is returning to Spain soon, and he's always promised to take me with him." When Marta Carolina laid the cool rag on her bruised and cut face, Teodora winced. "Today he called me a slut and said he wouldn't take me home with him. He has his other family."

Teodora had no tears left; she was too happy, but she still had a role to play, one final scene to enact. She lifted the rag and settled supplicating eyes on Marta Carolina.

"I want to go home to my grandmother."

"The children?" Marta Carolina asked as she liberally applied ointment on the cuts. "What about the children?"

This was the first that Teodora had thought about her children. She nodded. "I will take them to her." The answer to another problem, she thought. The old lady may lose all her jewels a second time in her life—first to Desoto, now to his granddaughter—but Teodora would leave the children with her. "The—the children, they do not live with me and Manuel," Teodora said. When she saw the glower of disapproval on Marta Carolina's countenance, she hastily added a vindication for herself, "He—he was mean to them, so I moved them to the village . . . for their safety."

Marta Carolina wondered how this cold, callous woman could be Night Star's granddaughter. Then something else caught her attention—a movement from the window. She glanced over in time to see the face quickly blend into the shadows. White Blossom! She had recognized her earlier today. That's what had nagged her memory all day. White Blossom was in St. Augustine, dressed as a Timucuan. White Blossom had come to kill her . . . perhaps the granddaughter . . . and if she knew about the children, them, too.

"Until we go," Marta Carolina said, fear rushing the words out of her, "I will keep the children and treat the boy in the infirmary."

Teodora nodded. Anything to appease the woman. "Whom do we contact and when?" she asked.

Marta Carolina's dislike for the woman was growing quickly. Teodora's only concern was herself. "We can't leave tonight. I must first contact Wise Owl who's waiting outside the fort for a message from me. And we'll have to find a way to get you out of here without suspicion."

"Please hurry," Teodora pleaded, allowing her excitement to show for the first time. "I want to see my grandmother. Are you sure you cannot lead me?"

Feeling guilty about her uncharitable thoughts, Marta Carolina shook her head. "Your grandmother is a crafty old woman who has taught her people well. When we were brought into the city, the guide marched us around in circles for one entire day; Wise Owl did the same thing when he led us out." Marta Carolina patted Teodora's arm. "Can you return to Manuel? Can you stay with him a few more days?"

Teodora nodded and said in her pitiful voice, "I can."

"Good," Marta Carolina murmured. "I will send word to you as soon as I hear from Wise Owl."

"I will wait to hear from you," Teodora said as she stood and moved to the door.

"You must speak of this to no one," she admonished. "To absoluetly no one but me. Do you understand?" Teodora nodded. "I'll send word to you as soon as I know something."

Once Teodora was gone, Marta Carolina turned to Consuelo. "Come," she said, "we must get to Justo and take him to the infirmary. I want to give him some medicine that will help him rest better tonight."

"What about supper?" Consuelo cried as she ran behind her mistress.

"I'm not hungry," Marta Carolina called over her shoulder, "and I am worried about the child. If something isn't done for him, he won't survive the trip to Chicora."

When Marta Carolina and Conseulo reached the village, they didn't take long in locating the children who lived in a small wigwam by themselves. Concepción was sitting on the mat floor beside the platform on which Justo lay, his frail body curled into a tight little ball. The silence was marked only by his heavy breathing and a hoarse metallic cough.

"Come," Marta Carolina said to the girl, "you're going to stay with me."

"What about my mother?" Concepción asked.

"She has given her permission. As soon as we can, you, Justo, and your mother are returning to your grandmother in Chicora."

Concepción's face remained immobile, her eyes unchanged. "I did not know I had a grandmother. What is she like?"

Although Marta Carolina was small, she was strong, and determination made her even stronger. She scooped Justo into her arms and said, "Consuelo, we must take him to the bathroom."

Consuelo silently questioned Marta Carolina but for only a second. When she saw the flinty resolve in her mistress's eyes, she nodded her head. Grabbing the girl's hand, she said, "Come with me, Concepción. I'm going to need your help. Mistress Marta Carolina will take care of Justo."

Several hours later, Marta Carolina sat on the wooden floor of the steam-filled wigwam, an empty cup by her side. Her wet clothes were plastered to her body, and damp tendrils of hair clung to her face and strung down her neck and back. On a blanket Justo lay on the platform, for the first time sleeping—induced in part by the medication Marta Carolina had given him, induced more by the steam that was clearing up his chest and throat. Tightly in one fist, he clutched Marta Carolina's hand.

With the other she pushed the moist black hair off his forehead and outlined the beautiful contour of his oval face. Such a beautiful child, she thought. Too young to die. She couldn't stop the tears that rolled down her cheeks to merge with rivulets of sweat. She reached for the jug of water, which Consuelo conscientiously kept refilling, and poured it on the hot stones. Huge puffs of steam hissed through the small room

When the door opened, Marta Carolina whispered,

"I'm out of water again."

"Darling girl." Will's endearment cloaked her so sweetly that she began to cry in earnest. He knelt by her side and pulled her into his arms, cradling her against his broad chest. "Don't cry, little one," he soothed, brushing kisses over her sweat-moistened brow. "I'm here now."

"The child," she said, "I don't know if he will live or not, my darling. He's so frail, so weak. I don't know if he can endure. I am doing all I can . . . and it's not enough."

"All we can do is enough," he told her. He shifted her and reached out to touch Justo's forehead. "And it shall be enough to make the lad live." His hands came down on her shoulders, and he pulled her to face him. "And you, young lady, are going to your room right now and get some rest."

"I can't," she said dully. "I can't leave him alone." More tears fell. "Except for Concepción, he's been alone all his little—little life." Her sobs deepened. "He's—he's Night Star's grandson."

"I know," he gently replied. "Consuelo told me. She also told me that the lad's sister, Concepción, was staying the night in her parents' wigwam." He brushed his hands across her cheeks, pushing the curls from her face. "If you don't get some rest, you'll be sicker than he is, lass," Will softly persuaded. "Then you'll be of no use to any of us." The gentle tones and the sweet smile took all rancor out of his words. "And I don't propose to leave the child alone. I shall stay with him the rest of the night."

"Oh, Will," Marta Carolina sobbed, throwing herself into his arms, "I love you so much."

"And I love you, my darling." Both of them kneeling,

he held her tightly and rubbed his hands up and down her back in calm, reassuring strokes.

"I'm glad you're back. I've missed you so." She pulled her head back slightly and looked into his face. "Where have you been?" She laughed shakily.

"We'll talk about that later," he said. "Right now, I want you to rest."

"White Blossom is in St. Augustine" came the dull tones. "I saw her tonight. She's dressed like a Timucuan."

"Aye," he said, "I knew she was around. She followed us from Chicora."

"What does she want?" Marta Carolina asked. "Me or Teodora or the children . . . or all of us?"

"A short while ago, *querida*, I thought she wanted you and Teodora. Now I'm afraid she wants all of you." Will whispered his fear, his arms protectively tightening around her.

Entr'acte

"Thank you, Rodrigo, for coming so quickly." His Holiness stood in front of the window and gazed at the placid harbor in Havana. His hands were bridged, cathedrallike, in front of his face. "I need your help."

"Of what service might I be, Father," Rodrigo Fernandez asked.

"I received communication from St. Augustine in which Lieutenant Bustamante tells me that a woman, Marta Carolina Lucas de Santiago, who was traveling from Spain to her *repartimiento* in New Spain aboard the ship *El Salvador*, has arrived."

Marta Carolina Lucas de Santiago!

The name haunted Rodrigo, and his fingers nervously kneaded the black velvet cap he held. She was supposed to be dead. When the corsairs were captured, they reported only two nuns having escaped. The other woman along with everyone else on board was killed— they said! He had all Marta Carolina's personal effects; he had gone through them meticulously time and again. Still he hadn't found the papers which he sought.

Only a thin glimmer of perspiration on his bronzed face betrayed his turmoil as Rodrigo waited for the bishop to continue. He was accustomed to these long periods of introspection into which the old man lapsed when he was planning, but today Rodrigo was in no mood for patience.

"I wish you to go to St. Augustine as my ambassador, Rodrigo," His Holiness eventually said. "This young lady has requested an audience with me, and I wish to give it to her. Also I shall grant her refuge and help her reach her family in New Spain."

"Do you know who she is, Your Holiness?" Rodrigo exclaimed, wondering why the Holy Father was being so lenient with Marta Carolina. Did he not recall who the Lucas de Santiagos were? "Do you remember the name?"

"Of course, I do, my son," the priest snapped. "I'm old, not daft. Her aunt and uncle were hanged for treason." He turned and walked to his desk, his robes rustling as he moved. "But you must also remember her father was a holy man, totally dedicated to God, and no evidence has been found to incriminate Marta Carolina!" With colorless eyes—yet eyes that had ability to slice through every barrier, visible or invisible—the bishop stared at Rodrigo. "Well, did you?" he demanded. "When you confiscated the smuggled goods from the corsairs and learned that she was one aboard the ship, did you find the documents in any of her possessions?"

"No, sir." The words came out as an extended sigh.

"Also," His Holiness continued in a soft monotone, "Lieutenant Bustamante informed me that another of our countrymen has taken shelter in St. Augustine."

Rodrigo's heartbeat quickened.

"One called Guillermo Lucero." The bishop waited,

then asked, "Do you know him?"

"I do not know him by that name, Father. But I think this is the man whom we await—the man whom I know by the name of Will Dare."

"You think," the bishop grumbled. "You think."

"I shall know if he is Will Dare when I see him."

His Holiness now sat at his desk, his elbows propped on the top, his hands once again bridged in cathedral fashion in front of his face. He lightly drummed his fingertips together.

"He would recognize you?"

Rodrigo nodded his head.

"That I cannot permit. It would ruin our chances of apprehending him." He waved his long, slender hand through the air. "What has happened with this Timothy Turner fellow?"

Rodrigo pulled a face. He despised the Englishman who pretended to be Spanish and who was quickly insinuating himself into Alejandra's life. "He is still around. I promised that I would help him catch this Spanish spy."

"Well, then . . ." the priest drawled only to lapse into quiet introspection. "Well, then, Rodrigo," his voice snapped at the same time that his body did, "I think it is time for our Captain Ignacio Tello to apprehend this notorious Spanish spy." He laughed, the raspy sound filling the large study. "What do you think, my son?"

"I think you are right, Father." Rodrigo's voice smiled. "But I have one request to make as I also offer some advice." Father Simon lifted thick bushy eyebrows. "As you have already pointed out, Will Dare knows me by sight as well as by name; therefore, if I travel to St. Augustine with Turner, we are taking a chance on losing this opportunity to rid ourselves of El Desafiador."

"Yes! Yes!" the priest agreed impatiently. "Get on with it!"

"I suggest we enlist the help of another government official, sir. One of the minor port officials such as Don Diego, one who is innocent of subterfuge and one whom Will Dare would not suspect."

"I see. I see." The bushy white head bobbed up and down in agreement. "What do you suggest we do with our illustrious governor?"

Rodrigo spread his hands wide. "As I see it, Your Excellency, the governor will present no problem. At present he is leading an expedition up the coast of Florida, making sure the English do not have a settlement in Virginia. We will have apprehended and killed both El Desafiador and Turner before the governor returns. Emilio is easy to handle; he's rather slow-witted."

"Do you think Don Diego will object to going to St. Augustine?"

"Not if he thought the trip were worthwhile, sir."

The bishop laughed appreciatively. The old adage is true, my son. Gold speaks loudly, authoritatively, and quickly; she finds few obstacles she can't surmount." The chair creaked as he leaned back. "What is the basic outline of your plans?"

"We shall not tell Emilio that we think Guillermo Lucero is really Will Dare, an English spy. Only Don Diego will know the truth, and he and Turner will sail into St. Augustine with instructions to bring both Marta Carolina and this Guillermo Lucero to Havana. Once this man has been identified to Turner as El Desafiador, our worries are over. Ignorant of his facts, one Englishman

431

shall kill another, and we shall be rid of all the vermin. As soon as El Desafiador is dead, Don Diego will inform Emilio that Turner is an English pirate. He and his crew will be arrested and executed on the spot. Then, my lord, we will be ready for the alternate plan—our answer to the failing of the Armada to depose England of that stupid woman heretic."

"At last peace," His Holiness sighed, closing his eyes, bringing his bridged fingers to lie against his mouth. "Take care of all the details, my son. I trust your judgment implicitly." When he heard the latch on the door sound, he said, "By the way, Rodrigo, how is Alejandra?"

"Fine, once I get this damned Englishman out of our life."

Chapter XIX

Will sat on the floor in the steamy room with Justo for the remainder of the night. At different intervals a Timucuan Indian, sometimes a woman other times a man, would quietly slip in to refill the empty water jugs. Each time the door opened, Will would start, and his eyes strained through the misty veil that hung over the room as he tried to distinguish the visitor, but he couldn't; the haze caused the features to blur together. He would listen for a word or touch that would identify Consuelo.

Because she was the only one whom he could trust, besides Anita, who was sleeping with Emilio, Will had sent her to find Wise Owl. He had to get the children safely out of the fort before Emilio found out who they really were and used them to bargain for the small cache of riches in Chicora. Will looked at the small tot who had been sleeping peacefully for an hour, his cough slackening and his breathing less labored. Will thought of the young girl now under the protection of Consuelo's parents and asleep in their wigwam. Innocent victims in the hands of manipulators—their mother! Manuel Pena!

Emilio if he but knew who they were!

But, Will decided, he would get them to Chicora and give them a chance to find happiness. When Night Star learned that she had two great-grandchildren she would welcome them into her home and would love and care for them. Will smiled as he thought about Night Star's reaction to the homecoming.

"Will Dare."

Wise Owl's voice came so low Will wasn't sure he heard it. He straightened up, tensed, and waited.

"Will Dare."

"Wise Owl."

The Chicoran moved carefully across the narrow platform that rounded the room until he squatted near Will. "You sent for me. I have come." The steam glistened on his face and cast him a shiny bronze, the angular lines of his patrician face sharp in relief.

"This is Night Star's great-grandson," Will said. "The great-granddaughter is sleeping with Consuelo's parents in their wigwam."

Even the Chicoran could not suppress his smile of happiness. "This is truly more than Night Star could have hoped for. Now we must get them out of St. Augustine safely."

"White Blossom knows."

Wise Owl nodded his head. He had feared as much. "Word came by runner that White Blossom has been banished from our tribe. She refused to undergo the purification rites, and she and her braves rose against the queen. Had it not been for Morning Dew, Night Star would have been killed. She is badly wounded, and many fear she will not recover."

The news saddened Will. He would never forget Night

Star, the Chicoran *mico,* who had impressed him with her majesty and touched him with her kindness. "Are you sure Night Star may die?"

"Yes" came the sad reply.

"And White Blossom was only banished," Will exclaimed, careful to keep his voice low. "Why was she not killed for her act of treason?"

"To live a life of dishonor is worse to us, Will Dare, than to die. White Blossom will never be received by any of our people again. She must wander the Great Forest with no place to call home, no people to call hers. Her token was taken away from her and will be given to another warrior of great stature. Such is a great punishment!"

"In the meantime, she's going to wreak as much havoc as she can," Will muttered. "She's set on revenge." When the boy stirred and turned, Will picked up the damp cloth to wipe the perspiration from his brow. "We must get these children out of here tonight," he said. "That's their only hope. Can Consuelo help us?"

"She is a brave woman who has already placed her life in danger for me," Wise Owl said slowly. "I hate to ask her again, Will Dare."

Will clasped Wise Owl's shoulder and squeezed. "I'm sorry, my friend, but we must ask those whom we trust and who can help us. We have few friends in the fort and many enemies."

"I fear the dogs getting her," Wise Owl said. "She is afraid of them, Will. She has seen so many of her people mauled and killed."

"We must get the children to Night Star before she dies," Will emphasized. "You must send word of them to her. That will give her the will to live."

435

Wise Owl nodded.

White Blossom walked quietly through the streets, careful to stay in the shadows and avoid moonlit spaces. When she came to Teodora's house, she slipped into the shadowed inner side of the building, brushed the curtain aside, and entered through an open window. Without tiptoeing she moved through the room so quietly, none knew of her presence. In the pale light of the moon that glimmered through the gauze curtains she studied everything. When she reached the bedroom, she stood at the foot of the bed and looked at the fat, repulsive man who lay there on his back, naked. His legs were spread apart, his hands flung above his head. His mouth was open, and he snored loudly. His nudity, White Blossom thought, was a disgrace to the dignity of any warrior. The woman did not sleep with him. So easy it would be to kill him, the Chicoran warrior thought, her fingers closing around the hilt of her knife. But he wasn't the one whom she'd come to see. Teodora. She must find Teodora.

White Blossom strained through the shadows to find Night Star's granddaughter. Finally in the corner of the room on a narrow couch she saw Teodora. White Blossom approached the couch and stood for a long time to look down at the woman. A malicious smile spread her lips and glimmered in her eyes when she finally knelt over Teodora and tapped a shoulder at the same time that she clamped a hand over her mouth to keep her from screaming.

"It is I, Teodora," she said quietly in Spanish. "I have come to get you."

Teodora's eyes fluttered open; she sputtered against

436

the hand, kicked the covers aside, and flailed an arm. The point of a flint knife sank into the tender skin where her chin and neck met.

"Do not scream and do not fight me," White Blossom quietly gritted. "I am your friend, but I will kill you before I let you create confusion and awaken the fort to my presence." Only when Teodora's petty resistance ceased and she nodded, did White Blossom pull her hand away from the woman's mouth.

"I wasn't expecting you this soon," Teodora whispered. "And—I—" her gaze swept the feminine form "—I wasn't expecting a woman."

"I am a Chicoran chief," White Blossom replied in that voice that was softer and quieter than a whisper, that was more deadly and painful than the bite of a poisonous snake. "I have been sent to escort you and your children to Chicora. The queen wishes to see you."

In her haste to acquire the fortune of Chicora which would in turn purchase her heart's desires, Teodora forgot Marta Carolina's warning. She sat up, her feet hitting the floor with a muted thud. "My man," she said, thinking she would have use of Manuel getting in and out of St. Augustine, "he would travel with us."

Having Manuel would be to her advantage until she reached Spain, Teodora thought. Then—a smile curved her drooping lips—before he could reach that family he wanted to see so badly, before he could share his riches with another woman, she, Teodora, would kill him. Slow and easy. She would enjoy watching him die little by little.

White Blossom was displeased with Teodora's words; she did not wish to be burdened with the man. Killing Teodora and the two children was task enough. Now she had to plan on killing him also, but she would rather do that than create a scene with the woman and risk getting captured in the fort. Also, she reasoned as did Teodora, the fat man could get them safely out of St. Augustine away from the dogs.

She nodded. "We must get the children."

"Only the girl," Teodora said. "The boy has not many days left to live. He is so sickly he will be a burden to us; he will only slow us down."

"Where are they?" White Blossom asked, although she knew. She had monitored every movement of the woman black robe. Nothing had gone unobserved.

"I'm not sure," Teodora answered with a shrug. "The woman said she was going to take the boy to the infirmary. I don't know what she's done with the girl."

"Get the man up and dressed, but do not light any candles. No one must be alerted to my presence or suspicion that you are leaving. I will be back with the children, and we will go."

When White Blossom reached the door, Marta Carolina's warning suddenly stirred to life. "My grandmother's necklace," Teodora said. "I want my grandmother's necklace. Get it from the woman when you get the children."

"I will," White Blossom promised. Then she was gone from the house as quietly as she had entered.

Marta Carolina was in such a deep sleep, White Blossom moved freely about the moonlit room. She walked in front of the throw-chair, past the settle. From the table against the wall on which the pewter basin and ewer sat, she picked up the pearl necklace. Teodora wanted Night Star's totem, and she would get it! The malicious smile on White Blossom's lips widened. How tightly her plan for revenge was fitting together. But she was disappointed when she stood at the foot of the bed and looked at the lone sleeper. Night Star's great-granddaughter was not with Marta Carolina. But, the Chicoran chief shrugged, perhaps it was better. Now she could kill Marta Carolina.

It may be too late for me to get Will Dare, but, at least, you won't have him either.

Marta Carolina mumbled in her sleep and stirred, turning to the other side. White Blossom watched as she brought her hand up and tucked it under her cheek; then the Chicoran warrior walked the length of the bed until she stood at Marta Carolina's head. She lowered her arm and tapped her on the shoulder.

"Marta Carolina," she whispered.

Marta Carolina heard the soft call, but she was too exhausted to respond. She shook the offending hand from her shoulder and rubbed her face into the pillow.

"Marta Carolina," White Blossom called a little louder this time. Her hand returned to the shoulder and gently shook Marta Carolina again.

Something vaguely familiar about the call haunted Marta Carolina; it intruded into the peaceful oblivion of sleep. Slowly she emerged to full cognizance. She opened her eyes and blinked them. She looked at the silhouette above her. Timucuan, she thought when she saw the hairdo. She breathed deeply, turned again, and pulled the coverlet over her shoulders. She drifted away, but not to sleep. Another thought nagged. Consuelo! And another: The children!

Marta Carolina bolted up. "The children!" she said.

"Are they all right?"

"Yes, Marta Carolina," White Blossom said, "the children are all right, but not so you." With pleasure she observed Marta Carolina's eyes as they opened wide, the silver light of the moon clearly reflecting the fright in their shadowed depths.

"White Blossom," she whispered.

"It is I." The Chicoran laughed, playing with the necklace, doubling the strand and holding each end in a hand as if they were a medium length thong. "I have come to finish what I began when you were in Chicora. You should have died then."

Marta Carolina reflexively squirmed away from White Blossom, but the headboard of the bed dug into her back. "You can't kill me," she said.

White Blossom's laugh deepened. With swift, smooth movements, she whipped the pearls around Marta Carolina's neck and twisted them as easily as she twisted a thong around an animal she was about to kill and with as little conscience. "Night Star gave you this totem to save your life," she jeered, her eyes on the strand of pearls. "Little did she know that I would use it to kill you."

She pulled both ends of the pearls tautly to choke Marta Carolina whose hands came up, her fingers clawing at the vise. She gasped for breath and was so dizzy the room swam around her, rendering her temporarily blinded; she blacked out only to come to immediately. All the time she kicked and fought White Blossom, but she was no match for the warrior-trained woman. White Blossom gave the pearls a final jerk and watched Marta Carolina's face as it contorted in agony and death.

"I have already been to see the queen's grand-

440

daughter," White Blossom gloated to the dying woman. "She and that fat man she lives with are ready to leave for Chicora. They are awaiting my return now." Low laughter grated on Marta Carolina's ears and concealed the swish of the door as it opened. "She made me promise that I would bring the necklace, and so I shall. After I've choked the life out of your body and killed that man and the children, I shall let her keep the necklace. I have no need for it."

The minute Will had heard White Blossom's voice in Marta Carolina's room, he had opened the door, lightly because he didn't want to apprise them of his presence. He had heard her words, but only now—now that he was fully into the room did he see her, did he realize she was choking Marta Carolina.

"No!" he shouted, lunging across the floor for White Blossom.

She heard the sound and turned at the same time that she dropped the necklace. She unsheathed her knife and leaped to her feet to face the intruder. Moving cautiously, their arms extended, their eyes on each other, Will and White Blossom circled the room, locked in battle stance.

"I shall kill you, too, Will Dare," White Blossom hissed more than spoke. "You and the woman have brought shame on me. Because of you I have been banished from my tribe. I have no home, no people, no clan or totem."

With quick gracefulness her hand flew through the air and sliced her knife across the room, the tip cutting through the material of Will's shirt, barely grazing his skin. Then she sensed another's presence in the lodging. She looked at the door.

"Wise Owl," she shouted.

She pulled back her arm and loosed her knife to sail across the distance. It fell short of its goal, but the one Wise Owl threw hit true and deep. It lodged in her shoulder, a dark circle staining her buckskin shirt. She gasped, and her hand instantly reached up, clasped the hilt, and withdrew the weapon. Immediately Will raced to Marta Carolina who slumped on the bed, rubbing her neck. Wise Owl raced to White Blossom, but she was quicker than he. She bolted through the open window and darted through the buildings to disappear into the dark. Rather than hunt her, Wise Owl returned to the door to retrieve Justo whom he had set on the veranda. Now he laid him on the bed.

"Sweetheart," Will whispered, going on his knees beside Marta Carolina, "are you all right?"

"Yes," she said, her voice bruised and husky. When she looked beyond Will's shoulders at Wise Owl and his burden, she rasped, "Why have you brought Justo here?"

"We were afraid White Blossom was planning to kill the children," Will answered, "and we need to get them to Chicora as soon as possible."

"You knew White Blossom would try to kill them?" Marta Carolina questioned.

"We didn't know when," Will explained, "but we knew. Wise Owl learned that White Blossom refused the purification rites, and she and her braves mutinied against the queen. Night Star was wounded and may not live."

"Oh, my Lord!" Marta Carolina exclaimed, leaping to her feet, unmindful of her state of undress. "What about Concepción?"

442

Will grinned. "Consuelo is bringing her."

Marta Carolina rummaged through the dark for her dress. "As soon as I'm dressed, we shall be ready to leave."

"No, little one," Will said, "you will not be leaving with us."

Marta Carolina ceased her searching, turned, and walked back to him. She looked up at him, her eyes wide in the silver light. So thoroughly aware of Marta Carolina, Will could see the irises change from blue to indigo.

"Of course, I shall," she whispered.

Will took her hands into his and shook his head. "You and I, love, must remain here in the fort to keep from arousing Emilio's suspicion." He looked at Wise Owl and spoke. "I had wondered how we were going to get out of St. Augustine, but I see White Blossom has given us an answer. The queen's granddaughter and the man she lives with are ready to leave. He will get you out of the fort alive."

"What are you going to do about White Blossom?" Marta Carolina asked.

"My people will take care of that," Consuelo answered as she came into the room, Concepción following behind. "I will send word to Silver Bow; he and his warriors will find her and see that she receives her punishment." She looked at Wise Owl. "May I come with you to help care for the children?"

Wise Owl shook his head. "You must stay here, Woman-of-Joy." He called her by her Timucuan name. "I will come back for you, and we shall be married at the spring festival."

"I will wait," Consuelo promised.

"Be careful with the children," Marta Carolina cautioned, kissing and hugging both of them good-bye.

"I will," Wise Owl replied. "And do not worry. I have built a litter on which we will carry the boy. Once he's in Chicora, our shaman will give him medicine that will make him better. Soon he will walk without the help of the arm of the tree. He will grow into a strong brave." Wise Owl laid a hand on each of the children's heads. "These children will be the queen's delight. They will give her the will to live."

"But White Blossom and her warriors—" Marta Carolina muttered. "I'm worried about them. They may be a threat to you."

"No, mistress," Wise Owl answered, "they will be no threat. Silver Bow and his warriors will escort us to the edge of Chicora Land; there we will be met by Strong Bear and his warriors, who will take us home."

"Strong Bear," Marta Carolina murmured. "How sad for him! Will he, too, turn against the queen because she banished White Blossom?"

"Strong Bear is a Chicoran chief," Wise Owl answered. "He loves his people; he will not turn against them or the queen. Also, mistress, the queen did not banish White Blossom. The Council for All the Chicoras did. The queen simply voiced their judgment." He picked the boy up in his arms. "Come, Concepción, we must go get your mother. My friend," he addressed Will, "I will leave at the first light of dawn. My chances of passing as a Timucuan will be easier."

Consuelo caught Concepción's hand. "I will walk with you as far as I can," she said to Wise Owl.

Marta Carolina crossed to the window and stared at the eastern sky, ribboned in various shades of blacks and grays. She lifted a hand to her throat, gingerly touching the burn marks.

"I hope no harm comes to them," she said in a small, teary voice.

Will moved to stand behind her, his hands settling on her shoulders. He pulled her so that she rested against him. "The Chicorans would not have sent Wise Owl had he and his warriors not been capable of bringing Night Star's granddaughter back against all odds. Besides, Silver Bow will assist him."

"Now what?" she asked. Now that her most prevalent concern was lifted, she felt bereft, lost. "When will we get to Havana? The lieutenant is determined to keep us here. It seems to me that we move from one kind of imprisonment to another."

"We will be leaving soon," Will said. He understood how she felt. "Yesterday a galleon coming from Havana and headed toward St. Augustine was sighted. Emilio said it would anchor sometime this afternoon."

Marta Carolina turned in his arms, brushed her palms up his chest, and locked her hands about his neck. Although mauve semicircles underscored her eyes to emphasize her exhaustion, Will thought she was one of the most beautiful women he had ever seen. Certainly one of the bravest and most courageous. She smiled, her lips moving in that familiar gesture that lit up every corner of Will's heart.

"You and I then, sweetheart, will be free to live our own life. We shall be married and sail to New Spain to claim my *repartimiento*."

"Yes," Will murmured, wishing he could unload his last burdensome secret, wishing his past was as innocent and untarnished as hers.

Ironically, the only obstacle that lay behind them now was the one which lay ahead of them—the monster called his past. And he knew the past was sailing into the harbor to greet him head-on. His only uncertainty was the guise which it would wear.

"Now lie down," he said, guiding her back to the bed, "and get some sleep."

"What bout the infirmary?" she asked as he tucked her into bed.

"The natives can take care of that. You've trained them well." He leaned down to plant a kiss on her brow. "When you awaken, you'll feel refreshed and ready for tonight's dinner with our guests."

"Don Diego." Emilio bowed low and waved his hat through the air as he enthusiastically greeted the port official from Havana. "How delighted we are that you came to see us?"

"Thank you, sir," Diego said, stifling a yawn behind a delicate hand that was clothed in a beautiful leather glove.

He was bored with the entire situation before it ever began. Had not His Holiness, the bishop, insisted on his coming, he wouldn't have. He had no tolerance for the primitive, and St. Augustine could be described as nothing else but primitive.

"This—" he said with a wave of his handkerchief toward Timothy Turner "—is Capitan Ignacio Tello. He was kind enough to convey me here in his ship so that I might bring Mistress Marta Carolina's lost baggage to her and escort her to His Holiness. Do have one of your men take her things to her immediately."

"That I will, sir," Emilio gushed, bending low again as he bowed to Turner. "And you, Captain, we welcome to St. Augustine."

"Thank you," Timothy murmured, his gray eyes skimming the small settlement. He smiled broadly. Only two years ago was it that Drake razed this fort to the ground. When he left, he would leave them an even more bitter memory; St. Augustine would long remember Timothy Turner.

Later after Diego and Timothy had been assigned their quarters and Timothy was resting, Diego visited the garrison commander. A glass of wine in hand, he walked the length of the study and back again.

"I come on a matter of top priority," he said. "We are about to capture a nest of villainous Englishmen, corsairs—some of the most villainous in all the world."

Emilio was excited about this. His capture of the pirates would look good on his record, would gain him favor with the governor, and would perhaps bring him a monetary reward. He was sick of this pest hole with its mosquitoes and swamp fever. It was not honor to be in command of the soldiers stationed at St. Augustine. Were it not for Anita!

"Captain Ignacio Tello is dead," Diego imformed the lieutenant. "The man to whom I introduced you is an imposter who killed the captain and took his ship. This man's name—" Diego pointed toward Timothy's quarters "—is Timothy Turner. He has come to St. Augustine for the purpose of killing El Desafiador."

"I knew it!" Emilio pounded the table with his fist. "I knew he must be El Desafiador," he said, his mind on Will. Emilio squinted at the port official. "What are we going to do?"

"Patience, my dear lieutenant. Patience. We must take one step at a time. First, we must ascertain that this man whom you have here with you, this Guillermo Lucero, is in fact El Desafiador."

"Then we must protect him at all costs," Emilio blustered.

"No, my good man," Diego corrected him. "We shall aid Mister Turner in killing El Desafiador."

"We shall?" Emilio's mouth gaped open. He couldn't follow Diego's reasoning.

"El Desafiador is an English agent of whom we must dispose without anyone's learning his true identity. All must think he is a Spanish spy. The English queen, particularly, must never learn that El Desafiador was really one of her staunch supporters and that he was framed for murder and treason." Diego lifted his glass to his lips and drained it of the rich red wine. "So, my commander, you will await further orders from me."

"My clothes," Marta Carolina squealed that evening when the soldiers delivered her trunk.

She knelt beside the large chest, unfastened the leather straps, and opened it. She lifted gown after gown and buried her face in their rich softness. She breathed the fragrance of her perfume and powder. She dug for her favorite gown. She would wear it tonight, she thought, as she touched the golden silk, embroidered with beautiful threads and fine jewels.

Later she sat in front of her looking glass, brushing her curls around her face and tucking the combs and pins into her thick braid. "Tell me again, who's come?" she demanded of Consuelo as she settled the lace cap on her head and straightened the jewel that was secured to the point of the double crescent.

"Don Diego Jorge and Captain Tello," Consuelo replied.

"What do they look like?"

"I do not know, mistress," Consuelo answered. "I have not seen them. They went directly to the lieutenant's residence. Had it not been for the boy who helps Anita in the kitchen, I should not even know their names."

"How do I look?" Marta Carolina asked, standing to her feet and slowly turning around so Consuelo could inspect her.

"Beautiful, mistress, Very beautiful."

A knock, then Will's voice: "Marta Carolina, are you ready for supper?"

Marta Carolina swept open the door, her ivory and gold fan in hands that were covered in exquisite black leather gauntlet gloves. She greeted an equally grand gentleman, splendid in his rich trappings. He, too, wore new clothes, no doubt borrowed from one of the gentlemen who had put into port today, Marta Carolina thought with a twinkle in her eyes. As her eyes swept the dark green, French cut doublet with the high wings to the shoulders and the embroidered sleeves, she could not contain the small chuckle. How Will hated such garments.

"You look wonderful, my lord," she whispered, tucking her hand into the bend of his arm. "Why, the neat little ruff is no more than a stiff cup for your handsome face."

"And you, my lady, far outshine the queen herself."

"Thank you, good sir. Which queen—yours or mine?"

"Both," he returned.

Engaging in happy banter, the two of them walked to the lieutenant's residence. Once there the introductions were made and Marta Carolina found herself the center of attraction. While she had to admire the golden masculinity of Captain Tello—as she and Will knew Timothy Turner—she preferred the dark handsomeness of Will or Don Diego. But, she thought, fluttering her fan back and forth in front of her face, Don Diego was a little too soft for her. Yet it was he who managed to sit beside her through supper and to sit next to her afterward in the parlor. Marta Carolina tapped the fan over her mouth to hide her grin as she remembered the glowers Will had cast her throughout the meal.

"And were you frightened, madam?" Diego asked as he inquired about her harrowing escape from the ship.

"I was quite frightened," she replied, "but I did what had to be done. I have learned most recently that when we are frightened we are bravest. Sister Maria Theresa and I, without question, climbed into the smaller vessel and watched our ship burn." Sparing him a lot of details, Marta Carolina went on succinctly to describe her subsequent rescue by Will and the time she and he spent with the Chicorans.

"Quite a wealthy people, according to Emilio," Diego said, crossing one stockinged leg over the other.

"Not according to our standards of wealth," Marta Carolina pointed out practically. "They had a few pearls and some gold, but not in the quantities that we have in our other colonies in New Spain. Certainly nothing to warrant our endangering our soldier's lives for."

"Agreed, my lady." Diego played gently with his pomander for a while, then asked, "What will you do once you've reached New Spain, mistress?"

"I shall claim my uncle's *repartimiento,*" she said. "I carry papers for such an agreement on my person." She shivered. "I am so glad they were not packed with my other possessions, else I would have lost them as I lost my aunt's priceless chess set." Her blue eyes clouded with pain. "Her last gift to me."

Diego leaned forward and laid his hand comfortingly on hers. "I am sorry, my dear. Truly I am. You are so young to have suffered so much."

Marta Carolina managed a smile, all the while pulling her hand from under the weight of his.

"A game of chess anyone?" Emilio's voice rang out so loudly everyone turned to him.

Because she wore the gauntlet glove, Marta Carolina did not notice that Will's ring came off her finger and slipped down the folds of her skirt to land on the floor. Diego did not notice, either. He leaned closer and whispered, "I am not a chess player such as Emilio, but I have the distinct feeling, mistress, that I shall be the one who sits up to the early hours of the morning, playing game after game with him." He placed his hand against the side of his face in mock horror. "Woe is me!"

"Aye," she said with a knowing nod, "the lieutenant loves to play the game. We have whiled away many an hour since I have been here playing."

"Ah," Diego breathed the praise, "you know how! Who taught you, mistress?"

"My aunt," she replied.

At last the hour approached when Will and Marta Carolina could leave. Relieved Will was. He had watched for the past four hours while the men pawed over Marta Carolina, touching her with their hands and ducking

451

their heads close to whisper in her ears. Irritable he was as he escorted her to the lodging.

"Did you find Diego quite the gentleman?" he finally asked.

Marta Carolina didn't bother to suppress the grin that twitched the corners of her mouth. "Aye, love, I found him to be quite a gentleman."

"More so than I?" came the indignant question.

"Much more so than you, my lord" came the amused reply. She taunted him a second longer before she said, "But I care not, my love, for a gentleman. I care for my rugged, primitive lover. I much prefer him, my lord."

In front of her room, Will hungrily took her into his arms and planted his lips on hers in a hard, demanding kiss. They had been apart too long; he needed her. Dear God, he wanted her. Every cell in his body was starved for her touch. He caught her hand in his and guided it to his crotch.

"Feel me," he murmured. "Feel how big I am with desire. The ache which you cannot feel is even larger." His lips spread sweet, drugging kisses over her face back to her lips. "I want you so, my darling."

"Then you shall have me," she whispered. She opened the door and swept into her room, Will behind her. With his foot, he closed the door, the slam reverberating through the room. Quickly they divested themselves of clothes.

Their first coming together was urgent and catalytic; their first completion was deep and throbbing. The second was long and leisurely, each playing the other's body as if it were a finely tuned instrument. They touched with hands, lips, and tongues; they murmured endearments. They teased each other, working up to the summit but not quite going over . . . again . . . and . . . again. Slowly they climbed passion's peak, but this time consummation would not be cheated. They reached the summit, hovered in that one euphoric second when both lovers reach the pinnacle of pleasure at the exact moment; then they convulsed with all the violence of an explosion. Drained, they collapsed on the bed, each falling into a wonderful, sated sleep.

Chapter XX

The chess game finally over, Diego stood and stretched; then he returned to the paneled chair near the fireplace where he had been sitting earlier with Marta Carolina. Before he sat down, he hit an object with the toe of his shoes, something so light he would have dismissed it had he not heard metal singing across the floor. He looked until he found the circle of glistening gold which he retrieved and turned over in his palm.

"Madre de Dios!" he softly exclaimed, hurrying to the candelabrum so he could look more closely. *"Madre de Dios!"*

Emilio rushed to Diego's side. "What is it, señor?"

Don Diego clutched the ring tightly in his fist. "This proves we have El Desafiador, Lieutenant. This man known to us as Guillermo Lucero is indeed Will Dare."

"How—how do you know?" Emilio asked. He was a man caught between two powerful men, Diego and El Desafiador, and he didn't know in which direction to move. He wanted to believe both of them, *in* both of them. And he hesitated to make a move on Guillermo

Lucero without word from the governor. Damn, he muttered to himself, why did the governor have to be sailing up the coast right now! Why wasn't he here to issue the order?

Diego unfolded his hand, the ring displayed on the palm. "This is the proof for which I've been searching."

Emilio leaned nearer and squinted. "But that is Mistress Marta Carolina's ring. I have seen her wearing it."

Diego's brow hiked expressively. "She and Guillermo Lucero are indeed close, are they not, Commander?"

Emilio nodded his head; his face screwed into a grimace, and he immediately shook his head. "Don Diego, I respect your position, sir, and I would do anything to help apprehend corsairs and enemies to the Spanish throne, but I cannot accept this as evidence that the man whom I know as Guillermo Lucero is—is—an English spy."

Emilio had never considered himself an acutely intelligent man like the governor or Don Diego, who could make judgments and decisions on the spur of the moment, but if given time he could sort through information and separate fact from fiction. At the moment, however, he was overwhelmed. Everyone in St. Augustine seemed to be wearing a mask and hiding behind several names. He didn't know what or whom to believe anymore. Certainly he wasn't clear-headed enough to make a decision.

He lifted a thickly muscled hand to wipe the sweat from his brow. He and a few of his men who had been serving His Majesty over here for thirty years or more were going home soon. He couldn't jeopardize that. He had to be careful . . . very careful.

"This, commander," Diego repeated, the soft murmur maturing into resounding firmness, "is all the evidence you need that Guillermo Lucero is Will Dare who is El Desafiador. By this ring Sir James Palmer identified the man who had been sent to rescue him from the Spanish prison."

"How do you know this?" Emilio asked desperately. He felt as if he were a stone rolling down a hill. Unable to help himself or give himself direction, he was gaining momentum and running wild.

"One of my valued friends, Rodrigo Fernandez, knew El Desafiador. He told me how I would recognize him," Diego replied softly. His eyes were blank and faraway as if he were in great thought. "Please believe me, Commander. On the morrow I shall prove it to you." He smiled. "I should like to break fast with Mistress Marta Carolina, Señor Lucero, and Captain Tello."

Marta Carolina and Consuelo had searched the entire apartment on hands and knees for the better part of an hour, but neither found the ring.

"I know I had it on last night," Marta Carolina murmured, tears pricking her eyes.

"Perhaps Señor Lucero took it with him when he left before the break of day," Consuelo suggested.

"Perhaps," Marta Carolina drawled, rising. "I do hope so." She sighed. "Oh, well, I can ask him. He'll be here any time now."

"Mistress" came the call from outside the door.

Surprised, Marta Carolina and Consuelo looked at each other, but neither opened the door.

"The lieutenant sent me to fetch you," the masculine

456

messenger called. "He wishes you to break fast with him."

Consuelo opened the door to the young Spanish soldier.

"We need to hurry, mistress," he advised. "The other guests have already arrived.

"Yes, of course," Marta Carolina said. She wondered why the soldier rather than Will had come for her, but she could not expose her curiosity to one of the lieutenant's aides.

When Marta Carolina walked into the parlor, she saw the three men, standing together in front of the window. Her curiosity piqued, she sensed the tension in the room, and as soon as she entered, it also enveloped her. Rather than resenting it, however, she welcomed it. She was strangely exhilarated and felt as if the suspense gave her an inner strength and purpose. She moved across the room, a pleasant smile on her lips.

"Good morrow, mistress," Diego greeted her. "Rising early seems to agree with you. You are as lovely this morning as you were yesterday immediately after your siesta."

Marta Carolina kept her eyes from straying to Will. She must play this game without his help. "Thank you, kind sir," she simmered and batted thick lashes against her cheeks, her gloved hand touching his lower arm. "Shall we adjourn to the draw-table for our morning meal?"

Will hid the grin that tugged on his lips.

"Indeed we shall."

While on the surface everyone was friendly and the conversation informative, Marta Carolina felt the tension grow. Her emotions grew tighter and tighter by the

457

moment. She felt as if she were wound so tightly she would spin out of control any minute. A perpetual scream lodged in her chest, and her hands were clammy. Out of the corner of her eye, she looked at Will. He was so calm and self-assured, his tone easy and light, his smile friendly. She also noticed the glances with which he and Diego measured each other.

"Ah, Señor Lucero," Diego said from his position at the head of the table, "I believe this is yours." He squirmed in the paneled, high-backed chair, dug into his doublet, and came out with the ring. As if it were a victory trophy he brandished it in the air. "I believe this is your ring."

Marta Carolina opened her mouth to claim it; however, before the words could come, she saw Diego's eyes light on the whitened indentation on Will's little finger. Then, quite deliberately, they returned to the golden circlet with the star crested on the top.

"Lucero . . ." Diego mused. "The morning star."

Marta Carolina's eyes flew back to Will. He smiled and reached for the ring. "Indeed, Diego, the ring is mine. Where did you find it?"

Diego's mouth curved into a fine-lined smile. "I found it near the chair where Mistress Marta Carolina sat last night when she and I were talking."

"Ah, yes." Will drawled, flashing Diego a look of gratitude. "Mistress Marta Carolina has been kind enough to wear it for me," he said. Unperturbed, Will smiled at Marta Carolina as he slipped the ring onto his finger.

"I'm sorry," she whispered, grief-stricken that she had lost his valued possession. "It—it must have slipped off my hand last night and rolled under the chair."

"An unusual ring," Don Diego taunted.

Will touched the star. "My family crest."

"I have seen such a ring as that before," Diego said.

"Have you?" Will countered.

"*Sí*," Diego returned evenly. "In fact, I wondered if it were the same one."

Will stiffened. When could Diego have seen his ring? As quickly, he relaxed. The two of them were playing a game. Diego was bluffing.

"But no," Diego said, "I don't think it could have been the same one. The one I saw was worn by a man who called himself El Desafiador."

By now Timothy was on the edge of his chair. After two years he had finally found the man for whom he'd been searching. He was so excited he was actually shaking. "And are you the one called El Desafiador?" he asked.

Will's gaze swung from Diego to the man called Captain Ignacio Tello. Because this man hid his emotions and thoughts so ably, Will did not understand him. But he feared him. Tello was not what he appeared to be on the surface. Yet Will could do nothing but confess the truth. The moment called for truth—no matter what the consequences might be. At this realization his eyes moved to Marta Carolina, and he silently apologized; he begged for her understanding, for her forgiveness.

Although she didn't understand the meaning of the conversation, Marta Carolina knew Will's answer was important. She observed the expectancy on everyone's face. She read the apology in Will's eyes; she saw the plea, but she didn't know how to respond. What must she understand? What must she forgive?

With an imperceptible sigh, Will dragged his gaze from Marta Carolina and answered Timothy's question. "Yes,

459

señor, I am the one called El Desafiador."

"If I may be so bold," Timothy continued smoothly, his hand playing with his beard, "I should like to know what El Desafiador is doing in the New World."

"Immediately on my leaving Brussels," Will said, not stopping his story when he heard Marta Carolina's swift intake of breath, "I was sent on another mission. Someone had made it appear that El Desafiador had killed the people whom he was to contact in a small village outside Dover, an innkeeper and his young daughter. His Majesty felt it would be better if I were out of the country for a while." Will moved in the chair, laying his arm on the table.

Timothy's hands, hidden under the table, balled into tight fists.

"With only the pilot on board ship and I knowing my true identity, I was sent to check on the military garrison the English were establishing on the Chesapeake." Without losing visual contact with Timothy, Will said, "You will not find my name on the ship roster, Don Diego, if you should check the records. Since it was not necessary for me to mix with the other passengers, I wasn't even registered aboard the ship."

"Commendable piece of work, I must say," Diego murmured. "Strangely, none of us has been apprised of your mission." He smiled and shrugged dismissively as if his thought were of no consequence. "What were you to do once you obtained information on the English colony?"

"You were not apprised of my mission, Don Diego, because its success depended on secrecy." Will paused for impact. "I have come to find an English spy who is hiding in Cuba, sir." His raven-black eyes centered

460

squarely on Diego's face. "This man is on pension to the Crown of England and is supplying the queen with information about all wealth-laden vessels sailing to and from the Spanish Main and Spain."

Diego's lids drooped over his eyes, and he pretended interest in his glass. "Do you know who this man is, sir?"

"Aye."

Diego nodded. "Excellent. Captain Tello and I are leaving for Havana in the morning. You are welcome to travel with us if you wish. You can give your report to the governor in person." He hardly waited for Will's affirmative answer before he turned to Marta Carolina, "Mistress, after the others have been dismissed to their chores, I should like to have a word with you." Marta Carolina nodded, too confused to do more. She heard Diego speak to Timothy. "Captain, perhaps you will show Señor Lucero your galleon—all of your galleon. Spend some time with him and get to know one another much better."

Marta Carolina had never dreamed that Will was a Spanish spy. Why couldn't he have told her? Why didn't he tell her? Why had he purposely tried to convince her that he was English? So many questions came to mind, but no answers. Then she felt Diego's hand on her elbow.

"Come, Mistress Marta Carolina," he said softly in her ear, "let's go into the parlor where we shall have privacy."

Once they were behind the closed door, Diego said, "I have a strong feeling, madam, that you are in love with Señor Lucero."

From the throw-chair where she sat, Marta Carolina looked at him, but she never answered. She may have had her questions and her doubts about Will, but she would not discuss them with this insidious little man.

Diego's eyes narrowed. Marta Carolina was going to prove more an obstacle than he had reckoned. "I feel that it is only right you should know the truth."

Marta Carolina was transported back in time. She sat with her aunt, Dona Karolina. She heard Tía Karolina's words: The truth, *querida,* is relative. It depends on who is telling it and how they look upon it as to what it really is.

"Lucero is a spy with two faces, madam. He is Will Dare; his code name is El Desafiador."

"The one who dares," Marta Carolina whispered.

"He works for both the English and the Spanish." Diego smiled when he saw Marta Carolina pale and her lips thin. "He works for the one who pays him the highest."

"But he claims someone made him look guilty of murder when he was innocent," she pointed out.

Diego lifted his shoulders. "Listen to me first, child; then judge." He walked to the draw-table and lifted the ewer of wine and poured two glasses. The one he handed to Marta Carolina, the other he kept for himself. "His double-dealing was brought to the attention of the Duke of Parma two winters ago. When faced with the accusation, El Desafiador claimed innocence. To prove himself to the duke, he turned in an English spy in Brussels who, with her husband, was later tried and executed."

Diego watched Marta Carolina as she took a swallow of wine. Momentarily he saw the march of grief across her countenance to be followed by anger, but when she became aware of his scrutiny, she lowered her face.

"El Desafiador left Brussels that night and traveled

onward to England where he killed an innocent innkeeper and his daughter in an effort to prove to the English that he was still working for them. However, the innkeeper did not die in vain. He revealed to the English that Will Dare was working for the Spanish, and the Duke of Parma, through one of his trusted servants, learned that Will Dare—his El Desafiador—was working for the English."

Marta Carolina finished the wine, rose, and walked to the blackened fireplace to set her glass on the mantel. Her back to Diego, she said, "The spy whom he revealed in the Netherlands—that was Dona Karolina Lucas de Santiago?"

"The same," Diego replied softly, a sad tenderness in his voice. He wished he could have spared the child this hurt.

Knowing that Will was a spy, that he had lied to her repeatedly, that he was responsible for her aunt's execution didn't make Marta Carolina love him any less. It made her hurt so deep and so badly she didn't know if she could stand the pain. Her grief was so great, it exceeded death. All that she had thought Will Dare to be, he was not. All she had dreamed that the two of them would do together, they would not.

Added to her grief was a fury such as she had never experienced before. The compounded emotions made her momentarily question Will's feelings for her. From the beginning he had insisted that he felt nothing more for her than lust. But she—the heat of embarrassment rushed over Marta Carolina's body as she remembered— she had wittingly played his game; she had allowed herself to be used and manipulated by him. He was the puppeteer, she the puppet, and the string she dangled on was her love for him.

From afar Marta Carolina heard Diego's words, "I'm sorry, mistress." When she said nothing, Diego asked, "Will you help us?"

Marta Carolina was surprised at how quickly she had matured. Only seconds—minutes at the most—had passed; yet she felt as if she had witnessed the passing of years. With beautiful grace she spread her fan and lifted it to her face. She hid behind a false smile. "I may not like all Señor Lucero has done or what he may be," she confessed, "But I love him."

"I'm not going to ask you to do anything to hurt him," Diego promised as he gazed at Marta Carolina through narrowed eyes. "But we do need your help."

Marta Carolina shrugged. She was surprised that she was not convulsed with tears; she was even more surprised that she was as controlled as she was. Strangely, she was calm.

"We must find the documents El Desafiador brought to Brussels for the English," Diego said, repeating the lie which Rodrigo Fernandez had invented for him; then he paused. Was the girl listening to him? he wondered. What was she thinking? "These papers—" he cleared his throat in an effort to break through the barrier she had erected around herself "—they detail a plot to kill King Phillip and important officials of the Church."

"And how can I help you?" Marta Carolina asked. "Do you think I am one of your spies also?" A viper's nest, Will had said, and truly she was in one.

"No, mistress, I do not. But Will Dare brought the papers to your aunt." Again this was a fabrication. El Desafiador was to have received the papers from Dona Karolina.

The documents which the Duke of Parma begged Donna Karolina to give up, Marta Carolina thought. But her aunt had disclaimed knowledge of them. "They will not believe that I no longer have the papers," she had said.

"And she was never alone from the moment Will Dare left her side," she heard Diego say. "The papers have got to be hidden in some of her belongings. With your permission may we check through your baggage?" They had gone through that which they confiscated from the corsairs; now all that remained was that which she had with her.

Marta Carolina nodded.

"Did your aunt give you anything which might lead us to the papers?" he asked.

She shook her head; then she remembered. "The last time I saw her, she gave me her most valuable chess set." On the verge of tears, she laughed instead. "Some of the pieces were missing. She—she gave it to me."

"May I see it?"

"I don't have it," Marta Carolina replied. "The corsairs stole it. You did not find it in my things?"

"No," he sighed, and his shoulders drooped with disappointment. Anything else?" he asked. "Can you remember her giving you anything else or saying something in code perhaps?"

In a low voice Marta Carolina repeated as nearly correctly as she could remember everything her aunt had told her the last time they visited together. She ended with, "I had the queen's piece pierced so that I could wear it around my neck on a gold chain."

"May I see it?" Diego asked.

"Señor Lucero has it," Marta Carolina replied. "He's

wearing it." She rose and said, "If you don't mind, Don Diego, I should like to be excused. I'm rather tired."

"Of course, mistress," he quickly responded. He hurried to the table, lifted the bell, and rang for Anita. When she opened the door, he said, "Escort Mistress Marta Carolina to her room, please."

"What's going to happen to Will?" Marta Carolina asked from the doorway.

"That depends on him," Diego lied. "If he cooperates with us, we shall be lenient with him. If he does not—" A shrug and a wave of his hands through the air completed his statement.

A few minutes after Marta Carolina walked out, the door opened, and Rodrigo Fernandez walked into the room. "Well, my friend, how are things progressing?"

Diego smiled. "Marvelous. Simply marvelous. At the moment we have your friend, El Desafiador, right where we want him."

Fernandez chuckled. "And where is that?"

Will heard the lock grate as soon as the door slammed. "And what are you getting out of this, Captain?" he asked, looking through the metal bars that comprised the top fourth of the door. "Or *is* it 'Captain'?" The raven-black eyes perused the face on the other side of the bars—the face that struck him as familiar but one that was elusive to recall.

"Yes, Señor El Desafiador," Timothy said, "it is captain, but it is not Ignacio Tello." With a grand flourish, he doffed his hat, swept a wide bow, and said, "I am Timothy Turner, sir. 'Twas my betrothed you killed at the tavern in Dover."

"Ah, yes—" Will nodded. Now he remembered. The beard had changed the lad's appearance, but this was the same person who had followed him into the tavern to discover the bodies of Henry and Betsy Smyth.

"And now, I shall have the pleasure of killing you. Slowly and most painfully."

Will laughed. "Good, sir, I wish you luck. I fear, though, you must wait in line. Others wish that pleasure themselves." In quite an indolent gesture of unconcern, Will reached up to stroke his chin. "You wouldn't believe me, Captain Turner, if I were to tell you that I did not kill your betrothed and her father."

"Lies are plentiful, sir."

"Aye," Will agreed complacently, "that they are." He reached into the doublet and his fingers circled the queen's piece Dona Karolina had given him as the two of them departed the church. "Does Diego know that you are English?" Will asked.

Timothy shook his head. "Only the queen's pensionary Rodrigo Fernandez knows. He is the one who helped me set up your capture."

A bitter smile twisted Will's lips, and his eyes slitted. "Rodrigo Fernandez, my good man, is not to be trusted. He is the one responsible for the death of your betrothed and her father, for the death of Marta Carolina's aunt and uncle, and—" Will pushed a finger through the bars and jabbed on Timothy's chest "—I'm sure he's planning on the capture of a ship full of English pirates for which he shall get full glory."

For the first time since he'd arrived in St. Augustine, Timothy's eyes lost some of their cocksureness. "You would say that," he accused at last, "because you want to escape."

"Nay, lad," Will answered, "I'm where I want to be. I'm on my way to face the man I've been hunting for the past two years." Gone from his face was the assumed casualness and the insolent mask of the spy and courier. "I ask one small favor."

Timothy observed the changed demeanor and tone of voice. He nodded his head without hearing the request. He intuitively knew he would grant El Desafiador's desire.

"Take care of Mistress Marta Carolina. In no way is she involved in these political intrigues. Take her away from Diego and Rodrigo Fernandez and see that she gets to her *repartimiento* in New Spain."

"I will," Timothy promised.

"Now, good captain, with your permission," Will said, his somber mood vanishing as quickly as it came. "I need some time to myself. I must plan and scheme my escape."

Diego and Rodrigo Fernandez went through all Will's belongings, tearing every garment to shreds as they searched for secret hiding places, but they found nothing.

"Nothing here." Fernandez slammed his fist through the air. "Nothing in Dona Karolina's house. We searched it inch by inch. Not one nook or cranny did we miss. And the papers we found at the tavern in Dover were senseless words written in Dutch." He lifted a hand and cupped his neck, his fingers biting into the tensed muslces. "Where could the document be? Someone has to have it!"

"We have searched everywhere but not everything," Diego told him. "We have only two more places to look." Fernandez looked at him inquisitively. "The girl's chess piece, the one her aunt gave her and the one Will Dare

468

wears around his neck."

The room resounded with Fernandez's jeering laughter. "Don't act daft, man! Do you expect a document to be secreted in a chess piece?"

Taking no umbrage at the scoffing, Diego said, "No, I don't, but you and I know how Dona Karolina loved to send messages through chess pieces."

The smirk instantly disappeared from Fernandez's face, and he nodded his head.

"Dona Karolina had to have had a reason for giving that chess set to Marta Carolina and for having picked up that one particular chess piece." He held his hand in the air, gently waving his index finger. "The queen's piece, my friend. The queen's piece."

"You're right!" Fernandez snapped his fingers as he remembered Will's words to him at the tavern that night two years ago. "The chess pieces are the answer to the puzzle, and Will Dare knows what they mean. All this time he has had the answer!"

Both men raced out of the lieutenant's residence to the galleon. They hurried aboard to be met on the quarterdeck by Timothy himself. "Don Diego," he greeted, "what can I do for you, sir?"

"The prisoner," Diego said, out of breath. "I want to see the prisoner."

Rodrigo lagged behind and talked with one of the Spanish officers, not boarding the ship until Turner and Diego were out of sight. Caught up in the excitement and the rush. Timothy led them down the narrow slant of stairs to the mid-deck below to the hold, stopping only once to light a candle. He unlocked the door and pulled it open, the small, dancing flame doing little to cast out the darkness. He set the pewter holder on the table and waited for Diego to come into the room. Fernandez remained in the companionway, nothing but a dark, undistinguishable silhouette.

Diego moved to the narrow couch on which Will reclined. "I've come to get the queen's piece," he said.

"Which one?" Will asked.

"Both of them," Diego replied. "The one Mistress Marta Carolina gave to you which you wear around your neck, and the one Dona Karolina gave to you when you met her in the church."

"What if I said I don't have them?" Will replied.

"We can search you."

"Go ahead."

"Where have you hidden them," Don Diego shouted, his patience ended. "Where are they, you bastard?"

Will looked at the face which loomed above his. The light behind them, he saw nothing but distorted features. It reminded him of someone he once knew—but again his memory played tricks on him. He remembered the elusive face . . . or voice . . . or movement one moment; the next he remembered nothing. The voice coming to him from the darkness . . . The voice! He remembered! He'd heard it somewhere before! But the face slipped into oblivion. He couldn't remember. He glanced around Diego to the man in the door. He recognized the stance, the width of shoulder, the height. He knew immediately that he was looking at Rodrigo Fernandez.

"Hello, Rodrigo."

"Hello, Will." Fernandez didn't move from the doorway. "Sit down, Diego. There's no need to get upset. We have him, and sooner or later we'll get the information we want. If not—" He shrugged.

Diego sat in the chair and laid one arm on the table.

With his other hand he reached into his doublet and pulled out his handkerchief, a beautiful piece of soft linen bounded by four inches of exquisite lace work. Lifting it, he wiped his face, the gauzy material falling across the table in front of his arm.

Spellbound, Will stared at the table. Through the thin material on which the light of the candle played, Will looked at the outline of Diego's arm, features and color both obscured. Will was transported back in time. He was sitting in the confessional, a small window with a gauzy curtain over it, the only thing between him and the prisoner. Darkness all around him. Only a voice and an arm, only shadows and a lace curtain.

"Diego," he said, memories returning. "Would it be Don Diego Romero?"

"Yes."

"You saw my ring through the confessional when I came to talk with you when I thought you were a prisoner. That's how you could make the final identification. All the time you were the one."

"Yes."

"I thought you were dead, Sir James Palmer."

"For all practical purposes James Palmer is dead," Diego replied and swept his hand toward the man who stood in the door. "With Rodrigo's help he died in prison at the hands of the Spaniards."

"So, Her Majesty, the queen was told," Will said. "Another one of your lies, Rodrigo?"

"I prefer to call it a necessary untruth," Fernandez quietly replied, no wit perturbed.

"Alive, James Palmer was in the way," Diego explained. "Dead he was most useful. I am now Diego Romero and will be from this time forward. However, I have one job to complete, one I began two years ago and would have completed had it not been for you."

Timothy wasn't sure what was happening, and he didn't understand all he was hearing. Too great a gap existed between the spoken and the remembered. But he felt his world closing in on him. He felt the door of a prison cell locking him in this small, dark room

"I must put into action my plan for the assassination for the vain woman who holds the throne in England."

"But you don't dare contact any of the people because you don't know what happened to the documents which Dona Karolina sent to the queen, do you? You didn't find them on her or in her house? Evidently you didn't find them at the tavern, either!"

"And you cannot have them," Diego pointed out, "otherwise, you would have vindicated yourself with them."

Will laughed, a quiet sound that infuriated Don Diego. "That's why James Palmer was in the way alive," he taunted. "His name is on the list Dona Karolina was sending to Her Majesty. If the Spaniards hadn't pretended to put him to death, the English really would have done so." The laughter grew stronger. "What are you going to do, James Palmer? The documents will be located sooner or later."

The truth goaded Diego into screaming, "You have the key. You have the key."

"At present we are going to do nothing," Fernandez answered for Palmer. With a flick of his wrist, two soldiers, wearing their breast-plate and helmet and armed with a sword and a matchlock, moved into sight, although they remained in the companionway. "You, Turner, and his crew will become our prisoners."

"What do you mean?" Timothy shouted to the retreating Fernandez. "Are you taking us back to Cuba to stand trial?"

"No," Will quietly interposed, "that is not what he means, Captain Turner. Fernandez is not a pensionary for the queen, but the English must continue to think he is. If I'm not mistaken—" Will glanced at Fernandez's back "—Señor Fernandez has included you in his plan to rid the English of the hated spy, El Desafiador. An English pirate attacks St. Augustine, kills the traitor, but in turn is killed by the Spanish soldiers."

"How perceptive you are, Will Dare," Fernandez softly said over his shoulder as he stepped out of the small storage room that had now become a cell.

"But not perceptive enough," Diego jeered. "Neither of you, or you wouldn't have been captured."

"Come, Diego," Fernandez said, his footfalls already echoing through the hold. "We must return to Emilio before he suspicions anything afoul."

Diego nodded, and he quickly followed his friend. The heavy door slammed, and the sound of the bolt sliding into place reverberated long after Diego Romero moved toward the stairs that would carry him to the quarterdeck. The flame of the candle flickered against the dark walls to illuminate him in a small circle of light. But he didn't notice the blackness that surrounded him. He was deep in thought.

He could not get Dona Karolina's last two messages out of his mind. The first had come with the bishop and had read: Beware the bishop! The second came the day she was executed, the note tied around the king piece. One word, it said "Checkmate!"

He reached into his doublet for the two ebony chess

pieces he had been carrying with him for two years. Everyone in Holland knew Dona Karolina loved the game so much she collected boards and chessmen from all over the world. Also a known fact was that she chose to relay messages through chess pieces.

What did they mean? he wondered, staring first at the bishop, then at the king. What did they mean?

Still no answer! Yet he knew he would live in fear of the answer to the day he died.

Chapter XXI

"What now Will Dare, Guillermo Lucero, or El Desafiador or whatever your name is?" Timothy asked in English, his face uplifted as he studied the timbers of the ship.

"Will Dare," Will curtly replied, also speaking in English. "We have to figure a way to get out of the hold."

"I'm open to suggestions" came the dry reply.

Will walked to the door, caught two of the iron bars, and shook. "Tight," he gritted as he tried to pry them loose.

"Everything about this vessel is in excellent condition." Timothy exhaled heavily. "I can vouch for that. Even if it weren't, what are you going to do about the guards outside the door."

"I worry about one thing at a time, my man. My first concern is to get out of this place. Then I'll think about the guards. Was this cargo area converted into a cell just for me?" he asked.

"At the time I thought it was," Timothy answered, "but now I know Fernandez had it built for you and me."

"How did you get involved with Fernandez?" Will asked curiously.

Sitting on the bench beside the table, Timothy started talking, not stopping until he had told Will about his life for the past two years. In careful detail he outlined his hatred and search for El Desafiador.

"When I learned from the colonists that you were on your way to St. Augustine and an English pensionary lived in Havana," he concluded on a bitter snort of laughter, "I thought my quest was over. Little did I know I was going to get caught in my own web." He paused only momentarily before he said, "Since all we have is time, and precious little of that, tell me about yourself. You seem to have led an adventurous life as well as I."

Moving to the cot in the corner of the room, Will sat down, reclining more than sitting. As leisurely as if he and Timothy had met at the local inn in Plymouth where their ships were docked and were drinking their ale, Will verbally sketched the past two years of his life for Timothy.

"I will tear Rodrigo Fernandez to pieces, limb by limb," Timothy snarled when Will finished his story. He was angry with the Spaniard, but he was furious with himself for having been ensnared in his own trap— caught by the very man whom he had been chasing for the past two years. "How he must have laughed at me!" Timothy grated, raking his hand through his thick golden hair. "How much a fool I was!"

"Nay, my friend," Will quietly admonished. "Don't take it so hard upon yourself. Rodrigo Fernandez is an accomplished spy, one of the best in Europe, and you're but a rank amateur. Besides, the good fathers who taught me were quite fond of saying all things work out best for them who love the Lord and who are called by Him."

"I've never been one to spend much time in church," came Timothy's reply, "so I doubt the good fathers would consider me called by God."

The two of them lapsed into silence; however, both were preoccupied with the same thought: escape. What seemed like hours later but may have only been minutes, both heard a scuffle and a thud.

"Did you hear that?" Will asked, quietly leaping to his feet and running to the door.

"Aye," Timothy murmured, right behind him.

They waited and listened but heard nothing else. They peered down the dark companionway but saw nothing. Disappointed, both returned to their respective places. Then they heard the scrape of metal on metal, the grate and the grind of the bolt. The door swung open.

"Now, my friends—" Slowly the candlelight filtered through the heavy darkness as Fernandez moved into the cell, four soldiers with their match-lock guns propped and aimed on Will and Timothy "—it is time for you to escape."

Will's soft chuckle echoed through the small room. "Nay, Rodrigo, I don't think I want to escape. You and I have played this game before, and I didn't fare too well. Besides, I'm looking forward to seeing Havana."

"In the beginning, Will Dare," Rodrigo said, "my plan was to take you to Havana; however, circumstances have altered it considerably. Our good captain is no longer performing as I had expected him to. Now I think you shall escape. Both you and the captain shall be leaving." Because he gestured with the candle the flame frantically danced around the wick. "But, alas—" he clicked his tongue sympathetically "—both of you will be killed in the attempt."

"And, pray tell, how am I going to meet my death?" Will asked.

"The dogs," Rodrigo replied.

"That's rather bloody," Will retorted. "Have I no choice in the matter?"

"None."

"Well, then—" Will slowly unfolded from the cot and stood. "I had just as soon take my chances with the bloodhounds as with you Spanish dogs."

Fernandez's face twisted in anger, and he drew back his hand and slapped Will across the face. "If I had my way about it, I'd kill you myself."

"You couldn't kill me, Fernandez. You're not man enough."

"You're right," Fernandez admitted, "I can't kill you, but I'll take the glory for it when I report to your Queen Elizabeth that El Desafiador is dead. At the same time, when the Duke of Parma learns that his most illustrious pensionary is dead, I shall take none of the blame."

"Does Palmer know what you're doing?" Will asked, but as soon as the question slipped past his lips he knew the answer. "No, he doesn't," Will drawled, "because you've turned the tables on him without his knowing it. Rather than your working for him as he thinks, you're manipulating him. Once you kill me and find Dona Karolina's documents you will have no further need of James Palmer, and since he's already dead in the eyes of Her Majesty . . ."

"You always were astute," Rodrigo hissed, unable to hide his admiration. "But I was always a step ahead of you."

Will laughed. "You can't straddle the fence all your life, Rodrigo. One of these days you're going to fall and hurt yourself in a bad way, if you know what I mean."

Fernandez threw back his head and laughed.

Timothy, his fists clenched to his side, moved closer to the Spaniard. "I will kill you with my bare hands," he gritted, "for what you did to Betsy and her father."

Fernandez's laughter grew louder, more boisterous. "You stupid Englishman, you're not going to kill anyone. You played right into my hand. Had I planned the capture of Will Dare myself, it couldn't have turned out better." He withdrew his sword and lightly jabbed the point against Timothy's chest. "Come, now. We must be going."

"Where are my men?" Timothy asked.

"They, my good captain, will be put to good use in the galley."

"You bastard!" Timothy lunged at Fernandez, but the Spaniard thrust the sword into the captain's chest and laughed when blood stained Turner's shirt crimson.

"A surface wound, but don't tempt me."

When they emerged on the quarterdeck, Will saw that it was nightfall. He heard the water quietly lapping and the chirping of the forest creatures.

"You're not going to give us the advantage of daylight?" he asked.

Again Fernandez laughed. "You ask too much, old friend. I am already letting you escape. That is enough."

"What about weapons?" Will asked.

Fernandez sheathed his sword, placed his hands on his hips, and contemplated Will. Finally he drew in a deep breath and nodded his head. "Yes, you shall have

479

weapons. I don't want it to be said that I didn't give you a fair chance. Whatever you want! Name it."

"Two hours' head start." Timothy gasped the words in between deep gulps of air as he and Will splashed up the river. "Hardly enough time to outrun those hounds." He could hear them braying in the distance. "The soldiers are smart enough to follow the river, and as soon as we get out those dogs will catch our scent."

"Aye," Will grunted, his chest hurting from the lack of oxygen. "So we've got to think of something else, some way of tricking them."

Onward they traveled, talking little, thinking a great deal. Every so often one of them would say, "We could—" Then he would shake his head. "No, we can't." And then they rounded a bend in the river, the clearing illuminated by the moon. Standing in the shallows were two majestic horses, packs rather than men on their backs; standing beside them were four Indian braves. Will and Timothy watched one of the Indians move toward them; they heard the dogs barking behind them.

"Hello, Will Dare."

"Silver Bow!" Will exclaimed when the brave was close enough for him to recognize. Doubts began to plague him. "What are you doing here?"

"My braves and I have joined the Spaniards in their hunt for escaped prisoners."

"Have you found them?" Will asked quietly, his eyes darting about as he sought a route of escape.

"I have."

"What are you going to do with them?"

"Turn them over to the Spaniards," Silver Bow replied.

Evidently White Blossom had been correct, Will thought. Silver Bow had been scheming with the Spaniards all along. "What are you receiving in exchange?"

"More weapons." He lifted his hand and waved to his braves who waited in the distance. When they neared, he walked to one of the horses and picked up an edge of the blanket to expose the body of Manuel Pena. "We have the Spanish soldier and Night Star's granddaughter."

"What happened?"

"We were attacked by White Blossom and her braves. These two were killed."

"The children?" Will asked,

"They escaped," Silver Bow replied, a rare smile touching his face. "Now we must go meet the soldiers with the dogs," he said. "This will stop them for a while and give you more time to escape. Follow Grandfather, the river, my friend. He is your friend and will lead you to safety. Stay there until one of my braves returns to tell you that it is safe to travel. Now go."

Glad that Silver Bow was not the traitor White Blossom had accused him of being, Will said, "Thank you, my friend."

Nodding, Silver Bow stared at Will for a long moment, and his smile deepened; then with a wave of his hand he and his braves moved, their tall, lean forms soon blending into the forest.

Will and Timothy stayed in the river, but still they heard the braying of the hounds which seemed to get louder. They topped an incline and stopped. Dead ahead of them was a large waterfall. Each veered from the river and moved up either bank in search of a path around the precipice, but none could be found.

"The dogs are getting nearer," Timothy finally said when he and Will stood together again. He looked over his shoulder in the direction from which the barking was coming.

"Aye," Will returned.

"What now, my friend?" As soon as the words slipped from his tongue, Timothy turned his head and gazed at Will. How ironic that the man he had hated for the past two years and had sworn to kill was now his ally.

As if the same thought passed through Will's mind, he grinned. Then his head swiveled and he was scanning the countryside—the river, the waterfall, the incline. "We'd better put some distance between us and them."

"Silver Bow was lying to you."

"No," Will yelled, a note of animation in his voice, "he wasn't. I know what he meant. Come on." He dove into the river and swam through the fall into the cave.

"I can't believe it," Marta Carolina whispered, her face ashen.

"You can believe it, señorita," Diego said. "Will Dare escaped last night while we slept."

"Did he—did he get away?" she asked.

"No," Diego replied sorrowfully, "he did not."

Marta Carolina remembered the braying of the hounds. "The dogs?"

"Yes," he softly said. "Captain Tello and I are sailing for Havana immediately. I shall have your baggage loaded onto the ship."

Marta Carolina looked at him rather blankly. "What?"

she murmured. Diego repeated himself and awaited her reaction. "I—I suppose so," she mumbled. She was too confused to think at the moment, but without Will Dare she had no future in Florida. Without Will Dare she had no future at all!

"I'm sorry, my dear," Diego softly said.

"I should like to be alone," Marta Carolina said.

"Of course," Diego smoothly replied, rising from the settle and moving to the door, "I can understand. This has been a great shock for you."

Marta Carolina was so numb, she couldn't grieve. She felt as if she were a person detached from herself. She was aware of all that went on around her, but she was not a part of it. She dressed; then she sat in the throw-chair and watched Consuelo pack her trunks.

"Here is your medicine bag," the Timucuan said as she gently laid the satchel in the chest. "Your recipes and your medicine cabinet."

"Thank you," Marta Carolina returned in a detached voice, her eyes on the rising sun rather than her bag.

Later, escorted by Diego, she walked behind the soldiers as they carried her trunks to the ship. She vaguely remembered their boarding and Diego's leading her to a cabin.

"Lie down, my dear," he kindly suggested, guiding her to the bed, "and rest. I'll come get you when we're ready to dine."

Marta Carolina had ceased to mark the advance of time. She lay on the bed and stared into space, remembering all the wonderful moments she and Will had shared. A smile trembled on her lips when she recalled the first time Will kissed her; she laughed softly when she thought about the bear. She hurt—she hurt badly when she thought of all the lies and the deceit that separated them in death. She burned with shame when she remembered the way she had so blatantly given herself to him and had allowed him to use her.

She heard the knock on the door. "Come in."

"It's time for us to dine," Diego announced.

"I'm not hungry." She turned dull blue eyes on him.

His heart wrenched for the poor child. Walking into the room, he sat on the bed beside her and took her hands into his. "I'm deeply sorry," he said. "I do not care for the traitor myself, but I can understand what a shock his death is to you. But you cannot stop living, my dear. You're a young and beautiful woman. You have so much to give."

"I have no intention of dying," she answered quitely. "I'm just rather tired. So much has been happening."

"Come with me," he invited. "Whether you eat or not, you need to get out of this stuffy room. Also I should like you to meet a good friend of mine."

When they entered the captain's cabin, Fernandez stood at the window looking out. He was splendidly dressed, and his black hair, burnished to a high sheen, gleamed in the light of the lantern immediately over his head. He turned to smile at Marta Carolina.

"Good evening, mistress."

"Good evening," Marta Carolina returned prefunctorily, extending her hand for his greeting.

"I have heard so much about you," he murmured, his lips grazing her glove-covered hand.

"I'm afraid you have the advantage, sir," she said.

"Rodrigo Fernandez," he said. "His Majesty's Port Official of Havana."

"To him you owe a great thanks," Diego interjected.

"After I received Lieutenant Bustamante's letter, I sent a list of your belongings to Rodrigo. He's the one who captured the corsairs that plundered your ship and rescued your baggage."

"Thank you," Marta Carolina murmured methodically.

Throughout the meal she listened to the two men talk, but she heard nothing of what they said. She tasted little of her food. While she sipped a glass of wine after supper, she watched the cabin boy as he cleared the table. Before she was aware of it, she was alone with Fernandez. Hastily she rose to make her departure, but he detained her.

"One moment, mistress," he pleaded. "Don Diego tells me that you are an excellent chess player."

"I play well," Marta Carolina slowly admitted.

Fernandez cast her a most winsome smile. "Please play a game with me. I have not had one worthy opponent since I left Spain."

Marta Carolina twisted her head to look at the black-and-white board that set on the table. The alternate squares of marble glistened in the candlelight. A woman in a daze, she walked to the table and stared at the familiar pieces. The queen's piece that Dona Karolina had given to her—that she had given to Will—was there; the black queen was returned. Gone were the black bishop and king.

"You," she turned, accusing eyes blazing at Rodrigo Fernandez.

He nodded his head. "Me."

"The Corsairs were not English."

"No," Fernandez admitted, quite proud of his deed, "they were my men."

Incredulously Marta Carolina said, "You had them attack our ship, kill everyone on board and plunder it. Then you ordered them killed as English pirates! Why?"

"The cost of war, dear lady," Fernandez explained. "When Diego received word from the Duke of Parma concerning your trip to New Spain, I conceived the plan to get rid of you."

"Me!" Marta Carolina could not believe what she was hearing.

"You," he patiently explained. "You have something that I desperately need?"

"What is that, sir?"

"The documents which your aunt was sending to England."

Marta Carolina was puzzled. "I know nothing about any documents."

Fernandez was losing patience quickly. "You must have them," he grated. "You're the last person she saw before she died."

"I don't."

Fernandez grabbed her by the shoulders and jerked her to him. "Then she told you where she had hidden them." She shook her head. "She gave you and Will Dare the two queen's pieces."

"No," Marta Carolina protested. "She gave me only one queen piece."

"The other she gave to Will Dare," Rodrigo grated. Reaching up, his fingers bit into her chin. He turned her face and lowered it over the checkerboard. "What do the coded pieces mean?"

"I don't know," Marta Carolina replied, hardly able to stifle her groan as his fingers dug deeper into her tender flesh.

The door opened and Diego walked into the room, an enigmatic smile hovering on his lips. "What about a secret compartment, Rodrigo?" he asked.

"A secret compartment," Fernandez murmured, dropping his hand from Marta Carolina's face and stepping back. He snapped his fingers. "Of course, the crazed woman was always saying 'God save the queen.' Why hadn't I thought about that?"

He turned Marta Carolina loose and raked the chess pieces from the board. Grasping the bottom of the board with his fingers, he thrust his thumbs on both queen's primary position. He pushed, but nothing happened.

When Fernandez was preoccupied with finding the hidden chamber, Diego withdrew his sword and waved his hand for two soldiers, who were hiding in the hall, to quietly enter the room.

"You've been quite busy since you've arrived in Havana, have you not, Rodrigo?"

Hearing the subtle change in Diego's voice, Fernandez laid the chess board down and looked up. When he turned, the movement brought his chest against the point of Diego's sword. His eyes darted about, and he immediately encountered the soldiers standing behind him, their swords drawn also.

"All this time, Rodrigo, and you haven't told me about your having the chess set." Diego stroked his beard contemplatively. "I wonder why? Could it be that you planned to betray me? You set up my fake death in Holland. Were you planning to make it a fact now, my friend?" He laughed and reached into his doublet to extract the black king's piece. "Well, I'm sorry to disappoint you, but I must live a while longer. You see, I have the key to unlock the puzzle. This is one time that

Dona Karolina outsmarted herself." Sheathing his sword, he moved to the table and grasped the checkerboard in much the same manner as Rodrigo had done previously. This time, however, the thumbs rested over the king's primary position. When he pressed, a drawer glided open.

Marta Carolina gave a gasp of surprise and her eyes widened.

Diego picked up the sheet of paper. His hands shook as he unfolded and laid it on the table to hand-press the wrinkles. "The document," he murmured. "At last, I have it." He turned to the soldiers and jerked his head toward Rodrigo. "Take him below to the hold and lock him up."

"What about the woman?" one of them asked.

"The woman?" Diego repeated absently, having forgotten about Marta Carolina. Then he said, "Lock her in the cabin." In almost the same breath he added, "Send the pilot to me. We shall sail at break of day."

Hours later, having removed his baggage to the commanding officer's cabin, Don Diego hunched over the desk, the documents—which he had so slowly and laboriously translated—crushed in one fist, the black bishop chess piece in the other. "No," he muttered to himself, "this cannot be. Even in death she has beaten me!" As if to prove something to himself, he laid the papers down and hand-pressed them. Again he read the document. Nothing but a lengthy letter in which she laughed at Sir James Palmer and promised his ruin. The last three words mocked him: "Beware the bishop!"

Chapter XXII

Because of Silver Bow, Will and Timothy were able to elude the hounds and circle back to St. Augustine, arriving as morning gray first streaked the sky. Quietly they slipped aboard the ship and past the guards posted on the quarterdeck. Because the Spaniards expected neither trouble nor the return of Will and Timothy and because they relied on their bloodhounds, the soldiers were lax in their watch and eager to be on their way to Havana. By prearrangement Timothy and Will each went in a different direction, Timothy to find and release his men, Will to rescue Marta Carolina.

In the darkness Will crept down the companionway past the first two cabins. These Timothy had told him would be for the commanding officer and the pilot of the ship. Marta Carolina would be in the second one on the right. Will stopped and quietly tried the handle to find the door locked. But evidently he hadn't been quiet enough. He heard footsteps, then pounding on the door from the inside and Marta Carolina's muffled shout, "Let me out of here!" Louder was a noise across the hall.

Uncertain who or what it might be, Will said nothing to Marta Carolina, and to avoid detection he ran to the adjacent cabin, silently opened the door, and slipped into the room. Flattened against the wall he waited and listened as footsteps echoed down the hall. Again the only sounds were Marta Carolina's cries and her banging on the door. No one seemed to be paying her any attention. Eventually Will looked around the large room that glowed gray in the first morning light.

He was surprised that it was empty. Where were Diego and Fernandez? The room had to belong to one of them— its size indicated the prestige of the occupant. What were Diego and Fernandez doing? He walked to the table and brushed through the papers that were scattered about. He picked up the small chess piece—a quite familiar black bishop, the only piece still missing from Marta Carolina's chess set—then found the time-worn note written in Dutch that said, "Beware the bishop." His glance fell to the floor where he saw the wadded papers, which he bent and picked up. Moving to the window, he opened them and read, a smile ghosting his lips. Dona Karolina had outsmarted her adversary even in death. This was nothing but a letter written in Dutch to Sir James Palmer, a letter in which she gloated her victory over him. Where then was the document? What had Dona Karolina done with it?

The quietness was shattered by the opening and slamming of doors and heavy footsteps in the companion-way. Diego Romero's voice carried above the others. "Yes, Señor Eduardo, we are ready to set sail. I shall accompany you to the quarterdeck."

During the flurry of activity outside, Will folded the paper and slipped it and the chess piece into the pocket of his jerkin. When the companionway was quiet, he hurriedly slipped out of the room into the adjacent cabin—evidently occupied by the man called Eduardo who Will presumed to be the pilot. He moved to the desk where he quickly located a ring of keys. As quickly he was out of the room into the companionway again.

He had to try several keys before he found the one to unlock Marta Carolina's door. Finally the door yielded to the pressure of his hand, but only silence greeted Will. He didn't hear or see Marta Carolina. Not sure what to expect, he didn't immediately call out. Rather he took a cautious step, his eyes running the small room. Then he felt her presence and instantly knew she was behind the door.

In one smooth movement he closed the door and turned, grabbing her arms before she could bring the small wooden footstool down on his head. "Nay, lass," he muttered in English, "this won't do."

"You!" Marta Carolina exclaimed when she recognized Will's voice and ceased fighting. She was so happy to see him that her arms immediately fell to her side, and the stool dropped from her slack hands to the floor.

And then she was angry—angry at herself for being so happy to see him, for so quickly forgetting that he had used her, for so quickly remembering only that her body responded to him.

To cover her conflicting emotions, she said, "You're not dead!"

"I certainly hope not." His eyes devoured her, and he wanted to take her in his arms, to hold her close.

"What are you doing here?"

The raven-black eyes twinkled. "I came to rescue you."

She was glad to see Will, even gladder that he was alive, but in the past twenty-four hours she had run the entire circuit of emotions, and she was spiritually exhausted. Even in her joy at finding him alive, she could not forget that Will had used her and her love for him.

"Did you come to rescue me?" she asked, "or to get the papers?"

She and Will stared at each other for a long time, and neither said a word. Finally Will bent to set the stool on its legs, and the chess piece fell out of his doublet to roll across the floor and land at Marta Carolina's feet. She touched it with her toe.

"The bishop," she said in a small, detached voice. "My chess set is now complete. All the pieces have been returned." She raised her head to look at Will. "If you're looking for the papers, Don Diego has them. He found the secret compartment in the chess board."

That wasn't what Will was looking for; he was desperately searching for the woman he loved—the woman who loved him. He took a step toward Marta Carolina, but she held her hands out to ward him off.

"*Querida*," he began, "let me explain—"

"Let me explain!" she mimicked, her voice rising with each word. "Just what do you take me for?" she cried, beyond caring who heard her. Hurt and anger melded into a grief she could hardly bear. "Some simpleton who—"

"No," Will quickly denied. "Never that, love."

"And don't call me 'love'," she gritted as she planted her hands on her hips and glared at him. "You don't have to use the endearments any longer. You don't have to pretend to love me. There's nothing else I can tell you or do for you. I know nothing about the documents which my aunt was supposed to have delivered to the English."

"Please, *querida*," he softly said. Marta Carolina was slipping away from him. The prophetic words of Ecclesiastes came back to haunt him: "A time to hate." He had to reach her, to explain to her. "Please listen to me."

"Why explain now?" she asked.

"I owe it to you" came the lame reply. He knew what she was thinking and feeling. All the evidence pointed to his guilt and betrayal.

"You owed it to me when you first learned who I was and who Tía was. Not only did you deceive the others, Will," she accused, her hurt shadowing her eyes, "but you deceived me." Her voice lowered to a whisper. "How could you?"

"I couldn't take the risk—" he started, but Marta Carolina interrupted him.

"You told me that deceit is like a viper's nest," she said in that sad, faraway voice, "but I think you were wrong. Deceit is the viper, and you, Will, are that viper—that perpetrator of lies and deceit." Tears washed her eyes, but she refused to give way to them. "Why couldn't you have told me the truth?"

"I didn't want you hurt."

"Did you—did you love me when you—when you—"

Having dealt in half truths and subterfuge for so long, the answer Marta Carolina wanted to hear came readily to Will's lips, but he couldn't say the words. The only way he could salvage their love was to tell her the truth.

"I love you, *querida*." He saw the tears in her eyes and wanted to go to take her in his arms; he wanted to love her doubts away.

When she spoke, anger firmed her voice. "That wasn't

my question." She waited for his answer.

"I cared for you."

"Did you love me?" she insisted, even as her heart shattered into a million pieces.

After a long moment—longer than any Will had ever experienced before—he said, "No, I didn't love you at that time."

"You're despicable!"

"I love you now," Will stated a little louder this time.

"What do you need from me this time, Will?" Marta Carolina paused fractionally, then said, "Don't tell me any lies this time. I'm not fool enough to believe you anymore. It couldn't be the papers. I've told you where they are. Don Diego—"

The door opened, slamming against the wall, and Diego Romero entered the room, a huge bloodhound on leash, his paws tapping on the floor. A malicious smile pulled the man's thin lips and glistened in his eyes.

"I thought I heard my name" came the silky greeting. "But, my dear señorita, as your friend knows by now, I found papers but not *the* papers. Your aunt was smarter than I gave her credit for being." Diego gave Will a searching glance. "What did you do with Dona Karolina's letter?" Then he shrugged his shoulders and dismissed the question as no consequence. To Marta Carolina he said, "It must be on him somewhere. He took it from my cabin."

The papers! Marta Carolina thought disgustedly, lengthening the distance between her and Diego. She eyed the dog warily—its flaming brown eyes were targeted on Will. Diego's hand snaked out, his fingers clawing into the tender skin of Marta Carolina's upper arm. He yanked her to his side.

"You, my dear, will remain with me. We have some unfinished business to which we must attend."

All the time that he spoke, Marta Carolina tugged her arm, trying to loosen it from his grip. "What about Will?" she asked as Diego jerked her through the door.

"Don't worry about your lover," he sneered. "I'm not going to leave him alone." He leaned over to unfasten the leash. "By the way," Diego said to Will, "Timothy has been captured and locked up again, so don't think he'll be coming to rescue you." He gave the attack command to the dog, then he lunged through the door, dragging Marta Carolina with him. "I hope you fare better with the dog than Rodrigo Fernandez did, Will Dare?"

Left alone, Diego's maniacal laughter filtering through the thick door, Will faced the dog, whose vicious snarl filled the room. The only distinguishing feature on the beast was his bared teeth, long, sharp, and lethal. Quickly Will looked around the room for a weapon, but he saw none. Then he heard a movement, the scratching of claws on the floor, and swiveled as the dog lunged at him, the weight and momentum knocking both of them to the floor. The sharp teeth bit into Will's shoulder, easily cutting through Will's body, temporarily blinding him. Gulping in fresh air, he doubled up his arm and, with all his strength, he elbowed the dog in the chest. Winded, the hound loosened his grip and fell limply to the floor. Blood seeped out of Will's wound, running down his arm and chest and quickly discoloring the shirt.

But Will had no time to think of his pain. He must find a weapon. Then he saw the small wooden footstool. Instantly he was on his knees, crawling across the room, but his progress was suddenly impeded. The bloodhound's mouth circled Will's left wrist, and excruciating pain immobilized him. His eyes shut, his face contorted in pain, Will stretched the last few inches until his fingers closed around the leg of the stool. At the same time that he gripped the stool, the dog's mouth locked on Will's wrist—he felt as if the dog were crushing his bones! Breathing deeply and fighting the nausea that threatened to overpower him, Will lifted the stool in the air and with all his strength brought it down on the dog's head.

The dog whimpered with pain once, whined, then convulsed in the throes of death. He rolled to his side, blood dribbling out the corner of his mouth to pool on the floor. Will supported himself on the side of the bed and levered to his feet to stagger across the room. Weak and nauseous, he stopped at the desk, his eyes fastening on the small dagger that Don Diego used for a letter opener. Will's fingers closed about the hilt, then he pushed out the door through the companionway. He had to get Marta Carolina away from Diego. The man was a maniac. No telling what he would do to her.

But Will also needed to free Timothy and his men so they could regain control of the ship. By himself he couldn't overpower Diego and the entire crew. Perspiration beaded Will's forehead and ran down his face. Dizzy, he reeled from one side of the narrow corridor to the other, his shoulder and wrist throbbing so badly he could hardly endure the pain. He had to make it to the hold first. The keys! The keys he had taken from Diego's cabin! Where were they?

Slowly he retraced his steps and found them, still hanging from the cabin door. Before he could pull them out, he heard Diego's voice.

"You're a hard man to kill, Will Dare. Looks like I shall have to quit relying on others and do it myself."

Diego moved forward, brandishing a superbly crafted sword, the blade gleaming in the dim candlelight. That Will had no weapon mattered not to him.

"Where is Marta Carolina?" Will yelled, as he stepped back, so Marta Carolina could hear him if she were near.

"Locked in my cabin," Diego replied. "When she understands me better, she will tell me where the document is hidden."

"She doesn't know," Will exclaimed. "Her aunt didn't tell her."

On hearing Will's voice Marta Carolina crossed the room and pressed herself against the door. Relief surged through her body in such proportions tears freely ran down her cheeks. Will was safe; the dog hadn't killed him.

Diego's blade swished through the air, the point cutting a long slash through Will's jerkin and shirt as he jumped out of the way.

"The documents couldn't have disappeared," Diego said, advancing, his movements fluid and graceful, as well as deadly. "Dona Karolina had to give them to someone."

"Even if you found the papers," Will said, the two of them circling each other warily, knife against sword, "you could do nothing with them now. You can never return to England or reclaim your title."

"But when I locate them, I will know if my people have been discovered or not. If not, I shall kill that woman who sits on the English throne," Diego said. "That will be reward enough."

"Just as you had Dona Karolina and Betsy Smyth

killed?" Will taunted, again keeping his voice loud in the hopes that Marta Carolina could hear him.

"Just as I have killed anyone who stood in my way," Diego admitted. "I have a plan that—"

An unfamiliar sound from the quarterdeck interrupted Diego, who momentarily lost his concentration. Taking advantage of the distraction, Will lowered his head, raced forward, and butted Diego in the stomach. They fell and rolled on the floor until finally Will jarred the sword from Diego's grasp. The Spaniard clamped his hand on Will's shoulder and sank his fingers into the gaping wound.

Will groaned with pain, his body grew slack with weakness, and the knife slid from his fingers. Diego threw his left arm out, his hand brushing against the cold metal. He closed his fingers over the hilt and gripped it tightly. He brought the knife up and over, the blade headed for Will Dare's heart. In one last surge of energy and strength, Will's fingers banded around Diego's arm, and he pushed. Not realizing the blade was redirected toward him now, Diego made a last lunge, only to fall on the knife. With a hiss and a gurgle of blood he fell dead to the floor beside Will.

Slowly Will pushed to his feet and staggered down the companionway to the door where the keys still dangled in the lock. He pulled them out and unlocked the cabin where Marta Carolina was being held prisoner.

"Will!" she cried, when she saw his pallor and blood-drenched clothes. Her hands went to his face, and she touched him, reassuring herself that he was indeed all right. Tears running down her cheeks, she pushed to her toes and pressed her lips to his; she rained kisses all over his face and murmured endearments. Then she felt the sticky, warm blood that seeped through her clothes; she saw his shoulder wound. "Let me help you," she cried.

"I'm all right," he gently replied.

"No," she protested, "you're not all right. I need to bandage your—"

"Aye, love," he whispered, planting kisses on her face, on her lips, "I'm fine. Knowing that you love me makes everything all right. Now we must hide Diego until we've taken over the ship."

"After we've taken over the ship?" Marta Carolina murmured.

"After we've taken over the ship, *querida*," he said, "we'll do anything you like."

"Anything?"

"Anything!"

The precious promise between them, they dragged Diego's body into the cabin and laid it on the bed, covering it with a blanket.

"Please, Will," Marta Carolina begged, "let me at least bandage your wounds."

"Not now," Will gritted. "There are more pressing matters to attend to. I must release Timothy and his crew."

"I'll do it," Marta Carolina cried. "You're too weak."

"It's too dangerous, *querida*. If any of the soldiers saw you, they would suspicion something foul had happened. You had best remain here in case someone comes looking for Diego."

"I'll be careful," she promised.

Will smiled and shook his head, not wanting her to be endangered any more than she already had. "You'll be more help to me by remaining here than moving about on the ship."

When he reached the door, she said, "I love you, Will Dare."

He turned, the gray lines of pain around his mouth softening into a smile. "I love you, *querida*."

Then he was gone. When he reached the small cell in the hold, he slipped the key into the lock and called through the bars, "Turner, are you in there?"

"Aye" came the reply, and in the darkness Will could hear the thud of feet hitting the floor. "Not only I but my men."

"How did you manage to get yourself locked up again?" Will asked as he pulled the door open.

"The damned dogs," Timothy returned, he and his men rushing out of the small prison. "I had no idea Diego would have them on board. He evidently expected us to return."

"Maybe he didn't expect us but was prepared in case we did," Will gritted, unconsciously catching his upper arm with his hand and squeezing in order to bear the pain. In disjointed phrases, he told Timothy what had happened, concluding with, "Must get . . . to . . . Marta Carolina. She's . . . in . . . captain's cabin." Weak from the loss of blood, he slumped to the floor unconscious.

Later, when Will came to, he was lying on a bed. He could tell by the gentle motion, they were at sea. He opened his eyes, and the first thing he saw was Marta Carolina, sitting in a chair beside him.

"Have you finally decided to wake up?" she asked softly.

Will nodded and tried to sit up, but Marta Carolina was over him, her hands on his shoulders, gently pressuring him onto the bed. He didn't fight her; he had just discovered the barest movement hurt him. His shoulder was bandaged, his left arm in a splint.

"Lie still, *querido*," Marta Carolina commanded in a gentle voice. "You're much too weak to be up."

"What happened?"

As she poured him a cup of water, she talked. "After you released Timothy and his crew, you passed out. They brought you here to me, then took over the ship." With one hand she supported the back of his head, with the other she placed the rim of the pewter cup to his mouth and let him drink. Then she picked up a bowl and spoon-fed him the broth she had prepared that morning.

After several swallows, he asked, "Where are we going now?"

Marta Carolina chuckled. "Captain Turner said we were going to plunder the Spanish Main to make up for all the wrongs the Spaniards had done to us." Her smile told Will that Timothy hadn't offended her.

"How long have I been unconscious?"

"Two days."

He waited a long time before he said, "Marta Carolina, I have so much I need to tell you."

Sitting down beside him, Marta Carolina shook her head and cupped his face in her hands. "No, my darling," she said, "you have nothing to explain. What I hadn't learned from you and Diego, my heart told me and Timothy confirmed."

"I have nothing to explain," Will agreed, "but I wish to." And Marta Carolina listened attentively as he confessed his part in the apprehension and death of her aunt. "I thought Rodrigo was an English pensionary when I told him about Santica, and I did not know

501

Santica was Dona Karolina Lucas de Santiago, *querida*. I had no idea Rodrigo was working for the Spanish government." His onyx eyes fixed on hers, Will asked, "Can you forgive me?"

"There is nothing to forgive, *querido*." She lowered her head and tenderly kissed his lips. "I only regret that Tía died in vain. The people whom she wished to expose as assassins will forever be safe because the papers cannot be found."

As the days passed Will grew stronger and soon was up and about, spending several hours on the quarterdeck with Timothy beneath a healing sun. Nights he spent with Marta Carolina, the two of them basking in their love for each other. One evening several weeks later, they insisted Timothy sup with them rather than stay by himself in the captain's cabin. After a delicious meal, the men drank their ale and talked. Marta Carolina sat quietly, listening. All too soon the visit came to an end. Timothy stood and crossed the room.

Smiling, he said, "I hate to depart such wonderful company, but I don't want to tire you."

His gaze inadvertently strayed to a small table on the opposite side of the room on which he spotted Marta Carolina's chess set—the chess set he had heard so much about and had not had the opportunity to observe closely. His steps quickened to the table, and he picked up the white queen piece.

"So beautiful," he muttered. "Such exquisite workmanship." He set the queen down and picked up the black king. An odd inflection in his voice, he said, "They look so familiar I would swear that I've seen them somewhere before."

"No," Marta Carolina softly answered, "you couldn't have seen them before, Captain Turner. My aunt had this set made especially for her; no other exists in the world."

Timothy set the second piece down, only to pick up the black bishop. The sightless eyes seemed to reach into his very soul. "I would swear that I've seen this before," he exclaimed. "This is so familiar." He closed his eyes, willing himself to place the figurine. "As if I've seen it before."

"I'm sure you haven't," Marta Carolina said, moving to where Timothy stood and also picking up one of the pieces. "The queen piece is a replica of Queen Elizabeth, the king her father, Henry VIII."

Timothy took the queen piece from Marta Carolina, the elusive memory a sudden portrait. Vividly he remembered the mantelpiece in Henry Smyth's inn—the queen's bust on one end, an exact replica of this chess figurine.

"The castle of course is Hampton Court," he heard Marta Carolina say, "and the bishop is—"

"—is identical to the black marble statue on the mantelpiece at the Boar's Head Inn," Timothy said. He could hear Smyth's booming voice: That, lad, is St. Peter, the first bishop of the Christian faith and my namesake. Aye, lad, I am Henry Peter Smyth. Aloud Timothy said, "St. Peter, the first bishop of the Christian faith."

"Are you sure?" Will asked, hastening to where Timothy and Marta Carolina stood. He, too, was locked in memories; he remembered the night so long ago when in his haste to blow out a candle and to hide, he had almost knocked over a black marble statue.

"Aye," Timothy muttered, "I am sure."

"Beware the bishop," Marta Carolina whispered.

"Captain Turner," Will asked, "could we postpone our plundering of the Spanish Main until we return to Smyth's tavern and find our bishop?"

Timothy smiled rakishly. "Of course we can. I'm a patriot first, Will Dare, a pirate second."

Later when they were in their cabin, Will asked Marta Carolina, "Do you mind our going to England first?"

"No," Marta Carolina said as she undressed, "I don't mind. I wouldn't have it any other way. I feel as if I am completing the job which Tía began."

Their clothes off, they moved to the bed and lay in a pool of moonlight that poured through the window.

"What are we going to do afterward?" Marta Carolina asked.

He picked her hand up and brought it to his mouth, his lips touching the ring he had returned to her. "First, *querida*, I want our marriage legalized. Then we shall go to your *repartimiento*."

"Do you wish to stay in England?"

"No," Will answered, sliding down the bed, his lips blazing a trail of fire from her shoulders to the tip of her breast, "since I've tasted the wonder of the New World, I have no desire to return to Europe." His warm breath splayed over her skin. "Since I've tasted the wonder of your love, my darling, I have no desire for anyone else. You are my life."

Epilogue

"I am indeed glad that you're happily married, lad!" Drake's voice echoed through the deserted building as he paced back and forth in the main dining room of the Boar's Head Inn and slapped the newly found documents in his hand. "But happier I would be if you'd take these papers to the queen yourself. When Her Majesty learns that her favorite lady-in-waiting is indeed a Spanish sympathizer and was working with James Palmer to kill her, she will be most grateful to you. A fine reward she would heap on your head—even so far as to knighting you."

Will sat atop one of the dusty tables, his booted feet resting on a bench. He fiddled with the base of the black marble statue of St. Peter, running his fingers over the eyes so that the secret compartment opened. "I don't want to be knighted," he said. "I have served my country and my queen well. I have no desire to be conscripted into her court life. It is now time for Will Dare to live his life with his lady-love—to leave a life of deceit to others." Will looked up to see Drake shaking his head in bafflement.

"Have you gone daft, lad?" Drake clearly was at a loss to explain his protégé's behavior.

Will set the statue on the table and jumped to his feet. "Nay, Drake, I haven't gone daft, but I do have a desire to return to the New World—a new land with a new promise. It is there I wish to take my lady-wife and to rear my family."

"'Tis a primitive, godforsaken land," Drake grumbled.

"Aye, 'tis primitive," Will agreed, "but hardly godforsaken."

"Your mind is make up?"

Will nodded his head.

"And what would you have me do?"

"A ship all our own," Marta Carolina murmured, standing on the quarterdeck in front of her lord-husband, his hands on her shoulders, both of them staring out to sea. The wind gently loosened her hair from the coil at the base of her neck and blew the soft tendrils across her face. She tasted the bite of the salted air. "Do you not regret having gone to court yourself to present your findings to Her Majesty, *querido?*"

"No," Will replied. "I have my heart's desire, and that's you." He turned her around in his arms, and his lips tasted the sweetness of hers. After a long while, he said, "After we check on the colony at Roanoake, my business will be completed, *querida;* then we shall concentrate on yours."

"I really don't want to go to the *repartimiento, querido.* Let Don Rafael have it."

"As for me, your cousin can have it, but we must think

of our children. We must establish ownership for them."

"I am all for thinking about our children," Marta Carolina whispered, her arms snaking around his shoulders. "One day we shall go there and claim what belongs to me, but for now, my darling, I want us to think of ourselves."

"Meaning?"

"After we visit your colony, *querido*, I would like to return to Chicora to see Night Star and her grand children."

"Ummm," Will droned, pretending to weigh her request. "I think we can manage that."

"Then," Marta Carolina said, inhaling deeply as his head lowered, his mouth trailing kisses over the satiny swell of her breasts. "Then—I want us to build a home in the lovely port city on the Caribbean—the one where Timothy lives."

Will straightened up and looked at her, hiking a brow in surprise. "Where the privateers live?"

"Yes—" Marta Carolina chuckled. "Having tasted the life of a privateer, *querido*, I have a mind to plunder the Spanish Main some more."

"Madam, the life of a privateer is dangerous," Will exclaimed, his heart leaping at Marta Carolina's suggestion. He could think of no better vocation, but was this a life for his lady-wife? "Are you sure you will not mind the endless days and months that you will be home waiting for me?"

"I thought, my husband," Marta Carolina said quite demurely, "that I should accompany you." She felt Will's chest rise with his protest. Before the words came, she pressed her lips to his. "You'll need an apothecary on board, sir, to take care of the wounded."

After a long, leisurely kiss, in which Will thoroughly plundered the richness of her mouth, he said, "I can think of a much more important reason for having you on board, *querida*."

"Would you care to explain?" came the breathless question.

He scooped her into his arms and made for the companionway. "No, my love, I don't think this is the time for explanations." Over his shoulder, he called to the pilot, one of the men who had sailed with Timothy Turner, "Mister Perkins, Madame Dare and I are going below. Set course for the kingdom of Chicora."

"What is this the time for, *querido?*" came the soft query.

"A time to love."

MORE BLAZING ROMANCES
From Zebra Books

FRONTIER FLAME   (1965, $3.95)
by Rochelle Wayne

When her cousin deserted the army, spirited Suzanne Donovan knew that she had to go and get him back. But once the luscious blonde confronted towering Major Blade Landon, she wished she'd never left home. The lean, muscled officer seemed as wild as the land — and made her think only of the rapture his touch could bring!

ARIZONA TEMPTRESS   (1785, $3.95)
by Bobbi Smith

Rick Peralta found the freedom he craved only in his disguise as El Cazador. Then he saw the alluring Jennie mcCaine among his compadres and swore she'd belong just to him. When he left his lawless life, he'd leave the enticing captive behind . . . but until then the hot-blooded Rick would have all of his needs fulfilled by his provocative ARIZONA TEMPTRESS.

PRAIRIE EMBRACE   (2035, $3.95)
by F. Rosanne Bittner

Katie Russell was shocked by her passionate reaction to her bronze-skinned, jet-haired Indian captor. The gorgeous pioneer reminded herself that he was a savage heathen and beneath her regard, but deep inside she knew she longed to yield to the ecstasy of his PRAIRIE EMBRACE.

PIRATE'S CONQUEST   (2036, $3.95)
by Mary Martin

Starlin Cambridge always scoffed that the ruthless pirate Scorpio would never capture her sleek, treasure-laden ship. But one day, the notorious outlaw overtook her vessel — and kidnapped its raven-haired owner. Furious that the muscular marauder has taken her freedom, Starlin is shocked when she longs for him to take her innocence as well!

MEMENTO   (2037, $3.95)
by Eleanora Brownleigh

Just one chance encounter with the compelling Gregory West settles Katherine's mind: she knows he is the man for her, even if it means forsaking her rich and comfortable New York City home to travel across the uncivilized continent,. And though the dark secrets of the past ruled out marriage for Gregory, nothing could stop him from savoring Katherine's whole body for a brief, intense fling that would forever be this most cherished MEMENTO.

Available wherever paperbacks are sold, or order direct from the Publisher. Send cover price plus 50¢ per copy for mailing and handling to Zebra Books, Dept. 2116, 475 Park Avenue South, New York, N.Y. 10016. Residents of New York, New Jersey and Pennsylvania must include sales tax. DO NOT SEND CASH.

CHILLING GOTHICS
From Zebra Books